Praise for

Ready & Willing

"[A] great paranormal contemporary romance . . . Well-written."   —*Night Owl Romance*

Fast & Loose

"[A] fabulous romance . . . Captures the spirit of the Kentucky Derby . . . With well-developed, entertaining characters and humorous dialogue . . . Will keep you reading until the end of the race."   —*Fresh Fiction*

"Engaging . . . Fans will enjoy this lighthearted romp."
                                                  —*The Best Reviews*

"This warm, easygoing story, set in the world of horse racing, has very likable characters, especially a hero who's basically a nice guy and some great secondary characters. The way the hero pursues the heroine is lovely."
                                                  —*Romantic Times*

continued . . .

Berkley Sensation Titles by Elizabeth Bevarly

FAST & LOOSE
READY & WILLING
NECK & NECK

NECK
&
NECK

• Elizabeth Bevarly •

BERKLEY SENSATION, NEW YORK

THE BERKLEY PUBLISHING GROUP
Published by the Penguin Group
Penguin Group (USA) Inc.
375 Hudson Street, New York, New York 10014, USA
Penguin Group (Canada), 90 Eglinton Avenue East, Suite 700, Toronto, Ontario M4P 2Y3, Canada
(a division of Pearson Penguin Canada Inc.)
Penguin Books Ltd., 80 Strand, London WC2R 0RL, England
Penguin Group Ireland, 25 St. Stephen's Green, Dublin 2, Ireland (a division of Penguin Books Ltd.)
Penguin Group (Australia), 250 Camberwell Road, Camberwell, Victoria 3124, Australia
(a division of Pearson Australia Group Pty. Ltd.)
Penguin Books India Pvt. Ltd., 11 Community Centre, Panchsheel Park, New Delhi—110 017, India
Penguin Group (NZ), 67 Apollo Drive, Rosedale, North Shore 0632, New Zealand
(a division of Pearson New Zealand Ltd.)
Penguin Books (South Africa) (Pty.) Ltd., 24 Sturdee Avenue, Rosebank, Johannesburg 2196,
South Africa

Penguin Books Ltd., Registered Offices: 80 Strand, London WC2R 0RL, England

NECK & NECK

A Berkley Sensation Book / published by arrangement with the author

PRINTING HISTORY
Berkley Sensation mass-market edition / August 2009

ISBN: 978-0-425-22903-3

BERKLEY® SENSATION
Berkley Sensation Books are published by The Berkley Publishing Group,
a division of Penguin Group (USA) Inc.,
375 Hudson Street, New York, New York 10014.
BERKLEY® SENSATION and the "B" design are trademarks of Penguin Group (USA) Inc.

PRINTED IN THE UNITED STATES OF AMERICA

10 9 8 7 6 5 4 3 2 1

· One ·

NATALIE BECKETT SURVEYED THE ARCHITECTURAL wonder that was the ballroom of Edgar and Clementine Hotchkiss's palatial estate and decided that only a complete loser could mess up a party thrown against a backdrop like this. It was as if she'd just walked into the court of Louis XIV, from the cloud- and cherub-spattered ceiling to the gilded moldings to the beveled Palladian windows that virtually completed the far wall. The late afternoon sun spilled through those windows, imbuing the room with a luscious golden light, but at night, all those crystal chandeliers hanging overhead would toss diamonds onto the inlaid hardwood floor. It would take an abject, absolute loser not to be able to throw an amazing, full-to-the-rafters party in this place.

That made Natalie an abject, absolute loser.

And Clementine Hotchkiss was the ideal client, one who had spoken those coveted words that every professional event planner longed to hear: "Money is no object." Even better, she'd meant it. Clementine had been Natalie's aunt Margaret's best friend since college, and she and Mr. Hotchkiss were soiled to their undergarments by their filthy lucre. Clementine had told Natalie to do whatever she wanted with regard to the party—theme, decorations, catering, you name it—that she was turning the event over into Natalie's trusted, talented hands, and please just let Clementine know to whom she should make out the checks and for how much. There was no way anyone could mess up a golden professional opportunity like the one Clementine had offered. No one except an utter, unmitigated loser.

An utter, unmitigated loser like, oh, say . . . Natalie.

She'd had plenty of time to plan the party, too, since Clementine had hired her eight months ago, the very week Natalie had hung out her shingle for Party Favors, her event-planning business. And Clementine was hosting the bash on the quintessential evening to have a party in Louisville: the night before the most famous horse race in the world, the Kentucky Derby. *Every*body in Louisville was in a party mood on Derby Eve. The two weeks leading up to the race were the city's equivalent of Mardi Gras. Derby parties were easier to plan than any other type of party, because there were no conflicting events. It was Derby. Period. Everyone kept that weekend open for celebrating. Only a party planner who was a pure and profound loser would crash and burn planning a Derby party.

That made Natalie Beckett a pure and profound loser.

Because even though the odds had been overwhelmingly in her favor from the starting gate when it came to planning Clementine's Derby Eve party two weeks from today, almost no one was planning to attend. Even though the invitations had gone out six weeks ago—and the allegedly unnecessary save-the-date cards had gone out six months ago—Clementine had received few RSVPs in the affirmative. The majority of the three hundred guests she'd invited hadn't bothered to return the cards at all.

Which, okay, one could interpret to mean those guests might still be planning to come. But Natalie wasn't going to bank on it, since the party was only two weeks away, and unreturned RSVPs at this point almost always were negative RSVPs. By now, even Clementine probably wasn't expecting much. But she was optimistic enough—or perhaps deluded enough—to pretend Natalie could still turn this thing around.

That delusion—ah, Natalie meant optimism, of course—was made evident when Clementine asked, "So what do you think, Natalie? Shall we put the buffet on the left or the right?"

Buffet? Natalie repeated to herself. Oh, she didn't think they were going to need a buffet. A tube of saltines and a box of Velveeta ought to take care of the catering very nicely. They probably wouldn't even have to break out the Chinet.

She turned to her client, who was the epitome of society grande dame relaxing at home, with her sleek silver pageboy and black velvet headband, dressed in a black velour running suit, which, it went without saying, had never, *ever* been worn to run. Clementine had rings decorating nearly every finger—she didn't abide by that silly rule about never wearing precious gems before cocktail hour—and clutched a teeny little Westie named Rolondo to her chest. Rolondo evidently didn't buy into that precious gems thing, either, because Natalie would bet those were genuine rubies studding the little guy's collar.

But then, Natalie was no slouch in the fashion department, at least when she was working. As she pondered her answer to her client's potentially loaded question, she lifted a perfectly manicured hand to the sweep of perfectly styled golden-blond hair that fell to her shoulders—perfect because she'd just had both done before coming to visit Clementine. Of course, by evening, when Natalie arrived home, the nails would be chipped and nibbled, and the hair would be in a stubby ponytail that pulled a little too much to the left. But for now, she used the same perfectly manicured hand to straighten the flawless collar of her flawless champagne-colored suit—which, by evening, would revert to jeans and a Louisville Cardinals T-shirt. Then she conjured her most dazzling smile for her client, the one she'd learned in cotillion class as a child and perfected long before she made her debut thirteen years ago.

Her parents had spared no expense when it came to bringing up their youngest daughter right, after all. And by *right*, Ernest and Dody Beckett meant *to be the pampered wife of a commodities broker or a commercial banker or, barring that, a corporate vice-president on his way to the top*. They'd thought she was crazy, pursuing something as frivolous as a college degree—in, of all pointless majors, business—when she knew she would have access to her trust fund upon turning eighteen and could then land herself a perfectly good husband like that nice Dean Waterman, who had been mooning over her for years, and where had they gone wrong, having a daughter who wanted to go to college and start her own business? Merciful heavens. Why couldn't she be more like her sister Lynette, who was the pampered wife of an investment analyst—which was *almost* as good as a commodities broker or commercial banker—and who spent her days volunteering for the Junior League and in the library of her children's tony private school?

"Clementine," Natalie said in the soothe-the-client voice she'd also perfected years ago—right around the time her first business venture was going under—"I think we should put a buffet on the left *and* the right."

Clementine's eyes went as round as silver dollars. "Oh, my. Do you think that's wise? I mean, considering how few RSVPs have come back in the affirmative . . ."

Okay, so clearly Clementine wasn't as delusional as Natalie had hoped. Ah, she meant *thought*. That just meant Natalie would have to be delusional enough for the two of them.

Piece o' cake.

She lifted a hand and waved it in airy nonchalance. "Pay it no mind, Clementine. People often wait 'til the last minute to RSVP. Especially for something like a Derby Eve party, when they have so many prospects to choose from."

Which, of course, was one of the reasons Natalie was such an abject, unmitigated loser when it came to planning this party. Clementine's Derby Eve party was vying with a dozen better-established Derby Eve parties when it came to attracting guests. Since those other parties had been around so much longer—decades longer, some of them— they were able to pull in the cream of local society, not to mention the bulk of visiting A-list celebrities. The guests to the Barnstable-Brown party alone—easily the most venerable of Derby Eve parties—could light up Tinseltown, Broadway, *and* the Grand Ole Opry. But the Grand Gala and Mint Jubilee were closing in for sheer star power.

So far, the brightest star Natalie had been able to harness for Clementine's party was a first-round reject of the now-defunct—for obvious reasons—reality series, *Pimp My Toddler*. And as it was, little Tiffany was going to have to be home by eight if she wanted to make her bedtime. It would all be downhill after that.

Oh, Natalie was *such* a loser.

"Then you think we should move forward as if the majority of the guest list was coming?" Clementine asked.

"Oh, you bet," Natalie assured her. She was, after all, way better at harnessing delusions than she was celebrities. "Just you wait, Clementine. By the end of next week, those RSVPs will be pouring in with the little 'Of course we can come' boxes checked." She smiled a coy smile that was even more convincing than her debutante one. "I have a little secret weapon I'm saving for the right time."

Clementine's overly painted eyebrows shot up at that. "What secret weapon?"

Natalie lifted her finger to her lips and mimicked a *shh*-ing motion. Then she whispered conspiratorially, "It's a secret."

Clementine's expression turned concerned. "Yes, dear, but don't you think you could share it with me? The hostess?" Then, as if that weren't enough, she elaborated, "The hostess who's signing all those checks?"

Natalie took Clementine's hand in hers and uttered those immortal words of self-employed people everywhere: "Trust me." Then, before her client could object further, she added, "I've been planning parties like yours for eight months now, Clementine. I assure you, I know what I'm doing."

Which was true, since Natalie knew that what she was doing was failing miserably. Although she had indeed been planning parties for eight months, Clementine's was by far the most ambitious, way outpacing the handful of birthday parties, two bat mitzvahs, one retirement gathering, and a series of bunko nights, at least one of which was best forgotten, since Natalie had misunderstood the hostess of that one and, thinking it was a bachelorette party, had sent a male stripper dressed like a gladiator into a roomful of octogenarians. Not that the party hadn't received rave reviews afterward, mind you, but Mrs. Parrish's Bible study group really hadn't come prepared for it. Beyond those events, Natalie had put together an eighth-grade graduation party, a kindergarten reunion, and one debut, which had mostly served to remind her how awkward and uncomfortable she'd been at her own debut.

Not exactly a success story, she thought. And not for the first time.

"Then the new business is faring well, dear?" Clementine asked.

"Oh, very well," Natalie said. Figuratively speaking, at least. Provided *very well* figuratively meant *absolute, unmitigated failure.*

Under any other circumstances—like, say, if Clementine Hotchkiss had never met Natalie's aunt Margaret—the question would have been perfectly harmless and in no way noteworthy. But there was every chance that Clementine was asking it on behalf of Natalie's aunt, who would happily report back to Natalie's mother, which meant she was fishing for information about the status of Party Favors. And there was no way Natalie was going to give her client information that might find its way right back to her mother. Especially since she'd been sidestepping her mother's similar inquiries for so long that Natalie had invented a whole new dance, the subterfuge samba. If her mother inhaled even the slightest whiff of the stench that Party Favors had begun to issue, she'd be circling the steaming pile of Natalie's latest business failure like flies on horse doody.

Because Party Favors was only one of many steaming piles Natalie had left in her wake over the past seven years—if one could pardon the extremely socially unacceptable metaphor. Ever since earning her business degree, Natalie Beckett had been trying to launch a business of some kind, always with disappointing results.

Okay, okay, always with disastrous results.

What was ironic, though, was that Natalie didn't have to rely on a business to make her way in the world. The Becketts were one of Louisville's premier families—Natalie's parents lived in Glenview, too, right up the road from Clementine, in the third mansion on the right—and she'd had access to a very generous trust fund from the time she turned eighteen. But Natalie didn't want to rely on a trust fund. She wanted even less to rely on a wealthy husband. Natalie wanted a career. She wanted to be something more than Dody and Ernest Beckett's daughter and Lynette and Forrest Beckett's little sister. She wanted to do more with her life than volunteer for (choose at least one) medical research, social awareness, artistic expansion, educational development, or all of the above. And she wanted to be more than a pampered wife and pampering mother. She wanted to be . . .

Successful. On her own terms. Make her own way, her own name in the world. Unfortunately, the only path she'd been able to hew through the jungle of life so far had led to failure, with a brief stopover at disaster.

As if she'd just spoken that last thought aloud, Clementine said, "I'm so glad things are working out this time. I confess I had to wonder about the last business venture you undertook. I just couldn't imagine there being a big demand for doggie massage."

"Well, there was a little more to it than that," Natalie

began to object. It hadn't been doggie massage. Good heavens. That would have been silly. What Spa le Fido had offered was Rover reflexology. Along with poochie pedicure, muttley manicure, hound hydrotherapy, and canine coiffure.

"And what was the one before the doggie massage?" Clementine asked. "Something about the Hanging Gardens of Babylon."

"Hanging Gardens of Baby Bibb," Natalie corrected. At the time, the name had seemed so terribly clever. Now it just seemed to make no sense. "Organic hydroponics," she clarified for her client. Not that that would probably clear anything up for Clementine, since the only hydro she probably knew anything about was the alpha hydroxy she bought at the Lancôme counter.

"That was it," Clementine said. She cocked her head thoughtfully to one side. "You know, Mr. Hotchkiss actually considered investing in that hanging gardens venture."

This was news to Natalie. Maybe if he had followed through, she could have done a little better with the enterprise, and it would have lasted longer than nine days. "Really?" she asked. "What made him change his mind?"

Clementine smiled, then patted her shoulder. "He sobered up, dear."

Ah.

"It's just as well those businesses didn't flourish," Clementine said now with remarkable tact. "Party Favors is something you seem much more suited to. Having been the darling of so many parties yourself over the years, it would make sense that planning them would be something you're good at."

Yeah, well, that had been the theory, Natalie thought. Unfortunately, it was working about as well as the theory of Communism. Of course, now that she thought about it, that could be because, contrary to Clementine's assertions, Natalie had never exactly been the darling of *any*one's party. Disaster? Yes. Darling? Not so much.

"You always were the center of attention at any celebration," Clementine recalled further.

That part was actually true, Natalie conceded. Because she'd been the center of catastrophe at every celebration. Now that she thought about it, that was probably something she should have taken into consideration before launching a party planning business.

Gee, hindsight really was twenty-twenty.

Her client sighed with much feeling. "I must confess, Natalie, that I still have a few misgivings about the party."

Only a few? Wow, Natalie had way more than that. But she told Clementine, once again adopting her soothing voice, "That's only natural. But don't worry. Everything is moving along exactly as it's supposed to." And although that wasn't completely true, there were a few things that *were* going right, and it wouldn't hurt to remind Clementine of those. "The caterers *I* hired for you *eight months ago*," she said, "are now running a restaurant that's become one of the hottest tickets in town. Everyone wanted them for their Derby Eve parties, but you already had them, Clementine. And I just found out this week that the jazz band *I* hired *five months ago* is going to be featured in the *Scene* tomorrow as the city's latest locally grown success who are about to sign with a national record label. Everyone will want them for their parties, Clementine, but you'll already have them."

And that, truly, was where Natalie's talents lay. She could spot talent and predict trends months before anyone else caught on—well, doggie spas and organic hydroponics notwithstanding. She had been hoping that would be enough to move her event planning business ahead of all the others. She really was suited to this. She really had planned an excellent party for Clementine. They just didn't have enough clout in the Derby Eve milieu to command big crowds, that was all.

Not yet, anyway.

But Natalie was determined that she would not fail in this venture. She *was* good at this. She *could* make a go of it. She *would* ensure that Clementine Hotchkiss's party was a rousing success and that Party Favors, by being responsible for it, would be a rousing success, too.

Just as soon as she figured out how to bring people to Clementine Hotchkiss's party.

"Don't worry, Clementine," she reassured her client again. "I *promise* your Derby Eve bash will be the social event of the season, and the one everybody is talking about come Derby Day. I *promise*."

It *had* to be, Natalie vowed to herself. It just had to be. Because if Clementine's party failed, then the next event she would be planning would be a wedding. Her own. To a man she'd rather bury than marry.

BY THE TIME NATALIE ARRIVED BACK AT HER FRANKFORT Avenue office, she'd managed to shove thoughts of the imminently more buryable than marryable Dean Waterman back to the furthest, darkest recesses of her brain, which was where they belonged. No, actually, the furthest, darkest recesses of her brain were still too nice a place for Dean. She didn't care how much her parents liked him or how convinced they were that he was the man she should be tied to for the rest of her life. And she didn't care that Dean had been saying since childhood that someday he would make Natalie his Mrs., and that, to this day, he continued to make no secret of the fact that he was convinced she would be the perfect wife for him.

Dean Waterman was the very definition of smarmy. And cloying. And supercilious. And icky. And he'd been that way since she met him at the age of ten, in cotillion class. Between the sweaty palms and the prepubescent complexion and the hair goo his mother had made him use all the time, Natalie had always been on the edge of her seat, waiting to see if Dean would slide out of his.

These days, he bore no resemblance to the rat-faced little kid he'd been. Braces had fixed his overbite, LASIK had corrected his myopia, and puberty had filled him out.

Natalie might have even considered him handsome if it hadn't been for the cloying smarminess. He was still plenty oily, metaphorically speaking. And he was still definitely icky. But in a moment of weakness, on an evening when her parents had been hammering her even harder than usual about making a go of Party Favors, she'd made a bargain with them. If Clementine Hotchkiss's Derby Eve party didn't come off as a *huge* success, then Natalie had agreed she would close up shop and refrain from plunging into another business venture for six months. Also during that six months, she had further promised, she would . . . she would . . . she would . . . Oh, God, this part was so hard— and awful—to articulate. She would . . . gak . . . date Dean Waterman. Exclusively.

Not that the *exclusively* part was any big deal, since Natalie hadn't dated anyone for any length of time since college. It was the *date Dean Waterman* part that made her stomach clench. God, what had she been thinking to agree to such a thing? She'd just been so tired of her parents harping on her, and so certain she would triumph profes- sionally with Party Favors. She honestly hadn't thought it would come down to actually having to go out with Dean. For six months. Exclusively.

Not to mention the fact that Clementine's party, like all the big Derby Eve parties, was a fund-raiser, and her choice of recipients was a local group dedicated to making sure at-risk kids were challenged and stayed off the streets. The one hundred and fifty thousand dollar check Clemen- tine had hoped to turn over to Kids, Inc., after charging five hundred dollars to each of her wealthy guests was looking to be more like a buck and a half. And a buck and a half wasn't going to go far in building a facility that would teach those kids about running a business or offering schol- arships to help them someday do just that.

The word *loser* began to circle through Natalie's brain again, so she shoved it back into the shadows alongside thoughts of Dean. Yeah. They went nicely together. Then she turned to her computer and pulled up the web page for the *Courier-Journal* to read about the latest celebrities who were slated to be in town for Derby. The newspaper began their Derby celeb watch in January, and Natalie had been keeping close tabs on who was coming and when they were arriving. Scoring major players in the sports, entertainment, and business communities was a big part of ensuring the success of a Derby party, but most of the famous people coming to town had already committed to parties, even before she opened Party Favors.

Every time she saw a new celebrity listed, Natalie contacted that person's representative to extend a personal invitation to Clementine's party, but it was hardly ever with good results. At best, she received a polite *"Thanks, but no thanks, we're already committed that night."* At worst, her invitation went completely ignored. At second to worst, it was accepted by some celebreality type who was so far down the list, they actually referred to themselves as a "celebreality." In addition to the cast-off from *Pimp My Toddler* for Clementine's "Yes" list, Natalie had scored an auditioner from *American Idol* who hadn't made it to Hollywood but who had risen to fame—fifteen minutes of it, anyway— because Simon had dubbed him with one of those sound bites that got airtime over and over again. This one involved a cattle prod to a part of the young man's anatomy that one normally didn't want a cattle prod anywhere near. She'd also added an actor who had once played a politically incorrect Native American on *F Troop*. And a college basketball player whom, it was rumored, might possibly, perhaps, maybe, if the stars were aligned, go in the fifty-sixth round of the NBA draft.

Today's celebrity pickings, she saw, were pretty slim, even though the race—and parties—were just two weeks away. A talk show host from one of those niche cable channels that hardly anyone watched, a sort-of-cute assistant carpenter from a daytime HGTV series, and a marginally successful podcaster.

Ah, what the hell, Natalie thought. It wasn't like she had a lot of choices.

She was about to head off to Google to see who repped whom when her gaze lit on the sidebar of today's headlines, and a name popped out at her. A name which, although written in the same tiny font as the rest of the news, and with the same dispassionate reporting, might as well have been etched in gold on her computer monitor in letters eight inches high. And they might as well have been accompanied by a crack of thunder and a bolt of lightning, and the skies splitting open to showcase a chorus of angels belting out a chorus of "Hallelujah."

Russell Mulholland had come to town.

The headline linked to the Business section page of the website instead of the Features section, which normally highlighted visiting celebrities, so Natalie hadn't seen the announcement right off. Clicking on the headline now, she discovered that the man who defined the term *reclusive billionaire* had shown up in Louisville at some point earlier in the week, without announcement or fanfare, because he owned a horse that would be running in the Kentucky Derby.

Meaning, she concluded, that he would be here for the two weeks leading up to the race, including Derby Eve. And since no one had known he was coming, there was a chance, however small, that he hadn't committed to any parties yet. In fact, due to the whole reclusive billionaire thing, even if he had been invited to other parties, there was a good chance he hadn't accepted any of them, because everybody knew that Russell Mulholland kept a profile that was lower than a wolverine's burrow, due to his wanting to keep both himself and his teenage son out of the spotlight.

At least, he hadn't accepted an invitation to any Derby parties *yet*.

Hungrily, Natalie read the rest of the article. Evidently, Mr. Mulholland and his son Max had been spotted crossing the lobby of the Brown Hotel yesterday, surrounded by a cadre of bodyguards, which was the first anyone knew that he had planned to be in Louisville. There was a photograph accompanying the article, but it was virtually impossible to see what Mulholland looked like, because, even if his head hadn't been bent the way it was, he was wearing a hat and sunglasses, and what was left of his face was obscured by a very large man wearing a very determined expression.

Strangely, it was that man and not the buried billionaire who really captured Natalie's attention. He stood nearly a head above everyone around him and somehow seemed to be looking everywhere at once. His hair was dark, quite possibly black, and he didn't appear to have shaved for some time. His clothing was fairly nondescript, what looked like khaki trousers and a dark-colored polo, and shouldn't have called attention to him. But his rugged good looks coupled with that wary expression simply commanded her gaze.

Security detail, she thought. The guy had to be one of Mulholland's bodyguards. No self-respecting reclusive billionaire would travel without security. Or, you know, *exist* without security.

She forced her gaze back to the billionaire, since that was where her attention needed to be. Russell Mulholland had catapulted onto the celebrity scene about a year and a half ago after designing what would become *the* game system of gamers everywhere. The Mulholland GameViper had been talked about for months before it was made available, the gossip and hype turning it into the holy grail of game systems before anyone had even laid a finger on it. When it was finally launched—strategically just a few weeks before Christmas—there had been a frenzy to see who could get their hands on one.

Natalie wasn't much into gaming herself, but she'd seen on the news how a lot of people had camped outside Best Buy and GameStop stores for days, in freezing temperatures sometimes, in the hopes of scoring a GameViper for themselves. Even at that, few had succeeded. In the year and a half since its introduction, there had been a handful of additional pushes for a limited number of systems, again

with the camping outside retailers in an effort to be one of
the sacred few who procured one. Between the sale of
those systems and the games designed specifically for it—
not to mention the way the stock for Mulholland Games,
Inc., went straight through the roof—Russell Mulholland
had become a billionaire virtually overnight.

He'd become a recluse nearly as quickly.

Natalie had seen photos of him where he *wasn't* ducking
the paparazzi and knew there was a reason why he'd been
voted one of *People* magazine's Most Beautiful People and
its Sexiest Man Alive. Blond and blue-eyed, with one of
those smiles that made a woman want to melt into a puddle
of ruined womanhood at his feet, even without the billions,
he was too yummy for words. Add to that the fact that he
was a single dad who'd lost his wife to cancer when his son
was a toddler, and it warmed even the coldest heart.

According to the article in the paper, one of the things
he'd invested his money in was Thoroughbreds, all of whom
were named after his games, and one of whom claimed
decent odds for winning the Derby. Mulholland had come
to town with his teenage son, Max, the article added, but
it also cautioned readers not to expect to catch too many
glimpses of him, since he had routinely declined all invitations to make appearances at a variety of Derby-related
events.

Oh, he had, had he? Well, she'd just see about that. He
hadn't received his invitation to Clementine Hotchkiss's
Derby Eve bash yet.

Her gaze strayed to the big bodyguard again. She wasn't
about to let a little thing like a security detail get between
her and Russell Mulholland. The billionaire would be the
perfect party favor for Clementine's gala. *Everyone* knew
of "the Mulholland." *Everyone* wanted to get a glimpse of
"the Mulholland." If Natalie could convince the Mulholland to attend Clementine's party, *everyone* else would
come, too. The Hotchkiss gala would be *the* place to be on
Derby Eve, and it would be all people talked about the next
day. Natalie would be lauded as the party maven of all

party mavens, and Party Favors would be a huge success. Clementine could hand over an even bigger check to Kids, Inc., and Natalie would have jobs out the wazoo.

And Dean Waterman, the slimy little jerk, would be nothing but an oil slick in the darkest recesses of her mind.

· Two ·

IF THERE WAS ONE THING FINN GUTHRIE HAD LEARNED in the eighteen months he had worked as head of security for Russell Mulholland, it was to never underestimate anyone: not the new housekeeper, who'd turned out to be a corporate spy; not the personal chef, who'd turned out to be an autograph hound; not the plumber, who'd turned out to be paparazzi; not the veterinarian, who'd turned out to be a gold digger. When it came to doing his job, Finn Guthrie didn't trust *anyone*.

Of course, that lack of trust wasn't necessarily a by-product of his job, nor did it have much to do with having worked for eighteen months as head of security for Russell Mulholland. It was an essential component of his personality. That was part and parcel for a guy who'd grown up on the streets of one of Seattle's more notorious neighborhoods, and who'd been paraded through the foster care system, and who'd had more than one run-in with the authorities by the time he turned eighteen. Hell, by the time he turned fifteen. What was ironic was that there had been a time when Finn himself was the sort of person he would in no way trust around Russell or Max Mulholland. But then, there had been a time when Russell couldn't be trusted, either. And Finn should know, since he and Russell had been friends since they were thrown together more than two decades ago in the same group home at the age of fourteen.

Over the past eighteen months, however, the two men had shared more dubious adventures—and more secrets— than they had even when they were kids. And a big part of Finn's job, in addition to keeping both Mulhollands physically safe, was guarding the Mulholland secrets. Unfortunately, that was becoming more and more difficult with every passing month. Because with each passing month, the Mulholland wealth and celebrity multiplied significantly, and the Mulhollands' retreat from society escalated accordingly. And because of that, the determination of the public to uncover everything they could about them became more ravenous.

It wasn't that Russell *wanted* to be reclusive or hinder his son's freedom, Finn knew. It was that Russell wanted to keep both of them reasonably sane, reasonably normal, and reasonably safe. When you were worth billions of dollars, there were *a lot* of people who wanted to be your friend, few of whom were actually friendly. There were even more who wanted to see you fail, some of whom so begrudged you your success that they did everything they could to undermine it. And there were some—thankfully, only a handful— who posed a threat. Those, of course, were the ones from whom Finn made it his priority to safeguard Russell and Max. But everyone was always on his radar. Nobody—but nobody—was safe from Finn's scrutiny or his suspicion.

That included the petite, blond woman standing on the other side of the hotel lobby who kept darting glances in his direction. So indiscreet was her observation, in fact, that she could have been a femme fatale in some film noir, sitting in a chair holding up a newspaper into which she'd cut eye holes. Talk about your screen sirens. Her Veronica Lake hairdo fell in an elegant wave over her forehead, nearly obscuring one eye, and dark crimson lipstick stained her mouth. Her straight black skirt hugged her hips like a second skin, and her low-cut red top hugged the rest of her even better. Throw in the smoky stockings and black, spiky heels, and she was ripe for bringing down even the most jaded gumshoe.

Oh, yeah. She was definitely up to something. No woman dressed that provocatively unless she wanted to provoke. Good thing Finn wasn't a jaded gumshoe. Good thing he was just a jaded head of security instead.

Nevertheless, as he made his way across the lobby, much less obvious in his approach than she was in her observation, he had to admit he felt kind of like one of those doomed PIs. The Brown Hotel, where Russell had booked rooms for all of them, was something out of a fabulous forties film, from the marble floors to the dark paneled walls and ceiling, to the lush potted palms and overstuffed tapestry furnishings. The place reeked of old money and even older reputation, of wealth and refinement and all the things that made the rich so very different.

Money really did change everything. Hey, just look at Russell. Even Finn, though not the owner of the Mulholland billions, had changed by being a fringe member of this world. For him and Russell, thankfully, that change had been for the better. He couldn't say that was necessarily true of everyone whose pockets suddenly became lined with cash. All the more reason to shield the Mulhollands—especially young Max—from . . . well, everyone.

The blonde glanced up again, and when she saw Finn drawing nearer, her eyes widened in a panic that was almost comical. Then, abruptly, she spun around. Oh, yeah. Like that wasn't obvious. But she didn't bolt, so she clearly wanted to talk to him. About what, Finn could only speculate.

He'd come down from his room because he'd wanted to get something to eat and to scope out an entertainment complex up the street called Fourth Street Live, since it was the sort of place Russell—and fourteen-year-old Max, for that matter—would at some point want to visit. They'd only been in town a couple of days but had spent most of that time getting Russell's horse TimberLost settled at a Thoroughbred farm in a neighboring county, where he was boarding the animal until they could stable him at Churchill Downs. Louisville nightlife would almost certainly be next on both Mulhollands' to-do list, though, thankfully, Max's nightlife would be significantly less lively and infinitely more manageable than his father's nightlife was bound to be. At fourteen, Max was nowhere near as worldly or as inclined to mischief as his father—and his father's head of security—had been at that age.

So unless the blonde over there had just been smitten by Finn at first sight, which was highly unlikely, since he hadn't shaved since his arrival, and he was wearing his most disreputable looking jeans and a T-shirt that said Talk Derby to Me—hey, he wanted to get into the spirit—there was a good chance she'd seen the photo in yesterday's paper and recognized him as a member of Russell's entourage. Considering the way they'd been hounded since their arrival had been made public, and considering the fact that nobody ever wanted to talk to Finn—which was, quite possibly, the best perk of his job—it was a safe bet that she was looking at him as a route to Russell, since Russell did everything within his power to be a destination that was way off the beaten path.

Finn studied the woman again, trying to guess her reason for being there. Standing as she was in a spill of late afternoon sunlight that made her hair color alternate from gold to platinum to bronze, she looked like one of those high-maintenance women few men could afford to maintain. If the way she was dressed was any indication—and it went without saying that it was—she was probably looking to offer her, ah, services to Russell while he was in town, and for some laughably exorbitant price. Prices went up for everything in Louisville this time of year, he'd been told. Hotels, restaurants, limos, you name it. Naturally, call girls would raise their rates, too.

Not that Finn wanted to jump to conclusions. Maybe

Blondie over there was a Sunday school teacher and the oldest living virgin who just liked to dress as if she were throwing herself on the market to the highest bidder and only wanted to ask Finn if he knew the way to San José.

She turned slightly and looked over her shoulder at him again and, when she saw Finn still approaching, she looked even more panicky than before. To her credit, however, she slowly turned back in his direction and feigned nonchalance. Though it was about as much nonchalance as a jackhammer operating on broken pistons. She lifted a hand to her hair to scoop it back and away from her face, but the gesture was in no way smooth. In spite of its awkwardness, however, Finn still nearly stumbled as he watched her complete it. Because when she tucked a shoulder-length strand of gold behind one ear, damned if her cheek didn't look stained by the evidence of a blush.

Okay, so maybe she wasn't a call girl. Call girls didn't blush, and their hands didn't shake when they brushed their hair out of their eyes. She was still plenty suspicious. Even more so now. Because if she wasn't looking for Russell to offer up her services—and if she wasn't going to ask Finn about the way to San José, which he was pretty sure was unlikely—then why was she sneaking peeks at him and being so obvious about not wanting him to catch her staring?

He covered the last bit of distance that separated them in three easy strides and came to a stop in front of her. Then, knowing he was about as good at being inconspicuous as she was, he asked point-blank, "Can I help you, miss?"

Before he even completed the question, he noticed a soft scent about her, nothing too overpowering or heavy, just a nice, delicate fragrance reminiscent of something that was unsullied and sweet. It was totally at odds with the va-va-voom look of her, and that just captured his interest even more.

"It's Ms., actually," she said. Her voice was in keeping with her femme fatale mystique, all smoky and whiskey rough. But her smile was more suited to the blush he'd noted a moment ago, way more virtue than vixen. Okay, maybe not a call girl, after all, he thought. More was the pity. Not that he'd intended to let her get near Russell, but hey, Finn had needs, too.

"Ms. Beckett," she added. "Natalie Beckett."

She extended her hand in a way that was surprisingly professional, and, automatically, Finn shook it. Also automatic was the way he dropped his glance to the left hand that remained at her side—to the ring finger of her left hand, to be precise—to see if she was wearing a wedding band. There wasn't anything resembling a symbol of marital bliss—or marital misery, for that matter—on that finger, but it, along with several others, were decorated with gemstones that might have indicated it was an engagement ring.

Although why he was even bothering to make note of that—other than that he was always curious about the status of beautiful women, and this one was certainly that—he couldn't have said. For some reason, though, he was oddly relieved to discover that she was a *Ms.* who wasn't a *Mrs.*

The relief was short-lived, however. Because since Ms. Natalie Beckett probably wasn't a fallen woman, there was an even better chance that she was something even more heinous, the sort of woman it was absolutely essential Finn keep away from Russell. Not the hookers, who were at least up front about having sex for money, and they called the price right off the bat. And not the gold diggers who were pretty much the same but behaved with more subtlety. It wasn't the bad girls who were Russell's downfall, even though the bad girls were the ones he sought out the minute he arrived in any given town. It was the *nice* girls Russell was most susceptible to. And it was *nice* girls Russell had made Finn promise to keep away. Very, very, *very* far away.

"What can I do for you, Ms. Beckett?"

"Call me, Natalie, please."

He hesitated a telling moment before asking, "Why would I need to call you anything at all?"

Her smile fell some, but she bravely rescued it. "Because, Mr. Guthrie, I'm going to make you an offer you can't refuse."

He arched a brow at that, but not because of her Mafia-esque announcement. "You know my name," he said.

"I do," she concurred. "And I know what service you perform for Mr. Mulholland."

Not that it took a genius to conclude he worked a security detail for Russell after the piece and photo in yesterday's paper, but his name hadn't been included in the article, nor had he been designated as a bodyguard. And although it wasn't impossible to find out who headed up security for Russell Mulholland, both Finn and his employer took great pains to keep as many of their security guards' names as private as possible. It was just another way to add an extra layer to the Mulhollands' safety. But even beyond all that, it bothered Finn that Natalie Beckett had learned his name before he learned hers. It made him feel like he wasn't doing his job.

"You're Finnian Michael Guthrie," she said, jarring him even more. Almost no one knew his full name. "And you work as head of security for Russell Mulholland. You both grew up in Seattle, so I assume your paths crossed there somewhere at some point." She smiled coyly, and something inside Finn twisted tight . . . though not necessarily in a bad way. "I assume that," she said, "because, well . . ." She smiled again. "Beyond the things I just revealed, it gets a little murky trying to learn more about the two of you."

She leaned in a little closer than Finn liked, and not just because it enabled him to fill his lungs with the sweet, clean scent of her, either. "I did manage to dig up a few interesting tidbits, though," she whispered conspiratorially. She leaned back again and added in her normal—husky, sexy—voice, "I must say, though, you and Mr. Mulholland have managed to keep buried just about everything that ever happened to either of you pre–Mulholland Games, Inc. It was only after the GameViper came out that you start showing up regularly on Google. What's really interesting is that you are almost every bit as Googleable as Mr. Mulholland, even though he is by far the bigger celebrity."

As she spoke, one by one, every alarm in Finn's ample arsenal began to go off. Russell paid an exorbitant amount of money to keep any references to himself pre–Mulholland Games, Inc., off the Internet. Had the guy realized how successful the company would someday be, he doubtless would have changed his name a long time ago. But it was what it was, and they'd had to make do. Thankfully, there were people out there whose life's work was keeping outrageously wealthy people outrageously hidden in cyberspace, as long as those people paid an outrageously large amount of money for the service.

Somehow, Finn managed to keep his own voice mild and conversational when he asked, "Are you a reporter? Or writing a book about Mr. Mulholland or something?"

She laughed lightly at that, the sort of laugh that normally made a man think he was about to pay a lot more for dinner than he had planned to spend on a first date. Clearly she was beginning to feel more comfortable with the situation. Whatever that situation was. Which was ironic, because Finn was growing more uneasy with every passing second.

"No," she told him. "I'm an event planner."

He relaxed at her admission. Some. Russell had been inundated with requests for personal appearances since his arrival in town had been discovered. Hopefully, this would be just one more thing to decline, and then Ms. Natalie Beckett, who may or may not have an engagement ring on her finger, would be on her merry way.

He and Russell had done their best to keep the Mulhollands' arrival in Louisville under wraps for as long as possible, just as they did whenever Russell and his son traveled together or when Russell traveled alone. Whenever either Mulholland had gone out, they'd done so with a bare minimum of security—at least, until the other day—and they'd all dressed and acted as if they were simply a group of friends out for a good time. They'd hired a handful of guys who looked ten years younger than they actually were to accompany Max, as if they were friends of the fourteen-year-old. They never booked rooms under anyone's real name, and they never booked them all at one time. But in spite of all the precautions, there was invariably someone on the staff of any given hotel or restaurant who recognized Russell, and once he was recognized, the vultures started circling.

Damn those *People* magazine lists, anyway.

"An event planner," Finn repeated blandly, hoping his tone of voice would prevent her from going into detail about whatever event she had planned that she wanted Russell to be a part of.

"That's right," she said brightly. Then, clearly not picking up on that tone-of-voice thing, she continued, "I've organized a party for Derby Eve that's going to be the hottest ticket in town, and I'd like to extend a personal invitation to Mr. Mulholland to attend." Before Finn could utter another word, she was whipping an envelope from her purse and extending it toward him. As she did, she added, "And do please tell your employer he's free to bring as many of his, ah . . . *friends*"—she punctuated the overly emphasized word with a quick wink—"as he'd like to bring. Normally, there's a five hundred dollar fee for the party, but—"

Finn wasn't able to mask his surprise over that. He interrupted, "You want to invite my employer to a party, and then charge him money, to the tune of five hundred bucks, to attend? That's nuts."

This time, she did pick up on his tone of voice, because she halted midsentence with her mouth hanging open and blinked a few times, as if a too-bright flash had gone off before her eyes. Then she stammered, "I . . . it's . . . I mean . . . the party is for a good cause. It's a fund-raiser. The hostess is donating all proceeds to—"

"Thank you, Ms. Beckett, but no thanks," Finn said, interrupting her again. It didn't matter where the proceeds of the party would be going. What mattered was that Russell *wouldn't* be. "Mr. Mulholland has a very full schedule while he's in town. Unfortunately, he won't be able to attend your party. But," he added as he plucked the invitation out of her hands, deliberately folded it into uneven quarters, smashed it down with both hands, and stuffed it with total disregard into his back pocket, "I'll talk to his assistant about sending around a check."

She looked nonplussed and not a little ruffled at his reaction. Her smile fell as quickly as her expression, and she studied him in unmistakable disbelief, as if she had been absolutely confident that a simple invitation accompanied by a sweet smile and plunging neckline would win her the outcome she'd expected.

Obviously, someone thought very highly of herself.

"Now, if you'll excuse me, Ms. Beck," he continued, deliberately calling her by the wrong name, "I was just on my way out for a bite."

And with that, Finn brushed past her without sparing her a second glance. Unfortunately, he didn't think he'd be quite so successful in not sparing her a second thought. Or a third thought. Or a fourth. Because Natalie Beckett really did have a sweet smile. And it didn't go with the plunging neckline at all.

Sugar and spice, he thought as he exited the Brown Hotel and began to make his way down Fourth Street. He'd never been able to resist either.

NATALIE WATCHED FINN GUTHRIE'S LEISURELY RE-treating backside until it disappeared through the revolving door that led from the Brown lobby to the street. And she thought, *Damn. His backside is even nicer to look at than his front side.*

Then she remembered how easily and carelessly he'd dismissed her. "It's Beckett," she said softly in the direction of the hotel exit. "Natalie. Beckett." To herself, she added, *Thanks so much for your consideration. Jerk.*

And she'd been so suave, too.

She sighed. She really hadn't thought it would be that easy to get Russell Mulholland to accept her invitation to Clementine's party. But she hadn't thought it would be as difficult as Finn Guthrie wanted to make it, either. She'd thought he would at least offer some vague assurance that he'd give the invitation to Mr. Mulholland, not Mr. Mulholland's assistant. And then, you know, actually pass it along to Mr. Mulholland. Not that Natalie didn't appreciate the offer of a donation, mind you, since it would up the buck and a half Clementine's take was looking to be at this point. But she had thought Mulholland's bodyguard would at least help get the invitation physically into the billionaire's hand. And then the billionaire would read the wittily written inscription, see the wittily conceived theme, and be unable to resist coming to the affair, if only for a little while.

Thirty minutes, she thought. If she could just get a commitment from Russell Mulholland to stop by Clementine's party for thirty minutes, it would be enough for her to spin it into a major event that would bring people out of the woodwork to attend.

She looked at the door through which Finn Guthrie had just exited and marveled again at what a very disagreeable man he was. Not only had he been rude, but he was unkempt. He'd gone so long without shaving that the lower half of his face was shadowed like a Mack truck. His blue jeans were more rip than denim, and his T-shirt had barely fit. Okay, so maybe that last was because they probably didn't make T-shirts in size XX*OMGX*B—X-tra, X-tra, *Oh-my-God-X-tra* Brawny—but that was beside the point. The point was . . .

She sighed heavily. The point was that she had once again been dismissed as if she were no more important than a piece of lint. And this time it was by a guy who had smoky gray bedroom eyes and silky brown tousled hair and arms cambered with swells of muscle. No, wait. That wasn't why she felt so hurt. It was because this time it was by a guy who was a worse dresser than Larry the Cable

Guy. And he hadn't even offered the slightest indication that he wanted to git 'er done.

How could someone of Russell Mulholland's stature trust his security—or, even more surprisingly, his *son's* security—to a man like that? And why hadn't she been able to find out more about either of them on the Internet? It was as if neither of them had existed prior to the launch of the GameViper. What was up with that? Even Natalie, when she Googled herself, showed up in links to websites where her name was on the guest list of a party she attended years ago, or on the committee of some function she had helped organize. But Mulholland and Guthrie? Nothing.

She glanced down at her watch and looked up at the door again. He only had a few minutes' head start on her. And he'd said he was going out for a bite. She did some quick mental math. There were probably a dozen restaurants between here and Fourth Street Live, and Fourth Street Live claimed more than a dozen more. Still, considering the way he was dressed, that narrowed the choices some. Maybe if she hurried . . .

Tugging her purse strap snugly over her shoulder and rising up on the balls of her feet, Natalie took off after him.

·Three·

FINN HAD JUST ORDERED SOMETHING CALLED A HOT Brown and an American pale ale at a place called the BBC Alehouse when someone sidled up on the stool immediately beside him at the bar, even though nearly all the other stools were empty at this hour between lunch and dinner. He didn't have to look over to know it was Natalie Beckett. No, he knew that by the soft scent that surrounded her—and then surrounded him, too. And also by the way his body responded to that scent. And even more by the way his body responded to the fact that she had sidled up on the stool beside him at the bar.

He swore silently to himself. Russell Mulholland wasn't the only one who was susceptible to nice girls. Probably because he and Finn had never been allowed anywhere near nice girls when they were growing up. Or when they were adults, either, come to think of it. Speaking for himself, nice girls generally took one look at him and gave him a wide berth. Speaking for Russell, it was the other way around. Russell wanted nothing to do with nice girls. At least these days. Mostly because he'd already met—and married—the nicest girl in the world and lost her. Marti Dennison Mulholland had gotten close to Russell in spite of Russell's best efforts to keep her away. And when he'd fallen, he'd fallen *hard*. Since her death . . .

Well, suffice it to say Russell had fallen even harder. But this time he hadn't landed in the sort of nice, stabilizing life that brought out the best in him, like he'd had with Marti. On the contrary. Finn would have liked to think that with Max in the mix now, Russell would have been able to keep going somehow. Instead, he'd reverted to his old ways—tenfold. His life these days was about as tumultuous as it could get. It wasn't that he was a bad or negligent father. It was just that . . .

Oh, hell. Fact was, Russell *was* a bad and negligent father. He loved his son—there was no question about that. The problem was, he loved Max too much. So much that he was afraid to let the kid get too close, for fear of losing him, too, the way he'd lost Marti.

Finn turned to look at Natalie—who, for some reason, didn't know enough to give him a wide berth—and was opening his mouth to shoot her down before she had a chance to start carping again about her "event." But he snapped his mouth shut when he saw that she wasn't even looking at him and was instead studying the selection of beers on tap. And she was showing way more interest in them than she had in him just a little while ago, when he'd been so certain she was showing him an inordinate amount of interest. She was also, he couldn't help further noting, glancing up to smile at the bartender with way more sincerity than she'd shown when she smiled at Finn a few minutes ago. The bartender who, Finn *also* noted, was smiling back at Natalie, and doing so in a way that went way beyond simple *this smile always gets me a better tip* friendly.

"What can I get for you?" the guy—who was easily ten years younger than Finn and had that clean-scrubbed, all-American golden boy look about him that women like Natalie Beckett probably couldn't resist—asked her.

"I'll have a Nut Brown Ale," she said with the sort of confidence that indicated she was not only familiar with the product but enjoyed it on a regular basis.

Something about that realization made Finn feel better. Because it meant that she'd doubtless known coming in here what she would order, which meant she had only been pretending to study the assortment of beers on tap in an effort to fake the sort of nonchalance she'd been faking before at the hotel. And that meant she *had* followed him in here to carp some more about the "event" she was trying to get Russell to attend, something that should have irritated the hell out of Finn but which, for some weird reason, made him not feel irritated at all.

That was his story, and he was sticking to it. Except for the part about not feeling irritated. Really, he was irritated. He was. Irritated as hell. Honest.

Ah, hell.

Ms. Natalie Beckett who wasn't a Mrs. then added, "And a bison burger, blackened, medium rare with havarti and peppers, garlic fries as the side." She ordered with great aplomb—and without looking at the menu, another indication that she ate often at this particular eatery. Her order also indicated she couldn't possibly have a date tonight—not unless the guy had completely lost his sense of smell—but Finn couldn't have cared less about that. Really, he couldn't. Honest.

Okay, he supposed her familiarity with the menu could mean she had in fact come in here not by design but because she was hungry, and that she really didn't realize she had seated herself next to a man she had, only moments ago, been trying to seduce—figuratively speaking—with a sweet smile and a plunging neckline.

But he doubted it.

He doubted it even more when she turned to look at him and brightened in the way women did when things were going exactly according to their plans. "Why, Mr. . . . Gustafson, wasn't it?" she asked, sounding surprised to find him sitting beside her in a way that indicated she was in no way surprised to find him sitting beside her. Nor had she forgotten his name, he was certain. She just wanted to rankle him, the way he'd wanted to rankle her earlier by deliberately calling her by the wrong name.

"Guthrie," he corrected in a way he told himself did *not* sound rankled.

"That's right," she replied affably. "Fitz Guthrie."

"Finn," he corrected her again, in a way he told himself did *not* sound *really* rankled.

She made a soft *tsk*ing noise and lifted a hand to nudge back that shaft of blond hair that kept falling over her forehead. The shaft of blond that Finn kept wanting to reach over and nudge back himself. "Silly me," she said. "I am so bad with names."

Right. That was why she'd been able to find out more about him and Russell than he was comfortable with her knowing. Would that she *had* been bad with names, he wouldn't be sitting here with her now, getting ready to shoot her down again before she started carping about her event again. Of course, if that had been the case, he reminded himself, he wouldn't be sitting here enjoying the soft, sweet scent of her, either.

Ah, hell.

"Look, Ms. Beckett—" he began.

"So you do remember my name," she interjected, her smile moving into the smug range now.

He ignored her statement. And her smugness. "I appreciate your . . . tenacity . . ." he began. With remarkable restraint, too, since the word he was really thinking was *pigheadedness*, which he was absolutely certain was not a word a man should use with a woman he didn't want hitting him with a brick. ". . . in your pursuit . . ." he continued with even more remarkable restraint, since the word he really wanted to use was *stalking*, which was another one of those words that put a woman on alert and also made her pick up a brick. ". . . of my employer. But as I told you at the hotel before—"

"You know, the way you say that," she interrupted before he could finish, "you make me sound like I'm pig-headed or a stalker or something."

"Don't be ridiculous. The thought never crossed my mind."

"But I'm neither," she assured him. "I simply want to give Mr. Mulholland the opportunity to enjoy the time-honored Kentucky tradition of celebrating the most venerable horse race in the world on the eve of its running, by attending a formal benefit surrounded by like-minded individuals, enjoying Louisville hospitality at its finest."

"That's a pretty inflated way to say you want Mr. Mulholland to come to a party," Finn pointed out. "Especially since it will be everyone except Mr. Mulholland who benefits, since he'd likely be the star attraction and everyone would want a piece of his time. Time, I might point out," he hurried on when she opened her mouth to interrupt him again, "that is worth more on an hourly basis than even your hostess could afford to pay him. Not that you've indicated he'd be paid, since you're also asking him to pay for the privilege of being taken advantage of."

"It's a fund-raiser," she reminded him. "And my client would be happy to cover Mr. Mulholland's contribution herself if he agrees to come. And the cause is an excellent one. My client is raising money for a group that—"

This time Finn was the one to interrupt, since the last thing he wanted to hear about was some bleeding heart organization whose contributions went to the sponsorship of self-important artists whose "art" was anything but, or to funding research for more environmentally friendly lipstick. He'd met enough society do-gooders moving in Russell's social circles to know that most of them picked niche groups whose work eventually found its way back to the original benefactor. "My employer has better things to do than be the centerpiece for a party full of strangers that will benefit him in no way."

"But Mr. Mulholland will benefit greatly," she quickly countered. "He has a horse running in the Derby, doesn't he?"

"Yes, but—"

"But the race itself is only a small part of the Kentucky Derby experience," she interrupted. Again. "The parties come close to stealing the limelight every year. If Mr. Mulholland comes all the way to Louisville for the Derby but doesn't attend anything but the race, he's going to miss out on so many wonderful opportunities."

"Really," Finn said wryly. "And here, all these years, I've been thinking the Kentucky Derby was the reason for the Kentucky Derby."

Actually, he'd never given the Kentucky Derby any thought at all. Not until Russell started investing in Thoroughbreds and was bitten by the racing bug. And even now, Russell had been infinitely more excited about coming to town for the next two weeks than Finn had. Which, in the long run, had just frustrated the guy, because he knew he couldn't get out and enjoy things the very way Natalie Beckett was suggesting he enjoy them. To do so would mean to be overrun by, at best, admirers and, at worst, psychos. Even in good times, celebrity wasn't all it was cracked up to be.

Of course, there were those who said, "Hey, if you want to be rich and famous, you have to take the good with the bad." Celebrities knew the job was dangerous when they took it, and many of them spent years courting fame, so they had no right to shun the limelight once they had it. True enough for many of them, Finn conceded. But there were others, like Russell—and, even more to the point, his son Max—for whom fame and fortune had come as an enormous surprise and was simply the result of doing something they loved that grew beyond their wildest dreams. And those were the people who did have a right to shun the limelight. Unfortunately—and ironically—by making themselves unavailable, they became even more adamantly pursued.

If Russell had it all to do over again, Finn knew, he would have handled everything differently. But there was no such thing as a do-over in life. You had to make choices one day and deal with them the next.

"Pshaw," Natalie said, and for a moment, he thought she was disagreeing with his life's philosophy, and that she believed life was nothing but do-overs. Then he remembered they'd been talking about a horse race. "There's the Derby," she continued, "and then there's the Derby *experience*. As any Louisvillian will tell you, they are two hugely different things."

"Really," Finn repeated even more wryly.

She nodded knowingly and was about to say more when the bartender returned with her Nut Brown Ale. To Finn's surprise, it wasn't a light lager, which he would have thought a woman would order, but a dark stout that she readily lifted to her mouth. And she didn't sip it daintily, the way he would have thought a woman would. Instead, she drank appreciatively and savored it before turning to look at him again.

"The Derby," she began again without missing a beat, "is a bunch of gorgeous horses with brightly clad riders running around a big oval."

"Oh, I'd say it's a little more than that," Finn objected.

"Yeah, yeah, yeah, there's a million dollar purse," she conceded dispassionately. "Whatever. The Derby *experience*, on the other hand, is something you absolutely cannot put a price tag on. For the next two weeks, every single day, there will be something going on—often several somethings—that run the gamut from elegant to eccentric. One day there will be a fashion show for enormous hats where they serve champagne cocktails and little Benedictine sandwiches with the crusts cut off, and the next day there will be people dressed up as rabid badgers and sock monkeys, racing tricked-out beds around a track at the fairgrounds and behaving like drunken satyrs." She met his gaze pointedly. "Now, do you really think Mr. Mulholland wants to miss out on stuff like that?"

Actually, Finn thought, that kind of stuff was right up Russell's alley. Well, maybe not the hat fashion show, but he'd down more than his fair share of champagne there. And sock monkeys and rabid badgers? Say no more. Not that he was going to give Ms. Know-It-All Beckett the satisfaction. So he said, "To be honest, Ms. Know . . . ah . . . I mean, Ms. Beckett . . ."

But she cut him off—again—before he could continue. "And there's a rat race. With real rats. And a wine race. And a balloon race. And a steamboat race. Both Mr. Mulholland and his son would enjoy *all* of the above. Well, maybe not the hat fashion show," she conceded. "But there is fun to be had for all ages and genders during the Kentucky Derby Festival."

"Really, Ms. Beckett, I don't think—"

"And the parties," she further interjected. "My God, man, it's party central here this time of year. *Every*one hosts a party for Derby, from the Dare to Care Food Bank and Make-A-Wish Foundation to *Playboy* and *Maxim* magazines. Not that I'd encourage the younger Mulholland to attend those last two, mind you," she added. She continued starchily, "Or Mr. Mulholland, for that matter, since to do so would be to betray my gender in the most egregious way, but hey, that's not up to me to make that call. All I can do is hope that your gender rebukes things that smack of disrespectful treatment of women and behave in a manner that is, um, respectful." Again, before Finn had a chance to say anything—and he really, really wanted to say something— she hurried on, "But that, unfortunately, is also out of my hands, other than by ensuring that I myself behave in a way that commands respect from the opposite sex, which is something, quite frankly, I really wish certain other members of my gender would pick up on, but I guess that's out of my hands, too."

By now, Finn's head was beginning to spin at the outpourings of Natalie Beckett's brain. Though he somehow did manage to grasp the fact that she was currently condemning the very behavior she'd just indulged in herself, dressing as she had and flirting with Finn just to convince his employer to attend a party she was throwing.

Right? Wasn't that what she was doing? At this point, he was so befuddled, he wasn't confident he could say for sure that the sky was blue and the grass was red.

Green, he quickly corrected himself. The grass was green. Right? Wasn't it?

Oh, for . . .

"Look, Ms. Beckett," he said more adamantly. At least, he tried to be adamant. But she lifted her beer to her mouth for another one of those luscious sips, and when she lowered it, there was a thin veil of foam on her upper lip that she immediately swiped away with the tip of her tongue, and Finn couldn't remember what he'd been going to say. Then her tongue darted out a second time, limning the entire outline of that succulent mouth, and all he could think about at that point was the succulence of that succulent mouth.

And holy crap, what did he think he was doing, looking at Natalie Beckett's succulent mouth when he should be telling her to take a hike? He reminded himself of all the reasons Russell had hired him in the first place—including the really big reason—reminded himself it was his job to ensure there was always a safe distance between the Mulhollands and people like Natalie Beckett. Or people like anyone else. It didn't matter that the rule didn't hold up for Finn himself, and that there was no one who said he had to keep a distance between himself and Natalie. In fact, there was no one who said he couldn't get as close to her as he wanted. Even closer than they already were, with her elbow nearly touching his on the bar. He didn't even mind if she smelled like Havarti and peppers and garlic later. In fact, if he wanted . . .

He bit back a mental sigh. Well, that was the problem. Finn couldn't allow himself to want. Because he wanted things he would never—could never—have. And for that reason, if no other, he really needed to get as far away from Natalie Beckett as possible.

"Ms. Beckett," he tried again.

"Please, call me Natalie," she said.

Telling himself that was the last thing he should do, he said, "Natalie." He hesitated only a moment before telling her, "I'm sure Mr. Mulholland would tell you thanks for the invitation, but no thanks. He's a very busy man, and his focus for the next two weeks will be on making sure his horse is ready for the race."

"But—"

"Now, if you'll excuse me . . ." This time he turned to the bartender. "Could I get that Hot Brown to go?"

NATALIE WATCHED FINN GUTHRIE'S RETREATING BACK-side for the second time in one day, with even more appreciation than she'd had the first time. Boy, that walk of his could start fights and stop traffic. Then she noted the edge of the carelessly folded invitation rising out of his back pocket and remembered that he'd once again refused to even pass it along to his employer. The door closed behind him, removing both the invitation and his backside from view, leaving her feeling doubly let down.

What was the guy's problem, anyway? Yeah, okay, as head of Russell Mulholland's security detail, he was obligated to keep people away from his employer, but still. Mulholland really was going to miss out on a lot of fun if he spent his entire stay in Louisville surrounded by bodyguards and never enjoyed any of the scores of events to be had this time of year. And it wasn't like Natalie was asking the guy to attend some minor affair where a bunch of yahoos would do nothing but make demands on his time and attention. Only the finest people would be at Clementine's party making demands on his time and attention. Provided, you know, he accepted the invitation. Otherwise there would be no one at Clementine's party doing anything.

The bartender placed her burger on the bar in front of her, and she turned to look at it dispassionately. Just as Finn Guthrie had done a moment ago, she asked the bartender if she could get it to go instead. She enjoyed a few more swallows of her beer as she waited for him to box it up, but left the glass half-full after paying for her purchase.

Half-full, she repeated to herself at the realization, brightening some. That was the way she always looked at things.

It was the reason she kept rebuilding after every disaster she'd created, both in life and in business. Natalie Beckett was not a quitter. Nor was she one to back down from a challenge. If things didn't go right the first time, then you tried again. And if they didn't go right the second time, then you tried *again*. And if they didn't go right the third time, you—

Well, anyway, *she* would just try again. Natalie Beckett had never been one to take no for an answer. Not unless no was the answer she wanted to hear. And certainly not when her livelihood—her entire future—depended on a yes.

Once again, she followed the same path Finn Guthrie had taken, exiting through the same door as he. But this time, she didn't follow him. She turned in the opposite direction of the Brown Hotel and strode toward the lot where she'd parked her car. Instead of returning to her Crescent Hill office, however, she opted for her Crescent Hill home, a creekstone Arts and Crafts–style house she'd purchased after graduating from college—okay, okay, with money from her trust fund—and which she loved even more now than she had the first day she moved in. It wasn't huge—three bedrooms, two baths—but it was the perfect size for her, and the open spaces, geometric lines, dark trim, and jewel-toned colors she'd chosen to fill it suited her. It was a far cry from the muted and overstuffed—in more ways than one—house in which she'd grown up, and in which she'd never felt comfortable. Where her mother's style could be best described as Colonial condescension, Natalie's was more cottage cozy. And that didn't relate just to their decorating styles, either.

After stowing her carryout in the fridge—not surprisingly, she hadn't actually been hungry when she ordered—she went straight upstairs to her bedroom to change clothes, opting for a baggy white T-shirt and even baggier pajama pants decorated with cartoon cats. Then she washed her face of the makeup she'd donned for Finn Guthrie's benefit—for all the good it had done—and made her way to her home office. Zip, her silver tabby, jumped into her lap the

moment she sat down in front of her computer, and Natalie
absently scratched her ear as she skittered the mouse across
the pad to bring up a screen. She clicked on her Internet
icon, which automatically opened on Google, but she hesitated a moment before typing anything into the search
box.

Finally, on a whim, she typed in the name Steve Jobs in
quotations. More than sixteen million hits came up. When
she'd done the same thing for Russell Mulholland earlier
in the day, fewer than one million had come up. Why
would that be? Certainly Steve Jobs had been around longer than Russell Mulholland, but the two men's success
was comparable, and the huge discrepancy hardly seemed
justified.

That was made more evident when she Googled Finn
Guthrie's name for a second time and realized again that
his name appeared nearly as often as Mulholland's did.
Why would a man who was worth as much as Russell have
only as many hits as a man whom he employed, even if
that man was constantly at his side?

One thing Natalie had learned early on about the Internet was that it was rife with complaint and misanthropy,
particularly where celebrities of any kind were concerned.
There should at least be a handful of websites—if not
more—devoted to bashing Russell and his game system,
thanks to malcontents who hadn't been able to get their
hands on one or who didn't know how to use it properly.
And those sites wouldn't include mention of Finn's name,
because people wouldn't know or care about him in that
context. There should also be plenty of business and financial articles about the billionaire that wouldn't include
Finn, because even if they mentioned his cadre of bodyguards, few would bother to specify any of them by name.

So why were Finn and Russell virtually always linked, and
why were there so many fewer mentions of the billionaire
than there should be? There could be only one explanation,
Natalie finally concluded.

Russell Mulholland was hiding something. The billionaire had a secret he didn't want getting around. And she'd bet every cent she had that Finn Guthrie's job was to protect that as much as he did the billionaire.

She'd read an article not long ago about a type of business that was beginning to thrive because the companies were able to, through finagling or bribery or outright threats, have removed from the Internet any number of pages or sites that referred to their clients in less-than-stellar ways. It made sense that someone who valued his privacy as much as Russell Mulholland did would pay for such a service. If Natalie could afford it, she'd pay for such a service herself. To this day, she continued to be mocked about the dress she'd worn to Sybil Garrison's twenty-first birthday party, because there were still photos floating around out there in cyberspace. Well, how was she supposed to know how enormous her butt had looked with that big-ass bow on the back?

Suffice it to say she could just sympathize with Russell Mulholland, that was all.

But what could a man like that have to hide? Then again, what she *had* read painted him as a man who was using his newfound wealth to live like an overgrown adolescent. In addition to racing horses, he liked to race Formula One cars—except that he employed jockeys to ride the horses, and he himself drove the cars. He'd also been linked romantically to a number of women—though none for any length of time—but that wasn't surprising, given both the nature of handsome, wealthy men and the often biased sensationalism of the media. Womanizing was in no way a secret when it came to business moguls, never mind acting like an overgrown adolescent. So that couldn't be what Russell Mulholland was worried about having revealed to the world.

She recalled again how she hadn't been able to uncover anything about him or his chief of security prior to the formation of Mulholland Games. No mention of him being an academic standout in high school or college, which one would think he had been, considering his current success.

She hadn't found so much as his name listed on the roster of the science or chess clubs of any schools. No marriage announcement. No birth announcement for his son. Not even an obituary for his wife.

Just to be sure, Natalie searched a variety of word combinations in an effort to rouse something like that. But there was nothing. She did the same thing with Finn Guthrie, telling herself it was only because she needed a comparison, and not because she was genuinely curious about whether or not he was married with children, or how old he was, or where he was born, or where he'd gone to school, or whether or not he'd been in the science or chess club at that school.

But there was nothing about Finn prior to his employer's business successes, either. There were only a few hundred thousand mentions of him at Mulholland's side, keeping away (choose any that apply) paparazzi, autograph hounds, gold diggers, corporate spies, all of the above.

Just who was Finn Guthrie? she wondered. Who was Russell Mulholland, for that matter? And more to the point, what was he—or what were *they*—trying to hide? Maybe if Natalie could figure that out, she'd have some leverage when it came to convincing the billionaire it would be in his best interests to come to Clementine's party.

She was brought up short when she realized what she'd just thought. Digging into someone's background to uncover things they'd probably just as soon leave covered, and then using those things to sway that person's actions wasn't leverage. It was extortion. What Natalie was thinking about was blackmail, plain and simple.

Could she really do that? Could she blackmail Mulholland into coming to Clementine's party if it meant ensuring her own success? That was pretty conniving. Pretty coldhearted. Pretty heinous. Even assuming she *could* uncover whatever it was the billionaire was hiding.

Good heavens, what was she thinking? Natalie asked herself. Of course she wouldn't—couldn't—blackmail anyone. Not unless, you know, she got really, *really* desperate.

And she wasn't desperate. She still had two weeks before

Clementine's party. Well, okay, one week to convince Russell Mulholland to attend and make the announcement, and then another week to have hundreds of people switch allegiance to attend the Hotchkiss gala instead of the parties to which they'd already committed. But hey, that was seven whole days she had to change Russell Mulholland's mind. Anything could happen in seven days. An entire universe could be created in seven days. And even if that was an allegory, Natalie was up for a decidedly *un*allegorical challenge.

All she had to do was find some way to convince Russell Mulholland to come to Clementine Hotchkiss's party that *didn't* involve extortion. If she could somehow appeal to the billionaire himself, in person, she was confident she could do just that. But appealing to the billionaire himself, in person, meant getting past his bevy of bodyguards first. And *that* meant getting past Finn Guthrie. Finn Guthrie, whose arms were roped with sinew, and whose chest was as broad as the Grand Canyon, and whose shoulders were roughly the size of Antarctica.

Oh, yeah, she thought sarcastically. No problem. Considering the way he'd succumbed to her today, she'd have him eating out of her hand in no time.

Okay, Natalie. Time to implement plan B.

There. The perfect solution to her problem. There was always a plan B to implement. Always. All she had to do now was, you know, remember what plan B was.

· Four ·

FINN WAS IN THE HOTEL SUITE BATHROOM TRYING TO get melted cheese off his Talk Derby to Me T-shirt—a Hot Brown, he'd realized in hindsight, wasn't the best thing to eat from a carryout box—when he heard the knock at his door. For one fleeting moment, he thought—even hoped—it was Natalie Beckett coming to bother him again. Then he reminded himself that there was no way she could learn what room he—or anyone else in Russell's party—could be in. Not if he was doing his job right.

It was only after he exited the bathroom and heard a second knock that he realized it was coming not from the door leading to the hallway but the door that connected his suite to the one Russell and Max were sharing. Nevertheless, he yanked a pinstriped oxford shirt out of the closet and shrugged it on before tugging the door open. It wasn't locked—Russell could have just come right in—but each man respected the other's privacy enough not to intrude without knocking first. It was a courtesy even Max remembered to uphold.

But it was Russell on the other side of the door this time,

looking like a man who was headed out for the evening. His pale blond hair was perfectly groomed, he'd just shaven, and he was dressed in khaki trousers, a white dress shirt, and a navy blue sport coat with brass buttons.

"What?" Finn said by way of a greeting. "Did you forget where you parked your yacht?"

Russell grinned. "No, it's anchored in Cinnamon Bay at the moment. I loaned it to Frøydis and some of her friends."

Frøydis was a supermodel whose name in Norwegian translated to "Goddess." Considering the fact that she was six two with ice blue eyes and white blond hair, the name should have been perfect for her. And it would be, were she not, in fact, from Hoboken and actually named Frances.

"You sure that's wise?" Finn asked. "The last time you loaned something to Frøydis and her friends, she sold it and they divvied up the cash between them."

Russell shrugged. "It was just a Bugatti."

Right. "You sure the yacht will still be there when you need it back?" Finn asked.

Russell shrugged again but said nothing.

Of course, Finn thought. It was just a Neorion. He shook his head slowly. "You're not even in love with her, Russell."

"No, but she's a hell of a lot of fun."

"No, she isn't. She sleeps twelve hours a day, then lets other people dress her and brush her hair and put on her makeup, then makes her living walking, then eats a meal that consists of two cabbage leaves, three peas, and a carrot sliver."

Again, Russell's only response was a shrug.

"Look, I know you're never going to find another woman like Marti," Finn said. "But the least you could do is date women who can hold a halfway coherent conversation with you."

This time Russell shook his head. "You're just jealous because you've never dated a woman whose name has an *o* with a slash through it."

"Neither have you," Finn pointed out.

Once again, Russell went back to his shrugging.

So Finn asked, "Where are you going tonight?" Russell had given him the night off, but Finn still wanted to know the other man's agenda.

"Dinner first, then a club or two."

Or ten, Finn added to himself. "Specifically?" he asked.

"I really don't know. I'm going to turn myself over to the capable hands of the driver you hired for me, since he's a native and should know where all the best places are located."

Right, Finn thought. Russell had specifically asked for a driver who could find all the best strip clubs in town, which meant it was going to be a late night for all concerned.

"Who's going with you?" Finn asked.

Russell sighed in the way that indicated Finn was hovering like an overprotective mom. *Too bad,* Finn thought. It was his job to be responsible for Russell. And since, for the past eighteen months, Russell had been using his newfound wealth to reclaim the youth he'd been denied as a youth, that left Finn to hover like an overprotective mom. At least, that's how he and Russell thought Finn was behaving. Neither had really had a mom who hovered over them when they were kids, which went a long way toward explaining why Russell was using his newfound wealth to reclaim the youth he'd been denied as a youth.

Finn could have done likewise, but, frankly, he had no desire to return to that time of his life, even if he could relive it differently. The man he was today was a sum of his life experiences, and he liked, for the most part, the man he was today. Had he been a happy teenager who never knew adversity, he would be someone else entirely. And he couldn't imagine being anyone else.

Russell, on the other hand, wanted to be *any*one else and had wanted that, probably, since Marti's death. During those too-short years with her, Russell had been the happiest Finn had ever seen him, and that was long before the Mulholland billions—or even the Mulholland millions—had started rolling in. He'd been wildly in love with his wife and baby son, and for a few months after Max's birth, it had just looked like his life would be perfect forever. Then came Marti's diagnosis, then her death, and after that . . .

Well, Russell had just started to pull away after that. From everything. And everyone. Even Max. Finn knew Russell loved his son. A lot. Which, maybe, was the very reason he kept his distance from the kid. Because he remembered how much it had hurt to lose Marti. And some part of him recognized that losing a child would hurt even more. Not that Finn was a psychologist by any stretch of the imagination, but it didn't take a degree in human behavior to figure that out. It only took watching your best friend go through the worst time in his life.

So while Finn was being a hovering mother to Russell, he did his best to be some kind of father figure to Max, too. So did the other guys who worked security. And Russell, to be fair, spent as much time with his son as he could. Or, at least as much as he dared. Their passion for gaming was the glue that bound them, and they shared as much as they could of that world.

Russell also did his best to set a decent example for Max, mostly by keeping his *in*decent behavior confined to after-hours. He rarely introduced his son to the women he was dating, and the low profile he did his best to keep prevented him from being the target of too many lurid tabloid stories. Anything Max might read about his father was easily dismissed as—and Finn had spent a lot of time wording this explanation—"rumor and innuendo generated by a disgruntled media." And, hey, anything printed about Russell *was* often rumor and innuendo generated by a disgruntled media.

Never mind that the reality was often rumor and innuendo for a reason, not to mention lurid. As far as Max was concerned, his father was no worse behaved than anyone else's. And really, considering the behavior of some of the fathers of the kids Max ran around with—and some of the mothers, too, for that matter—Russell was a paragon of virtue.

"Come on," Finn cajoled that paragon now. "Out with it. Where are you going?"

Russell ticked off a list of destinations whose names had enough *X*s and *Z*s in them to qualify for an obscure Eastern European language. Yep, it was going to be a loooooong night.

"And who's going with you?" he asked further.

"Stoller and Franklin," Russell replied obediently.

Finn nodded. Between the two of them, they ought to be able to keep Russell both safe and in line. "And what are Max's plans for the evening?"

"I believe he said something about checking out an extreme sports park not far from here," Russell told him. "It's supposed to be one of the best in the country. He left about an hour ago with Hernandez and Moseby, who both looked equally delighted to be spending the evening shredding. Whatever the hell that is."

Finn had already known about Max's interest in the park, so he'd sent Moseby over earlier to scope out the location. It wasn't the most secure place in the world, but Max ought to be okay with his entourage. It helped that the kid wasn't highly recognized, because he was almost never photographed by the media, thanks to everyone who worked security. And puberty had hit him so hard over the past year and a half that the fourteen-year-old Max bore little resemblance to the twelve-year-old who had been on the podium with his father on the much-publicized night Mulholland Games had announced the development of the GameViper. Max had shot up six inches in the past year alone and had dropped about ten pounds of leftover baby fat. His outdoor and beach life had bleached his hair from the dark brown he'd inherited from his mother to a sun-streaked chestnut that was nothing like his dad's. There was little chance anyone would peg Max as Russell Mulholland's kid. Still, Finn wasn't taking any chances. And neither would Russell.

"I told him he has to be back by ten," Russell said. "That tutor from his school who came with us isn't lightening up on the homework load just because Max is missing class for two weeks. So he still has to abide by his usual weekend bedtime."

"And what about you?" Finn asked. "Do you have a curfew, too?"

Russell tossed him a disgusted look. "I don't know, Mom, do I?"

"Just try to be home before dawn this time, okay?"

For the first time during their exchange, Russell grew serious. "With Max here? You know better than to even ask."

True enough, Finn thought. Russell only stayed out all night if Max was spending the night with a friend or his grandparents. And he never brought women home with him. Russell might stay out 'til the wee hours, but if Max woke up when he came in and saw how late it was, his father would tell him he'd just been having so much fun he'd lost track of time. Which would be true. He just wouldn't tell Max that the fun had been sexual in nature. Not that Max probably wouldn't be able to figure that out for himself. But at least Russell was trying.

Okay, okay, Finn thought. So Russell wasn't exactly in the running for the Father of the Year Award, and he was moving farther and farther away from it—and his son— every year. It was a defense mechanism on his part, Finn told himself. And anyway, now that Max was growing up and becoming more independent, he'd started to pull away from Russell, too, the way a healthy adolescent kid should. Of course, Russell had probably made that easier on the kid by never allowing him to get too close in the first place, but . . .

Well, hell, Finn thought. Suffice it to say that, these days, both Mulhollands were acting like adolescents. Which was weird on Russell's part, since Finn could remember plenty of nights when they were stuck in that group home where they had lain in their bunk beds—Finn on top, Russell on the bottom—talking about how much better their lives would be once they were grown-ups. How they couldn't wait to not be teenagers anymore, because no one took you seriously when you were a teenager, and the whole world was out to get you.

Then again, in some ways, the whole world was kind of out to get Russell now, so maybe he thought retreating back to that netherworld of adolescence would be a good place to hide.

Ah, screw it. Russell was who he was, and Finn was who he was. As happened so often in life, they'd taken different paths only to wind up at the same destination. To this day, they still approached things differently, even though they had identical goals. Keep the Mulhollands safe, and keep their secrets secret. Finn, at least, would do what he could to ensure that.

"Just behave yourself," he told Russell, hoping that would help him do his part, too.

"I always behave," his friend replied.

It was only after Russell had returned to his room and closed the door behind himself that Finn realized his last sentence could have meant anything.

AT ONE A.M., FINN WAS ALONE IN HIS ROOM, AND Russell still hadn't returned. He'd heard Max come in around nine, then the kid had spent a couple of hours playing Super Mario. Finn would recognize that overly cheerful, computer-generated music anywhere. Unfortunately. Try as he might, he'd never developed the interest in gaming that the Mulhollands had. Not even for the ones that weren't overly cheerful. Call him crazy, but he'd rather watch hockey anytime. Of course, you couldn't fire bazookas or blow people up in hockey—not and stay within the rules of the NHL, anyway—but at least the blood was real.

At the moment, all was quiet in the next room, indicating that Max was asleep and Russell still wasn't home. Finn ambled over to the minibar and withdrew a third beer, relishing the hiss of the cap as he twisted it off and savoring the first cold swallow. It was a rare Saturday night that he had off from work, mostly because weekends were when Russell was at his rowdiest, and he didn't trust his friend's safety to anyone but himself. But the last week had been especially grueling with all the preparation for the trip to Louisville, what with having to check up on everyone Russell and Max would be meeting with, and anyone they *might* be meeting with, and everyplace they were going, and anyplace they *might* be going. Add to it the fact that Finn hadn't taken a day off in more than three years, and Russell hadn't had to do much cajoling to get his head of security to take some time for himself.

And what had Finn done with that time to himself? He'd spent it cooped up in his hotel room—alone—watching TV. Yeah, okay, the room—*suite*, he corrected himself, still unaccustomed to staying in hotel *suites*, as opposed to hotel *rooms*—was pretty damned nice, with its dark wood paneling and Early Imperial Despot furnishings. And yeah, on the TV had been a boxing match he'd been looking forward to for a long time. But the point remained that Finn's nights off weren't exactly anything to write home about, which, now that he thought about it, might be why he took so few nights off.

For some reason, that made him think about Natalie Beckett, and he reached into the back pocket of his jeans for the invitation that was still jammed there. He set the beer on the desk and unfolded the heavy vellum paper, smoothing it out until the invitation lay open beside the beer. But where he would have expected there to be an elegantly scripted, formally worded summons for the prospective guest, instead, the card was inscribed in a funky font that described what actually sounded like a very good time.

A costume party, he thought as he set the invitation down on the desk. *Jeez, did people still have those these days outside Halloween?* Finn didn't think he'd ever been to a costume party, not even as a kid. He thought back. Nope. Not one. Then again, when you grew up the way he had, parties were few and far between. Whenever Finn got together with other kids, it had been to throw rocks at bottles in vacant lots or knock flattened cans down alleys with broomsticks. Then, later, to smoke cigarettes and drink vodka that someone had stolen, respectively, from his old lady's purse and his old man's liquor cabinet. To this day, Finn could not abide the smell of Virginia Slims or the taste of Smirnoff.

He looked at the invitation again and, impulsively, lifted it to his nose for an idle sniff. Yep, it smelled like her. Like Natalie. Soft and sweet. He wondered what she would be going to the party dressed as. Did party planners do that? Attend the parties they planned? Surely, they must, to make sure everything went according to plan and schedule. But would she dress up or wear street clothes?

Probably, he decided, she would dress up to blend in with the crowd. If it was a formal affair, she'd wear a formal. A barbecue or picnic, she'd wear something casual. Nobody wanted to stand out in a crowd, especially the person who was supposed to be keeping that crowd happy. So Natalie Beckett would almost certainly wear a costume to a costume party thrown by . . . He glanced at the name on the invitation again. Of course. Of course people who would throw a five-hundred-dollar-a-plate party would have names like Edgar and Clementine Hotchkiss.

So what would Natalie dress up as?

The answer came to him immediately. Hell, she could go as a screen siren from the Golden Age of Hollywood, and she wouldn't even have to change out of what she'd had on today. But she seemed like the type who would be more inventive than that. Maybe she'd go as a French maid. Or a Playboy bunny. Or a swimsuit model. Or wait . . . he knew. A harem girl. Yeah. That would suit Ms. Natalie Beckett to a T.

Well, okay, actually, it wouldn't suit Ms. Natalie Beckett at all. But it would suit Finn just fine. Except that, if he were her date, he'd have to dress like Rudolph Valentino, which wasn't going to happen in this life or any other. Then he realized he was thinking in terms of not just going to this party, but being Natalie's date, and that *really* wasn't going to happen in this lifetime or any other.

He inhaled deeply one more time of the invitation, breathing in the scent of Natalie and envisioning her in a skimpy, filmy Arabian Nights outfit. Then he closed the invitation and started to toss it into the trash can under the desk. He hesitated before completing the action, however. Just because Russell wasn't going to go to the party—or Finn, either—there was no need to be hasty. He had promised Natalie he would pass along the invitation to Russell or his assistant William, who normally took care of such things, and have a check sent around for whatever fund the party was raising money for. So he should hang on to the invitation, right? Just so he'd have a contact name and all that.

He started to fold up the invitation again, but something stopped him. Instead, he flattened his palm over the heavy paper and smoothed it out again, as well as he could. When he did, the scent of Natalie Beckett drifted up from it again. Or maybe that was just his imagination. Or wishful thinking. Or something.

He propped the invitation up against the lamp on the desk, to remind him to pass it along to William tomorrow. No need to bother Russell with something like this. There was no way he would accept the invitation. He hadn't accepted any of the other dozen or so he'd received since his arrival in Louisville had been made public. Hell, even in Seattle, he rarely went to parties anymore. Or anywhere else he might be recognized and/or photographed and/or glad-handed and/or hit on and/or all of the above. Russell much preferred being in places where there were other things that commanded attention way more than he did. Things like naked, sweaty women swinging around poles on a stage. And when he did his own entertaining, he did it in private.

Then again, there was a lot to be said for that.

Finn enjoyed another swallow of his beer and tried to think about something else. Something that didn't involve naked, sweaty women or entertaining in private or Natalie Beckett dressed as a harem girl. Unfortunately, that just made all those things become inextricably entwined.

Damn. It was going to be a long night.

AT TWO A.M. SUNDAY MORNING, NATALIE LAY IN HER darkened bedroom, wide-awake and staring at the ceiling, still trying to put her finger on plan B. But all she could think about was Finn Guthrie in his tight, X-tra brawny T-shirt and five o'clock shadow. Specifically, she was thinking about how it would be to peel that T-shirt from his X-tra brawny body and feel that five o'clock shadow abrading her tender skin.

Damn, would this night never end?

She tossed restlessly onto her side and checked the clock again. Two oh one. Nope, this night was never going to end. Not unless she got some sleep. And the only way she was going to get any sleep was to come up with a way to convince Russell Mulholland to attend Clementine's party. So far, she'd ruled out kidnapping (because it was illegal), seduction (because it was immoral), drugging him (because it was illicit), and conjuring him with herbs (because it was impossible). And, okay, fine, her morality was a little fluid in the seduction department when it came to gorgeous, wealthy men. But the problem was, it hadn't been Russell Mulholland she'd been thinking about seducing. It had been his head of security. And she'd already tried that once and failed abysmally.

She'd also thought about simply appealing to the billionaire's compassion for children, since he must have some compassion somewhere, but that would necessitate being face-to-face with him, and Finn Guthrie put an X-tra brawny obstacle between her and her target.

So what was she supposed to do now? Other than toss and turn some more and think about Finn?

She tossed and turned some more and thought about Finn. Hey, at least it was something.

She tallied everything she knew about Russell Mulholland in her head. One, he liked beautiful women and lots of them. Two, he liked fast cars and lots of them. Three, he had a teenage son she couldn't recall seeing him photographed with. Four, he was a game designing genius. Five, he owned Thoroughbreds. On and on Natalie went, listing facts and figures, rumor and innuendo. What she finally had at the bottom of the list was a man who used his billions to live life to its most extreme, who might need to work a bit on his fathering skills, who might have a teeny bit of a self-destructive streak, and who came across as not a little shallow and superficial.

She could work with that, she told herself. She might not be accustomed to mingling with billionaires, but she'd grown up amid wealth and people who enjoyed living life to its fullest. She knew plenty of fathers, including her own, who hadn't exactly lived up to their paternal potential, and she knew a lot of risk-takers—though, granted, most of them took risks with the stock market, not race cars that went a million miles an hour. And shallow and superficial? Pshaw. That was three-fourths of the social register, as far as she was concerned, from Arabella Abernathy to Zachary Zimmerman. Now all she had to do was figure out how to make her deductions about Mulholland work for her instead of against her.

Think, Natalie, think . . .

Unfortunately, instead of thinking about Russell Mulholland, she found herself thinking about Finn Guthrie again. Only this time the X-tra brawny T-shirt was gone. And so were the ragged jeans. And, dammit, so was the five o'clock shadow.

She turned to look at the clock once more. Two twenty-two. She sighed fitfully, tossed some more, and resigned herself to the fact that no, in fact, this night wasn't ever going to end. Nor was plan B likely to develop. Not unless it included a shirt-free, jeans-free, shadow-free Finn Guthrie.

·Five·

IT WAS AT SOME POINT DURING HIS THIRD LAP DANCE
that Russell Mulholland realized his boredom just wasn't
going to go away. Oh, certainly the young woman grinding
her pelvis against his chest at the moment was reasonably
attractive. At least, he thought she was reasonably attractive. It was hard to see her face the way her hair was flail-
ing around like that. Unfortunately, that was the only thing
that was hard at the moment. And what did it say about a
man when a scantily clad woman straddling him while he
sipped a fifty-dollar-an-ounce brandy did nothing to ap-
pease his ennui?

He glanced at Stoller on his left and Franklin on his
right, for whom he had also purchased a third lap dance.
Both men seemed to be entirely delighted with the goings-
on, though their dancers were no more, ah, gifted than
Russell's was. So why wasn't he enjoying himself, too?

Gentleman's club. That was how Minxxx referred to itself. And although the decor did a decent job of evoking the
feel of an English manor smoking room—provided English
manors today had taken to gaudy pink and purple neon,

disco mirror balls, and scratchy Eurotrash pop music—
few, if any, of the club's current patrons bore even a remote
resemblance to a *gentleman*. Russell himself included, of
course. And although the proprietors of Minxxx referred
to their acts as *cabaret*, few, if any, of the women who had
wrapped themselves around the pole tonight had looked as
good as Liza Minnelli in a halter top. Really, they didn't
even look as good as Joel Grey in a halter top.

The signs hanging outside of Minxxx had depicted a
juicy young blonde with a tiny waist and enormous hoot-
ers. But she must have been lifted from a piece of Internet
clip art, because none of the women who had graced—and
it went without saying that he used that word sardonically—
the stage tonight had claimed *any* of those traits. Well,
there had been a couple of blondes, but they hadn't been
natural blondes. He knew that by looking at their eyebrows,
not their—

Well, he knew it by looking at their eyebrows, because
Louisville had an unfortunate law about liquor not being
served in places where women disrobed completely. At least
professionally. And whoever had come up with that idea
should be taken out and flogged.

Oh, well, Russell thought. He doubted he'd be having a
good time even if the woman in his lap *wasn't* wearing a
hot pink thong, a couple of purple pasties, and a tattoo immortalizing someone named Phil.

"Thank you, sweetheart," he told the woman in an effort to make her stop, ah, performing. When she continued
with her gyrations, he added, "That was lovely. Brava." But
still she continued to bump and grind and slap her sweaty
hair across his face. He would have halted her by placing
his hands on her shoulders to get her attention, but he'd seen
other guys—ah, he meant *gentlemen*, of course—tossed out
on their keisters for laying hands on the women in their laps.
"Truly," he continued, raising his voice in the hope that she
might hear it over the raging cacophony of a band who obviously hadn't been able to afford a brand-name synthe-
sizer, "I had a delightful time, but I have an appointment

that I absolutely can't miss." At two a.m., he thought further. Then again, two a.m. was probably a time when a lot of these women had, ah, appointments.

When she still didn't stop dancing, Russell reached into his jacket and withdrew his wallet. At the sight of that, the young woman immediately ended her performance. He opened it to pull out a fifty—even though the dance itself had only cost twenty-five—when she looked in and saw a Benjamin gazing back at her.

Before he could stop her, she snatched out the hundred dollar bill and stuffed it into her bikini bottom. Then she met his gaze and smiled. "Hey, you can afford it."

Oh, if he had a dollar for every time he'd heard that, he'd be a billionaire. Again. He was hoping that would be the end of it, but she leaned forward again, brushing her pasties against his brand-new Hermès shirt with great intent. Instead of feeling aroused, however, Russell only hoped she didn't leave a stain.

"Thanks, babe," she purred. Well, okay, maybe not purred. There was that heavy smoker's rasp that turned the purr into something that sounded like fingernails on a chalkboard, punctuated by a clearing of her throat that could have put a dying giraffe to shame. "If you want, we could dance some more after my shift is over in an hour." She winked with all the enchantment of a wildebeest with a sty before further grating out, "If you know what I mean."

Alas, he was afraid he did know what she meant. And it would cost him even more than this so-called dance . . . not to mention a trip to a clinic for, at the very least, a penicillin shot in a week or two.

"I'd love to," he said, "truly I would. But, as I mentioned, I have an appointment." Just because it was an appointment to avoid an STD, there was no reason for him to elaborate.

"Shame," she said as she levered herself off his lap and tugged at her panties to readjust the thong wedgie she'd gotten as she danced. "We coulda made beautiful music together."

"Hmm," Russell replied noncommittally. He didn't know about that. Though he was sure they could at least do better than the outdated disco covers he'd been listening to all night.

He watched the dancer as she strode away, noting she had two more tattoos on her back, one immortalizing a guy named Sheldon, and the other immortalizing a woman named Dolores. Draining the last of his brandy, he looked around to order another and caught sight of a redhead near the bar dressed in the standard garb of Minxxx waitresses.

The waitresses at Minxxx wore only marginally more than the dancers, hot pink vinyl microminiskirts that barely covered their assets and purple vinyl halter tops that covered even less. The redhead at the bar, Russell couldn't help noticing, filled out her tiny costume better than any of the dancers, and he wondered briefly why the owner hadn't put her on the stage instead. As he drew nearer, he looked for one of the inevitable tattoos all the other women seemed to sport but saw none on her person anywhere—and he could see plenty of her person in that getup. And where the other women's complexions seemed sallow and insalubrious under the gaudy lights, this woman's was creamy and smooth, almost—dare he say it?—wholesome.

When she turned briefly to look at someone behind her, however, he saw that she was, like the other waitresses, wearing as much makeup as the dancers: bloodred lipstick and dark purple eyeshadow that made her look almost bruised. She was undeniably pretty, however, despite the garishness of her cosmetics, and surprisingly petite. Even in purple stilettos whose heels had to be four inches high, Russell gauged that she still wasn't tall enough to come up even with his chin. He watched as she loaded her tray with a dozen drinks of varying sizes and colors, noting with appreciation the way her breast pushed out of the side of the halter and how the soft curve of its underside peeked from beneath.

She was a symphony of curves, in fact. The full breasts

narrowed to a slender waist, then she flared out nicely once
again at her hips. Her arms bore the musculature of a woman
who hefted heavy trays for a living, her shoulders, biceps,
and triceps all clearly delineated as she went about her task.
Where Russell would have thought such an obvious sign of
physical strength in a woman would be off-putting, he instead found it rather . . . erotic. Her legs, too, were long
and muscular, from the camber of her calf to the arc of her
thigh.

And suddenly, he found himself thinking he might like
to dance after someone's shift, after all. Just not with the
dancer.

He lifted his glass to his lips again, then remembered
it was empty. Stoller and Franklin were still enthusiastically occupied with their dancers, so Russell didn't bother
to ask if they wanted a refill, too. Unfortunately, just as he
approached the redheaded waitress, she lifted her tray and
levered it onto her shoulder. So he watched her as she made
the rounds of her tables, setting each glass before its appropriate owner, amazed at the fluidity and ease of her movements as she completed the action. He winced as one of the
men at a neighboring table reached over and grabbed her
ass. But she was completely unfazed by the man's groping,
just reached behind herself to remove the offending hand
and returned to her drink deliveries.

Clearly, this was a woman who had made her living as a
waitress in seedy dives for some time and was utterly comfortable in the role. Better still, she didn't have any tattoos
immortalizing anyone.

Oh, yes. She was looking like the perfect *dance* partner
indeed.

Just as she relinquished the last of her drinks, the two men
seated at one of her tables rose to move closer to the stage, so
Russell made his way hastily to one of their vacated seats.
The waitress was about to move off in the opposite direction,
so he called after her, "Excuse me, miss?"

She turned at his summons, looking vaguely surprised
to be addressed as *miss*. Russell tried to guess her age, but

with all the face paint, it was hard to pin down. He could discern no lines around her eyes or mouth, however, something that suggested she was still in her early twenties, which made her even more attractive, because it meant he would have almost nothing in common with her.

She made her way back to the table, smiling at him in a way that was surprisingly charming, considering the fact that, barely a moment ago, a man had grabbed her ass in the most insulting way. Since it was safe to assume that that was probably a nightly—perhaps even hourly—event for her, Russell would have thought she wouldn't be particularly amenable to the opposite sex, even if her livelihood depended on it. Clearly, she wasn't saddled with something as heavy or inconvenient as self-respect.

In a word, *Yay*.

He noticed then that, like the other waitresses, her name was stitched into the vinyl of her halter top. *Amber*, it read. He wondered if that was her real name.

"What can I get for you, sir?" Allegedly Amber asked.

Her voice was touched with just a hint of a Southern accent, but it wasn't like the other accents he'd heard since arriving in Kentucky. This one was a deep Southern accent, the kind he'd heard in places like Georgia and South Carolina. She wasn't a Louisville native, he guessed, but a transplant. He found himself wondering what brought her here.

Then he wondered why he would care. She was a waitress in a strip club wearing a barely there outfit who didn't mind having her ass grabbed by strangers, and who was too young for him to be interested in what was going on in her head. *That* was what he cared about. Nothing more.

He held up his empty glass. *"Un autre Delamain cognac, s'il vous plaît,"* he said in flawless French. The fact that Minxxx even had it on the menu was the only concession he was willing to make that the place might, maybe, perhaps, possibly indeed be a gentleman's club.

He'd hoped his order would impress Amber the waitress— surely she was familiar enough with the menu to realize how expensive it was—but she only gazed at him blankly, her smile never faltering . . . or offering the merest hint that she knew what the hell he was talking about. Obviously, she didn't speak French—no surprise there—but neither had she figured out simply by hearing the brand name *Delamain* what he was ordering.

He smiled at her indulgently and clarified as simply as he could, "That means I'll have another glass of cognac from the bottle that has the word Delamain, spelled D-E-L-A-M-A-I-N, on its label."

She expelled a sound of relief and lifted a hand to her forehead, her smile now going supernova. "Thank you *so* much for translating that, sir. Sometimes those things just go right over my head." She punctuated the statement with a giggle that made something in Russell's midsection start buzzing with anticipation. "I'll get that for you right now, um . . . *monsieur.*"

She pronounced *monsieur* as *MON-sure*, something that delighted him even more, because it only hammered home that she was, ah . . . not the brightest neon light in Minxxx.

Still, it was better than being called *sir*, he thought as she turned to fill his order. *Sir* was how anyone who wasn't a friend or colleague addressed him. Employees, board members, the media, Max's friends, Max's teachers . . . everyone. Not once had Russell been comfortable with such address, but he tolerated it because he knew others expected him to. Somehow, it had bothered him even more than usual to hear *sir* rolling off of Amber's lips. Maybe because he knew she doubtless addressed all of her customers that way, and he didn't want to be lumped in with them. Even if, he made himself admit, he was here for the same reasons they were.

Stoller and Franklin joined him at the table then, each man wearing the sort of grin that indicated they were having a very good time, even with the bikini thongs and pasties covering up the good parts of their entertainment. Russell experienced a moment of envy, because he couldn't remem-

ber the last time he'd had as much fun as those two were
having right now.

Amber returned with his drink and asked what the other
gentlemen would be having, calling each of them *sir*, too,
when she addressed them. On her way to fetch those drinks,
she was summoned by a half-dozen more men, each of whom
who, at best, ogled her openly and who, at worst, tried to
cop a feel. But Amber ignored the ogling and deftly side-
stepped—or simply removed—the hands, moving fluidly
through all of it as she crossed the crowded room to the bar.
She had to thread her way through lap dances, reeling drunks,
and more than one flying beer can, but she remained completely unfazed by all of it.

Amazing, Russell thought. He'd met plenty of cocktail
waitresses in his day, but none who moved with that kind
of grace or whose charm was so infectious. She even managed to carry herself with dignity, in spite of the *in*dignity
of her outfit. Had he not known better, he would have thought
Amber the cocktail waitress spent her days as the reigning
monarch of some small, sovereign nation and never went
out without her white gloves, her unctuous entourage, or
her corgis.

Okay, now he was determined to, ah, dance with her.

He watched her until she returned with the other men's
drinks and placed them on the table before each, but before he could say anything, she asked him if he wanted to
run a tab.

"I'd love to run a tab, Amber," he told her. "Especially if
you add yourself to the total at the end of the night."

She didn't seem in any way shocked by the suggestion.
She simply smiled again and dropped her weight to one
foot, fisting her hand on her upturned hip. "Oh, MONsure,"
she said in a phony scolding voice that reminded him of
Minnie Mouse. To punctuate the fake censure, she removed
the hand from her hip to wag it at him playfully. "Now, you
oughta know that's not a service Minxxx provides."

"I'm not asking Minxxx to provide it," Russell said.
"I'm asking Amber to."

She shook her head and made a teasing little *tsk*ing sound. "Well, Amber is *very* flattered, but it's not a service she provides, either."

Russell met her gaze levelly and smiled what he knew was the most charming smile he claimed in his ample arsenal. "Oh, I bet you would if you knew who I am," he said.

Still smiling that adorable little smile, she bent over, *waaaay* over, holding the tray in both hands in a way that thrust her breasts together, a sight Russell found quite . . .

Well. Suffice it to say that Amber had accomplished with a single pose what whatshername the dancer hadn't been able to do grinding her pelvis into his lap and rubbing her pasties against his chest.

She moved her mouth right next to his ear, so close that he could feel her warm breath dampening his neck and could inhale the musky scent of her. Certain she was about to tell him that if he wanted the service he was clearly asking her to provide, then the two of them could arrange it out of earshot, he tilted his head closer to hers so that he could hear—and agree to—whatever terms she laid out.

Very, very softly, she said, "Oh, I do know who you are, Mr. Mulholland. We all do. The not nearly as reclusive as the media would lead us to believe billionaire. And where any other woman who works here tonight would be more than happy to take you up on your offer, I'm *not* any of the other women who work here."

Russell wasn't sure what surprised him more: the fact that Amber was turning him down or the fact that she'd known his identity all along and hadn't taken advantage of it. Usually, when people, especially women—especially women who worked in places like Minxxx—realized who he was, they went out of their way to either flirt with him or take advantage of him or out and out offer themselves to him in whatever capacity he needed them. Or just snatch a hundred dollar bill out of his wallet and be done with it.

There was one thing, however, that definitely did surprise Russell more than either of those things. And that was the way that Amber was suddenly speaking without a trace of the Southern accent he'd found so appealing, and with all the confidence and poise—and articulation—of that fictitious monarch he'd imagined her to be.

So astonished was he by this development, that, for a moment, he had no idea what to say. So Amber took advantage of that and added, even more quietly than before, "Don't make assumptions about people by the way they look or act, Mr. Mulholland. That kind of thinking will come back and bite you in the ass every time."

When she drew back again, she was smiling that vapid smile. And the Southern accent was every bit as convincing as before when she added, "Welcome to Louisville, *MON-sure*. Your tab." She slapped a scrap of white paper onto the table, and it clung to a wet ring near Russell's hand that had probably been there for a while. "One Delamain cognac, spelled D-E-L-A-M-A-I-N, one Johnnie Black on the rocks, spelled J-O-H-N-N-I-E-B-L-A-C-K, one Sam Adams, spelled S-A-M-A-D-A-M-S." She started to turn around, then added, "Oh, yeah. And *no* Amber. That's a big ol' *N* and a big ol' *O*." At that, she did pivot on her stiletto and gave Russell her back, then strode imperiously away.

And a very nice back it was, too, he couldn't help thinking as watched her departure. Seemingly acres and acres of silky skin marred only by the purple string of her halter and the hot pink miniskirt that twitched enticingly with every hip-swinging step she took.

"So what did she say?" Stoller asked eagerly.

"Yeah, and does she have any friends?" Franklin added.

Russell barely heard them. He was too busy wondering why a woman who seemed to have both intelligence and self-respect would be working in a dump like this, pretending to have absolutely no intelligence or self-respect.

"Sorry, boys," he told them as he reached for the tab, picking it carefully up by the corner. "I got shot down."

"Too bad, boss," Stoller said.

"Yeah," Franklin agreed. "She seemed like a nice girl."

Russell chuckled at that. Of all the things Amber the waitress might be—curvy, lush, unflappable, and, ultimately, halfway intelligent and in no way deferential—he could safely say that *nice* wasn't one of her qualities at all.

Which put Minxxx at the very top of his sightseeing list while he was in town. Because Amber the waitress, he thought, was just too lovely—and intriguing—a sight to miss seeing a second time.

GINNY COLLINS CINCHED THE LOCK ON HER LOCKER in the back room of Minxxx, the nightly ritual that officially transformed her from Amber Glenn back to her usual self. And, as she did every time she clicked the padlock into place, she reminded herself that her profession was a totally honorable one for women and had been for more than a century. She was, after all, an actress. Five nights a week, including weekends—especially weekends—she performed her role as a cocktail waitress in a strip club. And she performed it so convincingly that she should be nominated for a damned Tony. Amber Glenn, cocktail waitress, was every man's idea of a good time. Ginny Collins, on the other hand . . .

She made her way to the back door, pausing to inspect herself in the cracked mirror to double-check for any lingering traces of Amber. Her face was scrubbed clean of makeup, and the red wig was sitting atop its foam head in the locker, right next to the case holding her brown contact lenses. Her pale brown hair was in a ponytail now, and her faded blue eyes looked as unremarkable as ever. Her vinyl costume—because what good would a Tony-worthy actress be without a costume?—had been replaced with faded blue jeans and a loose-fitting black T-shirt, the stilettos traded for a pair of well-worn hiking boots. She was herself again. Thank God.

Now she could go home.

Two of the dancers had finished their shifts, too, so she

waited for them to get dressed so they could all walk out to their cars together. Even though the lot for Minxxx's employees was fenced and locked to keep out the riffraff, Ginny was hesitant to ever leave by herself. She waved to the other women as they all got into their cars—and locked them—with the precision of a Greek chorus, and they all waited to make sure everyone's engine started before heading to the exit to enter the code that would allow them to escape.

She turned off Seventh Street Road onto Dixie Highway, no longer surprised at how busy the area remained even at five in the morning, even on a Sunday. Some people were just heading home from a night out on the town—or, like Ginny, home from work—while others were up early for predawn shifts at twenty-four-hour places, their days just beginning. She was just happy it was still the weekend; otherwise, she would have had to go home and get Maisy ready for school, then head off for her own class at Jefferson Community College. After working weeknight shifts, Ginny didn't get to go to bed until almost ten a.m., then she got up at three to meet Maisy's school bus and start her day all over again.

It wasn't the greatest way to live, on five hours of sleep a day, doing her best to catch up on her nights off, but that was the way things were for Ginny Collins right now. She was halfway through her social work degree, having taken two classes a semester, including summer, for the last three years. In three more, she'd have her BS. She smiled every time she thought about it. Originally, she'd feared she would be graduating from JCC the same year Maisy graduated from high school. But now it looked as if she'd be able to start her new career while Maisy was still a junior. She'd make a lot less as a social worker than she was making now at Minxxx, but she'd earn something that was infinitely more valuable than money. And by then, there would be enough in Maisy's college fund to cover five years at Centre College, which was where Ginny was determined her daughter would go—the best damned college in the state, and one of the best damned colleges in the country.

As she let herself into her tiny house on Southern Parkway that was nestled less than a block from Iroquois Park, she tried to be as quiet as she could. But, just as it did every single morning when she entered, the kitchen linoleum squeaked under her first step. Then her second. Then her third. She glanced into the spare room off the kitchen to see Hazel sleeping soundly on the daybed, her glasses folded on the end table near her head, a fat paperback open on her chest. Ginny turned her head sideways to see the title and wasn't surprised to discover it was a grisly true crime book.

She smiled. The white-haired, blue-eyed, apple-cheeked Hazel Lenski looked and acted like the epitome of a cookie-baking, muffler-knitting, sock-darning granny. She was the kindest, happiest, sweetest person Ginny had ever met. Not that that was saying a whole lot, since Ginny hadn't met that many people in her life who rose above the pond scum level. But even if she'd grown up in Mayberry RFD, as she'd so often pretended she did when she was a little girl watching old reruns of the show, she'd still feel the same way about Hazel.

That wasn't why Ginny trusted her watching Maisy, however. She trusted her with Maisy because Hazel Lenski was a retired sharpshooter for the Detroit SWAT team. And because, before that, she'd been a prison matron, at a time when Hollywood was turning out movies like *Women in Cages* and *Barbed Wire Dolls*, which Hazel said were so true-to-life, it was scary. More than even that, though, Ginny trusted Hazel Lenski with Maisy because she'd done a hell of a job raising Ginny, once Ginny had allowed herself to be raised.

Hazel opened her eyes before Ginny even had a chance to turn around, instantly alert. Then she levered herself up on the daybed and smiled. "How was work?" she whispered to avoid waking Maisy, whose room was only a few steps down the hall.

"Fine," Ginny replied automatically. Also automatic was the additional lie, "But it was as boring as ever."

Well, except for the part where a gorgeous billionaire hinted that he would be willing to pay me an outrageous amount of money to do something a lot of women would have happily done for free, she added to herself. *But other than that, it was as boring as ever.*

No, she immediately corrected herself. It hadn't been Ginny that Russell Mulholland had made that thinly veiled offer to. A man like Russell Mulholland would never look twice at someone like Ginny Collins. But then, that was the way with most men.

And that was the way Ginny liked it. She'd been happier in her man-free life than she'd ever been before. She had Maisy, and she had Hazel, and she was supporting all of them now. Her life had a steady rhythm and a give-and-take that suited her. She never would have guessed that she would grow up to be the kind of person who could be relied on to hold everything together, but that was exactly the kind of person she was. Maybe working at Minxxx wasn't the greatest gig in the world, but the money was great, and the hours suited her. Ginny had been bringing home the bacon and frying it up in a pan for a long time now, thankyouverymuch. But unlike the song, she'd just as soon forget about any kind of man. A man would just muck things up. Interrupt her rhythm. Take and not give. She was better off alone. Because she wasn't alone. She had Maisy and Hazel, two people she loved more than anything else in the world.

Two people she'd been lying to for years.

Because as far as Hazel and Maisy were concerned, Ginny worked the night shift at the Ford plant, installing windshield wipers on F150s, and had been for the past five years—ever since going to work in places like Minxxx. There was no way she was going to let either of them know she was a cocktail waitress in a strip club. Not Maisy, because Ginny wanted to set a better example than that for her daughter, and not Hazel, because Hazel would be appalled, given how determined she'd been that Ginny would never enter into the same kind of lifestyle her mother had.

But there was no chance of that. Ginny had a few things her mother had never had the opportunity to find. Self-respect, for one thing. Self-confidence, for another. And the ability to kick anyone's ass who tried to mess with her. That was due in large part to Hazel, of course. And not just because of the Krav Maga lessons. But Ginny wasn't about to become like her mother, moving from one loser man to another. And she wouldn't end up in a missing person file, the way her mother had, either. Something else Ginny had that her mother hadn't was a love for her daughter that surpassed all else.

"Everything go okay with Maisy tonight?" Ginny asked. Not that she didn't already know the answer. Things were always okay with Maisy. It was Ginny's proudest accomplishment, her daughter's completely ordinary, uneventful existence.

Hazel nodded. "As always. She did her homework—"

"But it wasn't even a school night," Ginny interjected.

"I know, but that's the kind of responsible, self-motivated kid you're raising, Ginny." She patted her hand in mock sympathy. "You're just going to have to accept the fact that Maisy is a good kid."

Ginny smiled, too. She knew that. But she couldn't take complete credit for Maisy turning out as well as she had. Hazel's influence counted for a lot, too. And not just with Maisy.

"Then we watched some Johnny Depp thing," Hazel continued, "then Maisy downloaded a couple of new tunes for her iPod, and then she went to bed with her earbuds in." She smiled. "I can't imagine how that girl can fall asleep listening to all that screaming, but damned if she doesn't nod right off."

"Times change, Hazel," Ginny said. "Music changes with it. We can't expect Maisy to embrace *NSYNC with the same passion I once did."

"*NSYNC?" Hazel repeated, aghast. "I was thinking about Joni Mitchell. Now there's music to put you to sleep."

Ginny chuckled. "Oh, I couldn't agree with you more."

"Wait, that's not what I meant," Hazel said, at the same time, mirroring Ginny's laughter. "I just meant music should soothe, not incite."

"Hmm, I don't know about that," Ginny countered. "The music of your generation incited an awful lot of stuff."

"Something the music of *your* generation could benefit from," the other woman said smugly, evidently not realizing—or, more likely, not caring—that she'd just done a complete turnabout.

The two women chatted while Ginny started the coffee brewing and set out the accoutrements of Maisy's breakfast. Since it was Sunday, she'd have time to make waffles, her daughter's favorite. Ginny's, too.

It was only when Hazel excused herself to go shower— and while Maisy still slept—that Ginny removed her evening's take from her purse. The stack of bills was even fatter than usual, thanks to Russell Mulholland and his entourage who had tipped *very* well. This in spite of her telling him to back off, and in spite of turning the table over to another waitress after she'd presented him with that first tab. He'd stayed at Minxxx for another hour after that, and every time Ginny had looked at him, even though she'd done her best *not* to look at him—to no avail, dammit—he'd been sipping his unbelievably expensive cognac and watching her. Every. Single. Time. Then, when she cashed out for the night, Marcus the bartender had presented her with a couple hundred dollars more than she usually made on a Saturday. When she'd questioned it, he'd shown her the tab she'd presented to Mulholland for the three, admittedly way overpriced, drinks she'd taken to the table, and there it was in black and white: he'd tipped her roughly two hundred percent of his bill.

She'd halfway expected to turn the tab over and find some sexually suggestive message and the assurance that there was more where that came from, along with a phone number. But there had been nothing. In spite of his watching her all night, he hadn't tried to get her attention again. He hadn't approached her. Hadn't sent any messages via one of the other waitresses or one of the bartenders. At one point, she'd felt almost disappointed by that . . . until she'd mentally smacked herself upside the head and told herself to snap out of it.

She flipped through the stack of bills again, and for one insane moment, thought about how she could have made even more last night. And maybe tonight, too. Hell, maybe even for the whole time Russell Mulholland was in town. It would be for Maisy, right? It would go into her college account. Jeez, Ginny could probably squeeze enough out of the guy over the next couple of weeks for Maisy to go for her doctorate. It wasn't like it would be any hardship to get horizontal with a guy who looked like that. It wasn't like sex was any big deal in the first place. Ginny had never enjoyed it, anyway.

Enough, she told herself. If she was going to sell herself out to Mulholland, she might as well be riding one of the poles at Minxxx. The dancers made even more than the waitresses did. But her skills as an actress only went so far. It had taken her years to get into the character she played at work and to get comfortable showing as much skin as she did. Even now, there were some nights, like tonight, when she couldn't quite hold onto her character, and she let the facade slip. Damn Russell Mulholland and his blue eyes anyway. And when that happened, when she let herself think about how she was dressed and how the men looked at her—and groped her—she came all too close to quitting.

And she couldn't afford to do that, she told herself as she turned her attention back to the evening's take. She sorted the bills quickly by denomination, flattening them out as she went. Some guys thought it was funny to stuff their tips in the bottom of a glass that wasn't quite empty, meaning a few of the bills smelled like rank Bourbon.

Ginny didn't care. Tomorrow morning, she'd take them all to a branch of her bank that was miles away from her usual one to deposit them.

She did her best not to go to the same branch more than a few times a year, and she always went through the drive-thru. Nothing screamed "Working for tips in a bar" like a big ol' stack of wadded-up, Bourbon-stinking cash, and she didn't want to risk anyone at her regular branch—or any other—finding out what she did for a living. Beechwood was a chatty, friendly neighborhood, and it wouldn't be at all surprising if one of the tellers said something to Hazel about the piles of fetid money Ginny always brought in to deposit.

She pulled a shoe box from the very back of the closet and tucked the money inside, then returned it to its hiding place and placed a half-dozen other shoe boxes atop it. And, as she always did after handling the money given to her by groping hands—once she washed her own hands, she meant—she estimated what the total amount would buy. Half a semester's worth of textbooks, she figured. Provided Maisy majored in something other than law or medicine that required prolonged study.

Ginny sighed. Oh, well. If Maisy wanted to major in one of those, Ginny would find a way to pay for it. She always found a way to pay for whatever her daughter needed, be it school uniforms or organic food or orthodontics. Because Maisy Collins wasn't going to end up like Ginny. She was going to not just know her mother but love her and be close to her. And she'd never have to worry about how many more days they had before the landlord evicted them. And she wouldn't go to bed hungry. And she wouldn't have to listen to screaming and the back of a hand in the apartment next door.

Most of all, Maisy would never, *ever*, end up huddled behind a rancid Dumpster in the pouring rain, while at one end of the alley, cops were trying to find the Caucasian female, fourteen to eighteen years old, who'd just tried to break into the bakery, and at the other end, Mikey Malone was looking to bust up the girl who'd just told him she was pregnant with his kid. Never, *ever* would Maisy get that sick feeling in the pit of her stomach, wondering how the hell she was going to survive.

· Six ·

MONDAY NIGHT FOUND NATALIE SITTING AT A TWO-
seater table in the corner of the Brown Hotel's sumptuous
English Grill, awaiting her porcini mushroom ravioli and
sipping a predinner martini. She was still mulling plan B,
thinking surely *some*thing would come to her, when who
should fold himself into the seat opposite her but Dean Waterman. His appearance didn't come as a complete surprise,
however. She'd had a moment's warning before she saw him,
thanks to the fact that Dean was the only man she knew
who would pay five hundred dollars a bottle for cologne he
ordered from a tony fragrance shop in Paris. No one, but
no one, smelled as cloying and obsequious as Dean.

"Hello, Dean," she greeted him dispassionately, speaking into her martini rather than to him, suddenly wishing
she'd ordered a shooter instead, so she could toss it back in
one gulp and then order another. Double. "Fancy meeting
you here," she added. To her martini.

She was being sarcastic, of course. Dean worked on
the same block as the Brown and ate here with some
regularity. And since his condo on one of the uppermost

floors of Waterfront Park Place—which, Natalie had to
admit, had spectacular views of the Ohio and downtown—
was only minutes away, he ate here, or at another expensive downtown restaurant, even on the weekends. He saw it
as a testament to both his wealth and his health that he
could spend so much on a meal so often and eat so sumptu-
ously without hurting his wallet or his well-being. Natalie
saw it as a testament to how badly she wanted to score
Russell Mulholland for Clementine's party, if she would
spend so much time at the Brown and risk running into
Dean.

Apples and oranges.

"I'm not surprised at all," he told her, his blue eyes
twinkling. Honestly. Twinkling. How did someone make
that happen without special contact lenses or something?
And his black hair shone with bits of golden highlights
under the amber lighting that made it look as if he'd been
gilded. The effect was only enhanced by the amber shirt
and tie he wore with his chocolate-colored suit. What a
waste, that such good looks should encase such a creepy
guy. "What does surprise me," he continued, "is that you
feel it's necessary to resort to ruses like accidentally running into me at my favorite place to eat, dressed like that,
in order to attract my attention, when you know I'm yours
for the taking."

Natalie would rather take cyanide than take Dean, but
that was neither here nor there. And the reason she'd
dressed "like that" was because she was still stalking—ah,
she meant scoping out—the Brown for . . . Russell Mulholland. The sleeveless emerald dress was by far the most
flattering garment she owned, enhancing what few curves
she had and making her normally boring hazel eyes look
greener and larger. Just because it was more low-cut and
had a higher hemline than what she usually wore for stalking—ah, she meant scoping out the Brown—didn't mean
anything. Certainly it didn't mean she'd been trying to attract Dean.

Ew.

In response to his remark, however, she only smiled weakly and said, "Gosh, am I that transparent?" Because she'd learned long ago that the more she tried to convince Dean she was in no way interested in him, the more he took it as a sign that she was playing hard to get, and the more he stepped up his pursuit of her.

Again, she thought, *Ew.*

"Why don't you just stop playing games and marry me?" he asked. "Stop pretending at this career thing that you know as well as I do you're completely unsuited for, and spend your days doing the things women are supposed to do."

Since it was looking like there was little chance she would be getting rid of Dean anytime soon, Natalie decided to turn the encounter into a drinking game. Every time Dean said something stupid, she would have to take a drink. So, in response to his question, she enjoyed a healthy swallow of her martini and replied, "And what, pray tell, would be the things women are supposed to do, Dean?"

He smiled in a way that said she should already know the answer to that. And, of course, she did. Pretty much. But the workday for most people was over, and instead of being out enjoying some kind of entertainment with friends, Natalie was still working, because stalking—ah, she meant scoping out the Brown—for Russell Mulholland constituted work, and she was confident that no matter what Dean said, it was bound to be entertaining.

"Oh, you know," he began in that dismissive tone of voice that made her teeth hurt. She clutched her drink tighter, ready to swig at will. "Shopping . . ." he continued.

Swig.

". . . lunching . . ."

Swig.

". . . chatting on the phone . . ."

Swig. And, just for the hell of it, swig again.

". . . and organizing functions to help out sick and impoverished people and all the other wretched refuse from a safe distance."

Swig. Swig. Swig.

"The kind of things our mothers did," he concluded. "And still have the feminine decency to do."

Natalie took another generous swig of her martini, or, at least, tried to—wow, was it empty already?—and said, "But, Dean. I do *all* of those things. In fact, organizing functions is what I do for a living. It's my *career thing*." Even though it wasn't necessary to emphasize that last part, she did it anyway, because she knew it would make Dean's teeth hurt, too.

"Yes, I know," he said after grinding his teeth. "But I also know the only reason you have that ridiculous notion about wanting a career in the first place is because your life is so empty in other areas." He leaned forward and cocked a dark brow at her. "Other areas that I could fill quite nicely," he murmured in a way that he probably thought was sexually suggestive, but which really made him sound like he should be listed on an Internet offender site somewhere. "And, Natalie," he added, dropping his voice low enough so that only she could hear him, "I do mean I could *fill* those places. All three of them."

Oh, eeeeewwwww.

Without asking, she grabbed Dean's glass and drained what was left in it. Gak. Bourbon. That wasn't going to mix well with her martini. On the upside, maybe the combination would make her pass out. Or, better still, it might make her throw up. All over Dean.

A girl could dream, couldn't she?

She was about to say something in response to his odious remarks—something along the lines of "Help! Help! I'm being molested by this man!"—but the waiter arrived table side to inquire if the gentleman would be joining the lady for dinner. Natalie was about to correct his erroneous assumption about the gentleman thing when Dean took the liberty of ordering the lady another martini and himself another Bourbon on the rocks.

As much as she hated to ask, she knew the question—

and the answer, too, alas—was inevitable. "*Are* you going to be joining me for dinner, Dean?"

His reply was as immediate as it was inevitable. Alas. "Of course. Since I know it's what you so desperately want."

She looked up at the waiter. "You better make that martini a double." After another look at Dean—and that still-arched eyebrow—she turned to the waiter again. "And bring two of them."

Dean chuckled at that, and after the waiter left, murmured in that icky voice again, "Whatever puts you in the mood."

What it took to put her in the sort of mood Dean was talking about—at least with Dean—would take more than a couple of double martinis. It would take a veritable *case* of gin. And also a vial or two of Novocain. And a good solid blow to the back of her head. But she decided not to tell him that, since it would make him signal for the waiter to bring a few dozen pitchers of martinis and then run out for a hypodermic needle and a Louisville Slugger.

"Seriously, Natalie," he said as he leaned back in his chair again, his gaze fixed on hers. "When are you going to get over this idea that there's a businesswoman lurking inside you and take your rightful place in my"—now he grinned an icky grin—"home," he finished, even though she was sure he was talking about a very specific room in that home, and if he had his way, she'd never leave it. Except to lunch, shop, chat on the phone, and organize things. And possibly dress up like a shepherdess, but that was just speculation on Natalie's part. "If it's about the prenup," he added, "I've told you that's negotiable."

Somehow, Natalie refrained from laughing in his face. Her family was easily worth twice what Dean's was, and the amount in her trust fund was triple his. But if a disputed prenuptial agreement was the reason he wanted to cling to for why she wouldn't marry him, who was she to dissuade him of it? Especially since she'd already tried a half dozen times to dissuade him of it, only to have him not believe a

word she said. Probably because he couldn't imagine anyone putting that much money into a trust fund for a woman
who would just squander it on shopping, lunching, running
up a phone bill, and giving it away to undeserving sick and
impoverished people. So Natalie had just done her best to
avoid Dean when she could. And, in situations like this,
where that was impossible . . .

Well, if she didn't have access to martinis, she just suffered. A lot.

"You know, Dean," she said, deciding the best way to
avoid talking about both her business acumen and his marriage proposal was to avoid talking about both her business acumen and his marriage proposal, "I was just sitting
here thinking about that time in cotillion class when Miss
Leslie spent an entire afternoon teaching us about the
vastly different roles rim soup bowls play from footed soup
bowls. Do you remember that?"

To his credit, his expression changed not at all. "Um,
no. I don't remember that."

"Wow, I sure do," Natalie said exuberantly. On account
of she was beginning to feel exuberantly . . . ah, exuber-
ant, she meant . . . thanks to the effects of the too hastily
consumed martini. Not to mention the even more hastily
consumed Bourbon. "I never knew the history of the soup
bowl included so many fascinating anecdotes."

"Mmm," Dean replied, clearly not wanting her to repeat
any of those anecdotes. Not that Natalie would, since she
was making this up as she went along.

She nodded enthusiastically. On account of she was
beginning to feel enthusiastically . . . ah, enthusias*tic*, she
meant . . . thanks to . . . Well, she couldn't quite remember
why she felt so enthusiastically and exuberantly at the moment, but she was sure that, whatever the reason was, it was
a good one. "I gotta tell ya, Dean, that day changed my life
forever. Woo."

Fortunately, before she was forced to describe how, exactly, the history of the soup bowl had changed her life,
their waiter reappeared with their drinks and placed all

three of them—clearly he had realized she was serious about needing two, so he must have waited on Dean before—on the table between them. The two martinis looked delectably frosty and tempting, but she made herself wait. Oblivion would come soon enough, if not from alcohol, then from having to listen to Dean for more than fifteen minutes straight.

The waiter smiled at Natalie in a way that made her realize he had indeed waited on Dean before and understood her reason for needing two double martinis. In spite of that, he told her, "I took the liberty of putting a hold on your dinner, miss, so that the gentleman's would come out at the same time and the two of you could eat together."

At this, the waiter turned to Dean, rightfully expecting some show of appreciation from him. But Dean only gave the menu a perfunctory glance and said, "Bring me the filet. Medium rare. And a glass of the Silver Hill shiraz with dinner." Then he fairly flung the menu at their server without looking at him.

So Natalie smiled at the waiter as best she could and said, "Thank you. For everything."

He dipped his head in both acknowledgment and appreciation before departing, and, amazingly, didn't kick Dean in the shin under the table, which was what Natalie wanted to do.

She enviously watched their server leave, miraculously refraining from shouting after him, "Wait! Take me with you!" Then she looked at Dean, who was doing the eyebrow thing again. She pulled both martinis closer, curled her fingers possessively around one of them, and waited with great anticipation for Dean to open his mouth again.

IT TOOK FINN ALL OF TEN SECONDS AFTER ENTERING the restaurant with Russell to see Natalie Beckett seated at a table on the far side of the room. An intimate table for two, he couldn't help noticing, which she was sharing with someone who, judging by the guy's expression and that arched eyebrow, appeared to be pretty damned intimate with her. He was exactly the kind of man Finn would expect Natalie Beckett to be intimate with, too, from the expertly and expensively cut hair to the expertly and expensively tailored duds. Finn had been shopping with Russell often enough to recognize a suit with a four-figure price tag when he saw one. And the guy with Natalie wore one even better than Russell did. Probably because he'd been groomed for things like that since childhood, where Russell and Finn had spent their childhood doing things like, oh . . . trying to survive.

As luck—Finn's luck lately, anyway—would have it, the maître d' led him and Russell to the table directly behind the one where Natalie and her date were seated. And—of course—Russell claimed the chair that left Finn sitting where it would be impossible for him to miss watching Natalie and her date. Especially Natalie, who was facing him on the other side of the table she occupied with—had Finn mentioned this?—the guy who was her *date*. What was surprising was that Natalie didn't notice Finn right off. Uh . . . he meant she didn't notice right off that Russell, the man she wanted to score for her big to-do, was sitting at the next table. Clearly she was so besotted with her companion that the rest of the world had faded away.

However, with closer inspection—and, it went without saying that Finn inspected the couple more closely—he realized it might not be that Natalie was besotted with the guy who was her date so much as she was, well . . . sotted by at least one of the two martinis sitting in front of her.

Why would she have two drinks when the one she was drinking was only half-empty? Was it happy hour? Two-for-one cocktails? Finn looked around at everyone else in the restaurant, but everyone else who was imbibing claimed just one glass. Only Natalie had two. So, was the guy trying to get her drunk? If so, he seemed to be succeeding, judging by the dreamy look on her face. But then, why would the guy have to get Natalie drunk, when she was obviously there with him by choice, and—*Face it, Finn*—

Mr. Four Figure Suit obviously wasn't the kind of guy who had to resort to things like getting his date drunk to take advantage of her.

Inescapably, Finn glanced down at his own attire: dark khaki trousers and a white oxford with pinstripes that had put him back about fifty bucks at a Banana Republic sale. True, on his salary, he could afford a four-figure suit if he wanted one. *One* being the operative word, admittedly, but he could still afford one. But who in their right mind spent that kind of money on clothing, even if they could afford to? Other than Russell, but the rightness of Russell's mind had been in question ever since Marti's death. There were plenty of other things four figures could buy that would make the world a better place. For someone other than the person who had the four figures, he meant.

His thoughts were interrupted, thankfully, by the arrival of their waiter, who took their drink orders and, Finn couldn't help noting, said nothing about two-for-one cocktails. The movement must have caught Natalie's attention, though, because when the waiter departed, giving Finn visual access to her again, she was looking right at him. For a moment, she didn't react, her response time clearly dulled by the martini—martinis?—she'd consumed. Then, suddenly, her eyes went wide with recognition. What amazed Finn, though, was that, even after her gaze flew to Russell— and her eyes went even wider with recognition—it ricocheted back to Finn again, instead of remaining fixed on her quarry. And then, out of nowhere, the blush that had captured his attention the first time he'd seen her bloomed on her cheeks again. And damned if he didn't find it even more captivating this time.

For a moment, she only gazed at him; then she lifted her right hand and wiggled her fingers in greeting. That made her date turn around to see who she was waving at, and when he saw Finn looking at Natalie, he narrowed his eyes menacingly.

He did, however, turn more fully around and say, by way of a greeting, Finn supposed, "Dean Waterman." His

voice was edged with something that was anything but
amiable, however. Then he extended his hand without getting up, clearly expecting Finn to make the concession of
moving to shake it. "Are you a friend of Natalie's?" he
asked.

Russell turned around at Waterman's remarks, and when
he didn't recognize the man making them or the woman
with him, he turned back to Finn with a look of curiosity
etched on his face. Finn made a vague gesture that he didn't
know the guy—yet—then, realizing he would look like a
boor if he didn't shake the man's hand, he stood, rounded
the table, and gave it a quick shake.

"Not exactly," he said. "Ms. Beckett and I ran into each
other for the first time the other day." He turned to look at
Natalie then, only to find that not only had the blush deepened on her cheeks, but her mouth, too, seemed redder
than before, and her pupils had expanded to nearly eclipse
her greenish blue irises. "Ms. Beckett," he said with a dip
of his head toward her. "You're looking well."

Understatement of the century, he thought. Her green
dress hugged her lush body even better than the tight
sweater had the day before, and the neck was scooped even
lower. She also had the added accessory of a glittering
choker he'd just bet was real diamonds and emeralds—
he'd been around Russell's purchases like that enough to
recognize quality, too—the gemstones rivaling her eyes
for clarity and sparkle. Although they were probably winning in the clarity division for the moment, thanks to the
martini or martinis. In spite of that, she was able to manage a reasonably coherent greeting.

"Hello, Mr. Guthrie. It's, um, lovely to see you here."

Finn doubted that. She'd probably been hoping to find
Russell here without him. And how had she known Russell
would be eating here tonight, anyway? They always made
dinner reservations under a fictitious name, and never the
same name twice. He made a mental note to ponder that
later, then turned to look at Natalie's date again.

Thanks to Finn's making clear that he and Natalie had

just met, and thanks to the formal way they'd greeted each other, Dean Waterman had relaxed some, but his expression still held a wariness that suggested he wasn't comfortable with Finn's presence at the next table. It was something that made Finn think the other man might not be as confident of Natalie's affections as he ought to be, something that went a long way toward explaining the two martinis sitting in front of his date. Maybe he *was* trying to get her drunk so that he could take advantage of her.

Not that Natalie Beckett struck Finn as the kind of woman who would fall for a ploy like that, but, hey, he'd just met her a couple of days ago, so what did he know? Just because he'd formed an impression of her as an intelligent, sexy, witty, sexy, clever, sexy, beautiful, sexy woman didn't mean that she was one. Well, okay, she *was* sexy and beautiful—no one in his right mind could dispute that—but the other qualities might just have been his imagination. Or maybe that wishful thinking thing again. Or delusion, which seemed to also be a frequent companion of his lately.

Then again, if she was in a situation here where her date was trying to get her drunk so he could take advantage of her, then Finn ought to—

Nothing, Finn told himself. He should do nothing. Natalie Beckett was none of his business. She was a grown woman capable of taking care of herself. If she made bad choices like drinking too much and dating guys who would take advantage of that, then who was he to criticize? It wasn't like he was the poster child for upright, forthright, do-right behavior. He'd overindulged more times than he should have in the past and woken up beside women he shouldn't have. He was the last person who should be anyone's keeper.

Yeah, okay, he was Russell's and Max's keeper, he reminded himself. But he was paid to be that. Natalie hadn't hired him for anything. Not that he wouldn't mind if she hired him to—

Nothing, he repeated more adamantly to himself. He

was not now, nor would he ever be, anything to Natalie
Beckett, other than a thorn in her side if she kept stalking
his employer.

That thought made him look over at Russell, who, he
saw, had turned fully around in his seat and was eyeing the
group—and listening to their exchange—with much interest. The reason for that gradually became clearer when
Finn saw Russell's gaze flick from him to Natalie. Then
to her date. Then back to Natalie. Then back to Finn. He
grinned broadly, though for what reason, Finn couldn't begin to guess.

Until, out of nowhere, Russell looked at the other couple
and said, "Why don't you two join us for dinner? Any
friend of Finn's is a friend of mine."

Finn was about to point out that he'd just said he and
Natalie *weren't* friends, that they barely knew each other,
but she was out of her seat and folding herself into the one
beside Russell faster than you could say, "Ditch my date."
He noticed she only brought one of her martinis with her,
but it was the full one. Waterman, Finn noted, simply sighed
with something akin to resignation and mirrored Natalie's
migration. So what could Finn do but return to his seat—
next to Natalie—biting back a resigned sigh of his own.

"Ms. . . . Beckett, was it?" Russell said, extending a
hand toward her.

"Natalie, please," she replied, sounding more than a little flustered.

"Natalie," he said with the smile that had been the
downfall of many a woman. Natalie, Finn noted, was no
less immune. Dammit. "My name is—"

"Russell Mulholland," she interrupted before he had the
chance. "Of course I know who you are."

Evidently, Dean Waterman hadn't known who Russell
was, because his expression and demeanor changed dra-
matically at Natalie's words.

"Russell Mulholland?" he asked. "*The* Russell Mulholland? Of Mulholland Games?"

Where Russell had clearly been charmed by Natalie—

but then, he was generally charmed by anything that produced estrogen—his attitude toward Waterman's effusion was considerably cooler.

"I am," he said simply.

Waterman smiled brightly, but the effect on the whole was more of garishness than brilliance. "Dean Waterman," he said with way more enthusiasm than he'd shown when he introduced himself to Finn, thrusting out his hand with enough force to shatter a brick. Had there actually been a brick on the table, Finn meant. Russell gave it a single, less than enthusiastic shake. "I'm one of your investors," Waterman gushed further.

Well, hell, who wasn't? Finn wanted to ask the guy. Anyone who played the stock market invested in Mulholland Games, Inc. It was only one reason why the company was doing so well.

Even though Waterman hadn't asked—and Natalie hadn't offered, Finn thought, telling himself he was *not* bristling at the knowledge—he told Waterman, "I'm Finn Guthrie. I'm one of Mr. Mulholland's associates."

Natalie leaned toward Waterman and, in a theatrical whisper she didn't even try to hide, told him, "He's Mr. Mulholland's bodyguard. Well, one of them." She turned to Russell, wrinkling her nose in a way that should have been annoying but was actually kind of . . . Well, hell. *Adorable* was the word that came to Finn's mind, even though it was a word that he normally, manfully avoided. Then she leaned over toward Russell, and in the same too-loud whisper, said, "But don't worry, Mr. Mulholland. I won't tell anybody."

As if to illustrate that promise, she lifted her hand to her mouth and mimicked the locking of her lips with an imaginary key. Then, as if that weren't good enough, she made a big production of tossing it over her shoulder. Then she smiled in a way that indicated that yep, the martini was definitely not her first of the night.

Instead of being offended by her behavior, however, Russell was, predictably, even more charmed. "Please,

Natalie," he said. "Call me Russell. And don't *you* worry. As I said, any friend of Finn's is a friend of mine." Now Russell leaned in close to Natalie. Finn tried not to reach over and grab his best friend by the collar and shove him back into his seat. "Besides, I can tell right away that you aren't the sort of person who would betray a trust like that."

Oh, if he only knew, Finn thought. Then again, he was sure Russell did know. He just didn't care. Because Natalie was a beautiful, sexy woman, and that was all that mattered.

Dammit.

Russell signaled their server and asked that their guests' dinners be brought to their new table, and that their bill should be added to his own. Natalie started to object, but Waterman cut her off, thanking Russell with the same smarmy effusion he'd shown before.

"So, Natalie," Russell said when their server left again, even though Waterman had opened his mouth to say something more. Probably something really smarmy. "How do you and Finn know each other?"

Natalie looked flummoxed for a moment, her gaze darting from Russell to Finn and back again, as if she honestly wasn't sure how she and Finn knew each other. "Ummm . . ." she began eloquently.

She reached nervously for her martini and sipped it with all the daintiness of a debutante, which Finn was confident she must have been, once upon a time. Then she sipped it daintily again. Then a third time. By which point she nearly drained the glass. And by which point it wasn't just Russell eyeing her expectantly. It was Waterman, too. Hell, truth be told, Finn was feeling a little expectant himself.

Then, suddenly, her expression cleared. Sort of. "We, ah . . . we ran into each other in the lobby of this very hotel," she finally said. She looked at Finn. "Right? Isn't that where we met?"

Finn nodded. "Yep." No way was he going to help her beyond that, though. The last thing he wanted to do was jog her memory and have her recall that she'd been stalking Russell at the time. Not to mention he was having too much fun watching her get smashed. Of course, he immediately told himself he should be ashamed of himself, thinking it was entertaining to watch a beautiful, sexy woman slip into inebriation that way.

Because that would be wrong.

"That's right," Natalie said, setting her glass reluctantly on the table, but keeping her eye on it, presumably in case it tried to get away. "I was here that day looking for you, Mr. Mulholland, as a matter of fact." Somehow, she managed to pull her possessive gaze from the glass and shift it even more possessively to Russell.

"Me?" Russell replied with no small amount of astonishment . . . or amusement. Then, inescapably, he poured on the charm. "Why, Miss Beckett, had I known you were looking for me, I assure you you would have found me right away."

Natalie smiled at that, then turned to look at Finn, straightening in her chair—sort of—and treating him to a *very* smug expression. He halfway expected her to say "Toldja so" and stick her tongue out at him.

"Toldja so," she said.

He waited for the tongue, but, alas, it didn't appear.

She turned to Russell again. "See, Mr. Mul . . . Mr. Mulholl . . . Mr. Mullallalla . . . Russell," she finally managed. "There's this party I wanted to invite you to on Derby Eve. That's next week, on Friday, which is . . . How many days is that?" Since she seemed to be asking the question of herself, no one answered. Probably no one answered also because they wanted to watch her do math in her current state. She paused, lifting both hands to tick off the days on her fingers, mumbling, "Wednesday, Monday, Saturday . . . No, wait. I mean . . . Tuesday, Sunday, Labor Day . . . No, that's not right, either."

By now Russell was having a hard time keeping a straight face. "Next Friday," he reiterated to help her out.

"Yes!" she said with much relief. Then, with much hopefulness, she asked, "Can you make it?"

"No," he said decisively.

She gaped at him, as if she couldn't believe he would turn her down. "But it's a benefit," she tried again.

"No," Russell told her. Politely, but again, decisively.

She turned to Finn in a silent plea for help, but this time he was the one to look smugly at Natalie. "Toldja so," he said.

She blew out an exasperated breath and narrowed her eyes at him. Then she turned back to Russell, the epitome of grace and charm. Sort of.

"But the charity Mrs. Hotchkiss is trying to raise money for is an *excellent* one that does wonderful work."

"I'm sure," Russell said dryly. "Look, I'm sorry, Miss Beckett, but I never, ever, under any circumstances, attend such affairs. I'm sorry. But I'll have my assistant send around a donation if you'll leave the information with Finn."

"I've already left the information with Finn," she said morosely.

She started to say something else, but Waterman cut her off with a hastily interjected, "Well, now that that's settled, where were we? Oh, yes, we were talking about me."

Actually, they hadn't been talking about Waterman at all, but Finn figured it would be pointless to try and dissuade the guy of such an idea.

"I'm not surprised you ran into Natalie here at the Brown, Guthrie," he said, "since she actually spends quite a lot of her time here." At this, he threw her a salacious look that was nothing short of disturbing. "She actually spends a lot of time here. She's always hoping she'll run into me."

Finn looked at Natalie for confirmation, but she only picked up her martini and enjoyed another swallow, less dainty than before.

Waterman reached across the table and covered her hand with his. "She adores me," he told the two men.

Natalie had been about to put down her drink, but before it made it to the table, the glass was at her mouth again.

"In fact," Waterman continued, "ever since we were in cotillion class together as kids—"

Cotillion class? Finn echoed to himself. Jeez, she really *was* a debutante. Or, at least, had been once upon a time.

"—she's wanted me."

Back went the glass to Natalie's mouth again, only this time, it was empty. Which was just as well, since she'd obviously had more than enough. Nevertheless, when she lowered the glass again, she frowned at it in great disappointment, as if the martini had just betrayed her in the most egregious way. If she raised her hand to signal the waiter for another, he thought, Finn would intercept the drink before she could get to it. Hell, the way she was at this point, he'd be able to gesture over her shoulder and say, "Hey! Isn't that reclusive billionaire Russell Mulholland?" and she'd doubtless turn around and say, "Where? I've been looking all over for that guy."

Thankfully, she didn't signal the waiter for another drink. Instead, she seized what was left of Waterman's in both hands and, before anyone could stop her, drained it. And, judging by the amber color of the beverage, Finn was going to go out on a limb and say it wasn't the same thing she had been drinking all evening. Then she slammed the glass back down on the table and wiped her mouth with the back of her hand with all the decorum of Gabby Hayes.

Her gaze darting between each of the men, she said softly, "I have to go to the bathroom."

And then she was jumping up from her chair with enough gusto to send it toppling to the ground behind her. She didn't even seem to notice. She just grabbed the edge of the table for a minute, clearly needing to get her bearings, or something, then she carefully—whoa, *very* carefully— started making her way across the room.

Finn watched her pick her way cautiously—whoa, *very* cautiously—through the tables, working way too hard to find what should have been a fairly obvious straight line to the women's room. When she got to the little alcove nestled behind a couple of potted palms, she swayed into one of the plants, nearly knocking it over, but grabbed it before it went down completely. The action caused her to drop her purse, and when she bent to pick it up—bent, not stooped, the way any woman in a dress that short would do, were she in her right mind—she nearly took the same kind of tumble the palm almost had. She managed to right herself, but had to flatten one hand against the wall to steady herself before she could go any farther. Finally, she moved forward, putting one foot carefully in front of the other, and disappeared into the restroom.

For a really long time.

Best-case scenario, Finn thought, she'd make it back to the table—eventually—in much the same way she'd left it, down what was left of his and Russell's drinks, eat her dinner, then fall face-first into her tiramisu. Worst-case scenario, she was in one of those stalls right now, having an argumentative exchange with Ralph the porcelain god of regurgitation. And losing.

Somebody probably ought to check on her. And probably, that somebody should be Waterman. Finn looked over at the big jerk . . . ah, at the guy . . . ready to suggest just that, but Waterman, evidently used to this sort of behavior from Natalie—or maybe just not caring—was yammering at Russell about investments again, and Russell had an expression on his face that told Finn he was thinking about female mud wrestlers and probably had been for some time.

So what could Finn do but go check on Natalie himself?

"Excuse me," he said to his two companions, even though he was pretty sure neither one of them heard him or even noticed when he stood up. He followed the path Natalie had made toward the women's room, but halfway there, he saw her emerge . . . then bump into a small table beneath a mirror in the alcove before grabbing it with both hands to steady herself. Again. He smiled when she turned to the mirror and lifted a hand nonchalantly to her hair, as if she'd meant to slam her hip into the table all along. For good measure, she also opened her purse and withdrew a lipstick, then studied her reflection as she deliberately—whoa, *very* deliberately—refreshed the color on her mouth.

Her ripe, luscious mouth.

By the time Finn arrived in the alcove, she looked completely put together, if not entirely sober. Amazing. Even in her inebriated state, she'd managed to get her lipstick on perfectly. Her eyes still had that glazed look, though, and her smile was a little off-kilter. Then, when she saw Finn's reflection in the mirror behind her and spun around to look at him, the rest of her was off-kilter, too. He managed to catch her before she went down or knocked anything over, but where he would have thought she would immediately right herself again and pretend like nothing happened, she instead let herself fall against him. She flattened her hands against his chest and tucked her head into the hollow of his throat, tilting it back a bit so that her face was turned up toward his. Her eyes were closed, and her lips were curled into a soft smile, and when she sighed—with much contentment, he couldn't help noting . . . and liking—her warm breath caressed his neck, making something inside him cinch into a hard knot.

Not that he wanted to discourage her or anything, but . . .

"Natalie?" he said softly.

"Mmmm-hmmm?" she murmured against his neck.

"Are you, um . . . Are you okay?"

She nodded slowly. "Mmmm-hmmm."

She punctuated the statement by snuggling her body even closer to his, something he wouldn't have thought possible, making that knot in his belly pull tighter still.

"You sure?"

"Mmmm-hmmm."

Well, hell. Now what was he supposed to do? He told himself he should walk her back to the table, ply her with coffee, and instruct Waterman to take her home. Then he wondered if he could trust Waterman. Sure, the guy *said* Natalie was hung up on him. And she hadn't exactly disagreed. Then again, she hadn't confirmed it, either . . .

"So," he began experimentally. "What's the story with you and Mr. Four Figure Suit?"

She opened her eyes at that but arrowed her brows downward in confusion. "Who?" Then, before Finn could reply, she answered her own question. "Ooooh. You mean Dean."

Finn nodded. She nodded, too, but he didn't think it was for any reason other than that it was the only way she could stay focused on his face.

"Dino," she continued, smiling. Probably her pet name for him, Finn couldn't help thinking. Then she continued, "The Deanster. The Deanmeister. Dean-a-rino. Dean-o-mite." Okay, so obviously she had a lot of pet names for the guy. Probably just went to show how crazy she was about him.

The big jerk.

She started laughing, then halted abruptly. "The Deanmeister wants to marry me. In fact, my mother's already got the wedding date written on her calendar. In ink. The way she has it all figured out, by this time next year, I'll be signing in at the Junior League meetings as Mrs. Dean Waterman."

Finn was in no way prepared for the punch to the gut her announcement brought with it. What the hell . . . ? She was *engaged* to the guy? To be *married*?

He had no idea what to say in response to that bombshell. Nor did he have any idea why it even *was* a bombshell. What did he care if Natalie Beckett was engaged? To a big jerk? He'd just met her, for God's sake. And it wasn't like he was in any position to ask her out himself, anyway. He was only going to be in town for two weeks. And, hell, it was his job to keep her as far away from Russell as he could. He'd probably never see her again after tonight.

Before he could say anything, though, Natalie closed her eyes again. Then she went completely limp in his arms.

Finn enjoyed one brief, extremely satisfying moment when he thought maybe she was throwing herself at him, and he automatically tightened his arms around her waist. And he tried not to notice, really he did, how she was soft in all the places he was hard, and curved in all the places he was angled, yet somehow their bodies fitted together perfectly.

Then he realized that she hadn't gone limp because she was trying to get closer to him. She'd gone limp because she was passed out cold. Like boom-boom-out-go-the-lights cold. Which left him standing in an alcove holding an unconscious—and sexy and beautiful—woman in his arms, who belonged to another man. A man who was sitting just across the room. A man Natalie Beckett was engaged to marry.

· Seven ·

WELL, HELL. NOW WHAT WAS HE SUPPOSED TO DO?

Finn looked past the potted palm, across the restaurant to where Waterman was *still* yammering at Russell, and where Russell was lifting his hand to signal to the waiter that he wanted another drink. Evidently, it was an effect the guy had on everyone who encountered him.

Then Finn looked back at Natalie. Her head still rested against his chest, but now it was positioned the way a newborn's would be, as if her neck muscles were months away from maturity. Her face was still tilted toward him, but now she was quite obviously oblivious. In spite of that, there was a not-so-little part of him that wouldn't have minded standing here like this for the rest of the evening, because she just felt so damned good to hold. And what did that say about Finn, that even holding a woman who was unconscious of the embrace felt good? He was pathetic. Besides, if they stood here like this for the rest of the evening, it would just be courting neck cramps for both of them.

He dipped his head so that his mouth was just above her ear. "Natalie," he said softly. "Wake up."

She offered not even the slightest hint that she'd heard him. So he lifted his hand and cupped his palm against her cheek and tried not to notice how soft and warm her skin was beneath his palm. "Natalie," he said again, a little more loudly. "Come on, sweetheart, wake up."

Again, she offered no sign that she heard him. She just remained limp in his arms, her body pressing intimately against his. Well, it would be intimate if she was conscious, anyway.

He tried one last time to rouse her. Tapping her cheek lightly with the pad of his index finger, and trying not to notice how soft and warm her skin was beneath his, he said, "Earth to Natalie. Come in, Natalie. Your table is ready."

No luck. She was *out*.

There were more than a few ways he could play this. He could try dragging her around the alcove a couple of times in another effort to rouse her. Or he could drag her back into the women's room, out of the public eye, make her as comfortable as possible, then go tell Waterman what had happened so the guy could take her home. Or he could drag her back to the table so that Waterman could deduce the problem for himself and take her home. Or Finn could toss her over his shoulder and hope no one noticed, then take her up to his room where she could sleep it off in privacy and comfort. Of course, if he did that, she still wouldn't be in any shape to drive once she woke up, meaning he'd have to drive her home in her car and then take a cab back to the hotel.

Obviously that last idea was the most complicated, most likely to draw attention, and the least convenient to Finn. The best choice was probably the second one, where he moved her back into the restroom and told Waterman what had happened.

He looked past Natalie at Waterman again. Finn had no idea why, but he didn't trust the guy at all. He didn't care if he and Natalie were engaged to be married. There was just something fundamentally suspect about the guy. Finn had had good instincts about people since he was a kid—he'd had to, growing up the way he had—and he just couldn't quite bring himself to hand Natalie over to her fiancé in her current condition.

Okay. Option four—sleeping it off in his suite—it would have to be.

With another quick glance at the dining room to be sure no one—especially Waterman—was watching, he scooped her up and over his shoulder, firefighter rescue style. Then he did his best not to look too obvious as he made his way toward and through the restaurant's exit, to a nearby bank of elevators, where he thumbed the Up button.

Well, what the hell else was he supposed to do? This was the only way he'd be able to be sure that she made it home safely. It had nothing to do with his wanting to see where she lived. And it *really* didn't have anything to do with the possibility of spending a little more time with her. She was unconscious, for God's sake. Not exactly a stellar way to spend a first date. Not that this was a date, he hurried to remind himself. And even if she had been conscious—and even if this had been a date—it wasn't like he could have a meaningful conversation with her in her current state. And what else was there to do?

Don't answer that, Guthrie. Don't even go there. It's the very thing you're saving her from where Waterman is concerned, remember?

One of the elevators dinged, so Finn turned toward it. Before he could enter, though, a trio of people came out, all of them old enough to be his parents, and all dressed for some kind of major party. They looked curiously at Finn's face, then even more curiously at Natalie's ass, right next to his face. Then they looked at Finn's face again. Then Natalie's ass. Finn's face. Natalie's ass. Then back to Finn's face again, but this time, in place of the curiosity, there was clear hostility.

He forced a smile and cupped his hand possessively over her ass, trying not to feel too proprietary . . . and failing. With as broad a smile as he could manage for the other people, he said, "I *told* her that seventh mai tai wasn't a good idea, but did she listen to me? Of course not. And don't even get me started on what she said to the bride. My *sister*, the bride." He gave Natalie's bottom an affectionate pat. "Good thing I love her so much, huh?"

Then, without awaiting a reply, and before the elevator door had a chance to close—and before the partygoers had a chance to whip out their phones and call 911—he moved swiftly into the elevator and pushed the Close Door button. And he sent a silent plea up to every deity he could think of—including Bombay, the goddess of gin—that he didn't see anyone else on the way to his room.

He must have done something good in his previous life, because he made it the rest of the way without encountering a single soul. He shifted Natalie from his left shoulder to his right so he could fish his card key out of his back pocket, then let himself into the suite with a soft ding and clack of the lock. He carried her into the bedroom and dumped her unceremoniously onto the big, king-sized bed, trying not to notice how she landed with her little green dress hiked up a good bit higher than she probably would have been comfortable with on a first date. Not that this was a first date, he reminded himself again, but realizing that, too, probably would have made her *really* uncomfortable.

As carefully as he could, Finn tugged the hem of her dress down as far as it would go. Then he brushed her hair carefully out of her face and patted her lightly on the cheek.

"Natalie," he murmured, trying one last time to rouse her.

No response.

"Natalie," he repeated, a little more forcefully this time.

She did respond to his second summons, but the response was just a deep sigh, punctuated by a dreamy little smile and a quiet little . . . Well, there was no other way to describe it. A quiet little . . . yummy sound.

Then she rolled over onto her side, tucked her hands up under her cheek, and began to softly snore.

Great. For the first time in a long time, too long a time,

Finn had a beautiful woman in his bed—making yummy sounds, no less—and she was out cold.

This night wasn't turning out at all the way he had originally envisioned it. He'd figured he and Russell could go down and grab some dinner, then head to some sports bar up the street to watch the Seahawks game. Russell had said something about making an early night of it—which was another weird development, since Russell never made an early night of it, but that had been fine with Finn. He'd figured he could watch whatever was left of the game in his room. But now—

Oh, crap. Right about now, Russell was probably wondering what the hell had happened to Finn and where the hell he'd gone.

As if cued by the thought, the cell phone in his back pocket began to vibrate. He snatched it out, looked at it long enough to recognize Russell's number as the incoming call, then shoved the Talk button with more force than was necessary as he lifted it to his ear.

"I'm up in my room," he said before Russell could say a word.

There was a moment of silence from the other end, then, "Why?" Russell asked. "Aren't you supposed to be down here guarding my body? Keeping away people like Dean Waterman? Thank God he had to go answer the call of Nature, who I hope keeps him on the line for a while, because if I have to spend five more minutes with the guy, I'm going to shove his baked potato down his throat."

"I, uh, got a little sidetracked," Finn said.

"With what?" Then, before Finn had a chance to explain, Russell started to chuckle. "Or should I ask, with *who*?"

"With Natalie," Finn confirmed. "But it's not what you think."

"How do you know what I'm thinking?"

"Because when it comes to women, Russell, whatever you think has its basis in sex."

"And that makes me different from other men . . . how?"

"Look, she's out cold," Finn said, ignoring the question, since it was obviously rhetorical. "She came out of the women's room and pretty much passed out in my arms. I didn't know what else to do with her, so I brought her up to my room. She can sleep it off up here."

Russell had started laughing right around the part where Finn said "out cold," and he kept laughing, even when Finn tried to explain more about how it had all gone down. "Don't," he interrupted before Finn could get halfway through his first sentence. "I'm finding too much satisfaction in the knowledge that you have Waterman's fiancée up there in your bed."

The word *fiancée* brought Finn up short. "How do you know he's engaged to her?"

"He told me," Russell said. Then he hastily clarified, "Well, not in so many words. What he said was that he's making it his life's work to . . . How did he put it? Let me think. It was just so charming . . . Ah. I remember now. He said he was making it his life's work to 'tame the little vixen and show her who's boss' and said that he couldn't wait for the day when she finally accepted the fact that he was her . . . Oh, what were the words he used . . . ? Oh, yeah. 'Lord and master.' "

"What?"

"I know. He is *the* most delightful person to talk to."

Man. In a matter of seconds, Waterman had just upped his standing from big jerk to gargantuan asshole.

"So don't tell me Natalie is unconscious," Russell instructed him. "Just tell me she's in your bed . . . She is in your bed, isn't she, Finn?"

"Yep."

"Good. Just tell me she's in your bed, and that you're in there with her—we can be hazy about what exactly *there* means—and let me enjoy the cuckolding of Dean Waterman for a little while."

"Cuckolding?" Finn repeated. "Where did you hear that? My God, have you been reading *books*?"

Russell ignored the dig. "I gotta cut this short. Waterman's headed back to the table."

"Look, let me just write a quick note to Natalie, explaining what happened and where she is and what my cell number is, and I'll come right back down."

"Oh, no, you won't," Russell told him decisively. "You need to stay up there with Natalie."

Wow. Russell was being chivalrous? This was a new development. Finn was about to congratulate his friend on the birth of his new conscience when the other man continued, "This way, when I tell Waterman you and Natalie decided to go upstairs to your room, and that I just talked to you and you told me not to bother you again—"

"I never said that."

"Didn't you? I could have sworn you did. Anyway," he hurried on, "when I tell Waterman all those things, then, technically, I won't be lying. This is gonna be good . . ."

And then Russell was hanging up before Finn had a chance to argue with him.

But then, Russell had probably just been joking about telling Waterman all that stuff, Finn immediately reassured himself. That was Russell. Always joking around. Even he wouldn't be so crass as to screw up a perfectly nice woman's engagement to someone.

Even if the someone in question was a gargantuan asshole.

RUSSELL WAS CLOSING HIS PHONE, THINKING ABOUT how Fate wasn't always such a vindictive harpy and how sometimes she actually did smile down on people, when Dim Witterman pulled out the chair beside his and sat down, yammering just as incessantly and moronically as he'd been when he left. Okay, so maybe Fate was still being a vindictive harpy when it came to Russell. When it came to Finn, she was definitely feeling the love. It had been way too long since he'd had a woman horizontal in his hotel room. Just because the woman in question this time was passed out cold, that didn't mean anything. Eventually, she would have to regain consciousness. And surely Finn would be smart enough to keep her horizontal when she did.

"So, where were we?" Dud Wretchedman asked.

Russell sighed to himself. So much for hoping a couple of thugs in the men's room would take the guy for an extended swirly ride. "Well, you were telling me about that dazzling creature you're engaged to marry," he said, having realized by now that Natalie doubtless was dazzling when she wasn't drinking and had only been driven to excessive drink tonight because Damn Waterman just had that effect on people, "and I was about to tell you that I have to leave."

"Leave?" Dumb Waiterman echoed incredulously. "But we haven't even had coffee yet."

The objection bothered Russell on so many levels. As if the mere thought of spending another excruciating second in the man's presence wasn't enough to make him want to drive a fork into his eye so he'd feel better, Dweeb Watermoron was presuming Russell didn't mind adding to the already ridiculous amount he'd spent on his dinner companion tonight. Ever since Russell had told their server to add the newcomers' meals to his tab, Dull Waterhose had added enough courses to his that the PGA could host the next Ryder Cup at this very table. And it wasn't like the man couldn't afford his own dinner. He'd made clear—over and over again—that he had money to burn. Drip Wearyman just wanted coffee so he'd have a chance to waste more of Russell's time.

"I received an urgent phone call while you were, ah . . . while you were gone," Russell said diplomatically. "And I'm afraid I'm going to have to call it a night." Which was better than what he really wanted to call it, that was for damned sure.

Dork Wasteofman looked genuinely crestfallen. "But I didn't get a chance to tell you about some incredible investment opportunities you could take advantage of."

Ah, Russell thought. Now they were getting to the crux

of the matter. Dread Watermelon wanted to try to win him over as a client. Well, wasn't that just annoying as hell?

He hoped he sounded sincerely contrite when he said, "I'm afraid that will have to wait for another time, Dan." To himself, he added, *Like after a nuclear holocaust has left the entire planet in toxic flames.*

"Dean," Dildo corrected him.

"Right. Anyway, thanks, but I have to go." To punctuate that, Russell lifted a hand to signal their server, who was table side faster than you could say, *Get me outta here.* Russell signed the check with a flourish, generously tipping thirty percent for the waiter's having to put up with Watercan, and stood. "It's been such an interesting evening," he said as his companion stood, too. "I mean that sincerely."

And he did, too. The last couple of hours had been interesting in exactly the same way that olive loaf was interesting. When Waterbland began to look panicky, Russell hastily added, "I wish you and Miss Beckett all the best in your life together," and he turned to leave.

"Wait, Russell," Dirty Waterway said, immediately putting Russell's back up, because he hated it when people used his first name who had no business being so familiar.

"You don't mind if I call you Russell, do you?" Dip Wadderman added belatedly.

"Of course I don't mind, Don."

"Dean."

"Right."

"Listen, Natalie and I are hosting a little dinner party at my place Wednesday night, and it would be so great if you could come. Please. Just a handful of our closest friends, nothing major. Please. But you're more than welcome to join us. Please. And of course you should bring a date. Please," he said a fourth time, his desperation by that point making Russell want to cringe. "Let us repay your generosity tonight. Please."

"That's not necessary, really."

"I know, but it's the least we could do."

"Thank you, but—"

"My place is just minutes away from the hotel. It won't inconvenience you at all." He was starting to look as panicked as he sounded, but he managed to reach into his pocket and withdraw a business card case that Russell recognized as solid gold, not once pausing for breath. "Here, I'll write down the directions. Wednesday evening. Cocktails at six, dinner at seven. I won't take no for an answer."

Russell was about to shove the word *no* down the other man's throat when, suddenly, out of nowhere, he got an idea. A wonderful, awful idea. And like the Grinch, whenever Russell Mulholland got an idea, it took on a life of its own. So he smiled and said, "Thank you, Dale. That would be great. As it turns out, I'm totally free Wednesday night."

It was a lie, of course. He couldn't remember what he was doing Wednesday night, but he was sure he was doing something. And even if he had been free Wednesday, he would have made something up to assure Dismal Watercolor that there was no way he could make it to his party, even if Natalie was going to be there drinking herself silly again which, Russell had to admit, had been a very pleasant pastime while it lasted.

"Six o'clock Wednesday," Dunce Weaselman repeated, thrusting the card at Russell and giving it a little shake, lest he miss the way the other man practically stabbed him in the eye with it.

"I'll be there," Russell told him. He added to himself, *Or, as I do whenever I can't make a function, I'll send a reasonable facsimile in my place.*

GINNY WAS ON HER LAST HALF HOUR OF BEING AMBER Glenn when Russell Mulholland walked into Minxxx for a second time. Damn. So close. If he'd just come in thirty minutes later, she would have been headed for her locker and could have avoided him. But for some reason she couldn't begin to explain, she'd had a feeling he would come back, and she hadn't been able to keep herself from watching the door for his entrance, so she wouldn't be caught with her pants . . . ah, she meant so she wouldn't be caught off guard. And with each passing hour that he didn't come in, she'd—

Well, she'd taken drink orders from obnoxious men and hauled around overfilled trays of cocktails and removed groping hands from various parts of her body and dodged salacious demands. She'd continued to do her job, the same way she did it every night. Her lousy, demoralizing, pain-in-the-ass job. Her crap job that paid a lot more than she could make anywhere else claiming, or maybe lacking, the sort of skills she claimed, or maybe lacked. The way Ginny figured it, the only thing she was qualified for at this point was waiting tables and greeting discount store customers. And where that second might make her feel more like a human being and less like a piece of meat, it didn't pay enough to raise a kid to be anything more than a waitress or discount store greeter. So tonight, as always, she'd done her job.

What she *hadn't* done was care that Russell Mulholland never came through the door. She'd barely noticed he never came through that door. In fact, she'd been relieved he hadn't come through that door.

Yeah, that's the ticket.

Then she told herself not to flatter herself. Why had she been thinking Russell would walk into Minxxx a second night in the first place? There were dozens of other places in this part of town alone he could have chosen instead. There were plenty closer to where he was staying downtown, too. Not that she'd made a point of finding out where he was staying. She just remembered seeing his picture in the paper the other day where he'd been in the lobby of the Brown Hotel, that was all. Everyone in Louisville knew where Russell Mulholland was staying during Derby.

And even if he had come into Minxxx a second night, who said he'd come back because he wanted to see Ginny? Or, rather, Amber, since there was no way he'd bother coming back here to see Ginny. He might just want another lap dance from Mindy or Bunny or Cerise again. Not that Ginny had actually noticed which of the dancers he'd paid the last time. She just happened to remember, that was all. She had a very good memory, as evidenced by that Brown Hotel thing. She couldn't have cared less who Russell Mulholland paid to squirm in his lap. Just like she couldn't have cared less whose table he chose to approach.

So why did heat splash through her belly when she saw him take a seat at one of hers?

A seat all by himself, too, she noted further, wondering where his companions of the other night were. The men had tried to look like a trio of friends out on the town, but it didn't take a genius to figure out the other two guys had been there as security. Ginny shot her gaze quickly around the club. Nope, not a single guy there who looked like he was working for Mulholland.

Interesting. But she wasn't sure how.

She thought about handing off the table to someone else. Then she reminded herself how much he'd tipped the other night. Not that Ginny liked to think she had a price—except when it came to Maisy—but she wasn't stupid, either. She'd be leaving in thirty minutes and passing the table to someone else anyway. And in that thirty minutes, provided she didn't screw up, she could probably make enough from Mulholland alone for another textbook or two for her daughter.

Then again, she'd screwed up royally the other night by slipping out of character long enough to make clear to the billionaire that she wasn't the kind of girl he thought—and would have paid—her to be. Both Lenny, the owner of Minxxx, and Eddie, the manager, made clear to the girls almost nightly that the customer was always—*always*—right. No matter what the complaint or how unjustified, the bar's operators would always—*always*—find in the favor of whoever was putting the money in the cash drawer. But Russell Mulholland hadn't complained about Amber. He'd tipped her outrageously instead. Ginny still wasn't sure what to make of that. Other than that maybe he was one of those guys who got turned on by verbal abuse. In which case, ick.

She pushed the thought away, along with all the others, and emptied her brain so she could play Amber to the hilt. Amber, who wasn't the brightest bulb on Broadway, but who had a heart as big as all outdoors.

Cue the schmaltzy Hollywood music.

As she made her way to Russell's table, though, instead of a swelling symphony of heart-tugging strings, the music that erupted in her brain was more suited to a seventies' porno flick soundtrack. Damn. She hated disco.

Ignoring the music—for lack of a better word—she wove through the tables between her and Russell, double-checking her others as she went. One thing she liked about Mondays was that there were considerably fewer patrons, and they thinned out pretty well by midnight, since so many guys had to get up early to go to work. Ginny only had three other tables going at the moment, so, all in all, things were pretty well under control.

Until she came to a halt on the other side of the table where Russell was sitting, at which point almost nothing— at least where she herself was concerned—seemed in any way under control. Because those blue, blue eyes were assessing her in a way that was different from the way the other men in the club assessed her. Yes, she could tell he thought she—or rather, Amber—was sexy. Yes, she knew he was undressing her—or rather, Amber—with his eyes. Yes, she could see that he wanted to make her—or rather, Amber—another one of those offers she might find it harder tonight to refuse.

But he was also looking at her in a way that indicated he was just as curious about what was going on above her neck as what was going on below it. And not just where her mouth was concerned, either. Russell Mulholland, she could tell, wanted to know what was on her mind—and in it—too. He was trying to figure her out. *Her*, she realized with no small amount of shock. Ginny. He was trying to figure Ginny out. Because there was something about the speculation in his eyes that made it clear he knew she wasn't Amber, not really.

But then, Ginny was kind of curious about him tonight, too. Because Saturday night, he'd looked like one of those yachtsmen who whipped up a shaker of martinis while someone else sailed the yacht, something that had made it easier for her to dismiss him as shallow. Tonight, however, he looked like an ordinary guy. In place of the khakis and navy blue blazer, he was wearing faded blue jeans paired with a gray T-shirt and black jacket. He looked like the kind of guy who might do anything for a living, or be anyone under the sun. Like the kind of guy who *didn't* make it a habit of going to strip clubs. Like the kind of guy who would never grab a woman's ass without asking permission first.

Not that Ginny had ever been a good judge of men's appearances, as evidenced by the fact that every man she'd ever been involved with had turned out to be at best thoughtless and at worst vicious. But she'd heard the urban legends about how there might actually be decent men in the world. Somewhere.

"Mr. Mulholland," she said by way of a greeting, not bothering with the phony Southern accent that usually upped her tips a couple of percentage points, since he already knew it wasn't real.

"Miss, ah, Amber," he replied with a smile that—oh, dammit—made the heat in her belly surge higher.

She peeled off a cocktail napkin from the short stack on her tray and set it on the table in front of him. And she hoped she didn't sound too sarcastic when she said, "How fortunate for us to have you grace our little club for a second time."

He waited until she looked up from her task before saying, "Well, it's not because of the service, that's for sure."

She opened her mouth to reply to that, but he hurried on before she could get a word out.

"And it's not like there's a dearth of, ah, gentleman's clubs out there."

He said *gentleman* the same way Ginny did. With derision and rancor disguised as bitterness. Again, she opened her mouth to comment—still not knowing what she could say that wouldn't compromise her position—but again, he continued before she had the chance.

"It wasn't easy choosing which club to visit tonight. There are so many with such intriguing names. Minxxx and Foxxxy and Vixxxen and Chixxx and Trixxxie's. Any more triple *X*s, and I'd think I was in the land of moonshine."

"You are in the land of moonshine," she told him, finally finding an opening. Better still, it was an opening that allowed her to say something that wouldn't cost her her job. "Just go south for about an hour, turn left, and drive for a few hours more. Can't miss it."

"Is that an order?"

"Yep."

Damn. So much for not costing herself her job.

He looked stunned for a minute, then started to laugh. Ginny wasn't sure what was so funny, so she just continued to stand there looking down at him, one eyebrow arched expectantly as she waited to see if he would (A) take her advice and leave or (B) ignore her advice and leave. Either would be fine with her.

"That makes you two for two, Amber," he said once his laughter subsided.

"What do you mean?" she asked.

"Both times I've encountered you, you've told me to shove off."

"And?"

He sighed heavily but continued to smile. "And I'm not accustomed to being turned down even once, let alone twice. Not by anyone. But especially not by a beautiful woman."

Then his record was still reasonably intact, Ginny thought. Because under the wig and the layers of cosmetics, she wasn't a beautiful woman. Not that she was going to tell him that.

When she said nothing in response to his comment, he added, "But then, I'm going to be two for two, as well. Because for the second time, I'm not going to take you at your word."

As much as she wanted to reply to that, Ginny figured it was probably best not to. Not because she feared she would say something that would jeopardize her job again. But because it suddenly seemed kind of tempting to say something that would jeopardize herself.

So she only asked, "What can I get you to drink?" Belatedly, she remembered to add, "Sir."

He studied her in silence for a moment, then said, "What do you have on draft?"

The question surprised her, because, again, it made him seem like such a typical guy. "*What do you have on draft?*" was the most frequently asked question at Minxxx. Well, after "*You wanna earn a quick twenty bucks, babe?*" she meant.

She rattled off the four brands of beer—three overpriced domestics and one overpriced import—that they had on draft, and was amazed yet again when Russell ordered the least expensive, most plebeian of the bunch. She mumbled, "Coming right up," and turned to make her way to the bar, fielding a couple of requests for refills on the way, and wondering what had happened to turn Russell Mulholland from a shallow, cognac-sipping yachtsman into a regular, beer-drinking guy. Then she decided it would probably be best to concentrate on the drink orders and not ponder Russell Mulholland. Pondering too often led to preoccupation. And preoccupation too often led to passion. And that way lay madness.

She stopped twice on her way back to his table to deliver other drink orders, and each time, she felt his gaze on her. Sneaking glimpses of him from the corner of her eye, she saw that he never once seemed to take his eyes off of her. Other patrons of Minxxx did that, too, from time to time, so the open appraisal was nothing new. What was

new was how his open appraisal didn't give her a major
wiggins the way other guys' did. And not just because his
didn't involve licking his lips or grabbing his crotch or
mouthing offensive commands. He didn't look like he was
just appraising her body. He looked like he was trying to
figure her out.

Good luck with that one, she thought. Even Ginny had
trouble with that.

She set his beer on the purple cocktail napkin that was
decorated with Minxxx's disturbing line-drawing logo of a
woman's headless, limbless, naked torso, then started to
turn away, as she always did after delivering a drink. Except that where she usually smiled vapidly at the customer
and drawled out some Southern-fried platitude like, *"There
ya go, sugar dumplin',"* on her way, this time she said nothing, knowing it would be pointless and, for some reason,
uncomfortable to do so.

She should have realized Russell Mulholland wouldn't
let her get away that easily. "You know I lied to you a little
while ago," he said before she'd completed her first step.

Reluctantly, she turned around to look at him, but she
said nothing, since any reply the comment invited would
doubtless lead to trouble.

"When I told you I had trouble choosing which club to
visit tonight," he clarified. "It wasn't any trouble at all, really."

She remained silent, again unsure of what she could say
that wouldn't lead them down a path they probably didn't
need to travel.

Russell didn't seem as disinclined to the voyage as she,
however, because he continued, "I knew the minute you
turned me down that I'd be coming back here again."

At that, Ginny did know what to say. "Why? To give me
a second chance to turn you down?" At this point, she
didn't care anymore whether or not her job was at stake.
"Wow, that's really nice of you, Mr. Mulholland, but turning you down once truly was a lifelong dream come true

for me. And that tip you left after my turning you down was just icing on the cake. Really, I think you've done enough for l'il ol' me."

"Not to give you a second chance to turn me down on my offer," he told her. "To give you a second chance to take me up on my offer."

"Your offer to have sex with you in exchange for money?" she asked innocently. "Golly, that is just so—"

"My offer to have dinner with me Wednesday night," he interrupted her. "Sex with me afterward would be entirely up to you, but I refuse to pay you for it."

Well, that certainly brought her up short.

"You never let me tell you what my offer was the other night," he pointed out. "You simply assumed it involved something salacious."

"Yeah, well, it's easy to make assumptions like that in a place like this, when every offer you receive involves something that's illegal in all fifty states."

"With me, you assumed wrong."

There was something in the way he uttered the comment that made Ginny think he was talking about a lot more than just his offer of the other night. Which was all the more reason, she told herself, not to even consider it.

"Yeah, well, thanks, but no thanks," she said.

His mouth dropped open in obvious astonishment. "Are you serious?" he said. "You won't even have dinner with me?"

She shook her head. "Number one, why should I trust you? And number two, I'm busy."

"Number one," he said, "I may be a recluse, but I'm enough in the public eye for you to know who I am and that I'm not a serial rapist. And number two, you're not working Wednesday night. I checked." Before she could ask how he knew that, he told her, "The bartenders here are imminently bribeable."

"Number one," she echoed his own statement, "maybe it's not your criminal background I'm concerned about,

and number two, I didn't say I'm working. I said I'm busy."
And she was, too. Wednesday night was card night at the
Collins house. Not to mention Maisy had promised to teach
Ginny and Hazel how to play something called Trash, and
she was *so* looking forward to learning a game with a name
like that.

"They must be pretty major plans for you to turn down
dinner with a nice man who has money to burn and no
criminal background."

She smiled at that. "They are major plans. But they're not
engraved in stone." Which was true. Half the time, Maisy
was the one who changed them, often at the last minute, to
hang with a girlfriend or watch something on TV instead. "I
could potentially change my plans for dinner with a nice
man, should a nice man ask me out."

"You don't think I'm a nice man?"

To answer that question, Ginny did slip back into Amber
mode. "Sugar, look aroun' you. Do you think *any* of the men
who come to places like Minxxx could be called *nice*?"

He dipped his head forward, silently conceding the
point to her. "All right. Then change your plans to go out
with a man who could drop four figures on you in a matter
of hours."

She stiffened at that, dropping all pretense. "I already
told you I won't—"

"Think about it, Amber," he interrupted her again. "I'm
the definition of 'money is no object.' I can give you an evening like you've never had before. Like you'll never have
again. I'll show up at your front door dressed in a five thousand dollar suit, cradling two dozen long-stemmed roses in
my arms. I'll escort you to a stretch limousine with Dom
Perignon chilling in the backseat and a driver named Raoul
in the front. I'll take you to a restaurant that has a name
neither of us can pronounce, and we'll order one of everything on the menu, and a bottle of Cristal to go with. And I
will expect nothing in return except the pleasure of your
company."

As if, she thought. "Well, I don't know, Mr. Mulholland," she replied in her most vapid Amber voice. "You jes' kinda took the whole surprise out of it by tellin' me all that. Where would be the fun of goin' out and doin' it now?"

He smiled at her the way a man smiles when he knows he's close to getting exactly what he wants.

But he wasn't there yet.

Ginny told herself to turn him down, that no matter how much he assured her he wouldn't expect anything sexual in nature in return, no man—not one—ever spent that much on a woman he just met without there being the expectation of some spectacular sex at the end of the night. At least, no man ever took out a woman like *Amber* without expecting some spectacular sex.

Now Ginny smiled, too. It had been a long, long time since she'd gone out on a date with *any* man, let alone one who could afford anything more than Steak n Shake and a second-run movie at Village 8. And it wasn't like he was a total stranger. Everyone in the world knew who Russell Mulholland was. And he was definitely right about the fact that she'd *never* have another opportunity in her life to enjoy the sort of night he described. It really was an offer that was too good to refuse. Just because he was making the offer to Amber instead of Ginny . . .

Actually, that was the best part. Because assumptions went both ways, and if she showed up for the date as herself, instead of the woman *he* assumed *her* to be, not only would he not *expect* sex at the end of the night, he wouldn't *want* it.

"You don't have to pick me up in a limo," she told him.

His smile at that went supernova. "I insist."

She shook her head. "I'll meet you."

"But—"

"At a restaurant whose name I can pronounce just fine, thanks, called Vincenzo's. Make a reservation for five thirty. I want to get started early if we're going to eat our way through the entire menu." Because then, she thought, there would be plenty of leftovers to bring home in a doggie bag, and Maisy and Hazel both loved Italian.

Russell nodded his head with much satisfaction. "The Dom Perignon will be chilling when you arrive."

·Eight·

WHEN NATALIE AWOKE, IT WAS TO DISCOVER THAT A
lineup of rowdy hockey players was caroming through her
belly at full speed and rocketing pucks into her brain, leaving the mouth between little more than filthy, overskated
slush. Then the crowd, also apparently in her brain, went
wild. And then someone bodychecked her. Hard. Which
was really weird, because Louisville didn't have a hockey
team and hadn't for some time.

She opened her eyes to almost complete darkness, but
not before the steroid-crazed forward in her stomach did
some slap shot thing and beaned her squarely behind her
forehead with another puck.

"Ow," she murmured, lifting a hand to rub at the sharp
pain.

Vaguely, she heard what sounded like a hockey tourna-
ment raging in the next room, something that might have
explained how she had become a casualty of such, except
that she also registered the fact that she was still dressed in
the cocktail dress she'd donned the night before, and if
there was one thing Natalie Beckett had learned in life, it

was that one *never* wore cocktail attire to a sporting event. Unless, it went without saying, it was a fund-raiser.

What the . . . ?

Had she left the TV on before going to bed? And why hadn't she put on her pajamas? And what was with all the physical unfitness in her belly and brain? She started to lever herself up to sitting, but that just made the hockey players in her stomach turn into a pack of wild animals, all of whom wanted to be the enforcer, and it doubled the number of pucks—and their velocity—in her brain. So she lay back down again, cupping one hand over her forehead and the other over her stomach.

Okay, clearly something had happened last night that made her go to bed in her clothes, and—*okay*—she was obviously suffering from the effects of having had too much to drink. Natalie knew a nasty hangover when she felt one. Not that she'd felt one since her sophomore year in college during rush week, but that was beside the point. The point was that she'd obviously partied like a sorority girl last night, and the details at the moment were a bit, ah, sketchy.

Sketchy, ha, she echoed herself. *More like nonexistent. Think, Natalie, think . . .*

She remembered sitting in the English Grill stalking Russell—ah, she meant scoping . . . oh, what the hell . . . stalking Russell Mulholland—and then having Dean Waterman ooze into the chair opposite hers like the overripe contents of a septic tank. Then she remembered him saying something really stupid—no surprise there—and then she decided to—

Ooooooh. Now she remembered. She'd turned it into a drinking game. Whenever Dean said something stupid, she'd taken a drink. Well, hell, no wonder she'd passed out.

What a dumb idea, she thought. She should have realized she'd be under the table in no time. Dean rarely said something that *wasn't* stupid. No wonder she couldn't remember what happened after th—

She jackknifed up in bed, panic surging through her—
and pain knifing through her belly and brain again—when
she did indeed remember what had happened after that.
Finn Guthrie had come into the restaurant with Russell
Mulholland. And Mulholland had invited Natalie and
Dean to join them for dinner. After that . . .

She closed her eyes in abject humiliation. After that,
she must have gotten so snockered she didn't even remember what happened. She kind of recalled sitting next
to Mulholland and thinking he was even better looking
in real life than he was in his photographs. She also remembered thinking he still wasn't as attractive as Finn.
To her credit, she was pretty sure she'd tried to tell him
about Clementine's party. Unfortunately, she was also pretty
sure—dammit—she'd never gotten the words out. And
after *that* . . .

She opened her eyes again, thankful for the complete
and profound darkness. Because she could remember nothing after that, and she really hated to think that she'd made
a complete fool of herself in front of Finn Guthrie.

No, in front of Russell Mulholland, she quickly corrected herself. She couldn't care less what Finn thought
about her. It was his employer she'd been trying to impress.
Impress by getting so drunk, she couldn't even remember
what she'd said or done.

So how had she gotten home? Surely she hadn't driven.
Surely Dean would have been at least smart enough and
decent enough not to let her get behind the wheel of a car.
Surely Dean had driven her home and put her to—

Automatically, her nose wrinkled in disgust. If he'd
copped a feel while she was unconscious, she'd smack him
upside the head but good. With a brick. One of those big
cement bricks they used to build school gymnasiums.

What time was it, anyway? She turned to where her
clock with the big purple numbers should be, but it wasn't
on the nightstand. Unless maybe she was turned around
and had gone to bed—or been dumped there—backward,
with her head at the foot. So she looked where the clock

should be if that were the case. But there was no sign of it anywhere. Damn. She must have been ambulatory enough to make it into the bedroom but incoherent enough to run into things and knock stuff to the floor.

She reached over her head to feel around for the brass headboard, but her wiggling fingers met only thin air, telling her she was indeed at the foot of the bed. She did her best to scramble back up to the other end, looking first over one side of the mattress, then the other, to locate her clock. Ah. There it was on the floor, right on the side it was supposed to be on, having been toppled there by her plunge into bed—whoever had been responsible for it. But the fall had evidently slapped it out of whack, because not only were the numbers red instead of purple, they were half the size they normally were. Even worse, they were arranged in a way that indicated it was just after three a.m., and there was no way Natalie could have been passed out . . . ah, she meant asleep . . . for that long.

Just what time had dinner ended, anyway?

When she reached down to retrieve the clock, some of the hockey pucks in her brain toppled to the left, causing her center of gravity to shift—that was her story and she was sticking to it—something that made her, too, go toppling off the bed and onto the floor. The lushly carpeted floor with the thick, comfy carpet pad beneath it.

Waitaminnit . . .

Natalie didn't have carpet in her bedroom. She had a wool dhurrie rug rolled open over her hardwood—and very *un*padded—floor. Pushing herself up onto all fours, she crawled along the edge of the bed until she felt the bottom edge of a nightstand of some kind. Then she felt her way up to the base of a lamp, then farther up to a lamp cord, which, after only a small hesitation, she tugged.

"Oh, ow," she said again in response to the soft white light that spilled over her. She squeezed her eyes shut tight and lifted a hand to her forehead again in an effort to halt the pain that hammered her right between the eyes. Then her stomach lurched again, and she opened her eyes once more. She allowed herself a fraction of a second to look around, long enough to note the elegant furnishings and appointments of one of the Brown Hotel's most luxurious suites. Then—yes, there was a god—she saw the door of a bathroom ajar on the other side of the room. She had just enough time to reach the toilet before losing the entire contents of her stomach into it.

And just like that, hockey season came to an end. But, suffice it to say, Natalie did *not* win the Stanley Cup.

She flushed and continued to cling to the side of the bowl for another minute, just in case there might be a second-stringer or two still trying to leave the rink. Finally, when her stomach settled some and her head began to clear, she figured it was safe to stand.

Until she got a look at herself in the mirror.

Holy cow, she looked like the demon offspring of Marilyn Manson and RuPaul. Her mascara had smudged to raccoon eyes, and her lipstick had journeyed from her mouth up to her ear, leaving a few bread crumbs behind. Ew. Her hair was matted on one side to the point where it was significantly higher than the other side, making her look vaguely like the Matterhorn. Surely all that had happened *after* her dinner with Russell Mulholland. Surely.

As she ran some cold water into the sink, she noticed a man's shaving kit open on the vanity, and for the first time, she gave more than a moment's thought to wondering where the hell she was. Still at the Brown, obviously, but whose room? Had Dean taken one when he realized the severity of Natalie's condition? And if so, why had he had the foresight to bring along a shaving kit?

Why, that little worm . . .

Then she reminded herself that it was Derby time, which meant Dean probably wouldn't have been able to even get a room. Besides, his condo was barely five minutes away. He could have driven them to his place in the time it would have taken him to get a room and wrangle Natalie up to it.

So whose room is this? she asked herself again.

An answer came to her almost immediately, but she really

wanted to think it was wrong. Unable to help herself, she picked carefully through the shaving kit for some clue, but she found only the typical accoutrements of a man who traveled a lot. Travel-sized toiletries, comb, razor, toothbrush, an over-the-counter sleep aid that hadn't been opened. But nothing with a monogram that might offer her a hint. Nothing elegant. Nothing expensive. All of the toiletries were the sort that came from the grocery store, not a posh specialty store or even a department store. The shaving kit, too, was of the economically priced nylon variety that could have been purchased at a discount store. Clearly, even though she was in one of the hotel's most expensive suites, it wasn't Russell Mulholland's.

But then, it hadn't been Russell Mulholland whose suite she feared she was in.

She shut off the water, pulled a clean washcloth from the rack, and opened a box of soap. After washing her face, she reached for the little bottle of complimentary mouthwash and emptied its entire contents into her mouth. After a few good swishes and some gargling, the taste of her nausea was gone, and she felt good enough to go in search of her purse, which she found at the foot of the bed. The little fold-up brush that the size of the purse necessitated wasn't quite up to the task that was her hair, but she managed to at least divest herself of the Alpine look. After that, she *almost* felt like herself again. Well, except for the fact that she still had to confront the man who had brought her to his room and put her in his bed, even though she could remember none of it.

Steeling herself for the task, she moved to the bedroom door and, after only a small hesitation, pulled it open. Sure enough, there was a hockey game blaring on the television in the other room. And just as she'd feared, the man watching it was Finn Guthrie.

He lay on his back on the overstuffed sofa with his bare feet hooked at his ankles, one arm folded with his hand behind his head, the other dangling toward the floor with his hand loosely clutching the remote. He had changed out

of the khakis and striped shirt he'd been wearing earlier—
she did remember that, and recalled how incongruous she'd
thought the preppy attire had looked on him—into a pair
of faded navy sweatpants and a white, V-neck T-shirt. But
unlike the T-shirt he had worn before, this one didn't con-
tour to his X-tra brawny frame like a second skin. Except
at the shoulders, she couldn't help noting, where the fabric
once again strained tight enough to look as if it would rip
open any second.

Well, a girl could dream, couldn't she?

He was looking at the TV, even though Natalie was certain he knew she was standing in the doorway. He had to
have heard the sound of running water in the bathroom
and the rustle of her movements in the bedroom. Hell, he'd
probably even heard her getting sick. Damn him. Not to
mention it was his job to notice the presence of people. But
he didn't offer even a glimpse at her, only kept his attention
fixed on the game.

In spite of that, her stomach did a funny little flip-flop
that had nothing to do with having had too much to drink.
He was just an unbelievably beautiful man, from the dark
hair that fell over his forehead, tempting a woman to brush
it affectionately back, to the ginormous feet that invited
speculation about whether that size-of-the-feet-equals-the-
size-of-the-uh-other-thing legend was true.

The thought inevitably made her gaze wander upward,
over the long, long legs that were doubtless as roped with
muscles as his arms, to gaze in speculation at that very part
of him. After damning his sweatpants for being so baggy,
she drove her gaze higher still, over the belly as flat—and
probably as hot—as a steam iron, the chest that was roughly
the size of Rhode Island, the strong throat and jaws darkened by a day's growth of beard, to the eyes she knew were
the color of smoky quartz.

And she tried not to think about how nice it would be to
come home from work every night and have such a sight
greet her the moment she walked in the front door.

She pushed the thought away and asked, "Isn't it a little late for hockey?"

Still not looking at her, he replied, "Not on the West Coast."

"It's past midnight on the West Coast. That's too late for hockey even there."

"Not unless you're a big wuss."

She took a few steps into the room and trained her own gaze on the TV. Then she narrowed her eyes. "This isn't even live," she said. "It's a delayed telecast."

He did spare her a glance at that, but it was just that—a quick once-over before turning his attention back to the TV. "How do you know?"

"I watched it."

This time when he turned to look at her, it was for considerably longer than a second or two. "You like hockey?" he asked, his voice tinted with more than a little disbelief.

She shrugged. "Not as much as basketball, but yeah. I like hockey. When I was at Wellesley, I had season tickets to see the Celtics and Bruins both."

"You went to Wellesley?" he asked, sounding even more incredulous about that than he had about her liking hockey.

Feeling defensive for no reason she could name—except that maybe because Finn had just made her sound like she was too stupid to go someplace like Wellesley—she snapped, "Yeah. I went to Wellesley. What of it?"

He shrugged and turned his attention back to the game. "Nothing. Just that you don't seem like the Wellesley type."

"And what type do I seem?" she asked tersely.

He shrugged again. "I don't know. Just not the Wellesley type."

She was about to ask him what he thought the Wellesley type was, since Natalie had met dozens of types of women in college, but he pointed the remote at the TV and scooted up the volume a few decibels.

"The Thunderbirds are playing the Bruins right now," he said.

"No, they played them yesterday," she corrected him. "That's why I made sure to watch."

He opened his mouth to say something else, but the crowd on the TV started screaming. And so did he as he jackknifed up into a sitting position. "Yes!" he cried, pumping a fist in the air. "Seattle scores! Now it's tied with only two minutes left in the last period. We still have plenty of time to pull this thing through."

Natalie strode slowly into the room until she stood at the other end of the couch. "You didn't watch this live?" she asked.

He continued to watch the game instead of her. "I was working. Russell had to go to some meeting at Churchill Downs, so I went with him. I didn't get to watch it live."

She wasn't sure what made her say what she did next, since it was an incredibly mean thing to do. She only knew that Finn was sitting there on the sofa, looking all devilish and handsome when she looked so disheveled and haggard, and he'd questioned her suitability for one of the country's top schools, and he was making her body react in ways she really didn't want it to react. Not for him. Not for a guy who obviously held a low opinion of her. Not for a guy who was keeping her from doing her job. Not for a guy who was coarse and obnoxious. Not for a guy who would only be in town for a couple of weeks.

Before she could stop herself, however, she said, "Boston's going to score with ten seconds left. Unanswered goal. Seattle lost, four to three."

Finn clapped his hands over his ears the second she started talking, but she knew he heard every word she said, because he looked at her like she was the most heinous person to walk the earth since Genghis Kahn. Then he dropped his hands to thumb the Off button on the remote and tossed it unceremoniously onto the sofa beside him.

"Thanks a lot," he muttered.

"I was just trying to spare you the heartbreak you were in for," she replied.

"No, you weren't. You were deliberately ruining it for me."

She started to deny it, then realized she couldn't. "Well, you dumped me into your bed without with about as much care as you would have shown a bag of dirty laundry."

"Yeah, well, I wouldn't have had to dump you anywhere if you hadn't—"

He halted abruptly, right when he was getting up a good head of steam. Natalie had no idea why. She was behaving abominably, and he had every right to tear into her.

"Never mind," he said. The he grinned. Devilishly, damn him. "Can I fix you a drink?"

Her stomach roiled at the mere thought. "Not just no, but *hell* no."

He chuckled at that. "Hair of the dog," he reminded her.

She shook her head. "Fizz of the Alka-Seltzer, I think, would be a better choice."

"I'll see what I can do."

He made his way to a cabinet on the other side of the room and opened it, then rifled through a duffel bag until he found whatever he was looking for. When he lifted a little blue and white foil packet up for her approval, Natalie could almost hear a flock of angels lifting their voices in the "*Hallelujah* Chorus." Then he moved to where a couple of glasses sat by an ice bucket and upturned one to drop in a few cubes. He added a little water from a bottle of Fiji, ripped open the Alka-Seltzer with his teeth—*Oh, be still my heart,* she thought—and plopped the two white tablets in with everything else.

Her stomach took another roll suddenly, followed by a flare of pain between her eyes, so she took a seat on the couch at the end opposite the one where Finn had been sitting only a moment ago. Another stab behind her right eyelid made her lean her head back and cover her eyes with her arm, splaying one hand open over her still queasy belly.

But when she heard the hiss of the swiftly dissolving

Alka-Seltzer, she opened her eyes again just in time to see Finn's hand drop in front of her face, holding the glass that contained her salvation. Just as she started to reach for it, though, her gaze skittered to his thumb, where a scar that began just below his nail curved toward the back of his hand. As she took the glass from him, she circled the fingers of her other hand around his wrist and turned it, feeling the scar beneath her palm even before seeing how it ran all the way down the back of his hand and wrist. It didn't appear to be the result of anything life-threatening— she wasn't even sure it had been stitched up—but it was too strangely shaped to have been from a medical procedure, starting off deep and jagged, then narrowing until it was straight and smooth.

"My God, what happened here?" she asked before she could stop herself. It seemed like kind of a personal question to ask of someone she'd just met a couple of days before. Especially in the tone of voice she'd used, one that made her sound not just surprised by the size of the scar but by the fact that he'd been hurt so badly once upon a time and that she genuinely cared.

Then again, she *did* genuinely care, she realized. The thought that Finn had been injured like this at some point in his life made something inside her do a little hissing and fizzing of its own. And not in a way that promised to make her feel better.

Gently, he tugged his wrist free and held up his hand to inspect the scar, as if he'd forgotten about it until now. He flexed his fingers, relaxed them, then dropped his hand to his side, ignoring it. "I got that by stupidly breaking a window with my bare fist," he said in a flat voice.

Her eyebrows shot up at that. "What happened? Did you lock yourself out of your house?"

He shook his head slowly but said nothing.

"Your car?"

Another shake of his head.

"Your place of employment?"

This time he didn't shake his head at all, but his gaze

never left hers as he told her, "No, I was trying to break into the chemistry lab of Seattle Community College."

Now her eyebrows arrowed downward. "You locked yourself out of school?" she asked, confused.

This time he sighed heavily before shaking his head. But he did shake his head. Kind of. "No, some kid in the neighborhood told me and Russell that the chemistry lab of Seattle Community College had just switched over to Mac from PC, and we really, really wanted a Mac."

Natalie's lips parted fractionally as she tried to absorb that. "You were breaking in *illegally*?" she asked incredulously. "To *steal* something that didn't belong to you?"

He chuckled at that, a soft sound completely lacking in humor. "You say that like you've never met anyone who did anything illegal or took something that didn't belong to them."

"That's because I *haven't* ever met anyone who's done anything illegal," she told him. "Well, except for skimming off the books at work and cheating on their taxes. But that's not like . . ."

Now Finn nodded. "Ah. Got it. White-collar crimes. Much nicer crimes, those, than the kind of stupid stuff kids get themselves into. That's just people who are smart enough and old enough—and rich enough—to know better, stealing from their employers or employees or shareholders. Leaving retirees broke and people unable to send their kids to college. Robbing the government of tax money it could use for education and the arts. And here I had the nerve to try to steal a computer when I was a dumb-ass kid."

"Hey, that's robbing funds for education," she pointed out halfheartedly, knowing the argument was lame but reluctant to concede that he was right. At least to his face. "Those Macs cost way more than PCs, which aren't exactly cheap to begin with."

"My bad," he said blandly.

This time Natalie was the one to sigh. "Okay, okay. There's no such thing as a victimless crime. Crime is crime, no matter who's committing it, and at some point, somebody has to pay." When he said nothing more, she continued, "So what happened?"

He expelled another one of those impatient sighs. "Exactly what you might think would happen to a couple of dumb-ass kids who try to break into a community college, even without one of them slicing open his wrist."

"You got caught," she guessed.

"Yep."

"Did they at least take you to a hospital to get stitched up?"

"Eventually. They hauled us into juvie first. It was only when I passed out from loss of blood that they finally—"

"Finn!" she interrupted him, aghast. "Tell me you're joking."

He smiled at that, neither confirming nor refuting the comment.

So instead of pressing, she said, "You guys really ended up in juvenile court?"

He nodded.

"But for burglary, right? That's not such a terrible thing. Lots of dumb-ass kids try to break into places and steal stuff."

Not that any kids Natalie had ever known, dumb-ass or otherwise, had ever done that. Of course, had any of her friends wanted a Mac when they were kids—or anything else, for that matter—they either asked their parents for one or they tapped into their own money to get it. Then again, such crimes certainly weren't unheard of in the upper classes. They were just excused more often as kids being bored or being angry or suffering chemical imbalances in the brain—or just kids being kids—than they were for kids in the lower classes, who generally ended up getting hauled into places like juvie, instead of getting hauled in front of the old man to have a heart-to-heart. A heart-to-heart that more often than not ended up with a slap on the wrist or, worse, a pat on the back. Money really could buy anything, including good PR and even better spin. Natalie saw it happen all the time.

Then the first part of what Finn had said gelled in her brain. "You and Russell Mulholland have been friends that long?" Nowhere in her Googling had she uncovered how or where the two men had met. Part of that shadowy, pre–Mulholland Games thing that had so intrigued her. She'd just assumed Finn had worked for Russell in some capacity at the company, probably security, before he'd needed a body-guard and then got promoted to the position. She never would have guessed they'd known each other as juvies. Ah, as kids. And she sure wouldn't have suspected they'd led a life of crime, however youthful and however temporary.

Finn didn't answer her question right away. Instead, he cupped his hand under the one she was using to hold the Alka-Seltzer she'd all but forgotten about, and he urged it gently toward her mouth. Obediently, she drank, grimac-ing at the bitter taste. The moment it hit her belly, though, it started to settle her stomach. So she forced down a few more swallows, then lifted the glass as if in a toast and drained the rest.

"Thanks," she said softly after emptying the glass.

"You're welcome." His expression revealed nothing about what he might be thinking, and she wasn't sure if he was going to answer her question about him and Russell or not. Finally, he just said, "Yeah, Russell and I have known each other a long time."

But he didn't elaborate further, so she wasn't sure if that meant they'd known each other since birth, or elementary school, or high school. Then again, what difference did it make? In spite of her dubious plan B that may or may not have involved blackmailing Mulholland, Natalie realized then that she really didn't care if she uncovered some info that might allow her to do just that. She really didn't want to blackmail Russell Mulholland. She did, however, want to know more about Finn. Not because she wanted to black-mail him, either. She just wanted to know more about him.

"So how old were you when you and Russell started on this life of crime?" she asked.

"I never said Russell and I had a life of crime," he denied. "One broken window does not a crime spree make."

"No, but it's a good start."

He smiled at that. Then he dipped his head to look at the floor and rubbed the back of his neck in that way men do when they're not sure what to say next. What finally came out, though, was, "Russell and I have known each other since we were fourteen. We landed in a group home in Seattle after being, ah . . . relieved of our parents. Our mothers, anyway. Neither of us knew who our fathers were, which was a major bonding moment for us. Good thing, too, since the other four guys we had to share the room with weren't as squeaky clean as we were. Helped to have someone watching your back."

Whoa, Natalie thought. Where had that come from? Mr. Taciturn was suddenly gushing like an *Oprah* guest. Well, okay, maybe that was overdoing it, but still. Finn had just revealed a wealth of information that told her *a lot* about both him and his employer. Information she hadn't even specifically asked for.

"Finn?" she said.

He met her gaze, looking very, very tired. "Yeah, Natalie?"

"You do realize I'm sober now, right? And that I won't be forgetting all this stuff you're telling me in the morning."

"It is morning, Natalie."

"You know what I mean."

Instead of replying, he folded himself onto the sofa, leaving a solid foot of space between them. "Yeah. I know what you mean."

"So then . . . why the ritual spilling of the guts?" she asked. "I mean, even I don't tell a guy that much about me on a first date."

"Number one," he said, "I can't quite see you having stories to tell about breaking into a community college to steal a Mac. And number two, this isn't our first date."

She hadn't been thinking it was a date at all. Was he being sarcastic? It was so hard to tell with him. "Right," she said experimentally. "I guess that day at BBC was our first date."

His expression grew puzzled. "BBC?"

"The beer place."

He seemed not to remember for a moment—And, oh, didn't *that* inflate her ego to the size of a snow pea?—then he nodded slowly. "Right." He frowned again. "That wasn't a date, either."

She smiled. "Are you including that very first conversation we had in the lobby of the Brown? You romantic devil. I never would have pegged you for—"

"Natalie."

She sobered at his tone. "What?"

"We are not dating."

Okay, so then it *had* been sarcasm. Right?

She gave her head a mental shake and said, "So you and Russell were fourteen when you met. How old were you when you started on your maybe-maybe-not life of crime?"

He looked back up at her again, but his hand was still cupped over his nape, and she could tell by his expression that he really, really, *really* wished he'd kept his mouth shut. Nevertheless, evidently deciding the damage was already done, so what the hell, he told her, "We were fourteen."

Her smile fell. "Oh. That's young."

"Yes, it is. That's not to say that either of us was that age when we committed our first crimes."

Natalie wasn't sure what surprised her more. That he had been such a young offender or that he was actually telling her about it. "Meaning there were others," she said, stating the obvious.

"One or two." He squeezed his eyes shut tight. "Look, I shouldn't have told you any of that," he said. "It's not just Russell's body I'm employed to protect. It's . . . other things, too. I actually can't believe I just told you all that."

Neither could Natalie, frankly. But she was oddly flattered that he had. It was as if he trusted her, even after knowing her such a short time.

"Then why did you tell me all that?"

He studied her in silence for a moment with an intensity that bordered on palpable. Then he said quietly, "I don't know. There's just something about you, Natalie, that makes me forget who I am and what I should be doing."

She wasn't sure if she should be flattered by that or not. The words were good, but the tone of voice wasn't, as if he kind of resented her for making him feel that way. Or maybe he resented himself for letting himself feel that way.

He moved his gaze to the beer, holding it up to the light as if checking to see how much was left. "Now you'll probably go sell the info to the tabloids, and Russell's PR people will have to work overtime denying it and proving it's not true."

Okay, scratch that part about him trusting her. Clearly the guy had issues on that score. Then again, after everything he'd told her, she supposed she wasn't surprised. "But it is true," she told him. Before he could interject anything, she hurried on, "Despite that, I would never, ever betray a trust, Finn. Not from anyone." She paused until he was looking at her again, then added, "Friend *or* foe."

His gaze held hers for a moment, then he said softly, "And what am I, Natalie? Friend or foe?"

Something warm and wistful percolated through her at the way he asked the question. Just as softly, she replied, "You tell me."

For a minute, she thought he might actually choose one identifier or the other, and she found herself hoping it wouldn't be foe. Because she didn't want to be anyone's foe. And she especially didn't want to be Finn's. Funny, though, that had nothing to do with her needing to go through him to get to his employer. Even funnier, she'd hardly thought about his employer tonight. Only when Finn had brought him up had Russell Mulholland been on her mind. And the fact that she so desperately needed to speak to the billionaire hadn't even been on her radar.

Instead of answering her question, though, Finn said softly, "Finish up your Alka-Seltzer, Natalie, and I'll drive you home."

Her stomach did that little flip-flop thing at hearing him call her by her first name again. She thought about pressing him on the matter of his past, asking another question that might steer them in that direction, then decided it probably wasn't a good idea. There was no point in her pursuing anything with Finn Guthrie, no matter how much she might want to.

She extended the empty glass toward him. "Thanks," she said. "But I can drive myself home."

He shook his head. "I know how hangovers work. There's still the potential for dizzy spells and lightheadedness. You might get sick or even pass out again."

"I'm not going to pass out ag—"

"I'll drive you home," he interrupted, his tone of voice this time brooking no argument.

She started to tell him it wasn't necessary, that Dean could take her home, but she thankfully came to her senses. Wow, Finn was right. There *was* still the potential for getting sick again. All she had to do was think about Dean. And speaking of Dean . . .

"What happened to Dean?" she asked. Not that she cared, really, and not that she couldn't suspect, but it was a question worth asking. Especially if there was any chance he'd had anything to do with bringing her up to Finn's suite, in which case he probably had copped a feel at some point. "For that matter," she added, "what happened to me? After I . . . I mean . . ." She blew out an exasperated breath. "The last thing I remember is sitting down at the table with you and Mr. Mulholland. After that, it gets a little . . . fuzzy."

Once again, Finn's expression told her nothing of what he might be thinking or feeling. "Last time I saw your . . ." Strangely, he expelled what sounded like an exasperated breath, too. "Last time I saw Waterman, he was running his mouth to Russell about something. Not long after the two of you sat down, you got up to use the women's room, and you were gone long enough for me to wonder what happened to you."

"Dean didn't wonder?" she asked. Then she immediately answered herself, *What are you, Natalie, nuts? Of course Dean didn't wonder about you. Dean never wonders about anyone but himself. And even at that, he only wonders why a charming, handsome devil like him hasn't managed to acquire an entourage by now.*

Well, he *would* wonder that, she thought further. If he took time out of being self-absorbed to notice he didn't have any friends.

"Well, Dean was pretty wrapped up in his conversation with Russell," Finn said.

Yeah, he was probably doing whatever it took to ingratiate himself to the billionaire. When it came to people whose incomes had a comma more than Dean's did, he was always Johnny-on-the-brown-nose-spot.

"Just as I was approaching the women's room," Finn continued, "you came out. Then you passed out. I caught you before you fell, but it wasn't like I could just prop you against the door 'til someone came along and claimed you."

Why not? she wanted to ask. That was what Dean would have done. After copping a feel, she meant.

"So I brought you up here."

Natalie nodded, trying not to think about how he must have had to manhandle her to do that. Mostly because thinking about being manhandled like that by Finn didn't bother her nearly as much as it was probably supposed to. She was a twenty-first-century woman, after all. Manhandling couldn't possibly be PC, right? Not unless the woman in question wanted to be manhandled. Which Natalie didn't. At all. Of course. That little shiver of electricity that shot through her belly just thinking about it was the result of . . . of . . . of . . . revulsion. Yeah, that was it. The very idea of being slung over the XXX*OMGX*-Brawny shoulder of some guy with smoky bedroom eyes, a position that would probably require him to also have an XXXOMGX-Brawny arm wrapped around her waist. Maybe even an XXXOMGX-Brawny hand splayed over her, um . . . her, ah . . .

Well, suffice it to say that Natalie was just going to have to give the whole idea *a lot* of thought—like hours and hours of thought, after she went to bed, with the lights out, so she could really concentrate—before she decided what her reaction should be.

Um, where was she?

Oh, yeah. Dean never leaving the table so not being anywhere near her person while she was unconscious. In a word, *Whew.*

"So did Dean ever notice I was missing?" she asked anyway.

She figured she could use the information as ammo the next time Dean started going on and on about how he could take such good care of her, since she obviously couldn't take care of herself. She could say, "You're so right, Dean. Any man who would abandon me to two strange men he just met is the catch of a lifetime." And *okay*, so maybe he had some decent ammo, too, in that he could remind her of how she'd passed out in front of one of the most important men in the business world.

That was beside the point.

The point was that it had been Finn, not Dean, who had been concerned enough about her well-being to follow her; Finn, not Dean, who had taken care of her. And where Natalie should have felt, at best, embarrassed about that and, at worst, angry, what she really felt was kind of warm and fuzzy inside.

Finn didn't answer for a moment, then told her, "I'm sure he did eventually." And amazingly, he said it with a straight face.

Natalie nodded. "Yeah, I'm sure he did, too. That's Dean. Always putting me ahead of everything else in his life." Except for himself. And his personal wealth. And his condo. And his car. And, possibly, the jar of mayonnaise in his refrigerator door.

Finn didn't seem to realize she was being sarcastic, because he was looking at her like she was the most self-deluded creature on the planet. She started to explain her situation with Dean, then decided not to bother. Why waste that much time on something that was in no way important?

"If you still insist on taking me home," she said, "then we should probably get going."

Again, Finn hesitated before replying, and again, she thought he was going to say something other than what he did. "Just let me get my keys, and you're as good as there."

·Nine·

NATALIE BECKETT'S NEIGHBORHOOD WAS EXACTLY
what Finn had suspected it would be: warm, inviting, even—
and, as a manly man, he really hated to used this word—
cozy. The street down which she'd directed him to turn was
cobbled and hilly, and the streetlamps were old-fashioned,
probably original to the area. The houses varied in style
and size, but all of them had clearly been built before or
not long after the First World War. The trees were huge,
their branches canopying the road, and the yards were lush
with bushes and shrubs and recently planted flowers. He
knew they were recently planted because, driving along
with the window down, he could smell the freshly turned
earth mingling with a hint of honeysuckle. In the distance,
a dog barked once, lazily, as if he'd heard the approaching
car but felt in no way threatened by its occupants and wanted
only to reassure his owners that he was doing his job. This
was a quiet place, a peaceful place, the sort of place where
nice girls like Natalie Beckett blossomed.

Then Natalie was telling him to turn into the next driveway on his left, and there was her house, looking even warmer and more inviting—and, dammit, even cozier—than the neighborhood. The car's headlights swept over a facade that was, to Finn, the epitome of the word *cottage*, something stony and woody that was even better land-scaped than the other houses on the street. After he pulled the car to a halt and killed the engine, a good part of the house remained bathed in pale amber from the porch lights and driveway lamp, seeming to almost glow from within.

Jeez, it was like something out of one of those fairy tales his mother had never read to him when he was a child. He wouldn't have been surprised if Snow White herself was in there sweeping the floors and singing tra-la-las to Bambi. Well, he wouldn't have been surprised if it wasn't almost four in the morning, anyway. Snow White was probably sawing logs at the moment, with Bambi curled at her feet.

For one brief but not especially satisfying moment, Finn was transported back to his childhood, when he used to ride his bike the seven miles that separated his neighbor-hood from a Seattle suburb where houses like Natalie's were crowded nearly one on top of the other. A girl from his class—Becky was her name, just like in *Tom Sawyer*—had lived in one of those houses, and he'd told himself he only made the trip because he liked her and wanted to catch a glimpse of her outside of school.

But in truth, he'd been more attracted to the neighbor-hood than the girl. On school days, he would ride his bike up and down the streets of that neighborhood until dusk, watching the families arrive home to their cozy houses in shiny minivans and SUVs, the dads in dress shirts and ties that still looked professional at day's end, the moms toting bags filled with fresh produce from the market for dinner. The kids would all be wearing their soccer or hockey or scout uniforms, bickering halfheartedly the way siblings did when each wanted the other to think they were annoy-ing, or the whole family would be talking about how they wanted to spend the weekend, no doubt together.

Finn's plans for the weekends back then had mostly consisted of escaping from his own neighborhood and returning to that one, this time to watch the dads as they mowed the lawns and the moms as they planted flowers. The boys would always be playing street hockey, and Finn would deliberately plow right through their game, because none of them—even the ones he knew from school—ever invited him to join. And he'd do his best to ignore the girls who were invariably chatting on their porches or walking their dogs because they always ignored him, too. Including Becky.

But then, what kind of self-respecting parent would allow their offspring to associate with a kid from the part of town Finn called home? One that had crumbling sidewalks, spray-painted profanity, pockmarked cars, and a remarkable dearth of cottages.

"Thanks for driving me home," Natalie said from beyond the driver's side window.

Only then did Finn realize she'd already gotten out of the car and circled to his side of it while he'd been sitting there staring at her house and remembering things he hadn't remembered for a very long time. Things he wished he hadn't remembered tonight. With a sigh that he told himself did *not* sound yearning, he pulled the keys from the ignition and, after only a small hesitation—which he told himself was *not* the result of yearning—pushed open the car door. He started to hand Natalie her keys after emerging, but something made him hesitate. He noticed again the keychain and smiled, not having appreciated the significance before now of the Disney Cinderella all dressed for the ball.

Natalie really was a fairy-tale princess, he thought. And just like Cinderella, she'd found her Prince Charming in one Dean Waterman. She didn't need to worry about cozying up to frogs like him. Just because he thought Waterman was more suited to the role of the Wicked Queen didn't mean Natalie wasn't looking forward to playing cottage with him.

"I'll walk you to the door," he said, sounding like a high school senior bringing his date home from the prom. Not that Finn had attended his own prom. Hell, he'd been lucky to even make it through his senior year.

This time Natalie was the one to hesitate, as if his offer had surprised her. "Thanks, but you don't have to," she finally said. She pulled her cell phone out of her bag. "You want me to call a cab, or would you rather do it yourself?"

In other words, Finn translated, *Beat it*.

"I'll call," he told her. "After I walk you to the door."

"Really, Finn, it's not—"

"I know. But I want to."

She looked at him like she wanted to keep arguing but couldn't come up with anything to counter his proposal. Ultimately, she said nothing, neither accepting nor rejecting it. She only turned and began to make her way up the front walk. So Finn followed, closing his fingers carefully over the keychain as he went.

The moment she had both feet on the front porch, she spun around and said, "Okay, I'm at the front door." She held out one hand, palm up, in the internationally recognized body language for *Hand over my keys, man*.

Finn stopped abruptly before following her up, mostly because she'd situated her body in a way that made it impossible for him to do anything else. But even when she extended her hand closer to him—in the internationally recognized sign language for *I said, Hand 'em over*—he couldn't quite make himself release the keys. Even though he was a full step below her, he still had to look down to meet her gaze, something she must have noticed, too, because she straightened and tilted her head back, as if trying to make herself taller.

When Finn still didn't give her the keys, she repeated, "Thanks for seeing me home." And when he *still* didn't release her keys, she added, a little nervously, he couldn't help noting, "Good-bye, Mr. Guthrie."

It was the *Mr. Guthrie*, he decided, that made him do what he did next. All evening, he'd been Finn to her, and he'd liked the way his name sounded rolling off of her tongue. Even more, he'd liked the way she'd talked to him, the way she'd smiled at him. As if the two of them were . . . well, friends. Or something. Something more than Mr. Guthrie and Ms. Beckett.

He lowered his head to hers, until his mouth hovered scarcely a breath above her own, taking a moment to enjoy that soft scent of her that continued to tantalize him, even hours after she must have put it on. He enjoyed, too, the way she gasped softly and how her eyes went wide at his approach, because there was something in the two gestures that was more hopeful than fearful. He noticed how the tawny lighting made the hair sweeping near one of those eyes seem even golder, and how it ignited tiny fires in the blue green of her irises. Or maybe something else had ignited those fires, he thought hopefully. He dipped his head lower still, until his mouth was nearly brushing hers. Maybe . . .

"Maybe I ought to go in first," he murmured. "Just to be sure there's no one inside who might be a danger to you." And then he pulled back again, hoping the look in her eyes as he did so was disappointment, not relief. Nevertheless, he told himself he just imagined the way she seemed to sway forward as he retreated, as if she were trying to follow him.

No one inside who might be a danger to you, he repeated to himself. Hah. Like there was anything inside that house that could pose a greater danger to Natalie at the moment than Finn himself. Not that she wasn't plenty dangerous herself, looking all soft and luscious on the porch of her cozy house, gazing at him the way she was, as if she'd expected him to kiss her and maybe, just maybe, wouldn't have tried to stop him, making him feel like maybe if he did kiss her, he wouldn't turn out to be such a frog, after all.

Yeah, right. Like that was going to happen. Any of it.

"I mean, the place is dark," he pointed out when she only continued to look at him in silence. Soft, luscious silence. "You really should leave a light on inside before you go out."

After one more taut moment, she shook her head once, as if to clear it. "The, uh . . . the outside lights are, um . . . activated automatically," she stammered. "When the sun goes down, I mean. By the darkness. Or rather, twilight. Um, lack of sunlight." She gave her head another shake and pulled her body back a bit. "Besides," she added, still sounding a little flustered, "I'd planned on being home before dark."

Finn nodded. "I guess tying one on the way you did makes you forget good intentions like that, huh?"

Oh, yeah. That seemed to crystallize her thinking. Her eyes flashed fire again, but not the kind they had before. This was way hotter and way more dangerous. She opened her mouth to say something in retort, then seemed to think better of it and simply gritted her teeth at him instead.

He wasn't quite able to help the smile that curled his lips in response, and he hoped he didn't look too smug when he said, "Humor me with the seeing you inside. I'll feel better knowing you got home safely. *Totally* safely," he clarified before she had a chance to point out she'd already done that. "Inside *and* out."

"Fine," she said tersely.

She held up her hand for the keys again, but Finn nudged her gently aside and joined her on the porch, reaching for the storm door before she had a chance to get in his way. Cinderella twinkled in the lamplight as he inserted the key into the dead bolt and turned it, then he pushed the door slowly open. He reached blindly inside for a wall switch, but found both it and the one on its other side already flipped up in the On position, indicating they operated the outdoor lights.

"There's a lamp not far from the front door," Natalie said from behind him. She nudged him aside the way he had her only seconds before. "Allow me."

Even though it defeated the entire purpose of making sure she got in safely, since Freddy Krueger or Michael

Myers—or both—might very well be standing between her and that lamp, Finn let her go. Who was he kidding, anyway? He didn't fear for Natalie's safety. Not in a neighborhood as warm and inviting and—dammit—cozy as this one. He just wanted to see what the inside of a fairy-tale princess's house looked like, that was all.

Cozy, he realized when pale light flowed over the living room. And warm. And inviting. Wow, there was a shocker.

The room was painted the color of creamed coffee, its furnishings curvy and fat, in colors that reflected the rich jewel tones of the Oriental rugs spanning the hardwood floors beneath. Beaded, tasseled throw pillows swarmed over the overstuffed sofa cushions and chairs, and built-in shelves were strewn with books and plants and exotic-looking paraphernalia. The room, like the house, wasn't large, but its layout gave the impression of such. It was airy and open, with broad doorways and windows. To his left, a stairway led up to a second floor, and he could see just enough of a room at the top to know it was her bedroom. She had left a light on in there, he saw, and it afforded him enough light to see that the room was ridiculously feminine, with sage-colored walls and a bed that sported a fili-greed brass headboard and fringed bedspread the color of a ripe pomegranate. It was the sort of room in which a man would never feel comfortable. Hell, even from this distance, it was already making him use words like *ripe pomegran-ate*.

And damned if he didn't want to finagle an excuse to go right up there with Natalie in tow and find out what other ways it—and its owner—might make him even more un-comfortable.

On the other side of the living room, through wide French doors, was a dining area that housed a square, bare wood table and four chairs covered with some kind of em-broidered fabric. Through a door to his right was what looked like a home office: the glow of a computer screen was just bright enough to illuminate an open rolltop desk and a leather chair on wheels. To his left, beyond the stairs, he could see an entrance to a room that was bathed in the soft white light of a small appliance. The kitchen was nothing but shadows at the moment, but he'd bet it was just as inviting as everything else he could see.

A movement from his left caught his attention, and he turned to see a cat come running down the stairs past him, ignoring him completely as it wound itself around Natalie's legs. She stooped automatically to pick up the silver and black striped creature, and it bumped its nose under her chin before tucking its head into her neck and purring loudly enough for Finn to hear it from where he stood. She laughed at the gesture, in a way he hadn't heard her laugh before, completely lacking in inhibition and full of warmth and contentment and affection. It was the sort of laughter that fit perfectly in the place she called home.

Finn had never, ever, lived in a house like this. He'd never even known anyone who lived in a house like this. He'd gone pretty much from one extreme to another, riding on the Mulholland coattails. He'd grown up in a dingy tenement that was barely a step up from the projects, then, once he was turned over to social services, he and Russell had shared a bedroom with four other boys in a cramped house that was barely a step up from that. In college, the two men had rented an apartment that wasn't much better than the one Finn had known as a boy, and Finn had stayed there after Russell married Marti.

Not that Russell and Marti had done much better, pooling their meager resources to buy a house in a neighborhood that was rumored to be slated for urban renewal—though neither the rumor nor the neighborhood was ever quite substantiated. The first part of young Max Mulholland's life hadn't been a whole lot different from Finn's or Russell's. Oh, except for the small matter of his parents not being addicted to anything and loving both each other and their kid to distraction. And except for how his father's job as a game designer struggling to keep his small company afloat afforded Max the perk of sometimes having state-of-the-art game systems and games before his friends had a chance to sample either. It was little comfort to a kid who'd lost his mother early enough in life that he never really got to know her.

Then, boom, virtually overnight, after the launch of the GameViper, Russell and Max had moved into a plush mansion in one of King County's poshest neighborhoods. Immediately after that, Russell had put Finn on the payroll with a six-figure salary and benefits out the wazoo, moving him into the estate along with him and Max. The place was unbe-frigging-lievable, from its Greek Acropolis–inspired swimming pool to its Golden Age of Hollywood ballroom to the game room that put Disneyland to shame. Finn was still dazzled by the place—and by his suite of rooms within it—even having lived there for more than a year.

Extreme poverty and extreme wealth: those were the only environments Finn had ever known. And neither had ever suited him. In one, there had been so many things he wanted but could never have. In the other . . . Well, hell. There were still a lot of things he wanted but couldn't have. The difference was that, in his previous situation, money could have provided him with every one of those wants, and in his current situation, what he wanted couldn't be bought.

But Natalie's house was neither lacking in amenities nor overflowing with them. It was just . . . normal. Utterly, blissfully normal. This was exactly the kind of place Finn had wanted to live in as a kid, exactly the kind of life he'd wanted: a normal one. It was the kind of place—the kind of life—he wanted to live now.

The kind of place—the kind of life—he feared he would never, ever find.

But instead of saying any of that, he asked, "What's the cat's name?"

"Zippy," she replied without looking up, scratching the animal under its chin in a way that made it tip its head back in a silent request for more of the same. "Zip for short."

"Zippy?" he repeated distastefully.

"Yes, Zippy," she replied frostily. "Do you have a problem with that?"

He shrugged. "That's like naming your kid Algernon."

"Meaning?"

"It's like hanging a Kick Me sign on his back. You give a cat a name like Zippy, and it's just asking all the other cats to beat him up after school every day. He's gonna need therapy when he's grown up."

He wasn't sure, but he thought she tried to hide a smile at that. Relief washed over him. Rule number one in *The Big Book of Women's Rules for Men* was: never, ever, under any circumstances, insult my cat in any way. Every guy knew that. At least, every guy who wanted to get laid.

Not that Finn wanted to get laid tonight, he hastily reminded himself. Well, okay, he would have liked to have gotten laid tonight, especially since it had been so long. He just didn't want to get laid by Natalie. Well, okay, he would have liked to have gotten laid by Natalie tonight. He just didn't want to wake up next to her in the morning. Well, okay, he would have liked to wake up next to her in the morning—especially if it meant getting laid again. He just didn't want there to be any kind of consequences afterward.

And that, he knew, was the problem. With Natalie, there would be consequences. Women like her didn't just jump into the sack with a guy. Or, if they did, it was only because they had some ridiculous romantic notion that there was something between the two of them. Something personal. Something emotional. Something that transcended the mere joining of two bodies for the sake of having a good time. A really good time. A really, *really* good time. Women like Natalie thought there was more to sex than sex. And men like Finn knew otherwise. Sex *was* sex. It *was* the joining of two bodies for the sake of having a really, *really* good time. There was nothing personal, nothing emotional about it. Because once you introduced emotion into it, you were asking for trouble.

Still, he was relieved Natalie wasn't mad at him because he thought she'd given her cat a name that was, ah . . . unusual.

Natalie gave the animal one last scratch behind the ear, then stood and, as if his thought had cued the cat to do so, it suddenly dashed off at a speed he wouldn't have guessed a house cat could manage, careening off the sofa before leaping over the coffee table, nearly knocking over a candle as it went.

"That's why I named her Zippy," she said. "Because she zips around a lot." A loud crash in another room made her wince and glance over her shoulder in the general direction from which it had come. "And okay. Also because she can be kind of a pinhead sometimes."

That made him chuckle out loud. Then, "You have a nice place here, Natalie," he heard himself say, not sure when, or even why, he'd decided to make the comment.

She glanced back from the mystery noise, but her smile fell for some reason when her gaze lit on his. "Thanks," she said softly. "I like it, too."

Suddenly feeling nervous for no reason he could name, he hurried on, "What do they call this style of house? It has a name, right?"

"Arts and Crafts," she told him. "Or just Craftsman."

He nodded. "That's it. There are a lot of these kinds of houses on the West Coast, but I never knew what they were called." Mostly, he supposed, because he'd always told himself he didn't care. There had been a lot of houses like this one in Becky's neighborhood.

"There aren't very many in Louisville. I guess the style never caught on here. I felt really lucky when I found this one."

"Have you lived here long?" he asked, wondering why he was making small talk at four in the morning, when he should be calling a cab to take him back to the hotel and letting Natalie get some sleep.

She didn't seem that surprised or put off by the ques-

tion. "A little less than two years. Before that . . ." She
halted before elaborating, and Finn wondered why.

He was about to ask her to go on, wanted to know where
she'd lived before that. And before that. And before that.
He wanted to ask her why she wasn't shacking up with
Waterman since the two of them would be moving in together after their nuptials—just when was the wedding,
anyway?—not that anything containing the words *Waterman* and *nuptials* was an image Finn wanted to get lodged
in his brain.

Still, he was pretty sure he already knew the answer to
that. For some reason, Natalie Beckett didn't seem like the
type to live in sin—more was the pity. Unlike Finn, for
whom living *was* pretty much sin. Then again, it wasn't
just where she'd lived before now—or with whom—that
he was interested in. There was the small matter of everything else there was to know about her, too.

He started to ask her what she planned to do with the
house once she married Waterman, since her intended
didn't seem the cozy cottage type, but decided it was none
of his business. Not to mention the last thing Finn wanted
to talk about at the moment was Whatshisname. So he
withdrew his cell from his jacket pocket and said, "I guess
I should call that cab."

She opened her mouth to say something, but Zippy
zipped back into the room, banking off a chair this time
and tearing right between them, making Finn take a step
backward in self-preservation. The animal then circled
around and leapt up onto the back of the sofa, its legs splayed
wide, gazing at him in a way that made him think it was
trying to decide if he was a member of the pack or a wounded
wildebeest he should fell for dinner. For a split second, it
was man versus nature; then, as suddenly as the cat had reappeared, it disappeared again, darting back up the stairs,
as if its work here were finished.

As strange as the brief episode had been, it made Finn
feel weirdly honored that Natalie's cat would trust him

with her. But it was also a weird enough realization to
hammer home just how late it was and how much a lack of
sleep could mess with a person. For one thing, he didn't
give a damn about anyone's approval, least of all an animal. Especially an animal that didn't even have a job. And
for another thing, even if Natalie's cat did approve of him
on some arcane feline level, she wasn't the sort of woman
he should pursue since (A) he was only in town temporar-
ily, and she wasn't the temporary type, (B) she was engaged to be married, (C) she was engaged to be married,
and (D) she was engaged to be married.

"That's funny," she said as she watched the cat's hasty
departure. "She usually hangs around when people are
here." She turned and offered him a smile that looked a
little more anxious than it probably should be. "Once she's
zipped around the living room a few times, I mean."

In other words, Finn thought, maybe what he'd thought
was the cat's trusting him was actually its disliking him.

"Not because she likes people," Natalie added, seeming
to read his mind, "but because she doesn't trust them
around me."

Finn was about to ask how her cat liked Waterman but
checked himself. He really needed to get over this preoccupation he had with Natalie's fiancé. Of course, the best
way to do that would be to get over his preoccupation with
Natalie. And the best way to do that would be to leave.
Now. And make sure he never saw her again.

But then, he wouldn't be seeing her again, he reminded
himself. Not if he did his job right and made sure she never
got within a hundred yards of Russell, something that
would ensure she never got within a hundred yards of
Finn, either. So what was he worried about? Other than the
fact that he was never going to see Natalie again?

He started to punch a number into the phone, then realized he had no idea what number to dial. "You know the
number of a cab company?" he asked.

She shook her head. "No, but I have a phone book in the
kitchen."

She turned to walk in that direction, and even though she hadn't invited Finn to follow her, he followed her anyway. Hey, she hadn't told him not to. When she flicked on a switch inside the entry, the kitchen was cast out of shadow and into warm light, and he saw that it was indeed as welcoming as the rest of her place. Natural wood cabinets fronted with glass revealed dishes stacked neatly in alternating colors, softer versions of the colors in the other room. A small table tucked into one corner suggested she sometimes—maybe even often—ate alone, something that made Finn happier than it probably should have. There were enough pots and pans, copper at that, dangling from a grid overhead to indicate she was serious about cooking, something that surprised him, since she seemed the type who would prefer to have someone, someone like, oh . . . say . . . Waterman take her out to dinner.

Just who was Natalie Beckett, anyway? he wondered. One minute, he was thinking she wasn't the living-in-sin type, then the next, he was thinking she was the type who liked to be pampered by some overpaid, overbearing, overblown jerk like Waterman. At the restaurant earlier, she'd seemed perfectly at ease in her luxurious, elegant surroundings, as if she'd been born to the life, but at the same time, she was a businesswoman doing whatever it took to land Russell for what sounded like a pretty major fund-raising event she herself was organizing.

To look at her, he'd think she was little more than an expensive bit of eye candy destined to be some guy's trophy wife. But after talking to her, he'd formed an opinion of a woman who was reasonably smart, reasonably articulate, and who had a reasonably wry sense of humor. Despite the overindulging in drink tonight—which, hey, coulda happened to anyone—she'd impressed Finn as being anything but shallow.

So why the hell was she marrying Waterman, who was the very definition of shallow, and who clearly wanted nothing more than an expensive-looking bit of eye candy for a trophy wife?

His thoughts were pulled back to the present—and not a moment too soon—when Natalie opened not one, but two, cabinets, one above the countertop and one directly below. At first he thought it was because she didn't know where her phone book was. Then she kicked off her heels and stepped up onto the higher shelf of the bottom cabinet, pushing herself up from the floor to stretch her arm toward the top shelf of the upper cabinet.

"Oh, for—" he began impatiently when he realized what she was doing. He crossed the kitchen in a few quick strides. "If you needed help reaching it, why didn't you just ask?" He stopped immediately behind her, extended his arm up alongside hers, past where her fingers were trying to catch the edge of a fat phone book, then easily plucked it off of the shelf and set it on the counter.

And instantly he understood why she probably hadn't asked for help reaching it.

Because the moment his fingers bumped hers, he realized it wasn't just their fingers that, uh, bumped. Pretty much every inch of their bodies, uh, bumped. And thanks to the way she'd brought herself up to his height by boosting herself up on the shelf, their bodies, uh, bumped in ways that were pretty damned intimate, from the way his thighs pressed into the backs of hers to the way her fanny was cradled by his pelvis. Up this close, he could detect just a hint of that soft scent that had intrigued him since day one, along with something earthy and musky and end-of-the-day erotic that made him want to bend his head to that sexy curve where her neck met her shoulder and just—

Just remind himself that she was engaged to another man. Yeah, that was it.

"Um," she began softly, her voice catching even on that tiny sound. "I, uh, I didn't ask for help because I, ah, I don't usually need help. I usually do just, um . . . just fine. By, uh, by myself."

There were so many ways—too many ways—that Finn could interpret her words when he took into account their current position. And when she shifted just the tiniest bit against him, against the part of him she absolutely should not have shifted against, it was naturally the most salacious interpretation that exploded in his brain. An image of Natalie writhing naked amid tangled sheets, her golden hair flowing across the pillow, her fingers moving between her legs, her eyes closed in ecstasy, doing it by herself. And the way she was doing it went way beyond fine. In fact, it was pretty damned erotic. That didn't prevent his fevered imagination from introducing Finn into the picture, too, however. And once he entered it, things went even beyond erotic, straight to incandescent.

Telling himself he was only doing it to steady her, he cupped his hands over Natalie's hips and spread his fingers wide. The soft fabric of her dress warmed immediately under his touch, making him wonder if the skin beneath was even warmer. Not thinking about what he was doing—how could he, when that heady scent of her surrounded him the way it did?—he inched one hand forward, over her flat belly, splaying his fingers wide. At the same time, he pushed the other downward, along the slender curve of her thigh, toward the hem of her dress. It didn't take long for cloth to become flesh, and he discovered that her skin was indeed quite warm. Quite soft. Quite . . .

And then he was doing what he'd only thought about before, dipping his head toward her neck, toward that irresistible scent, toward that warmth and softness. When he nuzzled aside her hair, his cheek brushed hers, and it was only at her gasp of surprise that he hesitated. But that hesitation only made him aware of the fact that, instead of dissuading him, she had covered the hand he'd placed on her belly with her own and tilted her head to one side to welcome his advance. That should have emboldened him. Instead, it made him halt.

What the hell did he think he was doing? The woman in his arms was engaged to another man. And yeah, Finn could argue that her encouragement indicated her relationship with Waterman maybe wasn't on the most stable ground, but there were a host of other reasons not to do this. He'd only be in town for a couple of weeks. Natalie wasn't the type for a one-night stand. He had no room in his life for any woman who wasn't a one-night stand. And, in case he forgot, she was trying to get through to Russell, and it was both his job and his obligation as a friend to keep her away.

Somehow, he forced himself to rear back his head, pull his hand from beneath hers and, after only a small hesitation, remove the other from her thigh. Then he grabbed the phone book from the counter and took a giant step backward, turning his back on her as he flipped through it blindly and pretended the last couple of minutes never happened.

"So, do you think I should look under the word *taxi* or the word *cab*?" he asked, hoping he only imagined the uncharacteristic hoarseness in his voice.

He turned his head slightly to look at her out of the corner of his eye—because he didn't dare look at her full on—and saw Natalie step down from her cabinet perch, then grip the countertop with both hands and drop her head.

"Either one, I imagine, will get you what you need," she said, her own voice sounding a little hoarser than usual, too.

Oh, he didn't think so. What he needed right now couldn't be found in the Yellow Pages. The personals maybe, but not the Yellow Pages.

Hastily, he flipped around until he found the listing he wanted, then he pulled out his cell and dialed the first number he saw. He'd been indulging in a very nice delusion about having the taxi show up in the driveway, honking its horn impatiently, the moment he closed his phone so he could book it out of the house with nothing more than a hasty "See ya, Natalie." Then the dispatcher of the cab company asked to what address she should direct the driver, and Finn realized that, not only was he going to have to ask Natalie her address, but it was probably going to be a while before a car showed up, thereby necessitating even more conversation.

He asked her for the necessary information, which she

relayed in an automatic monotone, and relayed it to the dispatcher, then closed his phone. Alas, there was no portentous honking of a horn outside, however, so he resigned himself to pass what would probably be the most excruciating several minutes he'd been forced to endure in a very long time.

That resignation became dread, however, when Natalie said, without looking up, "Are we going to talk about what just happened?"

Damn. He should have realized she would be one of those can-we-talk types, since she wasn't a one-night stand type. One-night stands were always so cool with those eloquent lyrics Elvis once sang: "A little less conversation, a little more action." Though, admittedly, Finn actually preferred a lot less conversation and a lot more action, but that was neither here nor there.

Deciding it would probably be in his best interest if he just went with the obvious male reaction to situations like this one—deny everything—he said, "What do you mean? I needed a phone book; you got one for me. Why would we need to talk about that?"

She expelled a not-so-quiet sigh, then nodded her head. "Hoo-kay. Got it. I just wasn't clear on the rules there at first." She finally looked up at him and smiled. It was a forced smile, but at least she was making an effort to abet him in his denial, and that won her major points in any man's book. "You want some coffee or something while you wait? This time of night—or, rather, morning—cabs aren't too plentiful. They'll probably have to send one from the terminal or the airport or something."

Great, Finn thought. Louisville, for all its charms, was evidently a little taxi-challenged. Which meant his awkward several minutes could be significantly greater. As would be his awareness of Natalie. And his attraction to Natalie. And his desire to nuzzle Natalie's hair and neck and run one hand down her naked thigh while the other dove between her legs, then drive them both out of their minds with wanting until they weren't wanting anymore, they were taking and giving and giving and taking, and touching and tasting and licking and sucking and—

And he was *this close* to crossing the kitchen and pulling her into his arms again when a horn honked outside, signaling the taxi's arrival.

"Oh, wow," Natalie said blandly, completely unaware of Finn's agitated state, "maybe at Derby time it's a lot easier to get a cab. The driver must have been cruising Frankfort Avenue, looking for fares. Some places don't close 'til four this time of year."

She started to cross the kitchen toward the living room, but before she made it—and unable to help himself—Finn snaked out a hand and circled her wrist with sure fingers, halting her progress. When she spun around to look at him, surprise etched on her face, he realized he still couldn't look her in the eye, so he focused his gaze just over her left shoulder instead.

"Natalie," he said, still not sure what he wanted to tell her. For some reason, though, he knew he couldn't leave pretending nothing had happened between them. Although, technically, nothing *had* happened between them, something—something he hadn't expected and still didn't understand—had happened between them. Something he couldn't—and maybe on some level, didn't want to—deny. With any other woman, he could have. But not with Natalie. He couldn't pretend with her. Didn't want to pretend with her.

Which was all the more reason he had to make sure nothing—really nothing—ever happened between them again.

"Look, what happened just now . . ." he continued hesitantly, "well, let's just say it shouldn't have happened."

When she said nothing in response, he made himself meet her gaze, something she'd evidently been waiting for him to do, because she replied as soon as their gazes connected.

"Not that I necessarily disagree with you," she said, "but what's your reason for thinking that?"

Her question took him by surprise. Not just the question itself, but her frankness in asking it. He honestly wasn't sure what to tell her. Probably the truth, since that was what she seemed to want. He just wasn't sure what the truth was. Not the main truth, anyway. So he told her the obvious ones instead.

"Because I live two thousand miles away and will only be in town for a couple of weeks. Because I'm not at a place in my life where I want to get involved with anyone more than superficially. And because you don't seem like the type of woman who would be satisfied with a couple weeks with a superficial guy."

"No, I don't suppose I would be satisfied with that," she agreed.

She looked like she wanted to say something else, but she only continued to study him in a way that told him nothing of what she might be thinking. He, too, wanted to say something else, though he still wasn't quite sure what. Both of them were spared, however, when the cab honked its horn again.

"I guess you should get going," she said. "Otherwise my neighbors are going to be calling over here complaining about the noise."

Only then did he realize that not only had he not taken a single step in the direction of her front door, he was still clinging loosely to her wrist. With great reluctance, he released it, then, forcing an encouraging smile that felt in no way encouraging, he said, "Thanks for a nice evening."

She grinned at that. "Thanks for not pointing out what a disastrous evening it was."

"It wasn't disastrous, Natalie. Not by a long shot."

Again, she didn't reply, only arrowed her brows downward in a way that made her look strangely vulnerable. Telling himself it was because he wanted to get out before the cabbie honked his horn again, and not because he feared Natalie would say something that might make him think too much about whatever it was that was arcing between them, he impulsively leaned forward and kissed her on the cheek, mumbled a good-bye, and headed for the door. He never looked back once.

He didn't dare.

FINN'S KISS, HOWEVER CHASTE, HAD BEEN TOTALLY unexpected. Not so much because he didn't seem like the sweet-peck-on-the-cheek type—though certainly that was true—but because even sweet pecks on the cheek carried the suggestion of a certain amount of affection in them, and affection was the last thing he should be feeling for her. She'd made a fool of herself tonight, drinking as much as she had and passing out in his arms. And she'd inconvenienced the hell out of him, keeping him from sleep he doubtless needed very badly and making him drive her home.

That reminded her that she'd wanted to pay for his cab, so she hurried into the living room, hoping to catch him before he left. But he was already gone, the door closed firmly behind him. She watched through the living room window as he made his way down the front walk and into the waiting cab, alternating between hoping he would turn around and retrace his steps back to the front door to tell her he'd changed his mind about only being in town for a couple of weeks, and then hoping he would never look back and she'd never see him again.

For a moment, she honestly thought it would be that last, because he folded himself into the back of the car and leaned forward to tell the driver his destination, never once sparing a glance toward the house. As the car began to pull away, though, he did turn his head one last time. She told herself she imagined his look of surprise when he saw her still watching him, since it was too dark to tell anything of what might be on his face. But she could see the way he held up his hand in an uncomfortable gesture of farewell.

"Bye, Finn," she said softly. Her warm breath left a halo of fog on the cool window, obscuring what was left of the cab's red taillights as it drove away. "Thanks for seeing me home safely," she added.

At least, she'd been safe until he stepped up behind her in the kitchen. Until he'd roped his arm around her waist and pressed his hand against her stomach. Until he'd dipped his head into the curve of her neck, and she'd felt his warm breath stirring against her nape. She told herself it had only been wishful thinking when she'd felt his mouth skimming over her tender flesh. It had been so long since she'd felt a man's mouth on her skin that she wasn't even sure she remembered what it felt like.

She closed her eyes, trying to remember the last time she'd been intimate with a man, then snapped them open again when she remembered. Well, no wonder she'd been so susceptible to Finn. No woman should have to go as long as Natalie had without physical contact with someone who turned her on. Jeez.

And Finn did turn her on.

Something told her, though, that it wasn't the lapse in her sex life that had made her susceptible to Finn Guthrie. It was the simple fact that he was Finn Guthrie that made her so susceptible.

She told herself it was just as well that nothing had happened, other than a few intimate touches that she'd doubtless be feeling for a long, long time, since the lapse in her sex life was looking to stay lapsed for a while yet. And having even had that small contact with Finn—who was the sort of man who would be able to make a woman completely forget about any lapses—meant the lapse would probably last even longer, because after the intense, immediate way she responded to Finn, other, lesser men were going to be at a total disadvantage.

She made her way up the stairs, and a half hour later, she was showered and had changed into her pajamas and was lying in bed trying to steal a few hours of sleep before launching into another day. But her mind was racing too quickly with everything that had happened this evening, and every time her thoughts landed on Finn, she forced them to ricochet onto something else.

This close, she thought. She'd been *this close* to snagging

Russell Mulholland for Clementine's party. She'd been sitting at his dinner table, at his *invitation*, for crying out loud, and she'd still managed to mess everything up. It had been her best chance—hell, probably her *only* chance—and she still hadn't been able to make things work the way she was supposed to have made them work. Plan B had failed before she'd even realized what it was.

With a growl of discontent, Natalie shoved the covers off herself and jackknifed up in her bed. There was no way she'd be able to sleep with her mind racing the way it was, with recriminations in first place, guilt in second, and self-loathing bringing up the rear. Automatically, she headed downstairs for her office, thinking maybe a rousing round or two—or fifty—of spider solitaire would bore her enough to make her sleepy. But first, likewise automatically, she checked her e-mail, to see if maybe, by some wild miracle, George Clooney or Denzel Washington or Nicole Kidman had dropped her a line saying, why, yes, they'd be in town for Derby, and they'd love to come to Clementine Hotchkiss's party.

Hey, it could happen.

Unfortunately, it hadn't happened in the fifteen hours since Natalie had last checked her e-mail. Even more unfortunately, she *had* received a reply from Morty Hammerdinkle saying he'd be honored to attend, because she couldn't for the life of her remember who Morty Hammerdinkle was. But what was most unfortunate of all was that a quick Google check revealed that Morty Hammerdinkle was a ventriloquist who'd performed for children in Louisville decades before Natalie was even born, and all his puppets were racially insensitive stereotypes, which was why he hadn't performed in Louisville since decades before Natalie was born.

How the hell had he gotten on her list? she wondered. Man, she had to be more careful when she got desperate. Then she remembered. Dean had been the one to suggest him, telling Natalie how much his father had loved the guy when he was a kid. At that point, Natalie had been so hard up for talent, she hadn't bothered to do much research into anyone's background. If he'd been a local celebrity with kids back in the forties and fifties, she'd figured, then he would obviously have appealed to Clementine's social circle.

Yet another reason to never, ever, under any circumstances, pay heed to Dean or anyone else in the Waterman family. Because now, on top of everything else, Natalie was going to have to figure out how to uninvite a guy to a party no one was going to be coming to anyway.

Just to verify that, she scrolled quickly through her new e-mails, only to find that there were none, *none* from any celebrities—or any celebrealities, for that matter. Not even from the X, Y, or Z lists.

In a fit of despair, she dropped her head to the desktop and began to bang it gently on the surface. In time with the bonking, she told herself, "You are . . . such a . . . loser."

No one was going to come to this party. She might as well just accept it. She should call Clementine today and tell her the party was going to be a flop, so that at least Clementine would have a chance to make other plans for Derby. She should just confess to her client that she was an abject, unmitigated loser, refund the client's money, cancel the caterer, the band, and everything else, take a huge financial hit eating the nonrefundable deposits herself, and then slink under a rock to hide until it was time for her to make good on her agreement with her parents and date Dean Waterman for six months.

But then, if she was under a rock, Dean would already be right there with her, wouldn't he?

Strangely, it was more the thought of disappointing Clementine than going out with Dean that bothered Natalie. Then she remembered it wasn't just Clementine she'd be disappointing. There was that small matter of a six-figure check that wouldn't be going to Kids, Inc., because of Natalie's failure. So she'd cover that herself, too.

But even all that wasn't what disappointed her the most. What was most disheartening was the realization that she had failed abysmally again. Maybe she wasn't suited to a career, she told herself. Maybe her parents were right. Maybe even Dean was right. Maybe she should just forget about trying to be successful at anything, since the only thing she seemed to succeed at was failure.

As if cued by the thought, her e-mail alert chimed softly, and a disembodied voice that was supposed to sound like Clive Owen, but never quite did, announced that she had mail. And also that she looked sexy as hell in those pajamas, which would have been flattering had it not been for the fact that Natalie's tech guy had programmed the voice to say that at her own specifications. After seven a.m., which was when Natalie got dressed for work, Clive told her she had mail and that she looked ten pounds thinner in that outfit. And in the evenings, Clive told her she had mail and then insisted on letting him be the one to cook dinner and then give her a foot massage.

Hey, sometimes a computer-generated Clive Owen telling her that stuff was the only thing that got her through her day.

"Thanks, Clive," she said as she moused over to the mail icon and clicked on it. Maybe George Clooney had come through after all.

But it wasn't George Clooney this time, alas. It was Dean. Alas. Natalie told herself it was a sign of just how exhausted she was that she actually clicked on the mail to see what it said. Then again, she did wonder what Dean was doing up so early. Plus, the subject heading was a bit intriguing, since it was punctuated with about eighty billion exclamation points, and anyone who was the crème de la crème of society knew exclamation points were far too plebeian to ever use even one. Preceding those exclamation points was also the leading sentiment, "*You'll Never Guess.*"

Well, of course Natalie *could* guess, but she doubted Dean would be interested in her conjectures, since they would consist largely of things like guessing his sense of decency, his level of moral obligation, and his stage of

mental development, none of which she would place anywhere in the upper reaches.

What she *wouldn't* have guessed was that he had invited
Russell Mulholland to a dinner party Wednesday night
and that Russell Mulholland had accepted.

That *bastard*, she thought. Though she honestly wasn't
sure if the epithet was meant for Dean or for the billionaire. Ultimately, she decided it was for both. For Dean,
because he'd usurped her invitation—evidently pretty effortlessly, too—and for Mulholland, because he couldn't
be bothered to come to a fund-raiser for underprivileged
kids, but he jumped at the chance to hobnob with shallow,
pointless people who were obviously much like himself.

But what really toasted Natalie's melbas was that, as she
read Dean's e-mail, she realized he wanted—no, *expected*—
her to act as his hostess at this impromptu party, as if she
didn't have anything better to do with her Wednesday night.

Of course, she *didn't* have anything better to do with her
Wednesday night, but that was beside the point. The point
was that *she* was supposed to have been the one to win
Russell Mulholland's appearance at a party, not Dean. And
her party was way more important than Dean's was. Not
only did her career and Clementine's standing in the community depend on it, but so did a very worthy cause for
kids. What kind of man was Russell Mulholland that he
wouldn't even give Natalie a chance to tell him about all
the wonderful things the revenue from Clementine's party
would provide those children, but he would happily show
up at Dean's at the drop of a hat?

Well, she'd show both of them, she thought. She'd tell
Dean she'd be happy to act as his hostess—never mind that
she'd have to put up with his smug *"I knew you couldn't
resist me"* nonsense all night. And as soon as Russell Mulholland showed up, she'd corner the man and *make* him
listen to how important his appearance—his incredibly
brief appearance—at the Hotchkiss party would be. How
much good he could do simply by stopping by long enough
to glad-hand a few civic leaders and sign a few autographs.

She would get Russell Mulholland to attend Clementine's party, Natalie told herself as she lifted her hands to the keyboard to type her reply to Dean. She would. She wasn't a loser. She wasn't. Whatever it took to get Mulholland to the Hotchkiss estate on Derby Eve, Natalie would do it. Even if it meant spending an evening with Dean.

The man with whom she would have to spend six months of her life that she would never get back if she didn't.

· Ten ·

IT WAS NO EASY FEAT FOR RUSSELL TO SNEAK OUT alone without anyone realizing it for one night, let alone two, but he managed as well Wednesday as he had before. Though not without making everyone incredibly suspicious at first by telling them he intended to spend the entirety of the evening in his hotel suite. Fortunately, by a stroke of amazing luck, he'd noted an item earlier in the day while reading the newspaper that said ESPN2 was featuring the first round of women's championship roller derby tonight, something that had gone a long way toward convincing everyone a stay in his suite wasn't so far-fetched. It was also something that made him set up his TiVo. Add to it the fact that he'd had such an exhausting week so far, what with hanging out at strip clubs until nearly daybreak and spending his days at the track and his evenings at some function or another, and he finally stopped getting the evil eye from Finn.

Still, he knew Finn hadn't been completely convinced, even knowing Russell's proclivities when it came to Spandex-wrapped, girl-on-girl action disguised as professional sports.

But he wouldn't worry about that right now. Because he had used his limited—read, nonexistent—knowledge of feng shui to choose the most intimate table in a corner of Vincenzo's, one that would be growing more intimate as soon as Amber arrived. He sighed silently with contentment, admired the handsome ivory elegance of the place, and checked his watch for the tenth time.

In spite of Finn not having pushed, Russell still halfway expected his friend to come storming through the entrance to the restaurant, hand on hip, one finger wagging, then grab him by the ear like Aunt Bee and drag him out to the woodshed for a whuppin' because he'd told a lie. He reminded himself that there was no way anyone had followed the stretch limo he'd hired for the night, because he'd paid the driver outrageously to keep an eye out for any suspicious cars that might be tailing them. He'd paid the driver even more outrageously to go by the name Raoul for the night, but that was neither here nor there, even if the guy had driven a very hard bargain on account of his real name was Butch.

Russell checked his watch for the eleventh time. Five twenty-eight. Technically, Amber wasn't late. Technically, he had just been early. Never mind that he was never early for anything and in fact went out of his way to be more than fashionably late, just to piss people off and because he knew he could get away with it. Amber wasn't going to stand him up. He was sure of it.

Well, okay, *almost* sure of it. But then, that was part of her allure, the fact that he had no idea what to make of her. Other than that she'd obviously been around the block a time or two—or ten—and that she would be a pushover by evening's end, because he intended to woo her as no woman named Amber who worked in a strip club had ever been wooed before. And that wooing would end in something that would make both of them go *Woo!* Hopefully more than once.

A movement near the restaurant's entrance caught his eye, and Russell snapped his gaze in that direction, only to be immediately disappointed. Although a woman did indeed stand framed in the doorway, it wasn't Amber. Even with the late afternoon sun glaring through the windows behind her, he could see that she was a pale, plain creature, as lacking in color and attitude as Amber was abundant with it. With an audible sigh this time, he dropped his gaze to his watch again, noting that it was now five thirty on the nose, so his bird of paradise should be striding through the door right about—

A movement on the other side of the table made him look up, and he saw that the pale, plain creature had taken it upon herself to join him. He hated it when people did that—assumed that because of his celebrity, they could approach him without a single concern for his personal privacy. It was why he employed bodyguards, why he kept to himself, why he was such a freaking recluse, for God's sake. Not to mention the fact that this woman, if she didn't beat it now, might give Amber the wrong idea if she strolled through that door and saw Russell sitting here with her.

Though, he had to admit, now that he got a better look at his uninvited companion, she wasn't quite as plain or as colorless as he'd first thought. Her eyes were a rather remarkable shade of blue, and her mouth was too full to be considered anything but erotic. The rest of her *was* lacking in color, however, from her pale brown, shoulder-length hair to her utter lack of cosmetics to her simple black dress—made of cotton, if he wasn't mistaken, a fabric that certainly had its place, but not in a restaurant like this. The cut was a little off-the-shoulder, though, revealing skin that was smooth and unblemished, so it wasn't completely unappealing. Her lack of makeup, too, didn't really detract from her features, he decided, because her skin was a creamy, flawless ivory, her cheeks were tinted with the bare hint of a blush, and her lashes were thick and dark.

Still, she was nothing like Amber, and the sooner he got rid of her, the better. So he pulled a pen out of his inside jacket pocket, grabbed the cocktail napkin the waiter had dropped in front of him when he first sat down, and scrawled his name illegibly over it. Then he extended it to the woman.

"Here you go, sweetheart," he said.

Her lips twitched with something of a smile, but she didn't take the proffered autograph. "Can't you at least personalize it?" she asked.

He expelled a sound he hoped indicated how much she was trying his patience, then pulled the napkin toward himself again. "Fine," he said tersely. "Who should I make it out to?"

When she didn't reply right away, he looked up at her again. Her smile now was broader, and something about it made him think she was having a joke at his expense.

"Miss?" he prodded, his voice in no way courteous. "Who should I make it out to?"

"Amber," she told him. "Amber will be fine."

And with that, she pulled out the chair opposite him and seated herself, setting a tiny black purse on the table. As she scooted herself forward, she said, "You know, a lot of guys do this chair thing for their dates instead of making them do it themselves." She folded her hands—as unadorned as the rest of her—on the table in front of herself. "You never get a second chance to make a first impression and all that. Then again, I guess we've both already had our first impressions of each other, haven't we? So I don't suppose either of us has set the bar very high this evening."

Before Russell had a chance to say a word, their server appeared table side and withdrew the champagne that had been chilling in its silver bucket since his arrival ten minutes earlier. As Russell continued to study Amber in stunned silence, the waiter poured a small amount of effervescent gold into his glass and, without even thinking about what he was doing, he lifted it to his lips for a taste. Then he silently nodded his approval, even though the champagne could have tasted like sawdust for all he could have said at that point. Their server then filled an elegant crystal flute with the pale gold wine for Amber and set it on the table in front of her. She thanked him softly and lifted the glass to her lips for an exploratory sip.

"It's lovely," she told their server with a soft smile and all the dignity of that monarch Russell had once imagined her to be.

The man turned to Russell again, holding up the bottle and asking if he'd like his glass filled, as well. Since he wasn't even halfway through the Glenlivet he'd ordered for himself along with the champagne, he shook his head. The waiter returned the bottle to its nest of ice, asked if there was anything else he could do for the moment, and when Russell shook his head—silently again—the man dipped his own head deferentially and conveniently disappeared.

Amber smiled and sipped her champagne again with all the grace and sophistication of a debutante. Then she said, "And hello to you, too."

Russell looked for something—anything—that might have clued him in to her identity. But there was nothing. The big red hair had obviously been a wig. The brown eyes—and he'd always been a sucker for brown eyes—had clearly been contact lenses. And the cosmetics . . . well, evidently cosmetics really could transform a woman.

"I bet your name isn't really Amber, is it?"

This time she was the one to shake her head, punctuating the gesture with a quiet laugh. Everything about her was quiet tonight, he noted. Her looks, her voice, her laughter, her actions. Though she was still able to hold her own with him, so it wasn't the outer armor she wore as a cocktail waitress that allowed her to do that. It was some inner strength that allowed her to do that.

"No, my name isn't really Amber," she told him. "But it will do."

He reminded himself that he'd seen her wearing next to nothing, and that the body he'd so admired couldn't have possibly been faked. So that was something. All he had to do was keep his gaze below her face, pretend she wasn't wearing a boring black cotton dress, and maybe the evening

wouldn't be a total washout. The wooing was looking unlikely, however. As was the *Wooing!*

Amber—or whoever she was—sipped her champagne
again and tucked a strand of boring brown hair behind her
ear. Only then did he note something Amberesque in her
appearance. Her ears were pierced a lot. Maybe a half-dozen
times. But she only wore simple hoops of varying sizes in
each hole. Black to match her dress, though perhaps that
was the only color she wore. At the club, her hair had covered her ears, so he hadn't noticed the hardware. How or
why a woman would allow herself to be stabbed so many
times like that he couldn't imagine. He told himself over-
abundance of metal should be off-putting. Instead, coupled
with the clean lines of her face and the simplicity of her
attire, the punk/goth thing was kind of erotic.

Of course, Russell was the sort of man for whom a stray
piece of lint on a woman's collar was erotic, so that wasn't
really saying a whole lot.

She set her glass back on the table, met his gaze levelly,
and said baldly, "I hope you brought a credit card with a
big line of credit. I'm planning to run up a hell of a bill tonight."

Russell chuckled at that, surprising himself. He hadn't
been thinking there was anything funny about the situation.
He'd been expecting a promiscuous, redheaded bombshell
he'd have on her back—or, even better, on all fours—before
the night was half over. Instead, he had a woman who looked
like Little Orphan Amber. Only with pupils. Thank God.
Not that he wasn't still perfectly willing to uphold his offer,
and not that the expense would be any more than negligi-
ble to him, no matter how much of a bill she ran up. Then
he realized he wasn't chuckling because he found the situation funny. Or even because of what she said, really. He
was laughing because what she'd said had made a ripple of
something surge through him that he hadn't felt in a very
long time: happiness. Her forthrightness, maybe even her
very presence at the table, made him feel good inside.

Well, wasn't that a kick in the ass? Maybe the evening wouldn't be a complete waste of time after all.

"Don't worry," he told her. "Like I said, money is no object. Order whatever you want. As much as you want. I can even send Raoul out for a cooler if you want to take a doggie bag with you."

She sipped her champagne again and grinned. "Tell him to get a big cooler. Tell him to get two of them. Maybe three. I'll be taking a lot of doggie bags with me."

"Have a lot of doggies, do you?" Russell asked as he reached into his other inside jacket pocket for his phone. He'd put Butch/Raoul on speed dial for the night.

She nodded. "Great big ones. Rottweilers. Let's see, there's Fang and Killer and the twins, Terminator and Eviscerator."

Russell arched his brows at that one. "Eviscerator?"

"He's actually a big softie most of the time. He only eviscerates when he thinks I'm in danger. They still haven't found the remains of the cable guy who came on to me that time."

Russell punched the button for the chauffeur and put the phone to his ear. "Good information to have."

He started to say something else, but his driver picked up at the other end, so he gave him Amber's instructions and told him to take his time procuring the biggest, baddest coolers—along with a few major doggie toys—he could find. Then he folded the phone closed and started to return it to his pocket. But before he completed the action, and after only a small hesitation, he pushed the Off button, something he normally never did. Not many people had this number—only the ones who would have to get in touch with him over subjects of a life-altering, earth-moving, or business-collapsing nature. For some reason, though, suddenly, Russell wasn't concerned about any of those things. So after returning the powerless phone back to his pocket, he forgot all about it.

He picked up his Scotch and leaned forward, and was

delighted when Amber mimicked the action. The table was small, since Russell hadn't wanted there to be room for anything more than the two of them, so the double action brought their faces quite close. Close enough that he marveled again at how smooth and lovely her skin was. At how blue and clear her eyes were. At how good she smelled, even though he recognized the scent as one from his childhood: Ivory soap. Whose slogan he could also remember from childhood. Ironic, since he could say without doubt that Amber was anything but ninety-nine and forty-four one hundredths percent pure.

He remembered how, the first time he'd seen her in Minxxx, he'd been struck by the contradictions in her. He'd been thinking that by removing her from the garish environment of the strip club, she would be less of a puzzle to him. That once the outer trappings of the cocktail waitress were gone, her true nature would surface. And he supposed, in a way, it had. Her outer trappings had actually been a disguise that, once removed, had revealed a completely new set of outer trappings. But instead of making Amber easier to figure out, now she was even more of an enigma.

An enigma, Russell thought as he lifted his glass to his mouth again, that he couldn't wait to unravel.

Or undress.

GINNY SAT IN THE SOFTLY LIT, ROMANTICALLY AP-pointed restaurant across from Russell Mulholland, pretending she knew what she was doing and trying to ignore the heat lashing her stomach and the erratic racing of her heart. What the hell had she been thinking to assume she'd have the upper hand tonight? Whenever she'd been with him before, they'd always been in her world, where she was comfortable, where she understood how everything worked, where she did indeed have the upper hand and knew perfectly well how to use it.

Tonight, though, they were in his world. A world with

which she was in no way familiar and whose rules she couldn't begin to understand. When she'd agreed to go out with Russell, she'd figured this would be her chance to take a walk on the less wild side. To see what made life so sweet on the moneyed side of the street. She'd thought it would be a lark. She honestly hadn't realized she'd feel so different, so uncomfortable. Not in his environment. And not with him.

She was beyond uncomfortable here, had no idea how to act, and had lost the upper hand the moment she'd taken her first step into the restaurant. Sure, she'd known it would be nice, but this . . . this was unlike anything she'd ever seen before. There was a woman in a velvet dress playing the piano in the lobby. The host was wearing a suit. The hostess was wearing pearls. And their server. Holy crap. The guy was wearing a *tuxedo*, for God's sake. With white tie and tails.

The minute the guy had approached the table, Ginny had been hit by the realization that, essentially, she and he did the same thing for a living. But he sure as hell didn't have to wear a plastic halter top, almost certainly didn't have to pull anyone's hand from his ass at any point during his shifts, and his place of employment probably hadn't even once been raided by the cops. And on top of all that, one look at the prices on the menu also assured her he probably took home twice as much in one night as she did.

And he even had an assistant to make the Caesar salad.

Nice work, if you can get it, she thought. But waiting tables in a place like this required way more refinement and panache than she had, and way more knowledge of food and wine than she had, not to mention the ability to describe said food and wine with words heard more often on *Jeopardy!* than *Wheel of Fortune.* But Russell Mulholland moved in a world where people probably didn't even watch *Jeopardy!* He moved in a world like . . .

Well, she thought, giving the restaurant another surreptitious once-over. He moved in a world like this. Full of linen and marble, velvet and pianos, and freshly sautéed garlic cooked by someone else. Not a world like hers, full of polyester and linoleum, cotton and radio, and garlic powder bottled under the supermarket label. And truth be told, Ginny didn't even use garlic powder all that often. It was easier to just pull something out of a box or bag and nuke it.

Her world for sure didn't put her into this kind of proximity with blond, blue-eyed, Adonis-type billionaires, even if they were morally compromised enough to frequent the sort of place where she worked. Yet here she sat, her head bent toward Russell's, close enough that she could inhale the fresh, clean scent of him, could note the glitter of amber highlights in his hair, could detect just a hint of gray at the center of his azure irises. As she sat in silence gazing back at him, he arched one brow and grinned, a gesture that hinted at a single faint dimple on his left cheek. She would have sworn the photos she'd seen of him had been retouched, because no man could be that handsome, that perfect. But he looked even better in person than he did in magazines.

What *had* she been thinking to agree to go out with him tonight?

As if he could tell what she was thinking, he asked, "Having second thoughts already?"

"Of course not," she lied, digging deep for what little bravado she had left. "Are you?"

He shook his head. "Not at all. In fact, I find myself looking forward to the evening ahead now even more than I was before."

"Before what?" she asked. Then mentally smacked herself for pushing her luck.

"Before a woman sat down on the other side of the table from me who looks infinitely more mouthwatering than anything on the menu."

Oh, now who was lying? she thought. No way did she believe that. Men who visited places like Minxxx did so because they relished the trashy, trampy side of women that society liked to keep behind closed doors, and Amber

Glenn personified that perfectly; Ginny worked hard on her costume to make sure of that. Ginny Collins, on the other hand, was about as plain and ordinary as they came. The sort of woman men never looked at twice. She worked hard to make sure of that, too.

Something on her face must have hinted at her thoughts— or maybe he really could read her mind—because he asked, "Why the disguise when you work? You're a lovely woman under all the paint and big hair. Do you really think an over-the-top redheaded bombshell would make better tips than a cute girl next door? Believe it or not, a lot of guys go for the wholesome look way more than the lady-of-the-night thing." He smiled. "Especially if the girl next door is wearing knee socks and a plaid skirt."

She chuckled at that. "Yeah, right. Spoken like the only guy in the world who goes for the wholesome look more than the lady of the night." Then, because that made it sound like Russell found her attractive—which they both knew wasn't true, as evidenced by his use of the word *lovely* for her, which men only used in reference to a maiden aunt— she hurried on, "It's not just for the better tips. It's for . . . protection." For both her and Maisy, but she didn't mention her daughter. "A lot of guys come into Minxxx. And a lot of them—most of them, really—are just your everyday, average sort of guy. They just have this icky side to them that makes them objectify women and visit strip clubs."

"Are you calling me icky?" Russell interjected.

She threw him a look that said he should already know the answer to that, since she'd just spelled it out for him. Nevertheless, she clarified, "Just one side of you."

His mouth dropped open in astonishment at that. "And you think I objectify women?"

Again, already answered, she thought. What was it with men that they had to have things hammered home so hard? "Oh, absolutely," she agreed without a qualm.

His mouth dropped open again, but he closed it quickly this time. He studied her intently, but his expression was bland, so she honestly didn't know how he was taking her assessment of him. But what was she supposed to do, lie? Any guy who visited strip clubs was icky on some level. And they did objectify women. At least a healthy segment of the female population. Or worse, they had that whole Madonna-whore thing going on, which was just as bad. Maybe worse.

"Anyway," she continued, "they're the kind of guy it would be very easy for me to run into in some other area of my life. If I worked in my usual skin, those guys would recognize me in my usual skin. I mean, I could just be standing in the grocery store, trying to decide between Froot Loops and Cocoa Puffs—" Or, worse, she thought, she could be at a parent association function at school. "And some guy could come up behind me, grab my ass and say, 'Yo, Am-BER! You looked great in that plastic miniskirt at the strip club last night. You wanna earn a quick twenty bucks now?' " She shook her head and reached for her champagne. "I mean, who needs that crap, you know?"

Still looking at her in that maddeningly unremarkable way, he reached for his drink and drained what was left in it, then held the glass aloft without comment or fanfare, only to have it immediately removed by a passing waiter whom he acknowledged in no way. Unbelievable, Ginny thought. He literally had people at his beck and call. The waiter then filled his champagne glass, topped off hers, and conveniently disappeared again.

Russell lifted his champagne glass as if he were going to make a toast, leaning it toward hers. Not sure what he was going to say, she mimicked his action anyway, carefully resting the lip of her glass against his.

"To sweet excess," he said.

She grinned. "To sweet excess," she echoed.

They both sipped their champagne, their gazes never disengaging. When Russell set his glass back on the table again, he asked, "Will you tell me your real name, Amber?"

"No," she replied immediately. When his mouth tightened at her response, she added, "Look, it's nothing personal. I never give my real name to anyone who's not going to be part of my life."

"That protection thing you mentioned?"

She nodded. "A girl can never protect herself enough. Especially not a—" She'd started to say *a girl like me* but stopped herself. She'd learned a long time ago that the women who worked at Minxxx did so for a lot of different reasons. A lot of them were supporting addictions. But a lot of them were supporting kids. Or men. Or parents. You couldn't just lump them all into a group and say they were alike, any more than you could lump a bunch of anybody else into a group and say they were all alike.

But Russell finished for her, saving her the dilemma. "Especially not a cocktail waitress who has to wait on icky, women-objectifying men?"

She nodded slowly. "Yeah. Especially not one of those."

Still focusing his attention on her face, he traced the base of his glass slowly with his middle finger, an action that drew her attention downward. She would have thought he would have soft hands, sissy hands, all manicured and tended and never used for anything except holding cell phones and champagne flutes. Instead, they looked like a working man's hands, their nails clipped short, not particularly elegant, and the one holding the glass had a small scar on the back. They could have been a laborer's hands. They were just that sexy.

And the way that hand in particular was moving made it sexier still. With his middle finger, he made a slow circle around the glass's base, then skimmed it upward, along the fragile stem. At the lower curve of the bowl of the glass, he brought his thumb and index finger into the action, caressing the delicate flute as tenderly as he would a woman's breast.

And that was all it took for her to wonder what it would be like to have him touching her the same way, stroking the pads of his sexy fingers along her sensitive flesh. Which was weird, because Ginny never wondered about that kind of thing at all anymore. Not with any man. What was even weirder was that, thinking about it now, with Russell being that man, a flutter of something she hadn't felt for a very long time quivered to life inside her, sending a lovely rush of warmth purling through her entire body.

"Well then, shall we get our evening started?" he asked quietly. "I believe you said you wanted to order one of everything on the menu. And I'm sure you've made a list of other places you'd like to visit this evening?"

She nodded, tamping down the odd response he'd generated inside her. "All of them not far from here," she told him. "Crescent Hill is only a stone's throw, and there are a million places there: L & N Wine Bar, Volare, Varanese . . . lots of others. And then we can top off the night by circling back downtown to Proof on Main."

"I've read about that last," he said. "It's in a hotel, isn't it?"

"Yes, 21C Museum Hotel, to be exact," she told him. "The museum part is way cool."

"I'll bet the hotel part has a lot to recommend it, too."

Oh, she knew where this was going. Or where Russell *thought* it was going. Not that she was going to let that happen. She may have lost the upper hand a long time ago, and maybe her plan that he wouldn't find her attractive in her normal skin had backfired—obviously the only prerequisite he had for a woman was that she be breathing—but she wasn't so far gone that she had any intention of getting a room with the guy.

"I wouldn't know," she told him. "I've never visited that part."

This time, he was the one to grin. "Well, it sounds like it's going to be a night of firsts for you, doesn't it?"

She did laugh then. "Sorry, Russ, but somebody got to me a looooong time before tonight."

Of course, he had to have guessed that already. What he didn't know was how few men there had been since

then. Not that she intended to tell him that. Let him think
she was promiscuous and easy. For now, anyway. They
had a whole night ahead of them. And she intended to
take advantage of it—and of Russell—for as long as she
could.

·Eleven·

DEAN'S CONDO AT WATERFRONT PARK PLACE WAS A showpiece, Natalie had to concede, as she gazed out the wide windows that faced the river and made up nearly an entire wall of his living room. His was on one of the top floors, which meant he had not only stunning river views like this, but a spectacular vista of the city on another side, as well. And, as an added bonus, he could watch Bats games at Slugger Field across the way just by taking a beer out to his patio and pulling one of the chaises closer to the railing. Of course, he'd paid seven figures for the place, but then, he could afford it.

The interior was every bit as impressive as the views . . . and as different from Natalie's decor as Natalie was from Dean. Except that where Natalie, like Dean's decor, was tasteful and aesthetically pleasing, Dean, um, wasn't.

Ahem.

He'd eschewed the color Natalie liked in favor of neutrals, and the angles of her Craftsman style were Euro-chic curves here, the mocha-colored walls offsetting the taupe furnishings nicely. The only thing remotely resembling

NECK & NECK   181

color in the place was in the artwork on the walls—all
original, all by up-and-coming local artists, none Dean
had picked out himself, since he didn't know a thing about
art. But even there, most of the pieces were abstract geometric shapes or broad slashes of oil on canvas. One or two
were of objects Natalie could sort of distinguish, but since
she was pretty sure they were human body parts, she tried
not to look too hard.

She'd only been at his place twice before, both times as
a guest at parties he'd thrown to impress someone, so she
knew he went all out when it came to entertaining. She
also knew that because he'd asked her to arrange both of
them. However, he hadn't offered to *pay* her to arrange them,
even though both had taken place after she'd launched
Party Favors. He'd thought she would be flattered to play
hostess—and organizer—because he wanted to make her
his missus, and that was what missusses—missussi?—did,
even before they were officially missusses or missussi or
whatever they became after marrying Dean. Other than
irritable, she meant.

Tonight was no different, even though only a fraction of
his usual guest list was coming. (It was also no different in
that Natalie had told him no when he'd asked her to put it
together for free in exchange for that whole missus thing
again.) And it went without saying that he'd fabricated this
whole dinner party on the spur of the moment in the first
place after meeting Russell Mulholland. But he—or, rather,
his caterer, whom he *was* paying, since it was a guy, thereby
making the whole missus thing moot, not to mention illegal
in the state of Kentucky despite the Fairness Campaign—
had pulled it together quickly and with great excess. Dean
had ordered six courses—and a different wine for each—
along with hors d'oeuvres and cocktails before.

He had told Natalie that he could see right through her
hard-to-get act again with the not planning the party unless she was getting paid, but had deigned to allow her to
play hostess by his side anyway to show there were no hard
feelings. And he'd instructed her to come a half hour before

any of the guests, so that she'd be on hand when everyone arrived. So it went without saying that she'd knocked on his front door with barely ten minutes to spare before party time.

Still, it was ten minutes too many, as far as she was concerned, since the social circle she and Dean traveled in was always fashionably late. She probably should have arrived tomorrow instead. That way, Dean would be at work, and no one would have answered.

Gee, hindsight really was twenty-twenty.

Of course, then she would have missed her only chance for a second chance with Russell Mulholland, and she couldn't miss that. She'd taken special pains with her wardrobe and toilette tonight, but only because she knew he would be here, and she wanted to impress him after the debacle of Monday night. She'd paired black crepe trousers with a silk, sapphire blue wraparound top, had swept her hair into a sleek French twist, and fixed simple sapphire studs in her ears. Her only other jewelry was a sapphire solitaire pendant and gold watch. She'd also toned down her makeup, opting for just mascara and tinted lip gloss. She'd figured maybe understated elegance would win the billionaire over where a short hemline and scooped neck hadn't been able to—go figure, since the guy was a notorious womanizer, which was why she'd gone that route in the first place. She was also going to make sure she didn't touch a drop of alcohol tonight.

"Martini," Dean said as he drew to a stop behind her and extended a beautifully chilled, triangle-shaped glass toward her. "Bombay with a mere shadow of vermouth and two olives, just the way you like it."

"Thank you," she said, accepting the glass for the sake of looking the part of hostess and gritting her teeth against the irritation that rose in her belly at having to play second fiddle to Dean.

How had he managed to get Russell Mulholland to come to his place for a boring, last-minute dinner party when she hadn't been able to land him for Clementine's big, festive fund-raiser? It made no sense. Natalie may have had too much to drink the other night, but she'd been clearheaded enough at first to see Russell and Finn exchange more than one eye roll over Dean. And yeah, okay, so Natalie hadn't exactly been the picture of charm, drinking too much and being clearly inebriated. At least her invitation had been for a worthy cause. Dean just wanted Russell here so he could suck up even more than he had the other night.

"I'm so glad you could make it tonight," Dean said before lifting his own glass to his lips. He paused before completing the action, meeting her gaze levelly before adding, "Even if you didn't quite make it on time."

She drove her gaze deliberately around the room, then back to his. "Have any of your guests arrived yet?"

He shook his head. "No. But I could have used your help interceding with the . . . help."

He spoke the word *help* in the same tone of voice most people used for the words *child molester*. Because for Dean, there was nothing worse than having to talk to people who were paid by the hour. Even ones who were dressed in crisp white shirts and black ties and trousers, like the trio of servers standing at the ready for Natalie and Dean and the four other couples he had invited to come tonight, along with Russell and his guest. There was also a chef and his assistant in the kitchen putting together the night's courses.

Five people to entertain twelve, Natalie thought. That was a bit much, even for Dean. He really was in major suck-up mode tonight. She'd wager he'd even bought his charcoal pinstriped suit and discreetly patterned blue necktie for the event. The suit just had that crisp, fresh-from-the-tailor's-garment-bag look about it, and he'd called her yesterday to ask what color she'd be wearing so he could make sure his neckwear was sartorially coordinated.

She was rescued from having to continue the conversation by the chime of the doorbell. Evidently, even the people in her and Dean's social circle couldn't resist being in the same room as a billionaire, because over the next several minutes, all of his guests—save the aforementioned billionaire—arrived, two by two, just like Noah's ark. There was even a strange sort of animalistic resemblance to each of them. The Stephensons were bearish, the Mortons were bullish, Major and Mrs. Dugan were hawks, Dory Mitchell and her date Logan Butterworth were rats, and Tootie Hightower and her date—holy cow, was that Patrick Ellington, her ex-fiancé who'd cheated on her with a local punk band?— were pigs.

Natalie, of course, knew all of them—Tootie, in fact, was responsible for the photo of Natalie in her big-ass bow dress that was plastered all over the Internet—and Natalie, of course, liked none of them. Dean's friends were just like Dean: patrician, preening, and pompous, with a sense of entitlement that was nothing less than staggering.

Once everyone had their drinks in hand—and after Natalie set her still-full glass on the tray of a passing waiter— they all congregated in the main room, away from the windows, since no one wanted to admit the views were gorgeous, because that would make it seem like they were actually impressed by something. Other than themselves, she meant. But she naturally gravitated toward the windows again, because the sun was dipping low in the sky to her left, spilling over the Ohio and turning it into a ruffling ribbon of gold, flashing off the windows of southern Indiana on the other side and making them sparkle. A powerboat emerged from beneath the Second Street Bridge, and she smiled as she watched its wake widen leisurely into a golden triangle.

It was her favorite time of day, when the demands of life began to wane, and the pleasure of simply living began to trickle in. As much as she liked what she did for a living— what she hoped to keep doing for a living—Natalie was more of the "work to live" philosophy than of "live to work." And evenings were when that living generally began. Of course, her job often necessitated she work at night, but even that didn't feel the same as working during the day. As much as she flitted around keeping track of everything during the events she planned, she was still never quite able to avoid getting caught up in the festivity surrounding her.

As if cued by the thought, Dean's guests suddenly seemed to be surrounding her, because Dean had led them her way, and any chance for festivity went up in smoke. Even when they were all children, there had always been a kind of predation about this particular group that wasn't quite human. Suddenly, Natalie wished she was indeed working. Because it would have meant she would have had to decline Dean's invitation—nay, his edict—to be here tonight. Not that she was here because he'd decreed it. She just wanted to see Mulholland. Dean, however, was inescapably under the impression that it was the power of his charismatic charm that was responsible for her being here tonight.

Then again, Mulholland wasn't here yet, she noted. Not that he was *that* late. He'd just gone a bit beyond the *fashionably* thing at this point. Not that he probably cared. In fact, Natalie was beginning to wonder if the guy would show at all. Maybe she hadn't been the only one who'd overindulged that night. Who knew if Mulholland had even been sober when he'd agreed to come to Dean's party tonight? Who knew if he even remembered?

The realization hit her like a ton of overpriced hors d'oeuvres, followed by a gallon of Bombay martinis right to the face. She looked over at Dean, trying to think of a way to separate him from his guests to put forth the suggestion that Russell Mulholland had just been yanking his chain the other night when he said he'd come to this party. That way, he'd be out of eyeshot when she smacked him on the forehead and said, "Snap out of it!" because she sincerely doubted he'd believe that Russell Mulholland had just been yanking his chain the other night when he said he'd come to this party.

Before she had a chance to figure out how to do that, though, her nemesis from cotillion class—and the keeper of the big-ass bow picture—Tootie Hightower, sidled up next to Natalie and said the same thing she always said every time she saw Natalie at a party.

"I just updated my website. Have you checked it recently?"

Tootie's real name was Camille, but she'd been dubbed Tootie in seventh grade when she'd had an embarrassing gastrointestinal reaction to the gourmet garlic wienies at Heather Mortimer's pool party after eating way too many of them. In her defense, they'd been extra good wienies. On the other hand, Tootie's gastrointestinal reaction had been extra gastric and extra-extra intestinal. These days, she insisted on being called Camille, but everyone still called her Tootie. Well, okay, maybe it was only Natalie who still called her Tootie. But only because Tootie deserved it.

"You know," she told Tootie sweetly, "I keep forgetting you have a website. What's its purpose again? I mean, it's not like you have a career that you need a website for, like most people do." *Translation,* Natalie added to herself, *Like I do.*

Not that Tootie would even *try* to launch a career, since her parents, like Natalie's, had raised—and expected—her from day one to be a perfect society wife, and Tootie, unlike Natalie, had bought into it. But Natalie was pretty sure there were times when Tootie envied women who made their own way in the world. And there were a number of jobs Tootie would be perfect for. Important jobs, too. Jobs like gossip columnist and fashion police and fishwife were just crying out for applicants like Tootie.

"It's a society website," she said through what Natalie was sure weren't gritted teeth but just Tootie's unusual way of smiling. "The most visited society website in town. Anybody who's anybody checks it at least weekly. Usually daily."

Which was Tootie's way of saying that Natalie, by not looking at it, was a complete nobody. Not that Tootie needed any additional ways to say that, since she already had dozens she used regularly. In fact, many of them appeared on her website. Which was yet another reason why Natalie never felt compelled to check it.

"Ah," she replied without a trace of . . . well, anything.

"Well, I'll be sure to give it a look sometime when I'm not massively busy with my hugely successful career."

Tootie smirked at that. "It can't be too successful if Dean didn't even hire you to plan his party tonight."

Natalie smirked back. "Dean can't afford me."

Hoo-boy was that true. Just not in the way Tootie would interpret it. Not even Warren Buffett had enough money to make Natalie spend any more time with Dean than she had to. Bail out Wall Street, sure. Make Natalie spend time with Dean? No way.

What was ironic was that Tootie would have spent more than the gross national product of Denmark to have Dean pay as much attention to her as he did to Natalie. Even in cotillion class, Tootie had always wanted to dance with rat-faced Dean Waterman. Not because she had a crush on him—even Tootie wasn't that troubled—but because she had a crush on the Waterman fortune.

The Hightowers were nouveau riche, having claimed their millions for only the last three generations, and it would bring up their social standing considerably to be linked with the moldy old piles of filthy lucre the Watermans claimed. In fact, Tootie's grandfather's real last name had been Guberman when he invented the machine part that made him rich, and he changed it to Hightower because he thought it sounded more patrician, preening, and pompous. Which was unfortunate, because Tootie Guberman had a real ring to it.

Anyway, Tootie had always thought that marrying into the Waterman family would give the family formerly known as Guberman more social cachet. And now that Dean didn't look like a rodent anymore, she knew the two of them would photograph together beautifully, as well. And really, Natalie thought further, the two of them *were* perfect for each other. They were both condescending and supercilious and completely in love . . . with themselves.

Um, where was she?

Oh, yeah, she recalled. She was about to come up with some excuse for why she had to excuse herself from Tootie before Tootie could think of some comeback for that "*Dean can't afford me*" comment. Which, admittedly, considering the speed at which Tootie generally ran with ideas, would probably be sometime next week.

But Natalie was saved the trouble of planning her escape by the ringing of Dean's doorbell, a soft, elegant chime that utterly silenced the room. Not only that, but every person present turned to look at the front door, since everyone knew the only person missing from the party was the reclusive billionaire, Russell Mulholland. Even the black-tied servers paused in their serving, and the two chefs peeked out of the kitchen, all having been informed of the identity of the guest of honor so they'd all be on their best behavior. It was if the entire room was holding its collective breath in anticipation. The expressions on the faces of everyone would have been the same if they'd been told Dean was hosting the Second Coming tonight.

It was all Natalie could do not to shout, *Oh, lighten up, people! I've been three sheets to the wind in front of the man! He's no different from anyone else!*

Except for that stuff about how he could make or break her career. But there was no reason any of them had to know that. Especially Tootie.

The guests all waited another moment, evidently for a bolt of lightning or crash of thunder, Natalie couldn't help thinking, and when neither disrupted the gathering, Dean mumbled an "Excuse me" to everyone and headed for the door. But not before grabbing Natalie's wrist and dragging her along behind him, reminding her that she was supposed to be the hostess here, something she kept forgetting for some reason.

After straightening his tie and pasting on his brightest smile—and picking a piece of lint off of Natalie's shoulder and straightening her necklace, the big jerk—he wrapped his fingers snugly around the doorknob and began to turn it. Natalie wasn't sure, but she thought just about everyone present took a few steps forward in anticipation when he did, all of them craning their necks—as unobtrusively as possible, of course, though they were about as unobtrusive as a bunch of Mack trucks—to witness the arrival of the Mulholland.

As Dean tugged open the door, he jovially greeted his final guest with, "It is such an honor to have you here tonight, Mr. . . ."

But his voice trailed off before finishing—and heat splashed through Natalie's belly—when it became obvious that it wasn't Russell Mulholland who was standing on the other side of the door. It was Finn Guthrie. Nor was the person standing beside Finn Russell Mulholland. It was a breathtaking blonde in a satiny red dress that clung to more curves than Natalie had ever seen on another living creature, other than the Michelin man. But then, the Michelin man wasn't a living creature. And the blonde's curves were way more concave. Except around the top, where she gave new meaning to the word *consex*. Ah, con*vex*, Natalie meant, of course. Humpf.

". . . Guthrie, was it?" Dean finished, not even trying to hide his irritation. He even looked past Finn and the blonde in an unmistakable effort to locate the man he'd invited, dismissing Finn as security, a necessary but clearly unwanted evil.

Which was a fair assumption, Natalie thought. Except that she would have substituted the word *evil* with some other term. Something like *wickedly delicious sinfulness*. And she would have substituted the word *unwanted* with something like, oh, say . . . *hungered for*. Oh, and also except that Russell Mulholland was nowhere near Finn, and the blonde was way nearer than she probably should have been if she were Mulholland's date. Which meant that whatever security Mulholland's bodyguard was providing was pretty thin at the moment, except when it came to the blonde.

Not that Natalie noticed the blonde *or* her consexity. Damn her. Not when Finn looked as wickedly, deliciously sinful as he did, dressed in the wickedly deliciously sinful way he was dressed. Which wasn't like his usual way at all. At least, not the Finn she knew. So far, she'd seen him in ragged jeans and sweatpants and khakis and such, but tonight, his attire rivaled the elegance quotient of the rest of the guests. But instead of making him look elegant, the charcoal suit, slate dress shirt, and silver necktie only made him seem more dangerous somehow. It also made his smoky bedroom eyes even smokier and more bedroomy. He'd even shaved, she saw, something that brought out a long slash of dimple in each cheek that somehow made him look even more rugged than the stubble of beard had. And when he smiled at his host, even with the tightness and clear lack of warmth he held for Dean, Natalie very nearly swooned.

Truly. Swooned. Right there in the twenty-first century, where no woman had any right to swoon after all the social and political strides they and their mothers and grandmothers had made against women's swooning.

"That's right," Finn said crisply. "I'm Mr. Guthrie." Somehow, Natalie detected the silent *to you, buster* with which he'd wanted to end the statement but hadn't for the sake of . . .

Well, something. Not courtesy, that was for sure, since Finn Guthrie wasn't the type for that.

Dean didn't much bother with courtesy, either, when he asked, "Where's your employer?"

Not *Where's Mr. Mulholland?* Natalie noted. *Where's your employer?* As if he wanted to be sure to keep Finn in his place, relegated to the same status as the catering help.

Instead of answering right away, Finn shouldered his way past Dean without even being invited in, bringing the blonde with him. And when he finally did reply to Dean, he looked at Natalie instead of his host.

"Mr. Mulholland couldn't make it after all," he said. "He remembered this afternoon that he had a, um, previous engagement."

Oh, that was nice and vague, Natalie thought. That ought to piss off Dean royally. Which, somehow she was certain, was exactly what Finn had intended to do. What she couldn't figure out was why. Sure, Dean was smarmy and annoying as hell, but Finn had only met him that one time. It was enough to make anyone not want to cross paths with Dean again, but it wasn't enough to generate the kind of hostility Finn clearly felt for the guy. She could practically feel the waves of animosity flowing off of him.

As if he'd read her mind and wanted to hammer that thought home, he added, "It was something he couldn't miss. Something important."

Translation, Natalie thought, *Your party isn't important and is something Mulholland* can *miss.*

"And since he knew you were expecting another couple for this thing," Finn added dispassionately, "and probably paid some caterer through the nose for it, he didn't want to leave you hanging."

Translation, Natalie thought again, *He knows you're spending a lot of money on his behalf and* still *doesn't care enough to show up.*

"So he sent me as his representative," Finn concluded with even less concern. He nodded toward the blonde. "This is Danetta. She would have been Mr. Mulholland's date for the evening. He didn't see any reason why she shouldn't enjoy herself."

Yeah, since he'd probably already bought and paid for her, anyway, Natalie thought uncharitably. In one way or another. Why shouldn't Russell pass her along to his best friend for the night if he wouldn't need her services himself?

"Hello," Danetta said in a voice that sounded genuinely nice, with a smile that seemed genuinely warm. Damn her. "Thank you for having us, Mr. Waterman. It was so thoughtful of you. Russell is heartbroken that he couldn't make it."

Oh, fine, Natalie thought. *Just be sweet and considerate and seem genuinely nice and warm. Damn you.*

Dean, too, seemed to notice her genuine niceness and warmth—not to mention all her generous consexity— because his annoyance lightened at her comments. And her consexity. "Call me Dean," he told her. Nicely. Warmly.

Something in his voice made Natalie brighten, because

his tone dripped with the same sort of unctuous toadying he normally reserved for her. Even better, he nudged Finn out of the way to take Danetta's hand in his, and Natalie could almost feel his smarminess oozing off of her and all over Danetta instead. And wow, did that feel good.

"Well, if Mr. Mulholland couldn't make it tonight," Dean said as he tucked her hand into the crook of his arm, "at least he was good enough to allow us the pleasure of your company."

And then he led her toward the other couples and began making introductions, completely blowing off Finn. Obviously Antagonism Avenue was a two-way street, where every vehicle was driven by testosterone. Way past the speed limit. With a total disregard for pedestrians.

Man, Natalie was glad she was an estrogen-based unit.

Of course, by leading Danetta off the way he had, Dean was blowing off Natalie, too, but that was A-okay with her. Finn, however, would probably be POed that Dean had left him in the dust the way he had.

But when she turned to look at Finn, he wasn't watching Dean steal his date—even if she was just a loaner. He was looking at Natalie, his gaze fixed on her face in a way that made him look . . .

Well, *hungry* was the word that came to mind just then. And of all the words that had appeared in Natalie's head in italics tonight, that was the one that should have also been boldfaced, too. And capitalized. And underlined. And followed by at least three exclamation marks. Because ***HUNGRY!!!*** was the way she was suddenly feeling, too.

But then, she'd been feeling that way in a lowercase, unitalicized, lightfaced way ever since the last time she'd seen him. Thanks to that touch that hadn't quite been a touch, that kiss that hadn't quite been a kiss, and that good-bye that hadn't quite been a good-bye, she'd spent the last couple of days visiting the states of confusion, annoyance, and irritation, and finding none of them particularly scenic.

Wow, had that last meeting just happened yesterday morning? she asked herself, amazed. Not even two days had passed? Funny, but it felt like forever. Nevertheless, she could still remember every detail of their time together, from the moment she woke up in his bed in his hotel suite—oh, all *right*, from the moment she *came to* in his bed in his hotel suite—to that too-brief, crystalline moment in her kitchen when she'd begun to think things between them were moving too fast and headed farther than either of them should probably let things go. When she'd realized she *wanted* things to move faster and farther between them than either of them should let them go. Because it had been way too long since Natalie had let herself do that. And because she'd never met a man like Finn before—so gorgeous and masculine and sexy and . . . and . . . and *potent*—and likely wouldn't again.

And now here he was again, more potent than ever, when she'd been expecting and wanting—and needing— his employer to be here instead. Funny, though, how she wasn't all that disappointed to see Finn Guthrie in place of Russell Mulholland. Funny how she wasn't even thinking about Russell Mulholland at all.

"Natalie," Finn said by way of a greeting, almost as if that were the only word he trusted himself to say.

Amazingly, she was able to stop herself from greeting him with, *Who the hell is the blonde?* and instead said, "Finn. What a surprise to find you here."

Though, in hindsight, she thought, even if Russell had intended to come, he probably would have brought one of his security people with him. So she should have been expecting to see him again. Which she hadn't been, of course. She'd just been hoping she would see him again, that was all. But it made sense that he would have been the one accompanying Russell tonight. Unless, she thought further with a mental chuckle, Danetta was—

The thought stopped right there. She turned around to see Dean still introducing her to his guests, looking for any telltale bulge under her dress that was anything but normal, natural consexity. Nope. No weapon there, unless it was strapped to the inside of her thigh, something that would have made her walk kind of funny, anyway, and the woman's movements were as smooth as her looks. And her beaded gold clutch was too small to hold anything bigger than a paramecium, so no weapon there, either, unless it was an exploding tampon Q whipped up for her in MI6's lab. But since she didn't have a British accent, that wasn't likely. Then again, she reminded herself, Finn didn't carry a weapon with him. Except for his steely sexual magnetism.

Nevertheless, when Natalie turned around to look at him again, he was smiling at her in a way that told her she was dead on target. Danetta was indeed a member of the billionaire's cadre of bodyguards.

"Every now and then," he said, "Russell needs a beautiful escort to some function where it would be out of place for me or one of the other guys to keep close tabs. With Danetta by his side, no one could get near Russell if they tried. Her specialty is Krav Maga."

Having no idea what that meant, Natalie told him, "Gee, I'll have to ask her for the recipe before she leaves."

He shook his head, his smile growing broader. "It's a martial art form. Developed by the Israeli army. Suffice it to say that Danetta doesn't need to carry a weapon. She *is* the weapon."

Yeah, well, Natalie had already figured that part out. She'd just been thinking in terms of a different kind of warfare, that was all.

"So then you and she aren't . . . ?"

His smile fell some. "Aren't what?"

"Ummm . . ." Natalie said, stringing the word out over several time zones.

Finn looked past her at the group behind them, then back at her. "What? You mean, like, dating?"

"Of course I didn't mean that," she lied, striving for indignant, fearing it sounded more like insecure.

Finn returned his attention to her and said blandly, "If

she and I were dating, don't you think I'd go over there and remove Waterman's hand from her ass?"

Natalie spun incredulously back around at that—even Dean wouldn't be that crass this early in the evening—but he'd moved to the bar to fix Danetta a drink and was standing nowhere near her. When Natalie looked back at Finn in confusion, what little smile that had been playing about his lips was gone completely, and his expression was one of unmistakable annoyance. Before she had a chance to wonder about not only his mood swing but his comment about Dean, the latter was summoning her to join him at the bar.

Natalie went, not because she felt compelled to obey Dean's edict, but because she thought maybe some distance between her and Finn might be a good idea at the moment, if for no other reason than that it might curb her *HUNGER!!!* a little. Unfortunately, her plan backfired, because Finn naturally followed, coming to a halt beside Danetta, and Natalie found herself wondering if the two of them might be an item despite his strange comment. Because he hadn't exactly denied that he and Danetta were an item, had he? And even though Danetta was speaking to Tootie when Finn joined her, she looped her arm through his with much familiarity, as if it were something she did often.

Dean finished mixing Danetta's drink—a Manhattan by the looks of it—but as he turned to deliver it, he murmured something about having forgotten to ask what Guthrie was drinking.

"Beer," Natalie said automatically. "Something domestic." She turned to look at Dean, who met her gaze with much suspicion.

"You asked him?" he said.

"Of course," Natalie lied again, noting something in his voice that made her think she should. "What kind of hostess would I be if I didn't ask your guests what they were drinking?"

Dean sighed with clear frustration. "I don't have any beer. What kind of person drinks beer at a dinner party?"

She patted his hand sympathetically. "Don't worry. I

called the caterer this afternoon and asked him to include a case of Sam Adams."

Not because Finn would drink an entire case, of course. Just because she'd wanted Dean to pay for a case of beer he'd never be drinking.

Now he eyed her even more suspiciously than he had before. "How did you know I'd need some?"

This time Natalie was the one to sigh with frustration. "Be*cause*, Dean," she said in the same tone of voice she might use for a two-year-old who'd just shoved a Lego up his nose, "Russell Mulholland is an *eccentric*. You never know what people like that will be drinking." And you never knew who they might bring with them, she added to herself.

Oh, all *right*. So maybe she had been thinking—hoping— that Russell would have a member of his security team with him tonight. Just not one who was blonde and consex, that was all.

Dean didn't look anywhere near convinced, but Natalie . . . Oh, what was the phrase she was looking for? Oh, yeah. Didn't give a damn. Instead, she went to the kitchen and withdrew a longneck from Dean's fridge—Oh, good; they'd unpacked the entire case, so the entire bottom shelf of his Sub-Zero fridge was stocked with beer he'd never drink—twisted off the cap, and returned to the party.

She was surprised to see that Finn had moved away from Danetta to take in the view outside the window. She was not surprised to see that Dean had swooped in to take his place at the blonde's side. Possibly, Natalie thought, Dean was thinking he could get even with Finn for not being his employer by moving in on Finn's date. Probably, he would indeed have his hand on Danetta's ass by night's end. Definitely, he didn't realize she knew Krav Maga. It almost made Natalie want to stay 'til the end of the party.

Almost.

But she would hang around until dinner was over—she didn't want to be rude, after all, unlike *some* Tooties—

and then make up an excuse for why she had to leave. By then, Dean wouldn't miss her. And Finn probably wouldn't, either.

She strode over to where he stood alone at the window and stopped beside him, and when he looked up, she smiled and extended the beer toward him. He smiled back—almost convincingly, too—and accepted it from her, enjoying a healthy swallow before murmuring his thanks. Then he returned his attention to the view beyond the glass.

Not sure whether he was silently dismissing her or if he just thought Jeffersonville was the most beautiful sight he'd ever beheld, Natalie said, "Nice view, huh?"

Still looking out the window, he said, "Yep."

"You should see it after dark," she told him. "The lights from Indiana on the other side stream across the river like different colored stripes, and the bridge is all lit up with purple. It's gorgeous."

He said nothing for a moment, which she thought strange, then turned to look at her again. "Seen this view at night a lot, have you?"

Not exactly the reply she'd expected, but at least he was speaking to her. Maybe not in the warmest tone of voice—and what was up with that, anyway, since he was the one who had both started and ended anything that hadn't happened at her house the other night?—but then, his tone with her since meeting him had rarely been warm. Only that night in his room, when she'd awakened—okay, okay, come to—in his bed had they spoken with anything even remotely resembling friendship. Or something.

"I've seen it once or twice," she answered honestly.

He nodded at that, then turned back to the great outdoors. "Look, Natalie, you don't have to stand here and keep me company," he said. "I know you and Waterman have other guests, and I'm not much of a mingler."

He pronounced that last word as if it were something distasteful he found on the sole of his shoe.

She ignored, for now, the fact that he had seemed to link

her and Dean together as an item, because she couldn't imagine where he would have gotten a ridiculous idea like that, even if she was acting as his hostess tonight. Lots of single men in society had women who weren't girlfriends or fiancées or anything else help them host parties. Some archaic throwback to days when women didn't have anything better to do. Well, they'd had better things to do. They just hadn't been allowed to do them.

Then she remembered Finn had seen her and Dean seated at the same table at the restaurant the other night, which might have made it look like they were on a date. But surely once he'd talked to Dean for, oh . . . a nanosecond, he'd realized what a jerk the guy was. He couldn't possibly think Natalie would actually go out—voluntarily, anyway—with a guy like that, could he?

"You're a guest, too," she pointed out.

"Only by default," he pointed out right back. But he turned to smile at her again when he said it, and this time, he didn't look quite so perturbed. In fact, he kind of looked like he was sharing a joke with her, though, for the life of her, she couldn't imagine what the joke might be.

He enjoyed another sip of his beer, then turned his entire body to face her. "Seriously, Natalie, I know I'm not who you and Waterman were expecting, and dinner parties aren't up there on my favorite ways to spend an evening, anyway, so don't feel like you have to give me special treatment. You can go hang with your friends. I'll be over in a minute." He shrugged a little self-consciously. "Like I said. It's a nice view."

She tried not to read anything into the fact that he was looking at her when he said that last, and not at the vista beyond the window. She mimicked his shrug and said, "I'd rather talk to you." She glanced over her shoulder and then back at Finn. "Besides, they're not my friends. They're Dean's."

His expression changed to surprise at that. "You and he are hosting a party, and you don't know any of the guests?"

Her back went up at the way he linked her and Dean

again. And because of that, she couldn't quite curb the bitterness that edged her voice when she told him, "Oh, I *know* all of them. I've known them since childhood. But they weren't my friends then, either."

·Twelve·

FINN STUDIED NATALIE AS SHE STOOD IN A PUDDLE OF soft light, her words barely registering as she spoke, because he was too busy trying not to be overwhelmed by how incredible she looked. Somehow, this cool, collected, in-charge version of her was even sexier than both the va-va-voom screen siren she'd been in the hotel lobby that day or the vivacious party girl she'd been the night she passed out in his arms. And he should know, since he'd spent the last few days remembering how she'd looked both times, right down to the last detail. Had he realized where he would end up this evening when Russell told him yesterday that he needed Finn to fill in for him at some function he couldn't make himself—"one of those endlessly boring cocktail things where you can be in and out in less than an hour," Russell had called it—Finn never would have agreed to come.

Not even if Russell had told him Natalie would be here.

Especially if Russell had told him Natalie would be here.

The last thing he needed was to find himself in close

quarters with her again, inhaling that delicate scent of her and stroking that soft skin, and thinking about how nice it would be to run his mouth over every last inch of her luscious—naked—body.

Like he was right now.

He pushed the thought away and focused on the conversation at hand. So Waterman's friends weren't Natalie's, he thought. Even though they'd all gone to the same school and still obviously saw each other now. Interesting. People like Waterman and his cohorts were the type who generally came out of some tony private academy that produced king makers, chiefs of staff, and Enron executives. So if Dean's friends hadn't been Natalie's, had she been the scholarship kid from the wrong side of the tracks who had never quite fit in? Who hadn't come from the right sort of family or neighborhood to win acceptance from the other kids? Who'd been dismissed as unimportant because she didn't come from money or good breeding stock?

In other words, had she been like Finn? Except that he hadn't gone to a tony private academy, and he still hadn't fit in.

Maybe that was why she was marrying Waterman. So she'd finally be a part of the society into which she'd never been welcomed. Not that Finn could see anyone in that society liking her any better or accepting her any more just because she changed her name and address. And who wanted friends that were only friends under those conditions, anyway? Especially someone like Natalie, who was pretty damned likable no matter where she came from?

"Not your friends, huh?" he echoed, more to keep the conversation going than because he really cared about anyone on the other side of the room.

She shook her head again, but said nothing, just turned to gaze out at the river.

"Then who *are* your friends?"

She opened her mouth to answer him, then closed it again. Finally, she turned to look at him, but it was with an expression that was colored with confusion. "I never really thought about it," she said. "I mean . . . every time I've ever gone to a party or something, all those guys"—she tilted her head toward the other guests—"have been there. And a lot of other people from the same group. I've always socialized with them. But I've never really thought of them as friends."

Finn amended his opinion of her with that. She didn't sound like the kid from the wrong side of the tracks now. Now she sounded like one of the society crowd, and probably had been since birth. Funny, though, how she didn't seem like any of the other people he'd met from the town and country set.

So he repeated his question. "Then who are your friends?"

She seemed to give her answer some thought this time before giving it. "Well, I guess there's Janice, the florist I use for some events. She and I usually meet over lunch to make arrangements."

"That's not necessarily a friend," Finn pointed out. "That's a business associate."

"But we talk about cute guys," Natalie objected. "And shoes. And the latest episode of *Bones*."

"Okay, so maybe Janice would qualify. Who else?"

She thought some more. "Leo. My favorite caterer." Before Finn could point out that Leo was also a business associate, she hurried on, "We e-mail recipes to each other all the time, and we always run into each other in restaurant chats online."

Meaning she and her pal Leo doubtless had more interface time than face time.

"Anyone else?" he asked, even though there had already been a pattern established. It never hurt to have a little extra ammunition when one was about to make a point.

"Myrna," she said. "She's the graphic designer I use for invitations." Hastily, she added, "We visit local galleries together all the time."

"All the time?" he echoed dubiously.

"Well, once we did that," Natalie conceded.

"And did you talk business during this trip to the gallery?"

"No, we did not," she replied a little more defensively than necessary. "In fact, I only brought along those agreements I needed her to sign because I knew I wouldn't be crossing paths with her for the rest of the week, and I needed them back right away."

Finn nodded at that. "Natalie," he said, "every friend you just mentioned you've made since starting your business."

"So?"

"So how long ago was that?"

"Eight months."

"And before eight months ago, you only had, as you call them, 'Dean's friends'?"

"Well, jeez, you don't have to make me sound like some abject, unmitigated loser."

"I wasn't trying to make you sound like that," he denied. "Just pointing out some facts, that's all."

"Yeah, so what's your point?" she asked, turning to gaze out at the river again.

So Finn turned to look at the river, too. It was a nice view, he had to admit. What looked like a dinner cruise of some kind was setting off on an excursion, its cabin and decks dotted with tiny white lights. The evening sky was unbelievable, stained a deep orange, the clouds streaking across it a gauzy pink. Cars were streaming across the bridge in both directions, headlights and taillights both bouncing along the highway. And under it all, the river, rippling slowly and tossing back every bit of light and color it caught.

"So what happens after you marry Dean?" he asked as he watched the dinner cruise coast slowly downriver. "He doesn't strike me as the type to tolerate a working wife. What will happen to all the friends you've met through your job after that?"

Natalie's reply this time was silence. But there was something about it that didn't lend itself to being the sort of comfortable, contemplative silence that a bride-to-be might make while reflecting upon her decision. No, this felt more like the sort of silence a deer in the headlights might make while reflecting upon her imminent death.

Finn discovered the reason for that when he turned to look at Natalie, because deer in the headlights was exactly how she looked. Along with appalled, disgusted, nauseated, revolted, and a host of other adjectives for which Finn would need to consult a thesaurus, most likely under the heading: *ew*.

"What do you mean, when I marry Dean?" she asked, her tone thick with her revulsion. "Who told you I was going to marry Dean?"

Her contempt for the suggestion heartened him way more than it probably should have. "Uh, you told me that."

"Me?" she asked incredulously, turning to face him fully now.

She did so with such speed and vehemence that a tendril of hair freed itself from the severe way she'd styled it, the silky gold tress tumbling down to her jawline. His fingers itched to tug free whatever was holding the rest of her hair in place, so that it could flow down over her shoulders like it had that first day he'd met her and again the other night at the hotel.

Instead, Natalie herself tucked the strand behind one ear and demanded, "When did I tell you I was marrying Dean?"

"Monday night," he said. "At dinner."

Her brows arrowed downward as she tried to remember. Which, okay, might be a little difficult to do, considering her state of intoxication at the time.

So he added, "When you came out of the ladies' room. You and I were talking, and you said you were marrying Dean."

She started to shake her head before he even finished talking. "That's impossible," she told him. "I'd never say that."

"Yes, you did," he insisted, wondering why he was being so adamant about this when he should be rejoicing in the fact that the woman he thought was bound to another man was suddenly free for the taking. His taking. Taking in a way that had nothing to do with driving her somewhere. Except maybe driving her wild.

But her insistence that she would never say she was marrying Waterman made him go back and replay their conversation in his mind. And when he did that, he recalled that her exact words hadn't been that she was marrying Dean.

"You told me Dean wanted to marry you," he said. "And that your mother was already planning the wedding."

"Dean does want to marry me," she agreed. "And my mother's been planning my wedding to him since she made him my escort at my debut without even consulting me."

Debut, Finn repeated to himself. He didn't know a lot about high society, but he knew that if a girl had a debut, it meant she came from money. Probably a lot of money. Having that fact confirmed, he wasn't sure what to think. It seemed like yet another reason for him not to get mixed up with Natalie Beckett. The two worlds they'd grown up in couldn't be farther apart. The night she was walking down the stairs at some country club in her white dress and tiara, he'd probably been stealing *Playboy* and a Colt 45 tallboy from the local drugstore before heading out for a night of petty mischief.

"But there's no way I'd ever marry Dean," Natalie said adamantly, bringing Finn back to the present. "Okay, look. Let me explain what happened Monday night before you and Mr. Mulholland arrived at the restaurant, and why I was in the shape I was in that night."

This ought to be good, Finn thought. "I'm all ears."

She hesitated for a moment, as if she were thinking hard about how to arrange her words. "I admit I was kind of waiting for your employer—"

"You were stalking him, you mean."

She toddled her head back and forth impatiently. "You say *potatoes*, I say *potahtoes*. Anyway, I was waiting in the restaurant because I figured sooner or later, he was bound to eat dinner there."

"You planned to do this every night until you ran into him?"

"If I had to, yes. Fortunately for me," she continued hastily, "I didn't have to wait long. *Un*fortunately for me, however, I ran into Dean before I ran into Mr. Mulholland."

"You really can call him Russell, you know," Finn said. "He hates being called Mr. Mulholland." *Especially by beautiful women,* he added to himself. But there was no reason to make this story last any longer than it had to.

"You have to understand something about Dean and me," she went on as if Finn hadn't spoken. "Ever since we were kids, he's been adamant that someday, he was going to marry me. When I was a kid, the thought of being married to Dean was, like, totally grody. As an adult woman, the thought of being married to Dean is, like, singularly revolting."

Finn tried not to smile too big at that.

"By the time you and Russell saw me Saturday night, I'd been playing a drinking game to make my proximity to Dean more tolerable. Every time he said something stupid, I took a drink."

Okay, there was no way he couldn't smile at that. "And how long had you been playing when Russell and I showed up?" he asked.

"About fifteen minutes."

He arched his brows in surprise at that. "You got that drunk in fifteen minutes?"

"Finn. I had to take a drink every time Dean said something stupid. It's amazing I lasted as long as I did."

Good point.

"So if you think Waterman is a jerk," he said, "and if his friends aren't your friends, and if the only reason you're here tonight is because you thought Russell was coming, and now you know Russell *isn't* coming . . ."

She grinned. "Then why am I staying?"

He grinned back. "Why are *we* staying?" he corrected her. "Hell, I wasn't even invited."

She looked over at the other guests again, then frowned. "But what about Danetta? You can't leave her here alone. Dean will—"

"Dean will never know what hit him," Finn said. "Literally, if there's any justice in the world. Just let me talk to her," he added. "She seems to be getting along fine with everyone over there, and she doesn't get the chance to attend many parties like this. She might want to stay. Even if it means having to talk to Waterman all night."

Finn caught Danetta's eye and dipped his head toward the bar, and she excused herself from the crowd and met him there. He started to explain the situation to her, then realized he honestly wasn't sure what the situation was, other than that he and Natalie wanted to be somewhere else. Though he was pretty sure they both wanted to be somewhere else alone. So he only told Danetta that Natalie wasn't feeling well, and he'd offered to take her home. Instead of seeming inconvenienced, however, Danetta seemed obviously delighted by the news.

"No problem, Finn," she said. "I'm having a surprisingly good time. The way you made it sound, I thought Dean was going to be an asshole."

"Danetta, Dean *is* an asshole."

She made a soft *tsk*ing sound and pursed her lips prettily. "I think he's just misunderstood," she said.

When she looked over at the man in question and smiled, Finn turned his gaze in that direction, too. Waterman was giving her what was probably supposed to be a smoldering look, but which actually made Finn think of those FBI Most Wanted websites, under the heading, "*Sexual Predators.*" Danetta gave him a little one-finger wave, then looked back at Finn.

"Misunderstood," she repeated. "And a guy who just needs . . ." She arched her brows and smiled wistfully. "Who needs a firm hand."

That almost made Finn want to hang around to see what would happen later. Almost. But Natalie was waiting for him, and the night was young, and she looked and smelled better than a woman had a right to look or smell, and they were from two different worlds, which, on second thought, maybe ought to get to know each other better.

"Have fun, Danetta," he told her.

"Oh, I will, Finn. I will. As, I'm sure, will you."

They exchanged a final knowing smile—even though neither could really know what they were getting into tonight—and parted ways. Finn turned around to see that Natalie had already collected her purse and was edging her way toward the front door.

With luck, he thought, Waterman wouldn't even see them leave. And with a little more luck . . .

Well. Suffice it to say, he was suddenly feeling luckier by the minute.

NATALIE SUPPOSED IT HAD BEEN AT THE BACK OF HER head all night that she and Finn would ultimately wind up in his hotel room. It was probably what had made her want to leave Dean's party with him in the first place. Oh, sure, they'd made a big show of driving as far as Frankfort Avenue to have dinner at Varanese, her favorite restaurant in Crescent Hill, where they'd done a lot of talking about lots of important stuff. Stuff like movies and books and the latest episode of *Bones*. And then they'd strolled down to L & N Wine Bar to share a sampler there. And do a lot more talking about lots of other important stuff. Stuff like restaurants and favorite foods and the merits of wine versus beer.

But after that, even though they'd been closer to Natalie's house, they'd somehow found their way back to Finn's room at the Brown instead. Probably because both of them had been dancing around the inevitable all night, maybe even longer. And a man like Finn would want the outcome to be on his turf, not hers. Not that Natalie minded. The thought of . . . the inevitable . . . taking place at her house would make it much more intimate than if it happened at a hotel. Hotels were, after all, the very definition of temporary.

And temporary, she assured herself, was all this would be. Finn wasn't the sort of man to tangle himself up in a relationship. And hey, Natalie wasn't looking for a relationship, anyway. She and Finn found each other attractive. Neither was committed to anyone else. They were consenting adults. Two people who both wanted something and saw no reason to deny themselves. Just because, over the course of the evening—and the week—she'd come to like him . . . a lot . . . that didn't make any difference. She liked lots of people a lot. That didn't mean anything. Necessarily.

She pushed her thoughts away and focused on the man instead. They'd stopped by the bar long enough to order a bottle of wine, then brought it, and two glasses, up to the room with them. She watched as Finn opened the former, his big hands surprisingly graceful as he completed the task. She liked the fact that he could be so comfortable with beer and wine, appreciated how he seemed at home in both high society and low. Of course, he was the sort of man who could make hosing out garbage cans look like high art—not to mention really, really hot—but that was beside the point. The point was . . .

Ah, hell. Natalie had forgotten what the point was. Just that Finn was here with her now, and that was all that mattered.

"I like the city you call home, Natalie," he said as he splashed wine into each of the glasses.

She smiled. "Thanks. I like it, too. It's kind of a little-known secret, I think. People who visit for the first time are always kind of surprised at what a great restaurant scene and arts community we have here."

He picked up both glasses and crossed the room to where she stood, looking out the window at the city lights beyond.

She accepted the glass extended toward her and continued, "When I was a teenager, I used to think I'd move somewhere else after I graduated from college, but I honestly can't imagine living anywhere else now."

She hadn't meant for the comment to sound like she was fishing for what Finn's intentions might be, but somehow, it came out sounding that way. Finn seemed to think so, too, because he paused with his glass halfway to his mouth, then lowered it again, staring into it instead of looking at Natalie.

So she figured, what the hell, and went for broke. "I mean, everything you could possibly want, you can find it here. The winters aren't too harsh, and the summers aren't too unbearable, and the springs and autumns are spectacular. The people are friendly, and the community's diverse. It's a nice place to raise kids." She wasn't sure why she added that last. It wasn't as if she had plans to start a family at any point in the near future. Maybe she just needed to be clear on everything before they got started. So she'd know what she was getting herself into. If there was any chance—

"I'm a West Coast boy, born and bred, Natalie. I like Seattle, even if it hasn't always been the kindest city to me. It's where Russell's center of operations is. Where my life is."

She nodded at that. Okay. So now she was clear on everything.

Finn seemed to think it necessary to clarify it further, though, because he added, "Look, Natalie, I like you. I like being with you. I don't think I'm wrong in assuming we both know where this is headed tonight."

"No, you're not wrong about that," she agreed.

"Then I think you need to know that when my evenings end this way, it's without strings. It happens because of a physical reaction, not an emotional one." He smiled a little halfheartedly. "An itch that needs to be scratched, you know?"

She nodded again.

"And that's okay with you?" he asked.

Instead of answering him, she lifted a hand to his cheek, closed her eyes, and pressed her mouth lightly to his. Then, gingerly, she brushed her lips along the strong line of his jaw, down the column of his throat, and into the open collar of his shirt. He smelled so good, a fusion of heat and night and man, and his skin was warm and rough and weathered everywhere she touched him. He was so different from the men she normally met, so much more masculine, so much more confident, so much more daunting, so much more . . .

Just so much more. And he was hers. For tonight. And she told herself that would be enough.

When she moved her hand to his chest, he curled his finger beneath her chin and tilted her head back so that she was looking at him. Then he lowered his head to hers, slowly . . . slowly . . . oh, so slowly . . . and covered her mouth with his. As he deepened the kiss, he circled her waist with both arms to pull her against him, opening his mouth wider. She felt his hands skim lightly over her back, first tracing her spine, then curving over her shoulder blades, then caressing her nape, then tangling in her hair. Instinctively, she lifted her own hands to touch him, too, brushing her palms over his rough face, then along his muscular shoulders, through his silky hair, relishing the heat, the strength, the power that passed beneath her fingertips.

He seemed to touch her everywhere. Each time she inhaled, she filled her nose with the scent of him and her mouth with the taste of him. His heart pounded against hers, their pulses mixing and mingling until she couldn't tell which was whose. Their breathing became fierce and ragged when his kiss grew more possessive, until it was as if the breath that gave them life joined to become one, too.

With one hand still buried in her hair, Finn drove the other down to her hip, gradually inching it lower to curve

over her fanny and push her body into his. Natalie jerked
her hips upward, rubbing her pelvis against his, sinuously,
seductively, answering his growl of satisfaction with one of
her own. He pushed his hand higher, until he encountered
the buttons at the side of her shirt, and as he freed them,
one, two, three, he danced her away from the window and
closer to his bed. Then he bunched the silky fabric in his
fist and drew it upward, until she could feel a whisper of
warm air on her heated back. His fingers stole to the clo-
sure of her bra and made short work of it, and he splayed
his fingers wide over her naked skin and tasted her more
deeply still.

So Natalie tugged free his shirttails and dipped her hand
inside, guiding her fingers over the swells of muscle and
sinew on his back. Then she moved her hand to his front,
skimming the soft hair of his chest and the bumps of musculature along his torso. He was hard where she was soft,
planed where she was curved, rough where she was smooth.
But he was as hot as she was, as needy, as demanding.

She felt his hand at her waist, tugging down the side zip-
per on her pants, felt the airy crepe pool around her ankles
as it fell. He tucked his hand under the lacy fabric of her
panties, curving over her bare flesh, stroking her sensitive
skin until she grew damp between her legs. But when he
dipped one confident finger into the delicate cleft of her
behind, she nearly came undone.

"Oh," she murmured against his lips. "Oh, Finn . . ."

But he covered her mouth again before she could say
more. Not that there was anything else to say. Much better
to do. Do things to him and with him, and let him do
things to her in return. Seeming to understand, he filled
her mouth with his tongue and drove his other hand into
her panties, pushing her hard against his ripening erection.
In turn, Natalie wedged her hand between their bodies and
pressed her palm to the full length of him, rubbing him
through the fabric of his trousers until he murmured a satisfied sound. He moved himself against her, increasing her
rhythm, so she unfastened and opened his pants, too, and

dipped her hand inside to cover him, bare skin on bare skin, the way he was touching her. He was so big, so hot, so hard in her hand. She curled her fingers over the taut head of his cock, then circled them fully around his long shaft to caress him.

For long moments, they only kissed and touched, until one of them—and Natalie wasn't sure if it was Finn or her—finally started moving, slowly and deliberately over the short distance that was left between them and the bed. Finn skimmed her shirt and bra from her shoulders, then turned her around so that her back was facing him. He pushed her hair aside to place a soft, chaste kiss on her nape, then pulled her back against him, his hard cock surging against her back, sending fire through her entire body. When he nuzzled the curve where her neck joined her shoulder, she reached back with both hands to weave her fingers through his hair. She deliberately chose the position so Finn could cover her breasts with both hands, and when he did, she arched her back to push herself more completely into his touch.

He dragged his mouth along the sensitive flesh of her neck and shoulder, his hot palms squeezing and stroking and caressing her breasts. As he rolled her nipple under the pad of his thumb, his other hand brushed lower, along the tender skin of her torso, his middle finger slipping into her navel as he passed it. Then he pushed his hand into her panties, found her hot, wet center, and buried his fingers in the sensitive folds of her flesh.

She gasped at the sensation that shot through her, her fingers tightening in his hair. Still kneading her breast with one hand, he stroked her between her legs with the other, long, leisurely strokes that pushed her to the brink of sanity. He settled his thumb on her clitoris and furrowed all four fingers through her labia, first slow, then fast, then shallow, then deep. Her body went still as he touched her, her breathing coming in rapid little gasps. Bit by bit, he altered his movements, steering his hand back and forth, left and right, drawing circles and spirals until Natalie was rocked by an orgasm that seized her body and sent heat shuddering through her.

For a moment, she felt as if she would stay like this forever, her body fused to Finn's clever hand, her heart racing in time with his. Then the moment sifted away, and so did she, and she turned to just kiss him and kiss him and kiss him.

After undressing each other, they made their way to the side of the bed, Finn settling both hands on Natalie's hips as she curled her fingers over his shoulders. He sat and pulled her into his lap facing him, her legs straddling his thighs, opening her to him completely. He roped an arm around her waist and kissed her again, hungry and urgent and deep. She dropped her hand to the head of his cock, palming him again, using the wet release of his passion to lubricate her hand and stroke him, long, leisurely strokes, the way his had been for her. Finn murmured something dark and erotic under his breath, then curled his hands over her ass, matching his caresses to hers and mimicking both in the movement of his tongue inside her mouth.

He lay back, pulling her down with him, atop him, then turned their bodies so that Natalie lay on her back and he was on his side, one heavy leg draped over both of hers and his hand open wide over her belly. He kissed her jaw, her cheek, her temple, her forehead, then moved down to her throat, her collarbone, her breast. There, he took his time, flattening his tongue over her nipple before pulling it into his mouth, taunting it with the tip of his tongue and then releasing it to lick it more fully. He covered her other breast with his hand, catching her nipple between the V of his index and middle fingers, squeezing gently and lighting more fires inside her. Natalie spread her legs and lifted her hips and rubbed herself against his thigh, panting at the myriad sensations spiraling through her.

Finn seemed to understand, because after a few more hungry tastes of her breast, he continued his journey downward, this time tasting her navel as he passed it and tracing the skin beneath with his tongue. He pushed open Natalie's legs to duck his head between them, his tongue taking up where his fingers had left off, moving confidently over her without a single hesitation. He lapped leisurely with the flat of his tongue, then drew sensuous circles with the tip. He grabbed a pillow and shoved it beneath her fanny to lift her higher, parting her lips with his thumbs so that he could lick her more intimately and penetrate her with his tongue. Then he penetrated her with his finger, too, inserting it deep.

Ribbons of pleasure purled through her, starting low in her belly and rippling outward, until her body began to tremble. Sensing how close she was to coming, Finn moved again, this time kneeling before her. He grasped an ankle in each hand and opened her legs wide, then pulled her forward to bury himself *deep* inside her. Hooking her legs over his shoulders, he pulled her body up more, and for long moments jerked himself hard against her, his cock buried in her. Then he lowered their bodies to the mattress, bracing both elbows on each side of her and thrust himself forward again. Over and over, he bucked his hips against hers, going deeper with each new penetration, opening her wider to receive him. She wrapped her fingers tightly around his biceps as he thrust, taking as much of him as she could, until they both cried out with the their explosive completion.

For one long moment, they clung to each other, their bodies quaking with the final remnants of their climax. Then Finn fell to the bed beside Natalie, facedown, one hand draped over her waist, the other arcing over her head.

It was then that her confidence about what she had allowed to happen between them began to slip. Because she realized that what she'd been so sure would only be a physical release had instead been something else entirely. She knew then that one night with Finn would never be enough. She knew he would be leaving in a matter of days.

She knew that in a little over a week, he'd be back in Seattle, thousands of miles away.

And she knew that in a little over a week, her life would never be the same again.

· Thirteen ·

RUSSELL LAY AMID THE TANGLE OF SHEETS IN THE
king-sized bed and listened to the sound of the shower
running in the bathroom on the other side of the hotel
suite. He was trying to remember if even he had ever paid
for two different hotel rooms in one night and was pretty
sure he hadn't. But he and Amber couldn't have gone back
to the Brown Hotel after closing the bar at Proof on Main,
since Max would have been there, and it had been so easy
to simply get a room at 21C as the hotel was right above
them and certainly in keeping with his standards—i.e., as
expensive as he could find. Since he'd never been afforded
the luxury of spending money when he was young, he had
a lot of making up to do now. Though certainly the spare,
contemporary decor washed in the bright light of dawn
was the ultimate opposite of the Brown's dark, sumptuous
splendor, it had served his needs quite well.

As had Amber. And, all modesty aside, if her, ah, enthusiasm the night before was any indication, he had served
her needs quite well, too.

When she'd sat down across from him at Vincenzo's, he

honestly hadn't thought the night would end this way. Oh, he'd been certain it would after asking her out at Minxxx, since his modesty in that regard was nonexistent. But once he'd discovered that, outside her natural habitat, Amber's vivid plumage dulled and molted, he just hadn't thought he'd be interested. He liked bad girls. Women who wore too much makeup and too little clothing. Women whose morals were easily compromised and whose principles were conveniently forgotten. Or, better still, whose morals *and* principles were enjoyably nonexistent.

Not that Amber was a good girl by any stretch of the imagination, in spite of her clean-scrubbed looks. She did work at Minxxx, after all. And she had checked into a hotel for the sole purpose of having sex with a man she had known a matter of hours and met him in a place like Minxxx. And her sexual appetite had been as voracious as Russell's own, and as slow to satisfy. Even after that third coupling, they'd wanted more but had had to resort to oral gratification to achieve it.

Never in his life had he enjoyed sex more than he had last night. Not with a stranger. Not with a girlfriend. Not even with his wife.

And yet there was something about Amber that reminded him of Marti just the same. He had no idea why. The two women had absolutely nothing in common. Marti had been tall and willowy, her Mediterranean heritage evident in her olive skin and short black hair and eyes the color of espresso. She'd worn bright colors and lots of . . . stuff . . . with her clothes. Scarves, necklaces, long, dangly earrings. She had laughed loudly and a lot, had never judged anyone, had been the peacekeeper in every situation that grew tense. And once Max had come along, she'd become the quintessential earth mother, wrapping the baby to her body with bright batiks, buying only organic food, breast-feeding in public and turning the tables on anyone who expressed disapproval, asking them in that soft, sweet, conciliatory voice what they could possibly find distasteful about motherhood.

Amber was . . . Well, not the quintessential earth mother,

that was for sure. She was small and curvy and pale, es-
chewing all decoration on her person. She didn't laugh
loudly. She didn't laugh at all. Oh, there had been smiles
and chuckles during the evening they'd spent together, but
Amber kept a tight rein on her emotions that she never
once eased. And as far as being nonjudgmental or a peacekeeper, she seemed to have strong opinions—particularly
about men—and she'd spoken them freely and without fear
of reprisal during the hours they had been together before
checking into the hotel.

Then again, considering her line of work, Russell supposed her opinion of men would naturally be less than fa-
vorable. And, then again . . . again . . . he supposed he did
objectify women. Some women, anyway. Like those who
worked in strip clubs.

Amber, however, transcended objectification. Although
she had behaved predictably in some ways—like landing
in bed with him—she hadn't in others. Her openness and
uncompromising opinions and frank way of speaking was
a refreshing change from all the cloying yes-people who
normally surrounded Russell, telling him what they thought
he wanted to hear. Even if he didn't agree with her about
many of her convictions, he'd still enjoyed sparring with
her last night. Over the course of the evening, no subject
had been taboo. They'd covered politics (hers were considerably more liberal than his), religion (hers borrowed from
a variety of belief systems where his was nonexistent),
sports (she'd nearly thrown her drink in his face when he
told her he thought Mike Krzyzewski was the greatest
university basketball coach of all time), art (she liked the
Pre-Raphaelites where the only movement he could think
of was, um, none of them), and movies (her favorite was
Jean Cocteau's *La Belle et la Bête* where his was *Meet the
Fockers*).

But even more troubling than his enjoyment of their
time together was the fact that, the more he had looked at
her last night—and he'd looked at her a lot last night—the
more stunning she'd grown. Truly, stunning. There was

something about her quiet beauty that appealed to him even more than the overblown cocktail waitress disguise she wore for work that had drawn his eye in the first place. By the time they'd concluded their dinner at Vincenzo's—and loaded up nearly a dozen boxes worth of leftovers—he'd stopped seeing her as Amber. In fact, as the evening wore on, he'd stopped calling her by name, since he realized he didn't know it. Didn't know her. By the time they'd checked into the hotel, he'd barely been able to remember the woman he'd met at Minxxx.

So why had he checked into the hotel with her, when she wasn't the woman he'd asked out? And why did he find himself this morning wanting so desperately to know her real name?

He heard the water shut off in the bathroom and rose from the bed to locate his clothing. While he was looking, though, his gaze fell on the little black purse that had fallen to the floor the moment he'd kicked the door shut behind them. He strode over to collect it, and with a cursory glance over his shoulder to see that the bathroom door was still closed, flipped it open. It was so small, he found her driver's license immediately and pulled it out, quickly and effortlessly memorizing the information upon it before tucking it back inside and closing the purse again.

Virginia Collins. That was her real name. He smiled at the connotation. Who had named her after the virgin queen? Was that the name she went by, or had she or someone else shortened it to a nickname along the way? Ginny? Ginna? Gin? Yes, that last suited her much better. He laughed lightly. Gin Collins. Now *that* was the name of a woman who worked in a cocktail lounge.

Her address indicated she lived in a house, not an apartment, on a street called Southern Parkway, in the 40214 zip code. Shouldn't be hard to find, he thought. And now that he had her real name, it shouldn't be difficult to discover other things about her. Normally, he'd assign the task to Finn or one of his other security guys, but not this time. Virginia Collins was a secret Russell wanted to keep to himself for now. He had no idea why. Probably because he'd never asked anyone on his staff to look into the background of any of the other women he'd dated. He'd never cared about the background of any of the other women he'd dated.

And he was also still wondering about that phone call he'd seen her making in the bar, on his phone, when he returned from the hotel check-in the night before.

When he finally approached her, she'd claimed she was only playing Tetris while she waited for him to return, since she didn't have it on her own phone, but Russell had known she was lying. For one thing, her purse was too small to be holding *any* phone. For another, he didn't have Tetris on his phone, either. And for a third thing, he'd seen her talking into the phone when he'd reentered the bar, then had stepped out of her view to watch her and see how long the conversation lasted. Only moments before, the two of them had been necking and groping in a secluded booth at the back of the bar. As he'd slipped his hand between her parted legs and fingered her through her wet panties, she'd rubbed her open palm over the length of his cock, and almost in unison, they'd groaned something about getting a room. While Russell went to do just that, Amber—or, rather, Virginia—had made a call to someone, presumably to tell that person she wouldn't be coming home tonight.

So who might that person have been? A husband? A lover? And what reason had she given for not coming home?

He heard the hair dryer switch on in the bathroom, so he hurriedly pulled on his trousers and shirt, leaving the latter open and ignoring the rest of his attire of the night before. Except for his suit jacket. That he picked up off the floor and reached inside it to retrieve his phone, switching it on. Then he pulled up the last number dialed. A local call, prefix 363, made at 1:54 a.m. He pulled up the Internet and typed the number into a search engine, and wasn't much surprised to see that the number belonged to one Virginia Collins who lived on Southern Parkway in Louisville.

So Virginia/Ginny/Ginna/Gin—and the more he thought about it, the more she was definitely a Gin—had called home last night to tell someone she wasn't going to be home until morning. Somehow, Russell didn't think a husband or lover would have been too keen on hearing such news. A mother probably wouldn't be, either, unless she was used to that sort of thing from her daughter, in which case, why would the daughter, an adult woman who worked in a strip club, even bother calling home?

But, he thought further, a spiral of something he wasn't sure he wanted to identify curling up from somewhere deep in his belly, a child—or a child's caretaker—would need to know if its mother wasn't going to be home. And unless Amber had given birth when she was negative five, chances were good any child she had wasn't old enough to fend for itself. So she must have been calling the sitter.

Good God, he thought, looking at the bathroom door into which the most exquisite ass he had ever beheld had disappeared only moments ago. That exquisite ass belonged to a mother. He had bedded someone's mother last night. Had done unbelievably erotic things to and with a woman who had a child of some age at home. Had received unbelievably erotic gratification from her in return. Such a possibility had never occurred to him.

He waited for what should have been, at best, shock, and, at worst, revulsion, to wind through him. He waited to be appalled by the knowledge that he had aided and abetted in the corruption of a mother.

Then he reminded himself that he and Marti hadn't stopped having sex just because she'd given birth to their son. On the contrary, after Max's birth, because they hadn't had the leisure—or energy—to enjoy sex that they'd had before he was born, their lovemaking had taken on a new, more intense quality that had often been more satisfying than the hours-long lovemaking they had enjoyed as newlyweds. And there had been something about the knowledge that she had nurtured and created a life—albeit with a little help from him—that had provided a new, more powerful dimension to her that had inexplicably turned him on and made him even randier.

Even at that, though, the way it had been with Russell and Marti hadn't been anything like how it had been between him and Gin last night. Marti had never been as passionate, as enthusiastic, as adventurous as Gin. She had drawn the line at a few less conventional positions and actions that Gin had actually instigated herself. Last night had been . . .

He felt his cock twitch just thinking about it. Last night had been like no other night he'd ever experienced. And Gin wasn't like any woman he had ever met before.

He heard the hair dryer switch off in the bathroom. Twenty minutes ago, a woman had entered that room whom Russell had known only as Amber, a cocktail waitress at a strip club who was surprisingly interesting to talk to and extraordinarily passionate in bed. Now, without even talking to her, he knew so much more about her that he hadn't known before. What was beginning to bother him, though, was that he knew more about himself, too.

And for the life of him, he had no idea what to make of any of that new knowledge.

GINNY TOOK ONE LAST LOOK AT HERSELF IN THE bathroom mirror, trying to come up with any other reason for staying in the bathroom a few minutes longer. Russell had been sleeping when she first woke, his body spooning hers from shoulder to toe, his arm draped over her waist, his hand gently cupping her breast. His erection had been pushing forcefully against her fanny, making her instantly aroused, and she'd had to close her eyes and mentally fight back the waves of desire that rocked her. No matter how much she might want him again, there was no way her body would accept him without discomfort.

Good God, what had come over her last night? She had never, *ever* gone to bed with a man so soon after meeting him. And she'd never, *ever* had the kind of sex with any man that she'd enjoyed with Russell last night. Key word there, *enjoyed*. Because Ginny had never enjoyed sex, not really. Not even when she was a teenager, discovering it for the first time. The boys back then had been too eager to satisfy themselves than to bother with her pleasure. And the men since then . . . Well, they'd been too eager to satisfy themselves to bother with her pleasure, too. But Russell had seemed to enjoy the touching and kissing and caressing and tasting even more than Ginny had. He'd seemed to get off on watching her get off more than he'd enjoyed coming himself. She'd just never met a man like him, that was all. Even without the billions.

She wished she could explain away her behavior by having had too much to drink or simply being overcome by the larger-than-life man. But neither of those things was true. Whatever wine or champagne she'd consumed had been with large amounts of food and over the long course of the evening. She'd barely even felt buzzed at any point last night. And instead of being larger-than-life, Russell had seemed more and more down-to-earth with every passing hour. She even forgave him for the Mike Krzyzewski comment, which anyone in the commonwealth of Kentucky—Cards *or* Cats fan—would tell you was a pretty major thing to forgive. She wasn't sure when it happened, but at some point last night, she realized she'd forgotten all about the fact that he was Russell Mulholland, billionaire and former *People* magazine Sexiest Man Alive. He was just a nice, sexy man whose company she enjoyed. And then, that first time he kissed her in the bar downstairs . . .

Well, she guessed she just forgot who she was, too.

And when he'd suggested they get a room, she hadn't even hesitated in saying yes. Never in her life had Ginny wanted anything the way she'd wanted Russell in that moment.

When she'd hurriedly called home to tell Hazel not to expect her until morning, she'd hadn't been sure if her friend had been happy about the news or concerned. All Ginny had told Hazel before going out was that she was meeting a friend for drinks, something that could have meant anything. Hazel had been badgering her for years to find a nice man, start dating, and scratch the itch all normal women feel, but she probably hadn't meant Ginny should do all that in one night.

Ginny appreciated Hazel's encouragement, but she'd just never trusted any man enough to let him into her life. Not with herself, and not with her daughter. She'd always thought that someday, after Maisy was grown and on her own, she might, maybe, possibly, perhaps be open to dating. But she'd figured any guy she went out with would be like her. Working-class. A survivor of tough times. Rough around the edges. Not expecting too much in the opposite sex department. Never in her wildest dreams had she thought she would meet a man like Russell.

Never in her wildest dreams had she thought she would *like* a man like Russell. Like him more than she should. Like him in a way where she knew she would remember him for the rest of her life. In a way that made her realize that a working-class, survivor-of-tough-times, rough-around-the-edges guy would never be enough to make her content.

Because he had more than fulfilled his promise to give her one evening unlike any she could imagine. He'd more than fulfilled Ginny, too. Now it was time to tell him good-bye.

Maybe he'd be gone when she came out of the bathroom, she told herself. Maybe he'd awoken while she was in here, and when he'd heard the shower running, had seen it as the perfect opportunity to slip out without having to deal with all that messy morning-after cleanup.

Well, *duh*. Of *course* that was what he'd done. That's what guys like him always did. They got what they wanted, then they booked. The last thing they wanted to do was talk to a woman after a night like they'd had.

She waited for the ribbon of relief that should have wound through her at the knowledge there wouldn't be any awkwardness. Waited to feel the gratitude she should have experienced at not having to tell him good-bye. Instead, a spear of distress lanced through her. She really would never see him again. And she really would never forget him.

She gave herself a moment to let that settle in, her body feeling heavier and more unwieldy as it did. Then she cinched the sash of the white cotton robe tighter and, resigned to finding an empty room on the other side, strode slowly out.

Only to find Russell, half-dressed and smiling, sitting on the bed waiting for her, looking even more handsome and charming than he had the night before. Something else wound through her body then, but she dared not try to identify it. She started to move toward him, but his next words stopped her dead in her tracks.

"Good morning, Virginia," he greeted her. "Or do your friends and family call you something else?"

"Ginny," she answered automatically, her voice scarcely a whisper. How had he . . . ? When did he . . . ? Why was he . . . ? "I . . . I usually go by Ginny."

"Ginny then," he said amiably. "Though I've been thinking Gin suits you better. Can I call you Gin?"

She nodded, not sure she trusted herself to say anything. If he knew her first name, he already knew way more about her than she wanted him to. Then the first part of what he said gelled in her fuzzy brain. "Just how long have you been thinking Gin suits me better?"

"Since I saw your driver's license," he replied without hesitation.

She swallowed hard against the fear rising from her belly. "And where and when did you see my driver's license?"

"Just now. When I went through your purse."

"You went through—"

"Yes."

"Why?"

"Because I wanted to know your real name, and you wouldn't tell me."

"But I didn't think . . ."

"It was a good idea for me to know your real name?" he

finished for her. "Because I might turn out to be some kind of paranoid psychotic schizophrenic stalker?"

Actually, she hadn't thought he'd wanted it for any reason other than that it gave him more power over her. But that had been last night, before she'd willingly surrendered every bit of power to him, right around the moment he touched her for the first time.

It occurred to her then that if he'd seen her driver's license, then he also knew her last name and her home address. Normally, she'd freak out if a guy she'd just met had that much information about her. With Russell, though, the knowledge didn't strike nearly as much panic as it should. And somehow she knew that had nothing to do with his celebrity and reputation and everything to do with the way he'd made her feel last night. Even before the sex. Especially before the sex.

"I took the liberty of ordering some breakfast from room service," he said when she contributed nothing further. "Checkout isn't for another three hours, which gives us plenty of time. To talk," he finished, his grin growing devilish.

"About what?" she said. "We covered everything last night."

"Oh, I wouldn't say everything," he told her.

"Politics, religion, sports, entertainment," she reminded him. "What's left?" Then, feigning a *silly me* pose with one hand on her hip and the other tapping her forehead, she quickly added, "Silly me. Fashion. How could we have forgotten that?" She smiled in response to his own. "Probably because that's just *such* a controversial topic, and we didn't want to spoil the nice evening we were having."

"I know what we can talk about," Russell volunteered.

Afraid to even ask, but certain he wasn't going to drop the subject—whatever it was—she said, "What's that?"

He hesitated, but his gaze met hers intently. "Your daughter."

Something cold and oily settled deep in the pit of her stomach. How had he found out about Maisy? "I never talk about my daughter," she said adamantly. "Not with anyone." And although she figured billionaires had ways of finding out anything they wanted to, she still demanded, "How do you know about my daughter?"

He smiled again. "I didn't. Not until you confirmed it just now. I was only fishing."

She closed her eyes and shook her head. She was such a sucker.

"But I saw you calling someone on my phone last night before I returned to the bar and figured you were calling someone to tell them you wouldn't be home. And since that wasn't the sort of thing you were likely to tell a husband or boyfriend, I figured you must have been letting the babysitter know. As for the gender of the child . . . That was just a guess. I figured I had a fifty-fifty chance of being right. And even if I wasn't, I thought . . . hoped . . . you might slip up and say something like, 'Oh, no, it's a son.'"

Ginny opened her eyes again, her tension easing not at all. She wasn't sure why she didn't want Russell to know about Maisy, other than for the same reason she didn't want any men to know about Maisy. Because she worried about her daughter's safety in this age of predators and sexual advertising. But Russell wasn't any man. He wasn't a stranger now, and in a way, he hadn't been the night before. And he was a father himself.

Maybe her desire had nothing to do with Maisy and everything to do with herself. Maybe there was a part of her that still wanted him to see her as Amber, cocktail waitress at a strip club. Not because that made her sexier or more exotic or more attractive, but because Amber could handle men a lot better than Ginny could. And it would be a lot easier for Amber to part ways with a guy like Russell than it would be for Ginny.

"I won't ask why you didn't mention her last night," he continued. "A woman who won't even tell a man her real name certainly isn't going to reveal the fact that she has a child waiting for her at home. But this morning . . ." His voice trailed off, and he shrugged. "Well, I just thought maybe things had changed enough between us that you might be more amenable to talking about her. To talking about yourself."

That caught Ginny off guard. "Have things changed with us since last night?" she asked.

He seemed puzzled by the question. "Don't you think they have?"

Instead of answering, she turned the tables on him. "Do you?"

He opened his mouth to reply, then closed it again, as if he didn't want to be the one to play his hand first. Too bad, Ginny thought. She wasn't about to play her own hand first. She had way more to lose than he did. She didn't even want to up the ante any further.

"I'm a parent myself, you know," he replied instead.

She nodded. "I know."

"My son, Max, is fourteen."

"I know."

"He lost his mother when he was a baby. He doesn't remember her."

Ginny knew that, too, just as everyone else who'd read that *People* magazine article did. But there hadn't been much else in the story about his son. She'd assumed it was because he didn't have much time to spend with the boy while trying to run a multibillion dollar corporation. But maybe, like she, he just wanted to protect his child and keep him out of the eye of anyone who might take advantage of him.

So she relented some and told him, "My daughter doesn't remember her father, either. But that's because she never knew him."

"Does he know about her?"

Oh, yeah, Ginny thought. This was another reason she didn't want to talk about Maisy. Because people started asking questions like that. "Kind of," she replied.

Russell arched his brows in surprise at that. "Kind of?"

"I told him I was pregnant after I found out."

"And what did he say?"

She sighed heavily. "He backhanded me across my face a couple of times and told me to get rid of it. I took off before he could do anything more to help that along."

Russell said nothing in response to that, but his expression grew hard. So Ginny figured, what the hell. She might as well tell him the rest of it. Once he knew, there was no way he'd hang around. Then she wouldn't have to tell him good-bye. He'd be out of there faster than she could say, *Wrong side of the tracks.*

"It happened when I was fifteen. He and I had both run away from home and were squatting in a house with a bunch of other street kids. After he"—she expelled a shaky breath—"hit me, I knew I couldn't go back there. But I couldn't go home, either. I had this stepfather problem, you see, and a mother who had raised denial to an art form."

Russell's expression then turned as cold and hard as granite. "Did he—"

"No," she replied quickly. "But he tried. A few times. My mom didn't believe me when I tried to tell her, so I took off. I did okay on the streets until I got pregnant. Not great, but okay. But I knew I couldn't raise a kid. Not like that. So I got help from a cop who'd busted me a few months earlier for shoplifting. She set me up with some good people, and by the time Mai . . . by the time my daughter was born," she hastily amended, "I knew I wanted to keep her and raise her myself. By then, the cop had become a friend, and she was close to retirement, so she sort of unofficially adopted me. That's who I called last night, because she lives with me and takes care of Mai . . . of my daughter while I . . ."

She started to say, *Go to school and work,* but finished with a simple "work," because it was Amber who did that and Ginny who went to school. And right now, Ginny needed Amber way more than she needed herself.

Russell said nothing for a long time after she concluded her story, only studied her face and met her gaze fiercely, as if daring her to look away. But Ginny didn't look away. She would never apologize for who she had been or who she was now. Accept responsibility, sure. Be accountable, you bet. But apologize? Never.

"You were a street kid," he finally said, punctuating the comment with a period, not a question mark.

She nodded.

"Arrested for shoplifting." Another sentence. Not a question.

"Among other things," she admitted. "Nothing heinous like prostitution or drugs, but I've got more than one B and E on my record. A few burglaries. Mostly because I needed a warm place to sleep or something to eat."

He nodded at that. "You had your daughter when you were fifteen?"

"I was fifteen when I got pregnant. I was sixteen when she was born."

"That would make her how old now?"

"Thirteen." She smiled, unable to help herself. "Thirteen going on thirty-five."

"My son is fourteen." He smiled back. "Fourteen going on thirty-five. What does your daughter want to be when she grows up?"

Ginny crossed her arms over her midsection and took a few experimental steps toward the bed. When she'd first come out of the shower to find him there, she'd thought he just wanted to have sex one more time before leaving, to start his day off right. Now, however, she realized he wanted to have an, ah, intercourse of another kind. One that was even more intimate.

She climbed into the bed and piled a few pillows against the headboard the way Russell had, then curled her legs up beside her. "Maisy," she began, suddenly unafraid to tell him her daughter's name, "wants to be the CEO of a Fortune 500 company. How about your son?"

Russell smiled at that, too, but this time it was one of those full-blown grins that just about made a woman want to spontaneously combust. "Does she now?" he replied instead of answering her question about his son.

Ginny nodded, unable to disguise her pride in her daughter. "She's been involved with this group called Kids, Inc., since she was ten. It's *such* a wonderful organization, but so woefully underfunded. It teaches disadvantaged kids about entrepreneurship and business and how to take an idea and turn it into a viable product. She's become quite the little capitalist."

He nodded his approval, which didn't come as any shock. "My son, Max, wants to be a professional skateboarder," he said. "Or a professional surfer. Or a professional snowboarder. But if none of those things works out, he'll deign to play for the NBA."

Ginny laughed at that. Kids and their unrealistic dreams. Then again, she thought, when she was Maisy's age, she hadn't had any dreams at all. She started to say something else about her daughter, but a knock on the door halted her. It was punctuated by a muffled announcement of room service, so Russell rose from the bed to answer.

"Looks like we'll be finishing our conversation over breakfast," he said as he strode across the suite. "And then, afterward . . ." He paused before turning the doorknob. "We can make plans for the rest of the day."

"As long as I'm home by two thirty," she said. "That's when I have to leave to pick Maisy up at school."

"Not a problem," Russell assured her. "Maybe, eventually, we could even . . ."

"What?" she asked when his voice trailed off.

"Well. Maybe, eventually, we could even make an excursion as a . . . foursome."

Something inside Ginny warmed at that, a gentle, affectionate warmth for the innocence of the suggestion. He wanted her to meet his son, and he wanted to meet her daughter. She did her best not to feel too hopeful about that. Chances were good he just wanted his son to have someone close to his age to hang out with for a day. Maybe he just wanted Ginny and Maisy to take them sightseeing.

But maybe, just maybe, there was a little more to it than that.

· Fourteen ·

THE SECOND TIME NATALIE AWOKE IN FINN'S BED, things were very different from the first time. For one thing, where she'd awoken on top of the bedspread that first time, now she was tangled amid a bundle of sheets. For another thing, where she'd been dressed that first time, now she was, um, not. For yet another thing, where she'd been alone that first time, now she was, um, not. And for a still another thing, where before she'd been reasonably confident no one had copped a feel after dumping her onto the mattress, now she was *extremely* confident that there had been a lot more than feeling going on.

The problem—not that all those other things didn't present their own unique dilemmas, mind you—was that, at least in Natalie's case, the feeling had gone way beyond the physical.

And therein lay the biggest problem and dilemma of all. When it came to feelings, she sincerely doubted that Finn was of the same mind as she. For him, last night had been about the physical. He'd more than made that clear before their lovemaking.

Sex, she corrected herself. To him, it had been sex. To her, it had been . . . something else. Something more. Something she probably shouldn't even try to identify since there were so many reasons not to.

She closed her eyes and replayed the entire evening in her mind, trying to figure out where the road to physical attraction had taken an abrupt detour into emotional need. No, not detour, she corrected herself. Detour suggested that she would eventually come out safely on the other side and return to her normal route. After the night she'd spent with Finn, there was no way she could go back to her usual way of doing things.

Wrong turn, she amended. At some point last night, she'd made a wrong turn off Physical Avenue and onto Emotional Street, which appeared to be one-way. Then again, she was beginning to think her emotions had become engaged long before last night. Otherwise, last night never would have happened. Natalie wasn't the kind of woman to succumb to physical desire just because she needed to, as Finn had said, "scratch an itch." Oh, maybe she'd told herself that last night, but it had been her conscious mind speaking, not her subconscious. Because now that her itch had been scratched, she was in no way satisfied. On the contrary, she wanted more. Way more. More than Finn, she was certain, was willing to give. Last night hadn't been a physical response to a sexual attraction. It had been the physical response to feelings she'd been having since . . .

Well. Maybe since that first day sitting at the bar in BBC trading lighthearted jabs. Maybe since that conversation when he'd opened up about the past he shared with Russell. Maybe since that moment in her kitchen when he leaned in close behind her and his scent surrounded her. Maybe since last night when he walked into Dean's place with a breathtaking blonde on his arm.

Then again, the *when* of it really didn't matter, did it? Nor did the *why*, *where*, or *how*. What mattered was the *who*. And what Natalie was going to do now.

She opened her eyes again, waiting for her vision to

adjust to the semidarkness of the room. When it did, she saw Finn's face mere inches from her own. They were sharing a pillow—she remembered how he'd tucked the other one under her fanny last night to bring her closer to his voracious mouth—and he had draped both an arm and a leg affectionately over her body.

Affectionately, hah, she immediately chastised herself. Possessively was more like it. And he wasn't being possessive because he wanted to keep *her* by his side. He wanted to keep her *body* there. And only long enough for a repeat performance. Though now that he'd had her, now that he'd scratched his itch, he might not even want her body anymore.

Carefully, she turned over in bed, thinking maybe it would be easier for her to collect her jumbled thoughts if she wasn't looking at him. But the more she moved, the more, ah, *possessive* his embrace became, his arm curling more snugly over her belly, his leg bending to keep her firmly in place. He covered her breast with his hand just as she felt his taut erection pressing against her backside, and it was all she could do not to groan aloud her response.

In spite of her confusing thoughts, she wanted him now even more than she had the night before. Instinctively, she moved, too, pressing herself against him, so that they were spooned from shoulder to ankle. He tucked his other hand between her legs, stroking her softly until she was wet with wanting and breathless with desire. That was when he slipped inside her from behind, his hard length delving deep, and jerked his hips upward until he was buried fully inside her. Again and again he pumped her, the hand on her breast squeezing in time with his motions, his hot breath dampening the skin of her neck. He came quickly this time, her own orgasm rocketing through her on the heels of his release, and then they lay there quietly for long minutes, their bodies still joined, neither saying a word.

When Natalie tried to turn over again to face him, he hindered her movements with a soft "No. Don't move. I want to lie here inside you for a little while. This just feels too good to mess it up."

Yeah, it did, she thought. But she probably wasn't thinking that it felt good in the same way he did. To her, everything about the morning felt too good to mess up. The awareness of him—all of him—so close to her. The warmth of the sheet twining their bodies together. The softness of the pillow they shared. The musky aroma of their coupling. The gentle thumping of his heart between her shoulder blades. The simple joy of being with him. She wished they could have more mornings like this. Hundreds more. Thousands. Mornings where they shared themselves, utterly and completely, both body and soul. He was probably just thinking about how good it felt to have a breast—any breast—in his hand, and an ass—any ass—in his lap.

Still, she'd never know for sure if she didn't ask, would she?

She purred a soft sound of contentment, wriggled herself more intimately against him—eliciting an equally satisfied sound out of him—and murmured, "It does feel good. I wouldn't mind waking up like this . . ." She deliberately hesitated before adding, ". . . with you . . ." because she wanted to hammer that part home, then concluded, ". . . every morning."

She knew the hammer had hit exactly where she'd aimed it when she felt Finn stiffen behind her—only not in a good way this time—and the temperature in the room dropped fifty degrees. Evidently deciding their position didn't feel as good as he'd initially thought, he carefully disengaged his body from hers and rolled to the far side of the bed. By the time Natalie turned to look at him, Finn was sitting up, leaning against the headboard, studying her the way a chemistry professor must inspect a boron molecule under a microscope.

She wished she could be as dispassionate about him. But one glance at that brawny, naked chest sprinkled with dark hair, and those broad shoulders and arms cambered with muscle, and the shadow of rough beard, and the stormy eyes, and the last thing Natalie could be was dispassionate. On the contrary, even knowing he felt about her the way he did—specifically, that he seemed to have no feelings at all— she still wanted him. More than she'd ever wanted anything— anyone—before. With all her heart.

And that, she supposed, was the core of the problem. Maybe she didn't know exactly *what* she felt for Finn—this thing was still too new and tentative for that. But whatever it was, the feeling did indeed come from her heart. His feelings for her, whatever they were, came from someplace else in him. His libido. His testosterone. His sex.

"You can't wake up like this . . ." He hesitated the same way she did before continuing, ". . . with me . . . every morning, Natalie. For one thing, I'll be leaving in a little over a week. For another thing, it's never as good again between two people as it is the first time, so all the mornings after pale in comparison. And for another thing, I—"

"Don't want to," she finished for him, because she could tell by his expression that that was what was coming next, and she didn't want to hear him say it. It would be much less painful coming from her. Hah. "You don't want to wake up like this every morning. Not with me, anyway."

He said nothing to either deny or confirm her allegation, but that was pretty much tantamount to an agreement as far as Natalie was concerned. Sure, he'd like to wake up next to a woman every morning after a night of spectacular sex. It just didn't necessarily have to be Natalie lying there. But Natalie didn't think she'd ever be able to wake up again without thinking about the night she'd spent with Finn. There might be other men in her life someday—maybe, possibly, perhaps, in the far distant future—but none of them would make her feel the way Finn Guthrie did. Emotionally *or* physically.

"Natalie, we need to talk."

Whoa. Things were worse than she thought. It was supposed to be the woman who wanted to talk after lovemak . . .

uh . . . after sex. The man was supposed to get dressed and run out of the room, with a hasty, "Gotta go, but I'll call you," tossed over his shoulder. If the guy really liked a woman, he'd be sincere about that. But never, ever, under any circumstances did a man utter the sentence *We need to talk*. That was venturing way too deep into Oprahland. And it was encoded knowledge in a man's DNA that guys who visited Oprahland never returned quite the same. They started eating hummus and listening to Micheal Bublé and wearing oven mitts that *weren't* shaped like lobster claws. Guys who went to Oprahland were doomed. They'd never go there on purpose.

Natalie maneuvered herself to sitting, her efforts not as graceful as she would have liked, because she wanted to ensure the sheet was wrapped around all her parts that needed to be covered, on account of she was sure she'd be feeling more naked than ever after he said what he had to say. Although she mimicked his pose, leaning back against the headboard, one look at his face made her gaze ricochet away again, landing on the empty ice bucket on the other side of the room. She almost smiled when she realized where her attention had fallen. It was the perfect image for how she was feeling at the moment. Empty and icy and unnecessary.

"Talk?" she echoed, trying to inject a lightness into her voice that even she could tell fell flat. "About what?"

"About what happened last night," he answered immediately.

"We don't have to talk about that," she assured him. "You made everything crystal clear last night before we even started."

"Yeah, I did," he agreed. "And yet you seem to have misinterpreted everything."

"No, it wasn't that I misinterpreted," she said. "It was that I was mistaken."

He eyed her curiously. "Mistaken? About what?"

"About . . ." She punctuated the single word with a weary

sigh and looked down at her hands, tangled anxiously in the sheets. "About too many things to go into," she finally finished. "It's okay, Finn, really. I understand."

He said nothing for a moment, then, in a voice that was soft and solicitous and completely different from the frosty tone he'd had before, he asked, "Do you? Because I'm not sure I do."

That made her look up at him again, and for the briefest of moments, there was something in his face and in the hollows of his eyes that completely belied the cool aloofness he'd displayed until now. Something haunted and yearning and fearful, something completely at odds with the self-assured, disciplined, no-nonsense man he presented to the world. Something she hadn't seen in him before now. Something she wanted very much to bring out.

But the moment passed, and the shutters slammed shut, and all that was left was stark detachment. He was back to being the man she'd met in the lobby of the Brown Hotel that first day, the one who worked for Russell Mulholland and took his job—and pretty much everything else—very seriously. The one who was suspicious and wary and untrusting of everyone. He wasn't the man who had held her so tenderly the night before. Or the one who had revealed snippets of himself and his past in his room the other night. Or the one who had called her house cozy and made it feel that way.

That was the man she'd made love with last night. The man sitting beside her this morning was the other one. He was the one who'd had sex with her. And he was the one Finn wanted—maybe even needed—to be.

"You know, I don't get you, Finn," she said, once more speaking her thoughts aloud, unable to keep them to herself. "It's like there's this switch inside you that you can flick on and off to be whatever suits your needs."

He did respond to that, though only by arrowing his dark brows downward and narrowing his eyes. Part of Natalie thought he looked angry. Another part of her thought he looked hurt.

Ridiculous, she told herself. Men who spent their days being wary and suspicious weren't capable of feeling hurt.

"Flick the switch on," she continued, "and you're head of security for Russell Mulholland, a man who thinks everyone in the world is a threat. Flick the switch down, and you're an honest-to-God human being who talks about the mistakes he's made in life and what he'd like to do with the rest of it." She turned more fully to face him. "Last night—"

"Last night," he interrupted, "you and I both wanted something and, conveniently, were both in a position to provide. That's all last night was. An itch. A scratch. Remember?"

"Oh, I remember," she assured him. "In fact, I think maybe I remember better than you do. You think all we were to each other last night was convenient?"

He nodded once. Warily. Of course. "Among other things."

Oh, she couldn't wait to hear the rest of this. She hadn't thought he could make her feel any worse. But, wow, he was on a roll. Not able to hide her resentment, she snapped, "Well, gee, Finn, don't stop there. Tell me what else we were to each other last night besides convenient."

"Oh, no, you don't," he said. "No way are you going to pull me into a conversation like this."

"Hey, you're already in it, pal. And you're the one who said we needed to talk."

"Not like this," he countered. "Not where you're going to deliberately misconstrue everything I say and then feel insulted by what you think I'm saying."

"Oh, right. I guess there are a million interpretations of the words *convenient*, *itch*, and *scratch*, aren't there? And I suppose most women would find it unbelievably flattering to be considered any of those things."

"Hey, I called myself convenient to you, too. I said I was a scratch for your itch."

"Then I shouldn't be insulted," she deduced, "because you diminished not just me, but both of us, is that it?"

"See?" he said, oozing exasperation now. "You're deliberately misunderstanding what I'm trying to say."

"Then say it in a way that will make me understand."

He blew out another one of those aggravated breaths. Then, very carefully, he began, "I think it's fair to say that ever since you and I met that day in the hotel lobby, we've rubbed sparks off each other."

Okay, yeah, that was fair, Natalie thought. So she dipped her head forward in acknowledgment once.

"I think you're sexy as hell, and I'm reasonably certain you find me attractive, too."

Agreed, she thought. But she pulled a Finn on him and didn't say a word to either agree or disagree.

So he continued, "We managed to keep our distance until last night, when for whatever reason, and I don't know what reason that is," he hurried on before she could ask him, "maybe it was our shared desire to get as far away from Waterman as possible, or maybe it was just that Venus and Mars were all right last night. But for *some* reason, last night, we both gave in and let nature take its course." He met her gaze levelly. "And nature took us to some pretty amazing places."

True enough, she conceded again. But where he didn't seem to know the reason for that, she did. It had happened because she'd seen enough of him to know she liked him. Respected him. Trusted him. Wanted him. She'd assumed he felt the same way about her. Clearly, she shouldn't have assumed anything. But she still couldn't believe he honestly thought there had been nothing more to their joining than primitive animal attraction.

Before she could say that, however, he was talking again. "Look, Natalie, you and I met less than a week ago. I hardly know anything about you. Hell, for all I know, the only reason you slept with me last night was to use me in an effort to get closer to Russell."

She gaped at that, both incredulous and outraged. He was talking like they'd met in the bar the night before and hopped into the sack after sharing a drink without even exchanging names. He knew tons about her. He knew where she lived. What kind of car she drove. He knew she had a cat named Zippy and where she kept her phone book. He knew she liked hockey and that she'd gone to Wellesley. That she owned an event-planning business and had made her debut. The list could go on and on. He knew way more about her than she knew about him, and he still didn't care for her the way she did him. But obviously he'd either not been paying attention, had already forgotten, or just plain didn't care about the bits of her life she'd shared with him.

And even if he didn't remember any of those things, he should sure as hell have realized by now that she wouldn't use him the way he'd just suggested. He should have known her well enough to like, respect, and trust her, too.

Wow. Guess he was right. Guess they didn't know each other, after all.

More in an effort to burn off some of her own anger than to further what was fast moving from a tense conversation to an angry fight, she said, "And, hell, for all I know, the only reason you slept with me last night was because you want to keep me from telling the world about Russell Mulholland's dirty little secret." *Whatever it is,* she added halfheartedly to herself.

She had intended to further make the point that she didn't know or care whether Russell had a secret, and that even if he did, Finn could trust her, the way she trusted him. But the look that came over his face when she said what she did—one of disbelief, terror, and outright rage—halted her. As did the lightning-fast way he reached across the bed and grabbed her by both upper arms, hauling her against himself until they were literally eye to eye. She grappled with the sheet before it could fall to her waist, but his fingers bit tighter into her arms until she gasped and let it go. "Finn, you're hurting me," she whispered, fear welling in her belly.

He immediately loosened his grip enough that she could pull the sheet up over her breasts again, but he didn't let go of her. He did seem to notice her need to keep herself covered, however, and something akin to apology flickered in his eyes at the realization.

Nevertheless, his voice was part growl, part threat, when he demanded, "Who told you about Mac—" But he halted before saying anything more, looking sorry he'd said even that much. Instead, he said, "What makes you think Russell has a dirty little secret, Natalie?"

Gee, she hadn't thought that, not really. Not until Finn reacted the way he did. Evidently, she'd been right to be suspicious of the selective results her Google search on Russell's name had generated. But it wasn't Russell's name that popped into her head at Finn's question. His first one. He hadn't cut himself off with a shortened version of Russell's name. He'd cut himself off with a shortened version of Mac Somebody.

No, she realized then. Not Mac. He hadn't cut off the last part of a name. He'd cut off the last sound. The *s* sound.

Max. He'd been talking about Russell's son.

"Max?" she asked, puzzled. "Max is the one with a secret? But he's just a kid."

She hadn't thought it possible, but Finn went even more livid at that. "I never said a word about Max."

"You said Mac. There's no Mac in Russell's life."

"How do you know?"

"I've made it my business to find out as much as I can about your employer," she reminded him. "There's no Mac in his employ as far as I can tell. But there's Max. His son." She paused for another one of those point-making moments, then added, "His son, whom you are also employed to protect."

Finn set Natalie carefully down, placing her back on the opposite side of the bed, as far from himself as he could. But his gaze never once left hers. His cheeks were stained with evidence of his still simmering anger, and his chest rose and fell in slow, measured motion, as if he were trying very, very, *very* hard to keep his temper under control.

So there was a Mulholland secret to protect, Natalie

thought. It just wasn't Russell Mulholland's. It was his son's. His son who, at fourteen, was at an age where a secret was best kept in the family. Where, if the rest of the world found out and began to hound him about it, could affect his young, not fully developed self in a way that might not be nearly as devastating or as hard to fend off as it would be to an adult. Finn's anger now was in response to what he perceived as a threat to a fourteen-year-old boy. It had nothing to do with Natalie. And somehow, that just made her love him—or something—all the more.

"Finn," she said, her voice softer, calmer, and in no way angry now. "I don't know anything about Max other than that he's Russell's son. Even if I did find out about him whatever it is you and Russell are protecting, you have to realize that I would never, *ever* betray it to anyone else."

"Why do I have to realize that?" he asked, his voice flat and empty now.

Well, she would have liked to think it was because he trusted her. But hadn't she already realized that was impossible for him?

"Do you honestly think I'm only here with you like this now because I want to get closer to Russell?" she asked, returning to the place where they'd gotten sidetracked.

He said nothing, only met her gaze levelly, his jaw set tight.

"Do you?" she asked again.

"I don't know, Natalie," he finally said. "That's just the point."

She nodded, a quick, jerky action, her anger returning again. Anger that Finn couldn't see what was right in front of his face. Anger that he could think the worst of her. Anger that he didn't even want to try to explore whatever was happening between them. Because no matter what he said, and no matter what he denied, there was something happening between them. And if he'd just give it even the tiniest chance, it might be something wonderful for both of them.

But he couldn't do that, she reminded herself. Doing

that would mean putting his trust in someone. And trust was the one thing Finn had in very short supply.

"I see," she said, keeping her voice calm and soft when inside she felt anything but. "Well, there's one thing I *do* know about you. I know you're a rat, Finn Guthrie. Because only a rat would have sex with a woman without even knowing the reason why. Only a rat would experience what you and I experienced last night and wake up in the morning still not trusting the other person." She chuckled mirthlessly at that. "But then, what does that make me, since I made love with a man I trusted completely and woke up still trusting him? And now I discover he's someone I never should have trusted at all."

She didn't wait for an answer to that. Instead, she jerked the sheet off of Finn, ignoring both his nudity and his seeming lack of concern for it, and proceeded to collect her clothing from the numerous places it had dropped onto the floor. He didn't say a word as she went about her task, but she didn't know if that was because he didn't know what to say or because he thought the conversation had come to the end it should have naturally reached. It didn't matter, though. The only thing that mattered was that Finn Guthrie was a man who couldn't trust anyone and who never would trust anyone.

Not even the one person in the world he should know without doubt he could trust with anything. With everything. With all his heart and soul.

FINN WATCHED NATALIE COLLECT HER CLOTHES AND disappear into his bathroom, telling himself he didn't feel a thing. Because he never felt anything the morning after having sex with a woman. Except physically satisfied. Problem was, he didn't feel that, either, even after an entire night of what had to have been the most extensive, exhaustive, experimental sex he'd ever had. Of course, his mornings after always came to an end when the women were still sleeping, so he never had to have any conversation with them. So it must have been the conversation with Natalie, he told himself, that was making him feel the way he was at the moment.

Crap. Maybe he wasn't feeling physically satisfied, but he was feeling a host of other things. Things he really didn't want to feel. Concern for Max and Russell after realizing there was a possibility that Natalie had stumbled onto something she shouldn't have. Fear that Natalie knew more than she was letting on. Worry that he couldn't trust her.

Though, when he gave that more thought, he realized he actually wasn't too worried about that last. Not because he knew he could trust Natalie, though. No way. Finn couldn't trust anyone. It was just that there was no way she could find out the truth about Max, no matter where she looked or how hard she tried. That secret was ironclad and unknown to anyone other than Max, Russell, Finn, and a couple of extremely well-trusted—and even better-paid—attorneys. There wasn't enough money—or feminine wiles—on the planet that could get any of them to talk.

Not even Natalie Beckett's.

As if cued by the thought, the shower kicked on in the bathroom, and Finn was assaulted by a vision of Natalie, pink and naked and wet, with water cascading over her smooth flesh, and soap bubbles gliding between her lush breasts and over her flat torso, lingering in the dent of her navel before circling down into her . . .

He smacked his head against the headboard to dispel the image. Hard. Oh, man. How long was it going to take to get her out of his system? Instead of scratching an itch last night, all he'd done was wallow naked in poison ivy. His desire for Natalie now was a million times stronger than it had been mere hours ago. And there was no way she was going to let him get close to her again. Not after everything he'd just said to her.

But what was he supposed to say? He didn't know her that well. Just because he'd been to her house and driven her car, and met her cat, and just because she'd told him

things like where she'd gone to school and how she didn't
feel comfortable in the society where she'd grown up, and
just because she'd woken up in his bed—twice—and just
because he knew the exact place to touch her to make her
utter that incredibly erotic sound . . .

None of those things necessarily generated trust. Yeah,
maybe her cat liked him. And yeah, maybe they shared a
love of some things, like hockey, and a disdain for other
things, like Waterman. And okay, maybe she could relish a
good beer as well as he could, never mind garlic and peppers on a burger. Those were little things. They were noth-
ings. They damn sure weren't things that would make a
woman say she wanted to wake up every morning next to a
guy. What the hell was Natalie thinking?

More to the point, what the hell was he thinking? Because instead of getting out of bed and getting dressed and
getting the hell outta Dodge, the way he should be before
she got out of the shower, he was still sitting in bed, as if he
wanted to be here when she got out. As if he wanted to
pick up the conversation where they'd left off. As if he
wanted to explain himself a little better. Make things a little clearer. Tell her she had the wrong idea about him.

She had exactly the right idea about him. Once a street
rat, always a street rat. He might wear better clothes now
and live in a nicer place, and he might not break windows
or steal *Playboy* from the drugstore anymore, but deep
down, he hadn't changed at all. Deep down, he was still
that street rat who didn't want anyone getting too close.
Not just because letting people close meant they learned
more about you, but because it meant you learned more
about them. And learning about them—some of them,
anyway—meant caring about them. And Finn didn't want
to care about anyone. Bad enough he felt responsible for
Russell and Max. Caring for those two made him crazy
enough as it was. If he let Natalie in, feeling the way he did
about her . . .

But he didn't feel any way for her, he reminded himself.
He didn't. Not a single thing.

To prove it, he slung his feet over the side of the bed, gathered up his clothes from the night before, and hurriedly tugged them on. The shower cut off just as he was buttoning the last button on his shirt, so he grabbed his shoes, his wallet, his phone, and his hotel key and beat a hasty retreat through the door.

Natalie could find her own way, he thought as the door clicked softly closed behind him. The same way he always would.

· Fifteen ·

THE PARLOR OF THE HOTCHKISS HOME WAS AS
magnificent and majestic as the ballroom, Natalie noted
late Sunday afternoon as Clementine's maid invited her to
take a seat on the sofa while she summoned her mistress.
Except that instead of evoking the court of Louis XIV, this
room was more reminiscent of what his granddaughter-
in-law, Marie Antoinette, probably would have liked. The
color scheme and furnishings were unapologetically feminine, from the minty fresh walls to the powder-puff pink
chaise in the corner, to the pastel pastiche of Aubusson
rugs, to the flowered damask chair into which Natalie
eased herself to wait. There were even little flowered tea
cakes on the French Provincial coffee table, perfectly arranged on a china tray painted with red and pink roses. A
matching tea set awaited serving, its delicate little cups
limned with what Natalie would bet was fourteen-carat
gold. It was all so elegant and beautiful and gracious.
Even her mother didn't entertain with this kind of refinement. And Dody Beckett for sure wouldn't do anything
like this for someone she'd hired to work for her. Clemen-

tine clearly thought very highly of Natalie, to provide for
her like this.

So why was nausea rising in her belly and threatening
to jump out of her mouth to say howdy-do in the most *un*-
refined way imaginable? Why did she suddenly feel not
like a member of Louis's court, but like a prisoner who had
just been led into the dankest, moldiest part of the Bastille?
Why did she fear the petit fours and tea were just for show,
and that she was actually about to be fed weevil-infested
hardtack and fetid water from the Seine? And why did
Rolondo, Clementine's little Westie who cheerfully patrolled
the room, suddenly seem like a big ol' rat who wanted to
wrestle her for the last remaining crumb?

Her head snapped up when she heard the clatter of Clementine's shoes on the hardwood floor, telling herself they
did *not* sound like the kind of footwear any self-respecting
gendarme would wear. Then she had to squeeze her eyes
shut tight and open them again to make sure she was just
imagining her employer dressed as a *gendarme,* wielding a
blackjacques with which she intended to coldcoq Natalie
before dragging *la prisonnière* to *le donjon.*

Fortunately, that last was indeed her imagination, as
Clementine actually looked as if she'd just come in from
a Derby luncheon of some kind, dressed as she was in a
pale blue suit with matching pumps and a hat that was so
exuberant—read: ridiculous—that it would have looked
outrageous anywhere but Louisville during the week preceding Derby. As it was, the hat was actually a little on the
conservative side, since it didn't boast any kind of animal
or a tube for sucking in a strategically placed beer. And
Clementine didn't look at all like she wanted to coldcoq
Natalie with a blackjacques. In fact, she looked like she
wanted to give Natalie a big ol' hug.

And then Clementine was giving her a big ol' hug, and
Natalie was so surprised, she barely had time to duck her
head out of the way of the big feathers adorning her client's
hat, otherwise she might have lost an eye. Man, women
took their Derby chapeaux seriously in this town.

"Oh, Natalie, I just came from having *the* best time," Clementine said as she withdrew from the hug. She didn't go far, though, leaving both hands curved affectionately over Natalie's shoulders, gazing up at her through eyes that were shining with something Natalie could only describe as mischief.

Before she had a chance to ask Clementine where she'd had this best time, her employer was hurrying on, "Glenda Hightower had her Rose Garland Tea this afternoon, which, of course, everyone who's anyone attends, and which everyone who's anyone enjoys."

Everyone who was anyone in Clementine's generation, at least, Natalie thought. Glenda was Tootie Hightower's mother, and she'd been hosting the Rose Garland Tea annually since before Natalie and Tootie were born, always on the Sunday afternoon before Derby, to put all her friends in the proper festive mood for the week. Natalie's mother had never missed a year. Someday, Tootie would doubtless take up the reins and step in as hostess, inviting everyone who was anyone in *her* generation to attend, including Natalie. Not so much because Natalie was one of those everyones who were anyone, but more because Tootie could never have fun at these things unless she had a whipping girl to humiliate, and that, of course, was where Natalie would come in handy.

Not that Natalie cared. The Hightowers never scrimped on their parties, and several of the women attending would be her friends. Plus, she'd gotten very, very good over the years avoiding Tootie at such gatherings. And even better at leaving little surprises behind in Tootie's pocketbook if she ever gave Natalie a hard time. For example, at this very moment, there were a couple of especially pungent—and sticky—bits of blue cheese and salmon fermenting in the zippered pocket of Tootie's Michael Kors evening bag that she probably wouldn't open for at least another week, whereby it ought to be good and ripe. As should a number of other items in the closet with it. Well, could Natalie help it if she accidentally dropped an hors d'oeuvre into Tootie's bag when she was standing too close? And it would have been impolite to draw attention to the other woman's plight in a room full of other people.

Anyway, Tootie's taking over for her mother as tea party hostess was still a ways off, so Natalie cared even less about any of that right now. That evidently wasn't the case with Clementine, however, because she gushed for several more minutes about the party, and who was wearing what, and how the Benedictine sandwiches this year had been especially delicious and cut into little heart shapes, which had made them all the more enchanting, and how the most scandalous bit of gossip burning up the Glenview grapevine was that Darla Poindexter—wife of fashion-obsessed Frederick Poindexter, the city's equivalent of Beau Brummell—was engaged in the basest form of passive-aggressive behavior these days, buying all her clothes at a consignment shop on Frankfort Avenue, even if the dress she'd had on today, a gorgeous retro Givenchy reminiscent of Jackie Kennedy, was by far the most envied at the tea.

As Clementine had spoken, she'd seated herself on the overstuffed, rosy silk moiré sofa and invited Natalie to join her, had prepared each of them a cup of tea and tonged petit fours onto a plate for each of them to enjoy.

"But the absolute best part of the day, Natalie," Clementine said after pausing for breath, leaning comfortably against the sofa's back, teacup in hand, "was when Glenda asked me how my party plans were coming for this weekend."

It was the perfect opening for Natalie to tell Clementine what she had come over to tell her. That, actually, the party plans were going great, but the guest list . . . Well, not so much. That, actually, so many people had declined to attend that it would probably be best to cancel the party, because Natalie had kinda sorta lied about having a secret weapon, and hadn't been able to come up with a single idea that would lure guests away from the plethora of other parties going on that night. And she didn't want Clementine to be at home alone save her beloved Edgar, both of them all dressed up with a million other places they could have gone as guests, only to be feeling humiliated because no one had come to their own party. The party that, if Natalie let it go any farther, would cost Clementine thousands of dollars more than she'd already sunk into it, thanks to all those nonrefundable deposits.

Natalie opened her mouth to tell her client all those things, still not sure what the best wording for such a disastrous announcement would be, but Clementine hurried on before she had a chance to even start.

"But before I tell you how I replied to Glenda, Natalie, dear, I have to set up a little history that she and I share. We were both at Princeton years ago, you see."

Natalie's eyebrows shot up at that. She hadn't known Clementine attended Princeton. She hadn't thought many women of that generation really went to college, especially wealthy ones who, it was assumed, would marry and start families and become unpaid hostesses and caterers for all the parties their upwardly bound professional husbands would expect and require them to organize. Even Natalie's mother hadn't attended college. She'd toured Europe with a bunch of her friends for six months after high school, then had come home and . . . Well, mostly started going to parties and volunteering for a variety of causes, which was actually mostly an opportunity to socialize with friends and plan fund-raising events that were pretty much just more parties for them to attend and, hopefully, meet potential husbands. Natalie's parents had, in fact, met at such a society function.

"Oh, yes, I went to college," Clementine said when she must have noticed Natalie's expression. "I even graduated from college. So did Glenda. But my reasons for being at Princeton were quite a bit different from hers. Glenda's parents sent her because they wanted her to meet suitable young men in the hopes that she might marry one, which she ultimately did." Clementine lowered her voice a bit as she added parenthetically, "You see, Glenda had something of a, ah, reputation in Louisville by then that made her . . . Well, let's just say she was less than marriageable in the eyes of the boys in her own social circle. Her parents knew they'd have to send her where no one knew her for her to land herself a nice boy with lots and lots of money."

Natalie smiled at that. Sounded like Glenda's apple, Tootie, hadn't fallen too far from the tree. Tootie was a ho, too, but these days, that was by no means an impediment to marriage, even a profitable one. What made Tootie unmarriageable was the fact that she was a colossal bitch. "But that wasn't why you were at Princeton?" she asked Clementine. "To land a husband?"

"Oh, no, dear," her hostess said after another dainty sip of her tea. "I was at Princeton to study biology on a full academic scholarship."

Once again, Natalie's eyebrows shot up.

Clementine laughed lightly at her reaction. "I know I probably don't seem the type now, but there was a time when I wanted to become a doctor and open a free clinic for women and children in my old neighborhood. Teach them about family planning and birth control and give them a safe place to come if their situations at home became dangerous."

This time Natalie arrowed her brows down in confusion. "But I thought you grew up on Long Island. What would women in the Hamptons need with a free clinic?"

Clementine smiled, though there was something in the gesture that wasn't quite happy. "There's a lot more to Long Island than the Hamptons, dear."

"Like what?"

"Queens, for one thing." She smiled. "Well, Okay, maybe only geographically speaking. So I fudged a bit."

Although Natalie wouldn't have thought it possible, her eyebrows shot up even more. "You grew up in Queens?"

Clementine nodded but said nothing, only sipped her tea again . . . with all the elegance and finesse of a Hamptons *grande dame de la société*.

And just like that, Natalie understood why she'd liked Clementine so much from the get-go. They were a lot alike. Not that Natalie had come from a working-class background in an area where families were crowded into houses that were even more crowded atop one another or had needed an academic scholarship to attend college. It was that whole fish out of water thing. Ironically, however, Clementine was living in an environment now that was nothing like the one in which she'd grown up, yet she was comfortable and confident and fit right in. Natalie had grown up in this environment, but had never really felt any of those things.

"Anyway," Clementine continued, "Glenda Hightower was Glenda Melbourne then, and a meaner, more bitter, more self-absorbed girl didn't exist outside the Atlantic seaboard. And social climbing? My goodness, there wasn't a more socially voracious girl on campus than Glenda, and she didn't have a single qualm about stomping her competition into the ground." Clementine sipped her tea again. "So it goes without saying that a girl like me, whose father worked as a longshoreman, and who only had two skirts, three blouses, and one sweater to her name, and who paid the rest of her way through college working as a waitress at a diner off campus, was a very easy, and very frequent, target for Glenda."

And Tootie had obviously learned at her mother's knee, Natalie thought. For some reason, though, the realization didn't make her feel angrier at Tootie. Strangely, it sort of made her feel sorry for her old nemesis.

"But that's all water under the bridge now," Clementine said with what sounded like a genuine absence of malice. She smiled at Natalie again, with that twinkle of mischief in her eyes again. "Because after Glenda spent her entire time at Princeton doing everything she could to get her talons into the most sought-after boy on campus—he had gorgeous blue eyes and wavy blond hair and broad shoulders and the nicest eyes, Natalie, *and* he was the president of the Omicron Epsilon chapter of Zeta Psi—he asked me to marry him instead."

She lifted the teacup to her mouth again, but there was

no mistaking the smug little grin curling Clementine's lips as she enjoyed another sip.

Natalie couldn't help but smile back. Nor could she quite quell the chuckle that erupted when she said, "Clementine, you sly little campus vixen."

She settled her cup back into its saucer. "Well, as I said, that's all water under the bridge."

"For you, maybe," Natalie said, "but if Glenda Hightower is anything like her daughter—"

"Oh, she and Camille are definitely two of a kind," Clementine interjected.

"—then I'm guessing she saw that water take out the bridge like a big ol' tsunami," Natalie continued, "and hasn't even tried to rebuild it."

Clementine made a little sound that was a combination of both regret and satisfaction. "I'd say that's a fairly accurate way to put it. I do think the main reason Glenda includes me at her parties—aside from the fact that Edgar is the senior partner in her husband's firm—is because she enjoys having someone around to try to make feel small."

Natalie shook her head. Wow. The Hightower women really were poisonous little apples.

"But that only makes her look bad, doesn't it?" Clementine asked. "Everyone knows the reason Glenda acts the way she does around me is because she's a bitter, dried up old prune, and—"

Natalie nearly choked on the swallow of tea she'd been about to consume at that. She'd never heard Clementine, or anyone else in her mother's generation, talk like this.

"Well, she is," Clementine said.

Natalie tactfully refrained from commenting, picking up a napkin to wipe her mouth instead.

"Besides," Clementine added, "I always find some opportunity at Glenda's tea to accidentally misplace one of those cute little Benedictine sandwiches. And you know how, ah . . . pungent . . . cream cheese and cucumbers can get after a week or two."

Okay, that really did make Natalie choke on her tea.

She'd had no idea she and Clementine had so much in common. And anyone who could put up with the Hightower bullying and come out smiling was A-okay with Natalie. Not to mention anyone who countered the Hightower bullying with spoiled food was nothing less than genius.

Which, she thought with an even heavier heart than before, was going to make it doubly difficult to break the news to Clementine that her Derby party was going to come off reeking even more than bad Benedictine.

"Clementine," she began softly, still trying to sort out how she was going to break the news. "There's something—"

"No, wait," her client interrupted her. "I haven't told you the best part yet."

"But—"

"No, no, dear, you have to hear this. Since I know you go through the same thing with Glenda's daughter Tootie that I do with her—"

"How do you know that?" Natalie asked.

Clementine smiled kindly. "Everyone knows that, dear."

"Oh." She'd been hoping it was only everyone in her own generation that knew that. Evidently Tootie's condescension transcended generations. Then again, Clementine had called her Tootie, not Camille, so maybe it wasn't just Tootie's condescension that transcended generations. Maybe Tootie's tootiness did, too.

"Anyway," Clementine continued, "since you know what it's like to be high on the Hightower enemies' list, you'll appreciate what happened."

"But, Clementine—"

"No, really, Natalie, you'll love this."

Natalie told herself to try to interrupt again, that she really needed to tell Clementine the bad news before they went any further, but the woman was in such high spirits, she didn't have the heart to dash them. Not to mention any story about the comeuppance of a Hightower woman— which this was sounding like it was going to be—was A-okay with Natalie. Besides, there was still that pesky problem of having no idea how to break it to Clementine that her party was going to be a big, fat zero on the ol' social significance meter.

"As I said, it happened when I was on my way out. I was one of the first to leave the tea; you'll understand that, I'm certain," Clementine added with a knowing arch of one brow. "I was nearly out of the garden room, *this close* to making a clean escape, when Glenda called me back in because I'd forgotten to take my party favor with me. I actually did that on purpose," she continued parenthetically, lowering her voice, even though there was no one to hear. "Glenda is the biggest cheapskate on the planet, and the party favor this year was a huge bag of absolutely hideous gardenia potpourri. But being the gracious woman that I am, I feigned forgetfulness and went back to the table to get it.

"Of course, it goes without saying," she continued, "that Glenda had seated me as far away from herself as she could, so she was fairly shouting at me when she made the reminder. Which meant she was also shouting when she asked me how the plans for my party were going, and shouting when she made her apology for not being able to make it herself, because she and Sutton would be attending the Mint Jubilee."

Uh-oh, Natalie thought. Since Clementine was actually having fun telling this story, that meant she'd put Glenda Hightower in her place. And Natalie really, really, really didn't want to think about how she'd done that.

Clementine went on, "I shouted back that I was *very* excited, because my party planner had invited an extremely important person to the affair who had been delighted to attend for such a worthy cause, and it was someone everyone in town was going to want to meet."

Oh, no, Natalie thought. No, no, no, no, no. Here she'd come to tell Clementine that the VIP celebrity she'd invited wasn't going to be able to make it to the party after all, and Clementine had already told a room full of people— *shouted* to a room full of people—that said VIP would be there with bells on.

"Well, you can imagine the reaction that got from everyone in the room," Clementine continued.

Oh, yeah. Natalie could certainly imagine that. A gardenia-reeking room full of women whipping around in their chairs to look at Clementine fast enough to send all their humongous hats flying. God only knew what kind of damage millinery did to a garden room when it was flying at speeds like that.

" 'Who?' Everyone wanted to know," Clementine said in the same sort of voice the women must have used: surprised, curious and, alas, gossipy. " 'Who is it, Clementine?' they kept asking. Then all the speculation began. Was it someone from Hollywood? Broadway? Washington? *Dancing with the Stars*? And the names they threw out, Natalie," she added with a laugh. "Was it George Clooney? Was it Martha Stewart? Was it"—here, her voice grew reverent—"*Oprah*? Or was it someone like Angelina Jolie? And if so, did I think she would bring Brad Pitt? Or was it—and this was the best one, Natalie—was it our new president of the United States? Oh, Natalie, if you could have just seen their faces."

Natalie was pretty sure she was glad she hadn't. It was bad enough seeing Clementine's, all exultant and hopeful and smug. No, not smug, Natalie thought. Smugness wasn't in Clementine's character. What she looked was . . . happy. And not happy for herself, that her party was going to be a success, Natalie knew. But happy for the children of Kids, Inc., who would be benefiting even more.

"So now you have to tell me, Natalie," Clementine said with a grin. "I won't take no for an answer. Who's the big mystery guest? Who's the extremely important person everyone's going to want to meet?"

Natalie's heart sank to the pit of her stomach at the question. Then it dropped right through and went crashing to her toes. There was no way she could tell Clementine the truth. If she said the mystery guest was going to be a no-show now, Clementine would look like a big, fat liar. She'd never be able to go anywhere again without feeling uncomfortable. Glenda Hightower would make her social life a living hell. The same way Tootie could never see Natalie without mentioning the big-ass bow dress, Glenda would never be able to see Clementine without making some snide remark about the VIP who wasn't there. And although Natalie realized now that Clementine was made of sturdy enough stuff to handle it, Natalie also realized she herself wasn't.

Before she even realized she meant to speak, she heard herself say, "It's Russell Mulholland."

Clementine's eyes went as round as silver dollars. "Russell Mulholland?" she echoed incredulously. And damned if her voice wasn't even more reverent than it had been when she'd mentioned Oprah. "Really? You've met him?"

"I have indeed," Natalie said, grateful for not having to lie about that, at least.

"You've spoken to him?"

"I had dinner with him," Natalie confirmed, chalking up another tally for truthfulness. Just because she hadn't, technically, finished dinner with him—or quite started it, for that matter—didn't make it less true. They'd sat at a table in a restaurant and ordered food. That counted as dinner in anyone's book. Just ask Martha Stewart. Or Oprah.

Although Natalie wouldn't have thought it possible to surprise Clementine any more than she already had, she looked even more astonished at the announcement. Then she looked stunned. Then she looked delighted.

"Oh, *Natalie*," she said. "This is *wonderful* news. Russell Mulholland doesn't even appear on the big network talk shows. He won't talk to Barbara Walters. He won't talk to Oprah. He won't give interviews to the *Wall Street Journal* or *Vanity Fair* or anyone else. The women will want to meet him because he's so handsome and elusive. The men will want to meet him because he's so business savvy and elusive." She let that sink in for a moment, then launched herself at Natalie and hugged her even harder than before. "Natalie Beckett, you're *brilliant*," she said. "Everyone who's anyone really *is* going to want to come to my party. It's going to be a huge success."

Yeah, well, hold that thought, Clementine . . .

Clementine released her, looking absolutely giddy at the prospect, and ready to burst at the seams.

"But, Clementine," Natalie hurried on, injecting as much firmness into her voice as she could, "you have got to promise me you won't say a word to anyone until I've made the announcement public."

"But when do you plan to do that, dear?"

Natalie thought fast. The party was only five days away. If she was going to pull this off—and after everything Clementine had just told her, she was damned well going to pull it off, if she had to resort to duct tape and a burlap sack to ensure Russell Mulholland's appearance at the party— she was going to have to do it *tonight*. Before the eleven o'clock news. Tomorrow morning at the absolute latest to make the noon newscast. She could call Angie Fenton at WAVE and give her an exclusive. She wrote for the *Courier*, too, and she knew everybody who was anybody in the Louisville social scene. And Tamara Ikenberg. She could get the word out, too.

She could do this, Natalie assured herself. She *would* do this. For Clementine. For the children of Kids, Inc., who would benefit financially. For herself. It was time for Natalie to take charge of this thing. All she had to do was wrangle one billionaire for the lesser part of an evening. And, okay, wrangle his head of security, too.

That last, actually, was what finally brought the enormity of her situation crashing down on her like two tons of absolutely hideous gardenia potpourri. Because it wasn't Russell Mulholland Natalie was afraid to confront, and it wasn't him she was afraid she wouldn't be able to sway. It was Finn. Finn, who had kissed her so tenderly and made love to her with such passion. Finn, who had made her feel things she'd never felt before in her life.

Finn, who had pretty much told her he never wanted to see her again.

Well, that was just too damned bad. Because she *would*

confront Finn and his employer. And she *would* sway both of them to her way of thinking.

She just wished she could sway Finn to a whole lot more.

"Within the next twenty-four hours," she told Clementine fiercely. Because she *felt* fierce at the moment. Since, you know, Finn and his employer were nowhere around. "I just have a few more minor details to iron out. Time of arrival, how long he can stay, that kind of thing," she added, mentally crossing her fingers over the lie. "I'm heading over to his hotel right after I leave here to do that. And then, Clementine, you are going to see a media blitz unlike anything you've ever seen in your life."

She stood, straightening to her full height, feeling brave and militant, determined and strong. "By this time tomorrow," she said as she slung her purse over her shoulder, "everyone in Louisville is going to be talking about your party. And your phone is going to be ringing off the hook with all those people who haven't RSVPed yet with a whole mess of resounding yeses." She grinned. "And then it's going to be ringing off the hook with all those people who said they weren't going to be able to make it yet have suddenly had a change in plans that will allow them to attend your party after all.

"Just you wait, Clementine," Natalie concluded as she headed for the door. "Friday night, this house is going to be the place to be in Louisville for Derby Eve."

· Sixteen ·

JUST BEFORE ELEVEN O'CLOCK MONDAY NIGHT, Natalie was propped up in her bed with a stack of fat pillows behind her, wearing her usual springtime sleepwear of baggy striped boxer shorts and white undershirt, over which she'd thrown her usual pale blue silk kimono, currently unbelted. She was dividing her attention between the last few minutes of *CSI: Miami* and painting her toenails a color the bottle identified as Ocean Sunrise, but which looked more like the color of David Caruso's hair. Oh, well, she thought as she brushed the last bit over her little toe and capped the bottle. With all due respect to Mr. Caruso, she'd just wear closed-toed shoes tomorrow morning when she went to see Russell Mulholland. Again.

She'd had no luck reaching him since talking to Clementine. And there was no way she'd call Finn to ask for his help after the way things had been left between them the last time she'd seen him. All she could think to do now was go back to the Brown around six in the morning and wait around until Russell Mulholland showed himself so she could confront him in person. She figured that if Finn's job was to guard the billionaire's body, then the two men's rooms must be in close proximity, most likely right next door to or right across the hall from each other. Therefore she would simply park herself in the hallway outside Finn's door, as close to his room as she dared, until one of them stuck their nose out the door long enough for her to grab it.

Hopefully, the first nose she snagged would be Russell's. But if it was Finn's, then so be it. She had ceased being worried about seeing him again roughly two seconds after the last time she'd tried to leave a message for Russell and been assured by the hotel receptionist that she had indeed delivered all of Natalie's earlier messages to the billionaire. She still wasn't sure what she would say to change his mind, or what she would do if she had to confront Finn.

Well, she would say or do *whatever* she had to say or do, she immediately decided. Because she'd made a promise to Clementine—and, in effect, to every child involved in Kids, Inc.—that she would deliver Russell to the Hotchkiss estate Friday night. So to the Hotchkiss estate Friday night Natalie would deliver him.

Once the killer and her motive were revealed on *CSI*— But c'mon, Horatio, what woman *wouldn't* kill for a Hermès crocodile Birkin handbag?—Natalie stopped paying attention to the TV and turned her attention to her fingernails, this time opting for an old favorite from her manicure caddy. Until she heard the news anchor say the name "Russell Mulholland," which was when she snapped her attention right back up to the screen.

"That's right," the sleekly dressed blonde announcer said, smiling into the camera. "We learned earlier today that billionaire Russell Mulholland, who's in Louisville for Derby, but keeping a *very* low profile, will be attending one of this Friday's myriad Derby Eve parties. This after assuring everyone who asked, including our reporters, that he would absolutely, unequivocally *not* be making any public appearances while in town. And the party he's chosen to attend might just surprise you."

What followed, as far as Natalie could tell with her

brain jumping around in her head the way it was, was a film-at-eleven report filled with clips of Russell Mulholland ducking out of sight of cameras in a variety of local venues. There he was ducking out of sight at Fourth Street Live. And there he was ducking out of sight at Jack Fry's. Then at Lynn's Paradise Cafe. Then at Churchill Downs— there were two shots of him ducking out of sight there. Then at the Brown Hotel. In every image, he was covering his face with something—newspapers, menus, racing programs and, once, a Yorkshire terrier—and hurrying away in the opposite direction. One of his many bodyguards— usually Finn, Natalie couldn't help noting . . . and sighing about, damn her—invariably bringing up the rear. Those shots were followed by photographs of him taken at various press conferences and personal appearances for the GameViper and finally, inescapably, the cover of the *People* magazine issue in which he'd been dubbed Sexiest Man Alive. And over all of it, the reporter's voice yammering away about how reclusive he was, and what a hot prospect he was, and how *nobody* was supposed to land him for their Derby party and blah blah blah blah blah.

Somehow, in the far reaches of her brain, Natalie managed to translate all that blah blah blahing into a recognizable, if somewhat inconvenient, fact. The station—along with several other media outlets—had received word today that Russell Mulholland was scheduled to attend a by-invitation-only Derby Eve party hosted by local philanthropists Clementine and Edgar Hotchkiss, and—

And that was when Natalie's brain stopped jumping around and focused entirely on the phrase *along with several other media outlets*. That meant . . .

She fumbled around in the sheets for the remote, and hastily changed the channel from WHAS to WLKY, just in time to catch the end of their report about how Russell Mulholland would be attending the Hotchkiss affair. She pushed the button a couple more times, taking her to WAVE. Yep, they, too, were reporting on the social coup of the season. It was fair to assume that it would also be the centerpiece story on all the morning shows in a matter of hours, which meant anyone who didn't stay up late enough to watch the eleven o'clock news would be the early rising type who always caught the five a.m. news. It would doubtless make the front page of the Features section in the *Courier* tomorrow, too. Hell, they might already have the news up on their website.

By the time Natalie arrived at the Brown Hotel in the morning to beg Russell Mulholland to make an appearance at Clementine's party, every freaking mouth in Louisville would be wagging about how Russell Mulholland was going to be making an appearance at Clementine's party. There were only two words that could describe what was going through Natalie's head after that, and they inescapably made their way out of her mouth.

"Oh. Crap."

Clementine, what did you do?

Instinctively, she yanked the phone from its charger on the nightstand, but when she went to punch the numbers, she realized she wasn't sure who to call. The leak to the *several media outlets* must have originated with Clementine, because Natalie hadn't breathed a word to another soul, outside Finn and Russell. There was no way either of them had alerted the media to something both swore wouldn't happen. But Clementine wasn't the type to break a promise or go blabbing about stuff she knew she shouldn't.

Then again, Natalie thought, it hadn't necessarily been Clementine who said anything to the news outlets. She may have told someone else in confidence—even though that, too, had violated the promise she made to Natalie—and that person had flapped their lips when they shouldn't have. It may have even been an innocent slip of the tongue that Clementine uttered in her excitement before realizing what she was doing. Besides, even if Natalie did accuse her client of having broken her promise to keep the info about Russell confidential until further notice, Natalie hadn't exactly been in a position to extract that promise in the first place, seeing as how she'd been lying through her teeth with that info about Russell.

When she looked down at the phone in her hand, though, she realized it hadn't even been Clementine that her first impulse had dictated she call. It had been Finn. If she'd intended to call Clementine, her finger would have been on the two, which was the first digit of her client's home phone number. Instead, her thumb was placed firmly on the nine. That was the first digit of Finn's cell.

As if cued by that thought, someone—and she could just bet who—leaned against her front doorbell hard, punctuating the sound with a rapid *thumpthumpthump* against her front door. And then, as if that weren't enough to rouse her—which it evidently wasn't, because she still sat frozen on the bed, her phone clutched to her belly—she heard a male voice shout with all the anguish of Stanley Kowalski, "Natalieeee!"

"Oh. Crap."

Not that she wanted to be redundant or anything, but really, what else was there to say?

She had two choices. Either she could stay here in her bed with the covers pulled up over her head and hope one of her neighbors called the police about Marlon Brando out there, or she could face the music, cacophonous though it may be, that she herself had written.

"Natalieeeee!"

If he kept this up, in that tone of voice, he was going to make every dog in the neighborhood go deaf.

With a heavy sigh, she dropped the phone back into its charger and made her way out of her bedroom, checking her appearance in the cheval mirror as she passed to make sure she didn't look too—

She sighed again when she saw what she looked like. No makeup, her hair piled haphazardly atop her head with a loose clip, and the sleepwear of a thirteen-year-old boy. Then again, any woman who lounged around in the sort of stuff Victoria's Secret models lounged around in was nuts.

At least those women were paid big bucks for smiling seductively while a stocking garter bit into their flesh and all
that lace made their boobs itch.

Besides, what did she care if Mr. Finn "Issues with
Trust" Guthrie saw her looking like, well, herself? He
didn't have a very good opinion of her anyway.

Belting her robe over the ensemble and hoping it covered the battered boxer shorts, Natalie waved a defeated
hand at her reflection and fled. She deserved this, she told
herself as she padded barefoot down the steps. After the
whopping fat lie she'd told Clementine, she'd just been
begging karma to come dump something rancid on her.
Not that Finn was rancid or anything, but the situation in
which she found herself certainly was.

Your own fault, Karma reminded her.

Yeah, yeah, yeah.

He was still pounding on the door when she approached
it, and leaning into the bell again for good measure. She
paused for one more fortifying breath before gripping the
knob, then, resigned to her fate, she turned the dead bolt
and tugged the door open.

Forcing both a carefree smile and a breezy tone of
voice—neither of which she felt, of course, but a big part
of her job was spin, after all—she said, "Wow. That was
fast. You must have slid right down the ratpole in the rat-
cave and rushed over in your ratmobile. Did you wear the
ratbelt filled with rattools to battle my untrustworthy,
criminal mastermind self?"

One look at Finn, however, and her flippancy fled. He
was furious. His hair looked as if he'd been running both
hands through it with way more force than was necessary,
his brows were arrowed downward over narrowed eyes,
and his jaw—unshaven again, now there was a surprise—
was clenched so tight, she could see a vein throbbing at his
temple. He looked as if he'd thrown on clothes that had
previously lain in a pile on the floor, so wrinkled were both
the pinstriped, untucked oxford and faded jeans.

He dropped the hand he'd been using to pound on the

door and withdrew the other from the doorbell, then stood with both hands settled menacingly on his hips. When he leaned forward, crowding himself into her space, Natalie took an involuntary step backward. But all that did was open up enough space for him to enter uninvited, slam the door behind him, and glower at her some more.

And God help her, in spite of his threatening pose, the only thing she felt in that moment was completely turned on.

So he'd been right after all, she thought. Whatever it was burning up the air between them, it was founded in the physical, not the emotional. Oh, sure, there was a thin line between love and hate and all that, but no woman in her right mind would be turned on by a guy who was angry at her.

"I started over here ten minutes before the news came on," he began, grinding the words out through gritted teeth, "after picking up my messages and seeing about two hundred from eighty different media outlets asking me to confirm Russell's appearance at a party this weekend."

"Oh, stop," she said, waving a dismissive hand and hoping he didn't notice how much it was shaking. "We may be the seventeenth largest city in America—or maybe it's the sixteenth, I can never quite remember, though I think Rand McNally might have proven it's more like twenty-third— but we don't even have eighty media outlets here, so you couldn't possibly have had two hundred messages from anybody. We *have* been named one of the top twenty best places to live, though," she added. "At least, I think it was the top twenty. Maybe it was the top twenty-five. And we have two— or is it three?—high schools on *Time* magazine's list of the three hundred best public schools in the nation. Did you know that? Isn't that cool?"

"Oh, no you don't," he said, holding up both hands now, palm out, in an obvious gesture of self-preservation. "You are *not* going to mess with my head again with that weird, roundabout way you have of talking. It's not going to work this time."

Ignoring him—What was he talking about anyway?—

Natalie continued, "But getting back to the media outlets, let's see . . . There are the three local network affiliates, two—or maybe three now—independent stations, two educational channels, one daily newspaper, several weeklies, though the two biggies there would be *Velocity* and *LEO*, and let me tell you, if you haven't picked up a copy of *LEO* while you've been in town, you absolutely have to, because it's so funny and well-written and irreverent. And here's a tidbit I bet you didn't know. *The Louisville Eccentric Observer*—that's what *LEO* stands for—was actually started by one of our congressmen who—"

"Stop," Finn interjected before she even paused for a breath.

"But this is—"

"Just stop, Natalie."

"But this—"

"No. No more."

"But—"

"It's my turn to talk now."

"B—"

"And then," he interrupted her again, "*then*—"

"You didn't let me finish," Natalie interrupted him right back. "There are a bunch of local magazines, too. *Louisville* magazine, of course, but also *Today's Woman* and—"

"And then," he repeated, clearly not going to let her finish. Damn. A perfectly good stalling tactic ruined. "*Then* when I tried to call them all back to tell them that no, as a matter of fact Mr. Mulholland would *not* be making an appearance at the aforementioned party, all I got were recordings telling me to call back during regular business hours, or people's voice mail because it was too close to airtime for any of them to be answering their phones." He dropped his hands to his hips again and glared at her some more. "I ought to sic Russell's attorneys on you."

"*Me?*" she exclaimed. "*I'm* not the one who told everybody Russell was coming to Clementine's party."

He arched a dark brow at that, clearly not believing a word. "No?"

She shook her head, but the look on his face made her want to shrink into the floor and never come back. Because even if it hadn't, technically, been her to spill the beans to all the newspeople, she had been the primary source of the information. Still, if Clementine had kept her promise, none of them would be in this situation right now. They could have put this situation off for at least another twenty-four hours.

"I, um . . ." she hedged. "I, ah . . . Well, see . . . It's like this . . . I mean, what happened was . . ." As she stammered, she shifted her weight from one foot to the other and back again. Then she lifted her hand to the back of her neck and rubbed it anxiously. "Actually," she tried again, "it's kind of a funny story."

"Oh, I'll just bet it is."

She expelled an impatient sound. "Okay, so maybe funny is relative in this situation."

"I don't know, Natalie. *Truth* seems to be relative in this situation as far as you're concerned."

Yeah, okay, so he had her on that one. "The point is," she tried again, "that I only told *one* person that Russell would be attending Clementine's party. But I swore her to secrecy until I had all the kinks ironed out."

"One of those kinks being that you knew Russell wouldn't be attending."

"I thought maybe if I had another chance to talk to him, explain about the party and the charity it's raising money for, he'd change his mind."

"I promise you, Natalie, he won't change his mind about this. Russell never, ever, attends this sort of function. At best, it takes too much out of him to be nice to a bunch of strangers for any length of time. At worst, the security sucks at these things, and it's too dangerous for him to attend."

"But if I could just talk to him, Finn. I know he'd change his mind if he heard more about the charity Clementine's sponsoring."

"No way. The last thing Russell ever wants to hear about is disadvantaged people."

"And why is that?" Natalie asked pointedly.

"Don't try to change the subject."

"I'm not. I—"

"Who did you tell that Russell would be coming to the party?"

She bit her lip, sighed again, and then made a defeated sound. "Clementine Hotchkiss. The one who's giving the party." She hurried on, "But, Finn, if you just knew the circumstances, you'd understand." She opened her mouth to tell him about Glenda Hightower, and how she could put her daughter Tootie to shame when it came to making people feel small, but he cut her off before she could get the words out.

"You lied to your client for the sake of monetary gain."

She prickled at that. A lot. "No, I didn't." That much, at least, was true. The fact that Clementine was a paying customer hadn't had anything to do with Natalie's actions this afternoon. "I told her what I did because . . ." She sighed heavily again, lifting a hand to her forehead, as if that might keep all her jumbled thoughts from tumbling out. "I did it because Clementine was in a tight spot, and I needed to help her out of it. And dammit, Finn," she added, her own anger bubbling up now, "I did it because the money her party's going to raise with Russell attending is going to an extremely worthy cause, one that Mr. Mulholland—and you—should want to see succeed, because he—and you—could have benefited from it yourselves when you were kids. If you would just let me talk to him one more—"

Instead of mollifying him, her explanation only seemed to make him angrier. Nevertheless, he said, "Oh, I'll let you talk to him, all right, Natalie. In fact, you can talk to him right now. I'll drive you over myself."

For one brief, euphoric moment, she thought everything was going to be all right. Even if Finn was still bent out of shape, surely once she had five minutes of Russell's uninterrupted time—sober this time—she would be able to at least make *him* understand, and he would be happy to make an appearance at Clementine's party. Natalie would be vindicated, Clementine wouldn't be humiliated, and Kids, Inc., would bank a nice, fat check that would go a long way toward making their new facility a reality.

Then Finn added, "I've arranged a conference call with his attorneys on the West Coast and, interestingly, it should be starting right about the time you and I arrive."

Her heart fell at that. Evidently, Natalie would instead be eviscerated, Clementine would be humiliated, and both she and Kids, Inc., might very well end up tied to a nice, fat lawsuit with Natalie and Party Favors. And it would be all her fault.

"Let me go change my clothes," she said despondently.

Finn grabbed her wrist and gave it a less than gentle tug. "There's no time. We're leaving now."

She gaped at him. "Shoes?" she asked sarcastically. "The Brown isn't the kind of place to tolerate bare feet."

He looked down at her feet, wrinkled his nose in disgust at the orange polish, then returned his attention to her face. "You have thirty seconds," he told her.

"Thir—"

"Twenty-nine," he corrected. And then, just to hammer it all home, continued, "Twenty-eight. Twenty-seven. Twenty-six."

"All right, all right," she muttered as she turned to take the stairs two at a time. Under other circumstances, she would have tried to steal a few minutes to get dressed, too. But knowing Finn, in his current state, he'd drag her out of the house halfway through her efforts and dump her in the backseat in her underwear—if she even got that far. So she searched her bedroom for her sneakers, found only her pink fuzzy bedroom slippers, and stuffed her feet quickly into those instead.

From downstairs, she heard the ominous sound of "Five . . . four . . . three . . ." so she grabbed her purse and hurried out of the bedroom. Sure enough, Finn was halfway up the stairs and looked fully capable of throwing her over one shoulder and hauling her out to the car that way.

"I'm coming!" she yelled as she hurried down the steps past him. She came to a halt by the front door with him still standing in the middle of the stairwell, then crossed her arms over her midsection and tapped her pink-fuzzy-slippered foot impatiently. "Well?" she said pointedly. "I'm ready for my command performance for the king. What's the holdup?"

Very slowly and very deliberately, Finn began to make his way down the stairs, his gaze never once leaving Natalie's. And with every thump of his foot on the next stair, her heart began to thunder harder in her chest. Because with every thump of his foot, his expression darkened, his mouth tightened, and his eyes grew harder.

And Natalie, God help her, just got more and more turned on. By the time he stood beside her in the doorway, towering over her, his scent and heat neatly enveloping her, she was near meltdown. When he bent his head until his mouth hovered right beside her ear, she could barely control the shudder of desire that skittered down her spine and pooled deep in her midsection.

"Don't push me, Natalie," he whispered, his voice as coarse as sandpaper. "Just don't . . . push me."

Push him? she thought wildly. That was a laugh. All he had to do right now was touch the pad of his finger anywhere on her body, and she would come apart in his hands.

He straightened and pulled the door open, tilting his head toward the night outside. "Let's go," he told her. "The king is waiting."

Natalie would just bet he was. And he was probably sharpening the blade of the guillotine himself.

FINN LEANED AGAINST THE WALL OF RUSSELL'S SUITE, feeling like the king's favorite fool. The conference call with Russell's West Coast attorneys hadn't materialized after all, because Russell himself was currently missing in action.

Okay, so maybe Finn should have checked to be sure the

guy was in his suite before he'd stormed off to drag Natalie back here and threatened her with legal action that might not even materialize because he wasn't sure she'd done anything illegal. He'd simply assumed that, because he'd been doing his job properly, Russell would be where he was supposed to be, where he'd assured Finn he *would* be, in his room for the entirety of the evening. Then again, he'd been assuring Finn of that nearly every night for the past week, and it wasn't like Russell to *not* go out. As reclusive as he was, he wasn't willing to give up the joys of nightlife, particularly when that nightlife involved the sort of tawdry activity that diverted attention away from himself and onto the—choose one—naked women onstage, naked women on poles, or naked women on one's lap.

He wondered how many other nights Russell had snuck out undetected. And he wondered where he'd gone. No place tawdry, because he wouldn't have risked it without security. Even though he could move in such environments with fairly little risk of detection, he was smart enough to realize the potential for, at best, mischief and, at worst, crime. Russell might not practice common sense in some ways, but in that way, he was definitely smart. So if he'd been sneaking out, without security, it was because he wanted to go somewhere—or be with someone—he didn't want security to know about. And he could only be going to places— or be with someone—where he felt safe.

Which made absolutely no sense, because Russell didn't consider anyplace—or anyone—safe. He was even worse than Finn when it came to not trusting people. Russell didn't even trust himself.

Finn withdrew his phone and punched in the numbers of Russell's private line *again*. But after one ring, it went right to voice mail, meaning the phone had been switched off. Hopefully, Russell was the one who had done that. Otherwise, he might be tied up in a car trunk somewhere, and any minute now, a note would be tucked under the door of the hotel suite composed of letters cut out of magazines demanding millions of dollars in unmarked bills, and Natalie's probably-not-illegal-anyway stuff would be nothing.

He flipped his phone shut and stuffed it into his back pocket. His gut told him Russell was fine, and his gut had never been wrong before. Well, except where Natalie Beckett was concerned. Because as much as Finn had told her—and himself—that he didn't, couldn't trust her, he realized now that he had. When he'd come in to find all those messages wanting to verify Russell's appearance at the party he had repeatedly assured Natalie that Russell wouldn't attend, something in Finn's chest had clenched tight, then frozen solid and dropped to the pit of his belly. He'd felt betrayed. By Natalie. Which was how he knew he'd placed his trust in her. Without even realizing it, he had. No matter what his conscious mind told him, somewhere in his subconscious, he *had* trusted her. For the first time in his life, he'd allowed himself to think the best of someone, allowed himself to believe in her integrity.

And now she'd gone and proved him wrong. He couldn't trust Natalie—should *never* have trusted Natalie. He was just relieved that her betrayal had been over something relatively benign. It would be awkward contradicting the news that Russell would be attending the party, but it certainly wouldn't be a PR nightmare. It could be excused as a misunderstanding, mixed messages or crossed wires. No harm, no foul. Just a disappointed hostess and a bunch of people who would go to a different party on Derby Eve.

In fact, he thought now, he'd probably overreacted going to Natalie's house the way he had, and dragging her back here to Russell's suite. And he was big enough to admit now that his reasons for doing so had little to do with the stories on the news and a lot to do with his feeling of betrayal. But then, he hadn't exactly been the most trustworthy guy himself, had he? Natalie had been right when she called him a rat that night. Not because only a rat would have sex with a woman he didn't trust. But for the very reason that Finn *had* trusted Natalie, and what they'd had amounted to way more than sex. He'd just been too . . . something . . . to admit that before now. And now . . .

Ah, hell. Now he didn't want to think about it. He just wanted Natalie to stop looking so wounded and vulnerable sitting in the oversized, overpadded desk chair dressed in what should have been the most off-putting outfit a woman could wear, but which, for some bizarre reason, Finn found kind of . . . sort of . . . cute. Dammit. She was sitting in a slumped position, her arms overhanging the arms of the chair, her fuzzy-slippered feet planted firmly on the floor, pushing just hard enough to send the chair spinning first slightly to the left, then slightly to the right. And with each new turn, the lopsided topknot on her head dipped in a different direction, something that made her look even . . . cuter. Dammit.

She hadn't looked at him once since he'd told her to park herself there and not move. And she hadn't spoken a word to him. Not that he blamed her. And looking at her now, he had to admit, she didn't exactly look like the untrustworthy type. In fact, she'd never looked like the untrustworthy type. Because she'd never *been* the untrustworthy type. Yeah, she'd made a mistake, committing Russell to a party he'd never agreed to attend. But she hadn't done it maliciously, of that Finn was confident. She'd done it, as she'd said, to help out her client, and because she'd genuinely thought she could convince Russell to change his mind.

Finn knew that because he trusted Natalie. Still.

Which was all the more reason he had to get her out of here. As soon as possible. Before he did something he'd regret. Like apologize. Like ask her forgiveness. Like touch her and kiss her and invite her back to his room, where he could make love to her again. The right way this time. Aware of the fact that he had nothing to fear from her, and nothing to hide, and that it wasn't just scratching an itch, it was something that went way deeper than that, bone-deep, in fact, and maybe if the two of them just gave it a chance they could—

"C'mon, Natalie, I'll take you home," he said abruptly.

Her head snapped up at that, her eyes narrowed in suspicion. Great. Now she was the one full of mistrust. Then again, whose fault was that? And maybe it was better this way. Because now there really was no way he'd make love to her again. Natalie *wasn't* a rat. She *wouldn't* make love with a man *she* didn't trust.

"Not that I'm complaining, mind you," she said, "but why the sudden change of heart?"

He almost smiled at her choice of words. Change of heart. That's what he was having. What he'd been having probably since Natalie Beckett walked into his life. That was the problem. His heart was supposed to stay out of stuff like this completely. There was no way the two of them could make anything work between them. They were the products of two entirely different worlds, separated by everything from geography to economics. It was pointless to pursue what was bound to end in disappointment.

He pushed himself away from the wall and made his way across the room toward her, but all he did in response to her question was repeat, "C'mon. I'll take you home."

"But what about Russell?" she asked, looking panicky now. "What about the party? What am I going to tell Clementine?"

Finn came to a halt in front of her. "Tell her you were mistaken. Tell her you misunderstood. You thought Russell had agreed, but he had his dates mixed up or something. Tell her whatever you want. Just tell her Russell can't make it."

"But what if he can?" she asked, sounding even more anxious now. "Finn, I need to talk to him. I need to tell him about Kids, Inc., the charity whose benefit Clementine is having the party for. Once he hears about all the good work they're doing, he'll change his mind. I know it."

"Natalie."

"He doesn't have to stay all night. Just thirty minutes of his evening. An hour, tops. And it can be anytime he wants. Early, late, somewhere in the middle—"

"Natalie."

"If he'll just commit that tiny little bit of—"

"Natalie."

She finally stopped, but her anxiety now was replaced by a sad sort of resolution that was almost palpable. "What?"

Finn sighed heavily. "He can't make it. It's not a matter of how much time he has. It's a matter of his personal privacy. Of his personal safety. It's just not the kind of function he attends. Ever."

"But—"

"Now c'mon," he said a third time. "I'll take you home."

She gazed at him in silence for a moment, then nodded silently in defeat. "Does this mean you're not going to involve Russell's attorneys?"

He nodded, then spoke aloud his earlier thoughts. "As long as you explain things to your client, and she sends a retraction to the media outlets. No harm, no foul."

"No harm," she repeated gloomily. "Not to you or Russell, anyway."

He wasn't sure what she meant by that, but he was probably better off not knowing. He was about to verbally prod her again, but she rose and collected her purse from the desk, then shuffled in her fuzzy pink slippers toward the door. Finn followed, noting the few errant strands of hair that had fallen from the haphazard twist gathered at the top of her head. When she halted at the door to wait for him to open it, before he could stop himself, he reached out to twine one silky tress around his finger, thinking to tuck it back into the knot. Once his fingertips skimmed the warm skin of her neck, however, he halted, because Natalie spun around, eyes wide.

Damn, she was beautiful. Even dressed as raggedly as she was, without a single effort at enhancement. In fact, at the moment, she was somehow even more desirable than she'd been before. There was no artifice here, no pretense, no wall. Only Natalie, the way she really was. Beautiful. Desirable. One of a kind.

He dropped the strand of hair and reached for the doorknob. "C'mon, Natalie," he said for the last time, "I'll take you home."

·Seventeen·

ON TUESDAY MORNING, AS RUSSELL SAT AT THE
scarred oak table in Ginny Collins's tiny kitchen, nibbling
an overly crisp, slightly blackened piece of bacon and washing it down with not-quite-dissolved frozen orange juice,
his gaze flicking around that table from the narrowed,
very suspicious eyes of a crotchety old woman; to the narrowed,
very puzzled eyes of a young girl; to the narrowed, very
worried eyes of the girl's mother; to the narrowed, very confused eyes of his son, he marveled at how much a man's life
could change over the span of a single week.

Not just because he'd abandoned the wardrobe of a
phony yachtsman and businessman and replaced them with
the accoutrements of his former life: blue jeans and a light-
weight, oatmeal-colored sweater. And not just because he
couldn't even remember the name of the woman to whom
he'd loaned his yacht, never mind what she looked like,
which was usually all he remembered anyway. And not
because he was dining in—or, rather, breakfasting in—
instead of eating out. And not because there wasn't a single
member of his security team in sight.

It was because he was finding more pleasure sitting at a scarred oak table in a tiny kitchen, nibbling an overly crisp, slightly blackened piece of bacon and washing it down with not-quite-dissolved frozen orange juice than he'd ever found sitting in a five-star restaurant savoring oysters Rockefeller and swilling Perrier-Jouët champagne. And it was because he was with a group of normal, *real* people—a family, no less—instead of with the suits and sycophants he normally surrounded himself with.

Ten days, he thought, still astonished. That was how long it had been since he'd first laid eyes on the miniskirted, overly made-up, redheaded bombshell named Amber, who had turned out to be the blue-jean-wearing, naked-faced, wholesome girl next door Ginny Collins. Not Gin. Not Ginna. Ginny. Because she was too nice, too sweet, too decent, to be anything else.

She should have scared Russell to death. She was exactly the kind of woman he had hoped never to meet again. Someone like Marti. Someone he might fall in love with. Someone he might lose again. Someone whose loss he would never be able to comprehend or overcome or forgive.

And although the last ten days had proved Ginny was exactly that kind of woman, those days had also taught Russell some important truths. That it was indeed impossible to comprehend, overcome, or forgive the loss of some people. He would never be able to do any of those things where Marti's death was concerned. But it was also possible to . . . salve . . . that loss, to temper the grief and buffer the pain, to leave it in the past where it belonged, by finding someone to love in the present. Someone to love in, and with whom to plan, the future.

Because love wasn't confined to one person, he realized now. And the loss of love didn't mean loving came to an end. The heart didn't manufacture a finite amount that had to be doled out sparingly over time to special, specific individuals. No, the heart was an amazing organ that could produce mass quantities of the stuff, and with fairly little effort. No matter who you gave love to, there was always more to give. For anyone who might come along.

He'd learned that about Max, too. Yes, he would always fear losing his son. No, not fear, he would be terrified of it, with a terror so profound it would cripple him emotionally if he allowed himself to dwell on it, with a terror that *had* crippled him emotionally since Marti's death, to the point where he hadn't allowed himself to express the love he should—and did—feel for his son, so great was his horror of losing Max, too. But spending time with Ginny this week, Russell had gradually begun to realize that living life as an emotional cripple was slowly killing him, too.

And he didn't want to die. Not when he was learning so many important lessons about life. There were too many reasons to live.

Which was how he and Max—his family—came to be sharing breakfast with Ginny and her family, Maisy and the Lenski woman. Who, Russell had to admit, scared the bejeezus out of him. Though he actually kind of liked that part. It made him feel like he was a teenage high school student meeting his equally teenage girlfriend's parents for the first time, and being weighed for his potential to overstep the bounds of propriety with her. Which was a situation, it went without saying, he'd never found himself in as a teenager. Mostly because he'd had no propriety then. And neither had any of the girls he'd dated. Of course, most of the girls he'd dated hadn't had parents, either. At least none with any propriety.

Hazel, he could see, had buckets of the stuff. She also, he'd been told—by Hazel herself, in fact—had a .32 automatic and wasn't afraid to use it. Talk about proprietary. Propitious. Whatever the adjective that went along with propriety was. Then again, he supposed those other two were kind of appropriate, too.

Anyway . . .

He was just glad to be here sharing breakfast with the others and grateful for Maisy's in-service day at school so that all five of them could spend it together, getting to know each other and doing the sorts of things families did when they had an entire day to spend together. Now, if only Russell knew what some of those things were . . .

"I, um . . . I think I heard the mail truck," Ginny said suddenly, alleviating what Russell had to admit had been a pretty long, awkward silence, since no one had said a word after she put the too-crisp bacon and undercooked eggs on the table. "I'll run out and get it, 'kay?"

Ah, there was a good start, Russell thought. Mail. That was something families all across America got, right?

Unfortunately, when Ginny, one of only two people in the room who was linked to the remaining guests, left it, Russell was the one upon whom fell the duty of keeping the conversation going. And since Ginny was much better at that than he, and he had so far failed abysmally, there wasn't much chance he would do any better. Still, if he intended for this family thing to work out—and for some reason he had yet to fathom, he did—then he would have to do the family man thing and, you know, talk to his family.

"So, Maisy," he began, choosing the non-gun-toting member of Ginny's family for obvious reasons, "what's your favorite subject in school?"

Maisy, who was a thirteen-year-old version of her mother, right down to the hauntingly beautiful eyes, concentrated very hard on moving her scrambled eggs from one side of the plate to the other and not looking at anyone. "It's not really a class, but I like it best when we go to computer lab."

Russell brightened. "A budding technological genius. Excellent."

She looked up at that and smiled at Russell, then glanced over at Max, who also seemed to be showing an unusual amount of interest in the food on his plate. Then her cheeks stained with red, her expression went kind of panicky, and she stared back down at her breakfast. "Well, I wouldn't say I'm a genius . . ."

"I would," Hazel volunteered enthusiastically, fairly beaming at the girl. "She's in the Duke University Talent Identification Program and the Johns Hopkins thingy for gifted students. She took the SAT this year, at thirteen, and scored higher than most outgoing seniors. Got a perfect score on her essay, I might add."

"Hazel . . ." Maisy said sheepishly, trying to shrug off the praise but looking delighted by it nonetheless. "I would like to own my own software company someday, though," she added more enthusiastically. "I've been involved in this local group called Kids, Inc., that's all about teaching kids how to be entrepreneurs. I have some great ideas for starting up."

"Really?" Russell asked, surprised that someone so young already had such a solid vision. "Designing what? Games?" he added with a smile.

She shook her head. "No, I'm more interested in piracy."

His mouth dropped open at that. Okay, this was something he was going to have to nip in the bud right here, right now. Before he had the chance, though, Maisy started laughing.

"Man, you should see the look on your face, Mr. Mulholland."

He would have told her to call him Russell, but since she was turning out to be a criminal mastermind . . .

"I'm interested in stopping piracy," she said with a chuckle. "I'm working on a project right now that would allow record companies to include code on their CDs that would make it impossible to upload them to the Internet without permission. I figure once that's perfected, I could do some tweaking for the gaming and publishing industries, too."

Oh, Russell thought. Well. That made a big difference. He smiled. "Listen, Maisy, you can call me Russell, you know."

She smiled shyly back. "Thanks. Russell."

"And that's interesting about Duke and Johns Hopkins, because Max is in both of them, too," he added of the university programs. "He's going to Tokyo this summer to study new technologies that are being introduced in Asia. Maybe you could both go."

Suddenly flustered, Maisy looked down at her plate again. "Oh, I don't think I'd be a good candidate for—"

"She'd be an excellent candidate," Hazel cut in. "But at four thousand bucks a pop for those programs, her mother can't afford to send her. Unlike *some* people," she added a little testily—oh, all right, *a lot* testily—"money doesn't flow from golden faucets in this house."

"It doesn't flow from gold in ours, either," Russell was quick to point out. "My designer preferred brushed stainless. Much easier to keep clean."

Hazel nodded gruffly. "Yeah, and unlike *some* people, you don't have to work nights and raise a kid and go to college and keep your own house clean, do you?"

He shook his head, completely unashamed. "No, I don't, Hazel. But there was a time in my life when I did. And I remember it *very* well."

She snapped her mouth shut at that, but Russell could tell she still didn't like him. Didn't trust him. Then again, he supposed he couldn't blame her. She really was the closest thing to a parent Ginny had ever had. And she'd helped Ginny raise Maisy. It made sense that she would feel protective of both of them. Especially when some interloper like him, who'd only known her "daughter" and "granddaughter" for a week was suddenly trying to edge his way into their tight-knit family.

He was about to say something to alleviate the tension the exchange had created, but the sound of Ginny's voice coming from the other room did that instead. At least for Russell. Just hearing her speak made him feel calmer, less stressed, better.

"Bill, bill, bill," she said as she came into the kitchen, sifting through the mail. She stacked those envelopes neatly on the counter, then continued, "Credit card offer, credit card offer, credit card offer." These she immediately tore into quarters and tossed into the trash. "Advertisement, advertisement, advertisement," she added, tossing those, too, into the garbage, "Maisy, you got your latest issue of *Wired* and, Hazel"—she lifted a folded bit of newsprint wrapped in plastic and concluded—"your *National Investigator* came."

"Oh, goody." The old woman fairly snatched it out of Ginny's hand as she passed by on the way back to her seat next to Russell. "I love the *Investigator*," she added as she slipped it out of its mailing sleeve. "It's the only news you can trust. But I gotta check my horoscope first."

Russell couldn't hide his smile. Ah, yes. There was nothing more touching than an apple-cheeked, white-haired, former sharpshooter for the Detroit PD sitting down with a quality publication like the *National Investigator*. It was just so all-American. There must be millions of families in this country who, at this very moment, had apple-cheeked, white-haired members sitting at their breakfast tables, reading about the latest celebrity breast implants, which heads of state were actually pod people from outer space, and the most recent sightings of the Chupacabra. Life just didn't get any better than—

"Dad?"

Something in his son's voice made Russell's sense of well-being evaporate. And when he looked over at Max to see his usually sunny face looking ashen, and his normally laughing eyes looking haunted, his stomach clenched with the very sort of terror he had hoped to never feel again. God help him, there was an irrational part of him that feared his son was about to echo Marti's words of more than a decade before: "*There's something I have to tell you that I wish I didn't,*" then repeat the diagnosis she'd received a month before and kept hidden from Russell for weeks before finding the words to tell him. Nausea rolled in his stomach at the idea, however implausible—*impossible*, he corrected himself—that his son was going to leave him, too.

"Max?" he asked, his anxiety evident in that one word. "What is it? What's wrong?"

Instead of blurting news of his ill health, however, Max only lifted a finger and pointed it at something on the other side of the table. Russell followed the direction until his gaze lit on the tabloid that Hazel had opened in front of her face. There, staring back at him, was a photo of Russell himself. But that wasn't what had caused Max's reaction. What had caused that was the picture of Max—taken within the last week, because he looked exactly as he did this morning—beside it. That, and the words screaming out from the headline above: *"Unlike Father, Like Son!"* And then, in only slightly smaller letters, *"14-Year-Old Max Mulholland is the REAL Brains—and CEO—Behind GameViper and Mulholland Games!"* And then, in smaller, but still very readable, even from a distance, letters, *"An Investigator Exclusive!"*

"Oh, crap."

The words were spoken in unison by Russell and Max. Like father, like son, he paraphrased from the headline. Great minds really did think alike. Except that the son's mind was infinitely better developed than the father's, allowing him to design a game system at the tender age of twelve that was more sophisticated than anything Russell could have come up with himself. He wasn't sure what shocked him more, that the story he and Finn had spent the last two years keeping quiet had finally broken or that the *National Investigator* was, for once, reporting the truth.

He waited for the alarm that should have burned him up inside, waited for the panic that should have had him grabbing his son by the collar and racing him to the airport so they could fly someplace where the press would never find them. This was going to be the mother of all media circuses, something that was going to invade and upend Max's life unlike anything had since his mother's death. Russell and Finn had tried so hard to make sure Max's life could be as normal as possible, had done everything they could to shield the child genius—and de facto head of Mulholland Games—from the spotlight so that he could spend his time being a teenager instead. With the news out now of the truth—and just how the hell had the news gotten out?—all of that was going to change.

But, surprisingly, Russell didn't feel any alarm. He

didn't feel any panic. There was concern, of course, for how this was going to impact Max. But there was also a certain kind of relief that the truth *had* come out. A part of him had always known it was bound to come out, sooner or later. But there was something kind of poignant, something kind of perfect, that it was coming out in this moment, in this place. Because in this moment, in this place, Max didn't have to face the crisis alone. And neither did Russell. They had family to help them cope. Family to help them stay strong. Family to provide shelter from what was sure to be a media storm.

Family. Their family. Five of them, right here at Ginny Collins's kitchen table. Whether any of them realized it yet or not.

WHEN NATALIE TURNED ON THE TV IN TIME TO CATCH the last half hour of the *Today* show, she halfway expected to see Matt Lauer and Meredith Vieira breathless with the news that Russell Mulholland would be attending Clementine and Edgar Hotchkiss's benefit party in Louisville, Kentucky, this Friday night, so fearful had she become of newscasts in general over the last six hours. Fortunately, there was a commercial on for erectile dysfunction—and how cool was that, that men now had something to be embarrassed about in advertising, too?—so she lowered the volume and sipped her coffee and opened the Tuesday edition of the *Courier-Journal* instead.

Which, inevitably, had a front-page piece about Russell Mulholland attending the Hotchkiss affair this Friday night.

"Oh, crap!" she shouted loudly enough that Zippy went zipping off the sofa to retreat to the kitchen. As soon as she caught the national news, Natalie would call Clementine to discuss how they were going to handle this. *This* being the operative word in that sentence, since Natalie still hadn't figured out exactly what *this* was going to be. A retraction to the several media outlets that had been notified, telling them a mistake had been made and Russell wouldn't be attending the party after all? A demand to know who had notified them in the first place so that Natalie could hunt down that person like a dog? Yet *another* attempt to go toe-to-toe with Russell Mulholland in an effort to convince him to come to the party no matter what Finn Guthrie might or might not have to say about it?

Why, yes, as a matter of fact, Natalie *was* having a lovely time visiting the land of Denial. Thanks so much for noticing.

On the ride back to her house last night, she actually had made one last-ditch effort to appeal to Finn for an audience with Russell, to explain the situation and beg for a tiny slice of his time. But, as always, Finn had shot her down. Oh, he'd been nicer about it this time—and where that niceness had come from, when he'd been Mr. I'm Calling the West Coast Attorneys only minutes before, she'd never know—but he'd still shot her down. Then he hadn't talked to or looked at her for the rest of the drive home. He hadn't even offered to walk her to her door this time, evidently hoping there *was* someone in the house who would do her harm. Sure would save him a lot of trouble. Humpf.

Quickly, she scanned the article about the Hotchkiss party, which was suddenly being dubbed "a ticket hotter than entrée to Millionaire's Row" at the Derby—Clementine's phone should be ringing off the hook about now—noting how careful the reporter was not to cite any particular sources and how much emphasis she placed on the fact that the reports were unsubstantiated. But she did both in a way that made the story sound completely true and the sources impeccable. Damn those wordsmiths, anyway. Then again, maybe that would make it easier to retract the story tomorrow and save Clementine some face.

Reading further, however, Natalie realized it wasn't just her client's face that would need saving. Because there, in black and white, were the words "Natalie Beckett, local event planner and owner and operator of Party Favors,

is . . . continued on page A7." Hurriedly—once the sentence
made sense to her suddenly flurrying brain—she turned to
the page in question and continued to read. ". . . reportedly
the woman of the hour, having single-handedly planned
the Hotchkiss affair and arranged for Mr. Mulholland's
appearance."

Oh, crap.

"Unfortunately," she read further, "Ms. Beckett couldn't
be reached for comment. Calls to her business were not
returned."

"That's because I was out of the office yesterday, trying
to figure out how to get Russell Mulholland to come to the
Hotchkiss affair!" she shouted in her defense. Then she
made a mental note to install call forwarding at the office,
something she probably should have done a long time ago.

Okay, Natalie, she said to herself, *let's review, shall
we? In less than two weeks' time, you've managed to mis-
lead a client, get involved with a man you never should
have gone near, create a media sensation without lifting a
hand, and generally screwed up a bunch of people's lives.
Now Clementine Hotchkiss, a perfectly nice woman who's
never done anything to deserve it, is going to be humiliated, a worthy charity that was counting on a significant
donation is going to wind up with nothing, you're going to
look like an imbecile, and your business is going to go
under. Oh, and you're going to have to date Dean Waterman exclusively for the next six months, something that
will turn you into either a pudding-brained ninny or a raging alcoholic. Does that about cover it?*

Yep. That about covered it.

She was trying to prioritize all of the above and decide
which fiasco to try and un-fiasco first when the *Today*
show came back on and went right to the news desk with
Ann Curry, behind whom was a photograph of billionaire
Russell Mulholland.

Natalie felt the blood drain from her face, thinking the
national news outlets were indeed reporting that Russell
would be attending a party in Louisville this weekend, and

now she had screwed up on a national, perhaps even global, scale. But then a photo of Russell's son Max appeared alongside his own, followed by a blowup of the latest issue of the *National Investigator*, a tabloid Natalie used to read for fun in college and hadn't looked at since—

Okay, okay. Since last Thursday, when she was standing in line at Kroger. So sue her. She liked being kept informed about which heads of state were really pod people from outer space. It gave her comfort knowing what was actually wrong with the world. Still, since the *Investigator* was a weekly that was mailed early to subscribers so that they could receive their issues the same day the tabloid went on sale in supermarkets—okay, okay, so sue her again since she had been a subscriber in college—they couldn't have had enough time to report on the news of Clementine's party. Not that they would, anyway. Unless it was a slow news week for pod people from outer space or something.

She thumbed the volume button on the remote just in time to hear that the issue of the *Investigator* hitting newsstands today was reporting an exclusive story it insisted was absolutely true, citing a "confidential but extremely reliable source" and their own, still ongoing, investigation. And her jaw dropped when she heard the particulars of what that story was. That Russell Mulholland, reclusive billionaire and the genius behind the mega-selling Game-Viper system was neither a billionaire nor a genius. Natalie could have told them he also wasn't especially reclusive these days, either, but that was neither here nor there. At least, he wasn't the genius behind the GameViper. That honor would belong, according to the *Investigator*, to his son, Max, who had designed the game system when he was all of twelve years old. The money Mulholland Games had made since then belonged to him, not his father, who had put it all into a trust fund for his son that Max would be able to tap upon graduation from college. Yes, the elder Mulholland was, technically, CEO of the company and still designed many of its games. And yes, he still raked in a generous seven figures annually himself. But it was young

Max who was now the real brains behind much of the operation.

"Holy cow," Natalie muttered as the story concluded. That was the big secret, she realized. The one Russell and Finn had worked so hard to keep under wraps. The one that explained why there was so much missing about Russell and his business on the Web. The one Finn feared Natalie had figured out that night the two of them—

The bottom dropped out from beneath her when she remembered that conversation. Finn thought she'd uncovered something about Max. He was going to think she was the one who had broken the story to the *Investigator*. That she was the "confidential but extremely reliable source" they cited. If he'd thought she could falsify a news report for monetary gain in the form of a simple party, he'd sure as hell believe she'd sold a story like this to a national publication that was notorious for sensationalizing, well, everything.

She tossed the remote onto the couch without even turning off the TV and ran to the kitchen for her phone. She told herself the only reason she had Finn's number memorized was because she'd called him so many times in an effort to get to Russell. But really, she knew it was because of another reason entirely. It was because . . . because . . . because she'd wanted to know everything she could about him, and since he only offered up snippets of himself in small portions, learning his phone number was one way of adding to the meager pile of knowledge.

Yeah, that was it. She'd just been curious about him, that was all. It had nothing to do with those pesky *feelings* she'd thought she had for him. Those *feelings* that had turned out to be nothing but some misguided notion that the two of them could create something beautiful together. Those *feelings* she didn't *feel* for Finn at all. She didn't. Really. No way.

Just because she wanted so desperately to make him realize she hadn't been the one to betray his trust didn't mean anything. That was just Natalie saving face. Defending herself against an unwarranted charge. Clearing her name. Maintaining fairness and balance in an otherwise topsy-turvy world. It had nothing to do with her being unable to stand the idea of Finn thinking less of her than he already did. And it sure as hell didn't have anything to do with caring about him and wanting him to care for her, too.

Saving face. That was all Natalie was doing as she punched his number into the phone. Defending herself. Clearing her name. But when she heard the buzz of a busy signal hammering her ear—all six times she tried calling him back—when she realized he was probably on the phone right now with those West Coast attorneys, telling them what a deceitful, conniving opportunist she was, she felt something welling in the pit of her stomach that felt very much like terror. But it wasn't the terror of being sued, or of confronting a cadre of attorneys, or being financially and professionally destroyed. It wasn't even the terror of having to date Dean Waterman exclusively for six months.

It was the terror that she had lost forever the one man she might very well be in love with.

·Eighteen·

FINN FOLDED HIS CELL PHONE CLOSED AND SOMEHOW managed not to hurl it out the hotel window and into the building across the street. But within seconds, the damned thing was ringing again. He glanced down at the number—by now he had the number of every media outlet in town memorized—and when he didn't recognize it, decided not to answer. Instead, he shut the phone off, shot a longing look at the window, and tossed the cell onto the bed instead.

All hell was breaking loose where Russell and Max were concerned, and Finn didn't even know where in the hell Russell and Max were. Nor did he know how in the hell all hell was breaking loose in their lives. The *National Investigator*, for God's sake. Of all the ways he'd played out the possibility of Max's secret getting out, the *Investigator* was the last place Finn would have expected the news to break. Yeah, they liked to dish the celebrity scandals, but they generally confined their trawling to Hollywood and professional sports. If Max or Russell had suffered some Botox accident or been arrested for 'roid rage, he could see the *Investigator* jumping on it. But something that would rock the business and technology worlds? Who'da thunk?

Damn those *People* magazine lists, anyway.

He crossed to the hotel phone and picked it up to call Russell again. He'd told the desk not to put through any calls, knowing Russell would use his cell phone to contact him, but everyone else was trying to contact Finn through that number, too, so the hotel phone would have to do. He could punch in the numbers without even looking at this point, so often had he dialed them this morning. Hell, his fingers cramped up when he did it, so often had they made the route. But, as always, after one ring, Russell's voice mail came up instead.

"Dammit, Russell, where are you?"

As if cued by the question, there was a sudden, muffled thump from the suite next to Finn's, sounding very much like a door opening and closing. By the time he crossed to the connecting door, he could hear Russell and Max talking on the other side, and he expelled a long, lusty sigh of relief. Then, forgoing the courtesy of knocking since, hell, Russell didn't deserve any courtesies at this point, Finn turned the knob and pushed the door open with enough force to send it crashing against the wall on the other side.

"Where the hell have you two been?" he bellowed by way of a greeting.

A twinge of guilt pricked him when he saw how Max flinched at the question, but his anger returned in a rush when he looked over at Russell and saw him looking in no way troubled. That was Russell. Even in the face of disaster, he could hide behind the carefree facade he'd been perfecting since Marti's death.

"Well?" Finn demanded, still standing on his side of the room. "Where the hell have you been?"

In response to the question, Russell extended a hand toward the door, then curled his fingers toward himself a few times in a *come on over* gesture to someone out of Finn's line of sight. At the same time Finn crossed the threshold into Russell's suite, a young woman who was pretty and

wholesome-looking came into view. She was followed by a
girl, an adolescent version of herself, and then by an older
woman who resembled her not at all, but who reminded
Finn, for some reason, of Nurse Ratched from *One Flew
Over the Cuckoo's Nest*.

"Come on," Russell said softly, as if he were talking to a
litter of puppies out for their first walk. "He won't bite you,
I promise. It's his job to be scary. This is Finn. He's my
head of security." At this, Russell looked back at Finn.
"And also my best friend. And the only person in the world
I've been able to trust." Now he looked back at the young
woman and smiled in a way Finn hadn't seen him smile for
a very long time. As if he were genuinely happy. "Until
now, I mean," he added softly.

The three women looked at Finn but clearly didn't take
Russell at his word. So Finn did his best to smile at them,
relaxed his stance a little, and said, as politely as he could,
"Ladies." Then, to Russell, his smile turning more to gritted
teeth, he added, "You have me at a disadvantage. Russell?
Would you care to make some introductions?"

"Absolutely," Russell replied. He curled an arm around
the shoulder of the pretty woman beside him, pulling her
close, something that made Finn arch an eyebrow. "This is
Ginny Collins, a very nice girl I met in Louisville last
week."

A nice girl? Finn echoed to himself. *A very nice girl?*
What the hell had Russell been doing this week that would
put him in the path of a very nice girl? Nice girls were the
last type of woman he wanted to meet.

"And this," Russell continued, indicating the girl next to
Ginny, "is Ginny's daughter, Maisy."

Finn had pegged them as sisters. Ginny didn't look old
enough to be the girl's mother. Not to mention that mothers
were right up there on the list next to nice girls when it
came to Russell's Women I Don't Want to Get Near list.

"And this," Russell said, gesturing toward the older
woman, "Is Hazel Lenksi. She's Ginny's, ah . . ."

Hazel seem fully able—and more than willing—to an-

swer that question herself. "I'll kick the ass of any man
who tries to take advantage of Ginny," she announced in a
coarse, no-nonsense voice. She looked pointedly at Russell
and added emphatically, "*Any* man."

In response to this, Russell looked back at Finn and
smiled that oddly happy smile again. "Isn't she delightful?"

"Uh, yeah," Finn agreed. Mostly because Hazel Lenski
would have probably kicked his ass if he didn't. "Delightful." Then he hurried on, "Look, as nice as it is to meet all
your new friends, Russell, we have a problem on our hands.
A big problem. I've been trying to call you all morning.
Since last night, actually, when we had another problem on
our hands. But that one doesn't seem like such a big deal
now, in light of the—"

"*National Investigator*," Russell finished for him.

"You already know?"

"Since breakfast this morning. Hazel's a subscriber."

Wow, Finn thought, now there was a shocker. "It's all
over the networks, too," he said. "And the Internet has become a living thing. There are already web pages set up
and conspiracy theorists."

"Oh, I do so love technology."

"Um, yeah. Look, Russ, we're going to have to release a
statement ASAP. I've already been on the phone with your
attorneys and your PR people. They're all waiting for word
from you." He tried to smile reassuringly at Max. "And
Max, of course."

Max asked, "Could you tell them we're on a retreat with
Tibetan monks in the Himalayas and can't be reached?"

"I wish it were that easy," Russell told him. "To just go
someplace else—or become someone else—and hide."

And then, doing something Finn hadn't seen him do
since Max was a toddler, he put his arm around his son and
pulled him close. The gesture seemed to surprise Max
even more than it did Finn, but he didn't balk. He only
slung his arm around his father's waist and leaned into
him. Finn hadn't realized until now that Max was nearly as

tall as his father. He'd grown a lot in the last couple years. And not just on the outside, either. The next few months weren't going to be easy for him, being thrust into the media spotlight, fielding interviews and photo ops, and running from the paparazzi. But he wasn't as young as he used to be. And hey, he had his dad now to watch his back.

"But you can't hide from things just because they're difficult to face," Russell told his son. He looked at Finn, smiled sadly, then turned back to Max. "Oh, maybe you can for a little while. Maybe you can for years. But, eventually, you have to accept that things change, often in life-altering ways. And you have to learn how to cope. And accept. And move on." Now Russell looked at Ginny. "Because if you don't," he said, tilting his head to press his forehead against hers, "you close yourself off to the possibility of something wonderful happening."

Man, Finn thought. Where had Russell been spending his time this week? He realized he'd fallen down egregiously on the job since coming to Louisville—or, more specifically, since meeting one Natalie Beckett—but he hadn't realized just how lousy his job performance had been. Not only had he not been keeping tabs on Russell, he hadn't known who the guy was even running around with.

Although, judging by the way he was looking at Ginny Collins, Russell's "running around" days were winding down.

"So, Russell," he said, "where did you and Ms. Collins meet, anyway?"

"That's what I'd like to know, too," Hazel Lenski chimed in. "'Cause this guy just shows up for breakfast this morning out of nowhere, and Ginny's not the type to bring home strays. Then I see his face on the cover of the *Investigator*, and I don't know what to think."

Russell and Ginny exchanged a look that Finn was hard-pressed to interpret. Then Ginny smiled, and Russell smiled, and together, they said, "Vincenzo's."

The restaurant? Finn thought. He'd known it was one of the places Russell wanted to visit, but . . .

"Why did you go there alone?" he asked. "Why didn't you take me or Danetta or Moseby or Hernandez?"

"Well, at the time," Russell said, "I wanted to be alone."

"And all those other times you went out without security?" Finn asked pointedly.

Russell smiled. "Those times, I *didn't* want to be alone."

Hazel strode around from the other side of Ginny's daughter and stood face-to-face with Russell. "Am I gonna have to kick your ass?" she demanded.

"No," Russell assured her. "Because I have no intention of taking advantage of Ginny. In fact . . ." His gaze skittered from Hazel to Finn to Ginny. And then there was that smile again. Jeez, the guy was grinning like an idiot. "In fact," he said again, "Ginny and I have a lot to talk about." He shot his gaze toward Max and Maisy. "We all do."

Finn was about to tell him there was no time like the present, but a loud thumping at the door to his suite prevented him. He lifted a finger in the internationally recognized sign language for *Hold that thought,* then strode back into his own room to answer the door. For a moment, he steeled himself for the possibility that it might be someone from the media, even though the hotel staff had been given express orders not to let anyone near Russell's suite. Or Russell's floor, for that matter. Nevertheless, Finn was surprised to discover it wasn't a member of the media on the other side of the door at all.

It was Natalie. A woman who'd been hovering at the back of his brain ever since he'd dropped her off at her house the night before, and whose face kept materializing in his brain every time Russell looked at Ginny the way he kept doing.

"Natalie," he said by way of a greeting, his surprise— and pleasure—evident in his tone.

Instead of looking happy to see him, the way he was happy to see her, she looked frightened and panicky. Instead of the always-well-put-together woman—well, except for last night, when he'd kidnapped her in the men's underwear he assumed was supposed to pass for pajamas—she was a mess. Her hair was in a lopsided ponytail, her blue jeans had a rip in one knee, and her sweatshirt, emblazoned with the words, I Bleed Red and Black, was about ten sizes too big. And her shoes . . . Well, evidently, she either didn't realize or didn't care that one was a black Converse All-Star sneaker and the other was what to his admittedly untrained eye appeared to be a clunky brown sandal of some kind. And both were meant for the left foot.

"Finn, you have to listen to me," she said breathlessly.

She splayed both hands wide on his chest and pushed him back a few feet, then came into the suite, slammed the door behind her, and shot the dead bolt, as if she intended to lock him inside. Then she did the splayed hands on the chest thing again.

"It wasn't me," she said, her eyes pleading, her fingers curling tight into the fabric of his shirt. "I wasn't the one who said anything. I swear it. You have to believe me."

He shook his head in confusion, covering her hands with his to tug them from his shirt. But she tightened her grip and jerked hard, pulling his head down until his face was a scarce inch away from her own.

"It wasn't me," she said again, more desperately this time. She punctuated the statement with a vigorous shake of his shirt. "You have to believe me."

"Natalie, what are you talking about?" he asked, concern rising in his belly. Had she run into Waterman again? Done the drinking game thing again? Then again, running into Waterman *without* the benefit of alcohol could probably do a person even more harm. "What wasn't you? Natalie, sweetheart, what's the matter?"

Her eyes widened at that, though whether it was a result of the question or the endearment, he wasn't sure. Then again, the endearment had come as a surprise to him, too, and he was the one who'd uttered it.

She relaxed her hold on his shirt some, but she still clung to him, close enough that he could inhale that soft scent of her that had haunted him since day one. "You haven't heard yet?" she asked.

"Heard what? What are you talking about?" he repeated.

"The story on the news. About Max."

"Oh, that."

Now she gaped at him. "Oh, that?" she echoed incredulously. "That's all you're going to say?"

"We're working on it," he told her. Hell, he was way more worried about her at this point. "What else is there to say?"

She finally released his shirt, dropping her hands to her sides. "What else . . ." she repeated, her voice trailing off. "Aren't you going to blame me for it?"

Finn circled back to confusion again. "Why would I blame you?"

Her mouth dropped open for a moment again, then she snapped it shut. "Oh, I don't know, Mr. How-do-I-know-you-didn't-sleep-with-me-to-get-closer-to-my-boss Guthrie. Maybe because—"

"She slept with you to get closer to me?"

Finn spun around to find that he and Natalie had an audience, and probably had since the minute Finn left Russell's suite to return to his own. Russell, obviously, had been the one who spoke, but Ginny and Hazel were staring, rapt, too. Russell gazed at Finn with laughing eyes, then turned his attention to Natalie.

"Natalie, you didn't have to seduce this reprobate to talk to me. You could have just picked up the phone and called me."

"I did," she said. "But you never returned my—" She broke off, shook her head as if to clear it, then said, "That wasn't why I slept with him."

"Then why did you?" This came not from Russell, but from Hazel. "I mean, I wouldn't throw 'im outta bed for eating crackers, but then it's been a while for me, you know?"

"Because I—" She halted again, her gaze moving from

Russell to Hazel, to Ginny, then back to Finn. "Who are these people?"

Before Finn could answer her, Russell said, "Family, Natalie. They're family. You can speak freely here."

She expelled a restless sound and lifted her hand to anxiously rub her forehead. "Maybe you can, Russell," she said. "But not everyone feels the way you do. Not everyone . . . is as trusting as you are."

Russell looked amazed at that. "You're not trusting, Natalie? See, that surprises me, because I'd trust you with my life."

Now Natalie made a strangled sound. "Yeah, well, I wasn't talking about me, but that shows how much you know."

"What do you mean?" Russell asked.

"You haven't seen the local news since yesterday, have you?" Finn asked him.

He shook his head. "Ginny and I were, ah, busy last night. And this morning, after we saw the *Investigator*, we came to the hotel. I asked Ginny and Maisy and Hazel to come, just in case someone made the connection between me and Ginny and started harassing them, too."

"Yeah, well, in light of that story, this other one is going to seem like nothing, but Natalie did get you into a little trouble yesterday."

She made another one of those strangled sounds, so Finn took it upon himself to explain about the announcement of Russell's appearance at the party Friday night, ending with "But Natalie has promised to get it all straightened out and send a retraction to the paper and news stations." He threw a meaningful look at Natalie. "Right, Natalie? You and Mrs. Hotchkiss are going to send out a retraction today?"

"Hotchkiss?" Ginny repeated. "Clementine Hotchkiss?"

Finn wouldn't have thought there would be that many people named Hotchkiss giving a party this Friday night, but he said, "I don't know. I guess so."

"Yes, it's Clementine's party," Natalie said. She started to say more, but Ginny inadvertently cut her off.

"That's the benefit for Kids, Inc.," she said. "It's supposed to raise like three hundred thousand dollars for the group."

Natalie nodded disconsolately. Equally disconsolate was her voice when she said, "Well, that was what Clementine hoped, but it doesn't look like it's going to happen."

"Why not?" Ginny asked. "Maisy's involved with that group. They're wonderful. And they could really use the money."

"Believe me, I know," Natalie agreed. "And I did everything I could to make it happen. But there's just too much competition for parties that night. I sent invitations to tons of celebrities, and they're all already committed elsewhere. Celebrities are what bring in the guests, and without them . . ." She shrugged. Disconsolately, Finn couldn't help noting. "No guests, no contributions. No contributions, no check for Kids, Inc. That's why I was trying so hard to get Russell to attend. He'd be a major draw. Mysterious, handsome, reclusive billionaire. Celebrity du jour just about every jour of the week. People would be lining up just to get a glimpse of him, never mind the opportunity to shake his hand."

Russell had been listening to the exchange with much interest, Finn noted, certainly more than he'd shown when Natalie had tried to pitch the idea before. "So, if I agree to go to this party, lots of money will go to this Kids, Inc., thing that's helping Maisy so much?"

"And scores of other kids, too," Natalie told him, sounding vaguely hopeful. "And now, with this story about you and Max breaking . . . Woo. I bet we could get twice as many people to come. Twice as much money for Kids, Inc.," she added, her voice moving from hopeful to coaxing. "Of course, it will mean a lot of last-minute changes, but hey, I'm a professional. I can handle it."

Russell smiled, "Well, Natalie, dear, why didn't you say so in the first place?"

She gaped at that. "You mean . . . ?"

"Of course I'll come to Mrs. Hootchimama's party." He turned to look at Max, in a way that Finn hadn't seen him look at the boy in a long, long time. With absolute, unmitigated love. "Maybe Max would like to come, too, to really stir things up."

Max went pale for a minute, then looked at his father, his mouth already opening to speak. But when he saw the way Russell was looking at him, he closed his mouth again.

"What do you say, Maxie?" Russell asked, using the nickname he hadn't uttered since Max was a toddler. "You want to go public with this thing in a big way?"

Max inhaled a deep breath and released it slowly. Then another. And another. Gradually, the color returned to his face. And, gradually, so did a smile. "I guess it has to happen sooner or later, huh?"

"I'm afraid so," Russell told him. "Finn and I did our best to protect you for as long as we could. But there's no going back now."

Max's gaze went from his father to Finn and back again. "And you guys did a great job. I guess it's pretty amazing that no one found out before now. And it's my own fault anyone did."

Finn supposed that, someday, they'd all look back on this moment and realize it was the one when Max went from being a fun-loving, innocent kid to a fun-loving, experienced young man. For now, though, he figured they should just let Max work through it.

The kid hesitated a minute, as if he were trying to work out a few things, then looked not at his dad or at Finn, but at Maisy. "I guess I'd need a date if I'm going to a party," he said.

Maisy's eyes went wide and her cheeks went pink. "Uhhh . . ." she began eloquently. "My mom says I can't date 'til I'm sixteen."

Her mother smiled and slipped an arm around her daughter's shoulders. "It's okay if you double with me," she said. "Assuming I'm invited, too?" she added, throwing Russell a meaningful look.

He grinned at her, again in a way that Finn hadn't seen in a very long time. "I figured that went without saying," he said.

"Good," Ginny replied. "Just so we're on the same page."

Russell took her free hand in his, lifted it to his mouth and placed a chaste kiss at the center of her palm. "Oh, trust me, sweetheart, we are *definitely* on the same page."

At the gritty, in no way delicate clearing of a throat, Russell added, "And of course, no party would be complete without the presence of the illustrious Hazel Lenski."

Hazel fairly beamed at that. Well, okay, maybe *beamed* was pushing it. But she didn't look quite as, ah, shady as before. "Thanks, Russ, you're all right. Guess I won't have to kick your ass after all." She thought for a minute before muttering, "You think I could get Johnny Depp to come to this thing with me? He's a Kentucky boy, you know."

Maisy still didn't seem any too comfortable with the idea of attending the party with Max, though whether that was because she didn't like the kid or because she did was anyone's guess. Thinking back to when he was that age, though, Finn was guessing it was the latter. Liking someone made you way more uncomfortable than not liking them.

And on that note . . .

As the others returned to Russell's suite, Finn turned to Natalie.

"Why did you think I would blame you for leaking the story about Max?" he asked. Though by the time he finished the question, he already knew the answer. Because he'd blamed her for leaking the story about Russell going to the Hotchkiss party. But then, she *had* been the primary source for that one. Then again, Russell *was* going to be attending. Still, it had never entered his mind that Natalie would be the one to—

It had never entered his mind, he thought again. Not once. Even though that night they'd been together, he'd been afraid she'd figured things out about Max, he'd realized later that she'd only been throwing something out wildly to counter his wild accusation about her sleeping with him to get to Russell. He knew Natalie well enough to know she would never do anything to compromise the safety or happiness of a fourteen-year-old boy. Hell, he knew Natalie well enough to know she would never do anything to compromise the safety or happiness of anyone.

In fact, now that he thought about it, he knew quite a bit about Natalie. He'd learned more about her in less than two weeks than he'd learned about anyone since Russell. And he hadn't even been trying. She'd just kind of gotten under his skin. Worked her way into the recesses of his brain. Walked into his thoughts when he least expected it and into his dreams when he couldn't help it. It was almost as if she'd become a part of him. Almost as if he'd fallen in . . . fallen for her.

"I would never suspect you of doing something like that, Natalie," he said in response to his own question. "Never."

Her brows arrowed downward, and she crossed her arms defensively over her midsection. "You've been suspicious of me since the minute you met me."

Okay, he'd give her that one. "But only for a minute," he told her, smiling, knowing it was true. "I stopped being suspicious once I found out you were an event planner." His smile grew broader. "After that, you became a nuisance."

"Hey!" She swatted him on the arm. "I am *not* a nuisance."

"Not anymore, you're not," he agreed.

"Then what am I now?"

He slipped his arm around her waist and pulled her close, dipping his head to press his mouth quickly, lightly, to hers. "Well, let's just put it this way, Natalie. Like Russell said, we have a lot to talk about."

NATALIE STOOD IN THE CENTER OF THE PALATIAL ballroom of the palatial Hotchkiss estate and smiled with much satisfaction at a job well done. Not only had she amended the party to include another hundred guests, but she'd handed out her business card to a good two dozen people tonight. The costume theme, which she'd worried might present a problem when people had to come up with something mere days before the party, was proving to be a lot of fun, and she smiled at the inventiveness of some of the outfits.

And some of the strangeness, too. For instance, Dean Waterman was there with Finn's friend Danetta, both sporting black leather and silver studs, making Natalie wonder if they were supposed to be members of Hell's Angels or some kind of S and M, B and D couple. Surely, it must be the motorcycle motif they were going for. Surely. And Tootie Hightower, who Natalie had hoped to see dressed as a giant gourmet weenie, was instead dressed in a harem girl costume that made her ass look a mile wide. And—hah—she had come stag.

Russell, appropriately, had come as the little tycoon man from the Monopoly game, and Max looked as if he were in his element as a surfer dude. Their PR folks had sent out a fairly detailed press release the day of the *Investigator* story, and father and son had made a handful of television appearances and given a couple of interviews to major newspapers, all with the promise that they would make themselves more available the following week when they returned home to Seattle. Where, Russell had mentioned to Finn and Natalie, Ginny and Maisy and Hazel would be summering with them once school was out. And maybe more than summering, too, he'd further hinted, not so subtly, much to Finn's amazement.

But not so much to Natalie's. She understood how easy it was to fall once you met the right person.

She glanced around for Ginny and found her, not surprisingly, at Russell's side. Dressed, interestingly, as a French maid. Funny, but that just didn't seem like the sort of thing a wholesome, girl-next-door type like her would be. Then again, a lot of people used costume parties as an excuse to be something they normally never would. Natalie had gone with Marie Antoinette herself, symbolically thumbing her nose at the idea of being so tragic a figure earlier in the week.

She searched the room for Finn, who had promised not to go far, then smiled when she saw him striding toward her with a bottle of beer in one hand and a flute of champagne in the other. He'd claimed he was dressed as Jack Kerouac, but he just looked like some guy in blue jeans and a white shirt to her. A copy of *On the Road* tucked into one's back pocket did not a costume make, as far as she was concerned, but she certainly wasn't going to chastise one of the guests. Especially one who had decided to lengthen his stay in Louisville for a little while longer. To explore the great restaurant and arts scene, he'd said. To see if the people were really as friendly and the community as diverse as she claimed.

And then, making her heart soar a little, adding that he wanted to see just how "not too unbearable" the summers were. She'd advised him that the true test was August, and he'd said that wasn't a problem, that he had a lot of vacation time coming, and Russell and Max would be on a speaking tour for the next few months, and he wasn't a big fan of being on the road, Kerouac costume notwithstanding. He'd said some of the other guys on the security detail could handle it. With any luck, Natalie thought now, she could get him to stick around for a spectacular fall, too. Or maybe he could show her a Seattle autumn, and they could visit with Russell and Ginny and what was looking to become their blended family.

Natalie wasn't picky. As long as she was with Finn, she

didn't care where they were. She knew Louisville like the back of her hand. She could plan events from anywhere, provided she came home for a while from time to time. And provided Finn came with her. And since he was head of security for Mulholland Games and could give himself time off pretty much whenever he wanted . . .

Oh, yeah. This was gonna work out just fiiine.

"I would have brought you some cake, too, Marie," Finn said as he handed her the champagne, "but they're running out."

Natalie sipped the bubbly wine, then snapped the fingers of her free hand without concern. "Let them eat Bourbon balls."

He laughed, looping an arm around her waist and pulling her close. Or, at least, he would have pulled her close, if it hadn't been for all the hoops in her skirt. As it was, he pretty much just wrestled the garment into submission, gave Natalie a quick kiss on the lips, then let her go before the hoops bounced back and sent her orbiting into the celestial ballroom ceiling.

He shook his head in disapproval. "What were you thinking when you got the costume with more clothes than for a Maine winter?"

"I was thinking how much fun it would be for you to help me take them all off later."

He brightened at that. "Oh. Okay. I can see the attraction now." He dropped his gaze pointedly at his watch. "How much longer do we have to stay?"

She laughed. "'Til the end, I'm afraid. I'm the event planner, you know. I'm the one in charge."

He nodded. "For now. But at the event *I* have planned later, Miss Antoinette, you're going to have to be a little more submissive."

She smiled. "I thought that was Dean's costume tonight."

Finn smiled back. "If Danetta has her way, it'll be his costume every night."

Oh, Natalie did so like it when everything worked out the way it was supposed to.

She looked down at her watch, too, then at the crowd surrounding her. The buffets—all three of them—were well-stocked, the servers were weaving their way through the crowd to keep everyone's refreshment, ah, refreshed, and Clementine was beside herself with Russell on her arm. Everything was exactly as it was supposed to be. Everything.

Finn moved as close as he could, then bent forward until his mouth was next to her ear. "You know, Natalie," he said in a voice she'd come to recognize very well by now. He looked down at her skirt, then back at her. "That's an awfully big skirt you have there. A man could get lost under a skirt like that." He leaned in closer. "Unless he knew exactly what he was looking for."

She glanced down, but her gaze halted at his waist instead of her own. "That's an awfully big something you have, too," she replied.

He grinned. "Maybe we wouldn't have to take all those clothes off just yet. Maybe, if you could just sneak away for a little while, we'd only have to take off one or two pieces."

"Just one," she said.

"All the better. So what do you say, Marie? Are you with me?"

She wiggled her eyebrows playfully. "Let 'im eat cake."

Turn the page for a preview of
the first book in the
Mindhunters trilogy by Kylie Brant

Waking Nightmare

Available September 2009 from
Berkley Sensation!

SUMMER GRIPPED SAVANNAH BY THE THROAT AND strangled it with a slow, vicious squeeze. Most faulted the heat and cursed the humidity, but Ryne knew the weather wasn't totally to blame for the suffocating pall. Evil had settled over the city, a cloying, sweaty blanket, insidiously spreading its tentacles of misery like a silent cancer taking hold in an unsuspecting body.

But people weren't going to remain unsuspecting for much longer. This latest victim was likely to change that, and then all hell was going to break loose.

Compared to Savannah, he figured hell had to be a dry heat.

The door to the conference room opened, and the task force members began filing in. Most held cups of steaming coffee that would only make the outdoor temperature seem more brutal. Ryne didn't bother pointing that out. He was hardly in the position to lecture others about their addictions.

Their voices hadn't yet subsided when he reached out to flip on the digital projector. "We've got another vic."

A close-up picture was projected on the screen. There was a muttered "Jesus" from one of the detectives. After spending the last two hours going through the photos, Ryne could appreciate the sentiment.

"Barbara Billings. Age thirty-four. Divorced. Lives alone. She was raped two days ago in her home when she got off work." He switched to the next set of pictures, those detailing her injuries. "He was inside her house, but we don't know yet if he'd been hiding there or if he gained access after she arrived. She got home at six, and said it was shortly after that he grabbed her. She's hazy on details, but the assault lasted hours."

"Where'd he dump her, the sewer?" Even McElroy sounded a little squeamish. And considering that his muscle-bound body housed an unusually tactless mouth, that was saying something.

Ryne clicked the computer mouse. The screen showed a photo of a pier, partially dismantled, with the glint of metal beneath it. "A cage had been wired to the moorings beneath this dock on St. Andrew's Sound. That's where he transported her to afterwards."

"Looks like the kennel I put my Lab in," observed Wayne Cantrell.

Ryne flicked him a glance. As usual, the detective was sitting slouched in his seat, arms folded across his chest, his features showing only the impassive stoicism of his Choctaw heritage. "It is a dog kennel," Ryne affirmed. The next picture showed a close-up of it. "Sturdy enough to hold a one-hundred-thirty-pound woman. The medical exam shows she was injected twice. It'll be at least a week before we get the tox report back, but from her description of the tingling in her lips, heightened sensation, and foggy memory, this sounds like our guy."

"Shit."

Ryne heartily concurred with Cantrell's quiet assessment. It also summed up what they had so far on the bastard responsible for the rapes.

The rest of the photos were shown in silence. When he

got to the end of them, he crossed to the door and switched on the overhead lights. "Marine Patrol wasn't able to get much information from her when they found her, so they processed the secondary scene. Her preliminary statement was taken at the hospital, before the case got tossed to us."

"Where's she at now?" This was from Isaac Holmes, the most seasoned detective on the case. With his droopy jowls and long, narrow face, he bore an uncanny resemblance to the old hound seen on reruns of *The Beverly Hillbillies*. But he had an enviable cleared-case percentage, a factor that had weighed heavily when Ryne had requested him for the task force.

"She was treated and released from St. Joseph/Candler. She's staying with her mother. The address is in the file."

"Where the hell is that other investigator Dixon promised?"

McElroy's truculent question struck a chord with Ryne. He made sure it didn't show. "Commander Dixon has assured me that he's carefully looking at possible candidates to assign to the task force." He ignored the muttered responses in the room. If another member weren't assigned to the group by the end of the day, he would have it out with Dixon himself. Again.

"We need to process the primary scene and interview the victim. Cantrell, I want you and . . ." His words stopped as the door opened, and a slight young woman with short dark hair entered. Despite the double whammy of Savannah's heat and humidity, she wore a long-sleeved white shirt over her black pants. He hadn't seen her around before, but given the photo ID badge clipped to the pocket of her shirt and the thick folder she carried, he figured her for a clerical temp. And if that file contained copies of the complete Marine Patrol report, it was about damn time.

"I'm looking for Detective Robel." She scanned the occupants in the room before shifting her focus to him.

"You found him." He gestured to a table near the door.

"Just set the folder there and close the door on your way out."

Her attention snapped back to him, a hint of amusement showing in her expression. "I'm Abbie Phillips, your newest task force member."

"Does the department get a cut rate on pocket-sized police officers?" There was an answering ripple of laughter in the room, quickly muffled. Ryne shot a warning look at McElroy, who shrugged and ran a hand through his already-disheveled brown hair. "C'mon, Robel, what is she, all of fourteen?"

"Welcome to the team, Phillips." Ryne kept his voice neutral. "We can use a woman to help us interview the victims. We've been borrowing female officers from other units."

"I hope to give you more assistance than that." She handed him the file folder. "A summary of my background."

The folder was too thick for a rookie, but it also wasn't a SCMPD personnel file. He flicked a gaze over her again. No shield. No weapon. Tension knotted his gut as he took the folder she offered. He gestured to the primaries in the room in turn. "Detectives Cantrell, McElroy, and Holmes. We had another rape reported last night, and I was just catching everyone up." To the group he said, "I'll need all detectives and uniforms at the scene. Holmes, until I get there, you oversee the canvass. I'll meet you later."

There was a scraping of chairs as the officers rose and made their way to the door. Abbie turned, as if to follow them. His voice halted her. "Phillips, I'd like to talk to you first."

She looked up at him. At her height, she'd look up to most men. She couldn't be much more than five foot two. And her smoky gray eyes were as guileless as a ten-year-old's.

"We could talk in the car. I'm anxious to get a look at the scene."

"Later." He went to the projector and shut it off. Pulling out two chairs beside it, he gestured toward one.

She came over, sat down. He sank into the other seat, set her file on the table in front of him, and flipped it open. He read only a few moments before disbelief flared, followed closely by anger.

"You're not a cop."

Abbie's gaze was steady. "Independent consultant. Our agency contracts with law enforcement on problematic cases. If you're worried about my qualifications, the file lists my experience. Commander Dixon seemed satisfied."

Dixon. That backstabbing SOB. "I think there's been a misunderstanding." Ryne delivered the understatement in a steady tone. "What our task force needs, what I requested from Commander Dixon, is another investigator. Preferably two. What we definitely do not need is a shrink."

There was a flicker in those calm gray eyes that might have been temper. "I have a doctorate in forensic psychology—"

"We need a *doctor* even less."

She ignored his interruption. "And since joining Raiker Forensics, I've been involved in nearly three dozen high-profile cases."

"Shit." He was capable of more finesse, but at the moment diplomacy eluded him. "Do you realize what kind of case we're working here? I've got a serial rapist on the loose, and with this latest victim, the media is going to be crawling up my ass. I need another experienced investigator, not someone who'll shrink the skell's mind once we get him."

She never flinched. "You'll have to catch him first, won't you? And I can help with that. I consulted on the Romeo rapist case last year in Houston. The perp is currently doing a twenty-five-year stretch at Allred. Of the cases I've worked, well over half involved serial rapists. I'm exactly what you need on this case, Detective Robel. You just don't realize it yet."

The mention of the Houston case rang a bell, but he didn't bother to pursue the memory. "If we have need of a psych consult, we can always get one from a department psychologist."

"And how many of them—how many of your department's *investigators*—have been trained by Adam Raiker?"

Ryne paused, studying her through narrowed eyes. He had no trouble recalling that name; few in law enforcement circles would. The former FBI profiler had achieved near legendary status until he'd disappeared from the radar several years earlier. "Raiker? I thought he was—"

"Dead?"

Maybe. "Retired."

Her smile was enigmatic. "He'd object to either term."

He was wasting his time. The one he needed to be leveling these objections against was upstairs, where the administrative offices were housed, playing political handball. His chair scraped the floor as he rose. "Wait here." He left the room and strode through the squad room. But halfway up the stairs leading to the administrative offices, he met the man he was seeking, followed by his usual entourage.

Ryne shouldered his way through the throng surrounding Dixon. Raising his voice over the din, he said, "Commander, could I have a word with you?"

Dixon held up a hand that could have meant anything. In this case, it apparently meant to wait until he'd finished the joke he was telling to a couple suits who seemed engrossed in his every word.

Derek Dixon had barely changed in the nearly dozen years since Ryne had first met him. The observation wasn't a compliment. He had pretty boy blond looks and the manner of a chameleon. Jovial and charming one moment. Sober and businesslike the next. He was the ultimate public relations tool, because he was damn good at being all things to all people. Ryne happened to know that his habit of trying to be *one* thing to all women had nearly destroyed his marriage.

But being a womanizing, narcissistic prick hadn't slowed the rise of his career. In Boston he'd been the department's special attaché to the mayor. He'd come to Savannah three years ago as commander of the Investigative Division. The fact that his wife was the chief's niece might have had something to do with his procuring the job, but Ryne was hardly in a position to judge. When he'd accepted Dixon's surprising offer of a job here a year ago, he'd hitched his career to the other man's.

It was a troubling memory, but not the one that kept him awake nights.

There was a loud burst of laughter as the suits expressed their appreciation of Dixon's humor, which, Ryne had reason to know, could be politically incorrect and crudely clever.

"Excuse me for a moment." Dixon clapped the two closest men on the shoulders. "I need to speak to one of my detectives." The crowd on the stairwell parted for him like a sea before a prophet.

"Detective Robel." He flashed his pearly caps. "Here to thank me?"

"I appreciate the extra person assigned to the task force." Whatever their past, whatever had gone between them, Ryne always maintained a scrupulously professional relationship with the man in public. "But I'm not sure bringing in an outsider is going to be as much use to us as another department investigator would be."

Annoyance flickered in the man's eyes. "Didn't you read her qualifications? Phillips has a background unmatched by anyone on the force. You've heard of Raiker Forensics, haven't you? They're better known as The Mindhunters, because of Adam Raiker's years in the fed's behavioral science unit. The training in his agency is top-notch. With the addition of Phillips, we're getting a profiler and an investigator, for the price of one."

"Price." They descended the stairs in tandem. "Resources are limited, the last interdepartment memo said. Seems odd to spend them on an outside 'consultant' when we have cops already on the payroll who could do the same work at no additional cost."

Although he'd tried to maintain a neutral tone, Dixon's

expression warned him that he hadn't been entirely successful. The man glanced around as if to see who was
within hearing distance and lowered his voice, all the
while keeping a genial smile pasted on his face. "You don't
have to worry about the finances of this department, Detective. That's my job. Yours is to track down and nail this
scumbag raping women in our city. If you'd accomplished
that by now, I wouldn't have had to bring someone else in,
would I?"

The barb found its mark. "We've made steady progress . . ."

"Don't forget that my ass in on the line right along with
yours. Mayor Richards has had me on speed dial since the
second rape."

Already knowing it was futile, Ryne said, "Okay, how
about adding another person to the task force in addition to
Phillips? Marlowe out of the fourth precinct would be a
good man, and he's got fifteen years' experience."

They came to the base of the steps and stopped. The
suits were standing a little ways off and, judging by the
looks they kept throwing them, were growing impatient.

Dixon's words reflected the same emotion. "You wanted
another person assigned; you got her. Work with the task
force you've got, Detective. I need results to report to the
chief. Get me something to take to him." His gaze moved
to the men waiting for him. "Have you verified the connection between this latest assault and the others?" Ryne had
updated Dixon and Captain Brown before the briefing this
morning.

"I've got CSU at the scene. My men are on their way
over."

"Good." It was clear he'd lost Dixon's attention. "Let
me know when you get something solid."

Ryne made sure none of the anger churning in his gut
showed on his face as the commander walked away. Keeping the mayor happy would have been the driving motivation behind Dixon's hiring an outside consultant. The
second victim had been the mayor's granddaughter, a col-

lege student snatched on her way to work and driven to her grandparents' beach home, where the attack had taken place. The man had an understandable thirst for results, and Dixon's hiring of Phillips was only the latest offering. Assigning another department investigator to the case wasn't as dazzling as putting a profiler to work on it, especially one affiliated with Adam Raiker, a man practically martyred for the Bureau some years back.

At least he hoped he'd read Dixon's intentions correctly. Ryne turned and headed back to the conference room. He sincerely hoped the man was just playing his usual style of suck-up politics and not engaged in a cover-your-ass strategy designed to leave his image untarnished if this case went bad.

Because if that was the situation, Ryne knew exactly who'd be left twisting in the wind.

WHEN DETECTIVE ROBEL REENTERED THE ROOM, Abbie could tell that his mood had taken a turn for the worse. It wasn't evident from his expression. But temper had his spine straight, his movements taut with tension. "Let's go," he said abruptly.

Without a word, she got up and followed him out the door. He made no effort to check the length of his strides. She almost had to run to keep up with him, a fact that didn't endear him to her. He stopped at one cubicle and dropped the folder containing her personnel information on the desk, then picked up a fat accordion file sitting on its corner.

"Here." He shoved it at Abbie. "You can catch up on the case on the way."

On the way where? To the scene? To the victim? She decided she wasn't going to ask. His disposition had gone from guardedly polite to truculent, and it didn't take much perception to recognize that she was the cause for the change. His attitude wasn't totally unprecedented. He wouldn't be the first detective to resent her presence on his team, at least initially. In her experience, cops were notoriously territorial.

Rather than trotting at his heels like a well-trained dog, Abbie kept the detective in sight as she followed him out of the building and down the wide stone steps. Almost immediately, her temples dampened. Though barely noon and partly overcast, the humidity index had to be hovering close to ninety percent, making her question how the majority of her assignments just happened to be located in walking saunas like Savannah. Houston. Miami.

The answer, of course, was the job. Everything she did was dictated by it. If there was room in her life for little else, that was a conscious choice. And one she'd yet to regret.

Robel paused at the bottom of the steps as if just remembering she was accompanying him, and threw an impatient look over his shoulder. Unhurriedly, she caught up, and they headed toward the police parking lot.

"Do you have any experience with victim interviews?" he asked tersely. "I want to talk to Billings before I stop by the scene."

"Yes."

"Follow my lead when we get there. We've developed a survey of questions I'll lead her through. If you have anything to add afterwards, feel free."

He led her to an unmarked navy Crown Vic, unlocked it. She slid in the passenger side while he continued around the vehicle to the other door. Before following her into the car, he shrugged out of his muted plaid suit coat, revealing a light blue short-sleeved shirt crisscrossed by a shoulder harness. He laid the suit jacket over the seat between them as he got in.

"I'm never going to get used to this weather." He slid her a glance as he backed the car out of the slot. "How do you stand wearing long sleeves like that in the middle of summer?"

"Superior genes." Ignoring his snort, she spilled the

contents from the file he'd given her onto her lap. Flipping through the neatly arranged photos and reports, she noted they were sorted chronologically, beginning with the first incident reported three months earlier.

She looked at the detective. "So if this latest victim turns out to be related to the others, she'll be the . . . what? Fourth?"

Robel pulled to a stop at a stoplight. "That's right. And she's almost certainly related. He's injecting them with something prior to the attacks, and they all describe the same effects—initial tingling of the lips and extreme muscle weakness. It turns the victims' memories to mush, which means they haven't been able to give us squat when it comes to details about the attacker. From the descriptions they give, it also does something to intensify sensation."

"Maybe to increase the pain from the torture," she murmured, struck by a thought. If that were the actual intent, rather than just hazing the memory or incapacitating the victim, it would be in keeping with a sadistic rapist.

The hair on the nape of her neck suddenly prickled, and it wasn't due to the tepid air blasting from the air-conditioning vents. The atmosphere in the vehicle had gone charged. She slanted a look at Robel, noted the muscle working in his jaw.

"What do you know about the torture?"

Feeling like she was stepping on quicksand, she said, "Commander Dixon told me a little about the cases when we discussed my joining the task force."

"This morning?"

"On the phone yesterday afternoon."

The smile that crossed his lips then was chilly and completely devoid of humor. He reached for a pair of sunglasses secured to the visor, flipped them open, and settled them on his nose.

Irritation coursed through her. "Something about that amuses you?"

"Yeah, it does. Considering the fact that the last time I

asked Dixon for another *investigator*"—she didn't miss
the inflection he gave the last word—"was yesterday morning, I guess you could say it's funny as hell."

Abbie stifled the retort that rose to her lips. She was
more familiar than she'd like with the ego massage necessary in these situations, though she'd never develop a
fondness for the need. "Look, let's cut through the un-
pleasantries. I have no intention of muscling in on your
case. Since I was hired by Dixon, I have to provide him
with whatever information he requests of me. But my role
is first and foremost to assist you."

His silence, she supposed, was a response of sorts. Just
not the one she wanted. Her annoyance deepened. According to Commander Dixon, Robel was some sort of hotshot
detective, some very big deal from—Philadelphia? New
York? Some place north anyway. But as far as she could
tell, he was just another macho jerk, of a type she was all
too familiar with. Law enforcement was full of them. De-
partments could mandate so-called sensitivity training, but
it didn't necessarily change chauvinistic attitudes. It just
drove them deeper below the surface.

Abbie studied his chiseled profile. No doubt she was
supposed to crumple in the face of his displeasure. He'd be
the sort of man to appeal to most women, she supposed, if
they liked the lean, lethal, surly type. His short-cropped
hair was brown, his eyes behind the glasses an Arctic shade
of blue. His jaw was hard, as if braced for a punch. Given
his personality, she'd be willing to bet he'd caught more
than his share of them. He wasn't particularly tall, maybe
five foot ten, but he radiated authority. He was probably
used to turning his commanding presence on women and
melting them into subservience.

One corner of her mouth pulled up wryly as she turned
back to the file in her lap. There had been a time when it
would have produced just that result with her. Fortunately,
that time was in the very remote past.

Ignoring him for the moment, she pored over the police

reports, skipping over the complainants' names to the blocks of texts that detailed the location, offense, MO, victim and suspect information. "I assume you're using a state crime lab. What have the tox screens shown?" she asked, without looking up.

At first she thought he wasn't going to answer. Finally he said, "GBI's Coastal Regional Crime Lab is here in Savannah. The toxicologist hasn't found anything definitive, and he's tested for nearly two dozen of the more common substances. Reports on the first three victims showed trace amounts of Ecstasy in their blood. All victims deny being users, and the toxicologist suspects that it was mixed in controlled amounts to make a new compound."

She did look up then, her interest piqued. Use of an unfamiliar narcotic agent in the assaults might be their best lead in the case. Even without a sample, it told them something about the unknown subject. "Have you established any commonalities so far besides the drug?"

"Their hands are always bound with electrical cord, same position. Never their legs. At least not yet. He stalks them first, learns their routine. For most, he gets into the house somehow. Different entry techniques, so he's adaptable. But one victim he grabbed off the street and drove thirty miles to her grandparents' empty beach house for the attack."

"Same torture methods?"

He shook his head. "The first victim he covered with a plastic bag and repeatedly suffocated and revived. The next he carved up pretty bad. Looked like he was trying to cut her face off. Another he worked over with pliers and a hammer."

"What about trace evidence?"

"Nothing yet." And all the tension she'd sensed from Robel since she'd met him was pent up in the words. "He's smart and he's lucky. A bad combination for us. After the second rape, I entered the case into the Violent Criminal Apprehension Program system, mentioning the drug as a common element. Only got a few hits. After the third one, I resubmitted, thinking the drug might be a new addition for this perp. I don't have those results back yet, but I'm guessing we're going to get a lot more hits focusing only on the electrical cord as a common element."

"It's unusual to switch routines like that," Abbie mused. "Some rapists might experiment at first, perfect their technique, but if you've got no trace evidence, it doesn't sound like this guy is a novice."

"He's not." Robel turned down a residential street. "He's been doing this a long time. Maybe he's escalating now. Maybe it takes more and more for him to get his jollies."

It was possible. For serial offenders, increasing the challenge also intensified their excitement. The last three victims of the Romeo rapist had been assaulted in their homes when there had been another family member in the house.

With that in mind, she asked, "Are there any uncleared homicides in the vicinity that share similarities to the rapes?"

He looked at her, but she couldn't guess what he was thinking with the glasses shielding his eyes. "Why?"

"He had to start somewhere." Abbie looked out the window at the row of small, neat houses dotting the street. "A guy like this doesn't get to be an expert all at once." She turned back to Robel, found him still surveying her. "Maybe he went too far once and accidentally killed his victim. Or something could have gone wrong and he had to kill one who could identify him."

"Good thought." The words might have sounded like a compliment if they hadn't been uttered so grudgingly. "We checked that. Also looked at burglaries. Nothing panned out." But her remark seemed to have splintered the ice between them.

"I'm not surprised the burglary angle didn't turn up anything. This isn't an opportunity rapist. Sounds like he goes in very prepared, very organized. His intent is the rape itself, at least the ritual he's made of the act."

Robel returned his attention to the street. "I'm still try-ing to figure out why he *doesn't* kill them. A guy with that much anger toward women, why keep them alive and chance leaving witnesses?" He was slowing, checking the house numbers.

She needed to familiarize herself with the file before she was close to doing a profile on the type of offender they were hunting. But she knew that wasn't what Robel was asking for. "Depends on his motivation. Apparently he doesn't need the victim's death to fulfill whatever twisted perversion he's got driving him."

"Maybe it's the difference in the punishment. Serial rapists don't face the death penalty, even in Georgia."

But Abbie shook her head. "He doesn't ever plan to get caught, so consequences don't mean much to him. He may be aware of them on some level, but not to the extent that they would deter him."

"I worked narcotics, undercover. Did a stint in bur-glary, a longer one in homicide." He pulled to a stop be-fore a pale blue bungalow with an attached carport. Only one vehicle was in the drive. "I can understand the moti-vations of those crimes. Greed, jealousy, anger." Switch-ing off the car, he removed the sunglasses and slid them back into their spot on the visor. "But I've never been able to wrap my mind around rapists. I know what it takes to catch them. I just don't pretend to understand why they do it."

Abbie felt herself thawing toward him a little. "Well, if we figure out what's motivating this guy, we'll be well on our way toward nailing him."

"I guess that's your job." Robel opened his door and stepped out into the street, reaching back inside the vehicle to retrieve his jacket. "You get in his head and point us in the right direction. That's what Dixon had in mind, isn't it?" He slammed the door, shrugging into his suit coat as he rounded the hood of the car.

Abbie opened her door, was immediately blasted by the midday heat. The rancor in his words had been barely discernible, but it was there. So she didn't bother telling him that getting inside the rapist's head was exactly what she planned on.

It was, in fact, all too familiar territory. She'd spent more years than she'd like to recall doing precisely that.